BLACK WIDOW

Laurie Breton

In memory of my sister
Lucille E. Brown
"Tete"
who walks with the angels now.

.

BOOKS BY LAURIE BRETON

THE JACKSON FALLS SERIES

Coming Home: Jackson Falls Book 1
Sleeping With the Enemy: Jackson Falls Book 2
Days Like This: Jackson Falls Book 3
The Next Little Thing: Jackson Falls Book 4 (A Jackson Falls MINI)
Redemption Road: Jackson Falls Book 5
The Miles Between Us: Jackson Falls Book 6

ROMANTIC SUSPENSE NOVELS

Final Exit
Mortal Sin
Lethal Lies
Criminal Intent
Point of Departure
Die Before I Wake
Black Widow

prologue

Elba, North Carolina
May, 1994

The Saab's air conditioner was on the blink again, and the drive down from Richmond had been long and hot. But it had been well worth the trip. His presentation had impressed the hell out of Walston Associates. Just four years out of architectural school, and he'd been chosen from a field of two dozen architects to design Richmond's newest skyscraper. At twenty-seven, Michael McAllister was about to hit the big time.

He unbuttoned his shirt collar and peeled damp cotton from sticky skin. The air was steamy, ripe with the scent of magnolias and heavy with the signs of an impending thunderstorm. His right hand strayed to the cellular phone mounted on the ten-year-old Saab's dash. *Kathryn.* He should call Kath and give her the good news. Michael hesitated, hand still on the phone, then decided it would be better to tell her in person. He wanted to see her face when he broke the news.

She'd been right all along. He had been terrified of going out on his own directly after college. It had been Kathryn who convinced him that starting his own firm was the right thing to do, Kathryn who believed in him so strongly that she'd never complained about surviving on the combined incomes of a struggling architect and a schoolteacher. If he had joined an established firm, he would have been buried in bureaucratic anonymity, and it might have been twenty years before a chance like this opened up for him.

Trying to keep the Saab's speed down to within ten miles per hour of the legal limit, Michael cruised the streets of the quiet residential neighborhood. He glanced at his watch as he turned in at the end of a long driveway flanked by twin yuccas and paved with crushed white limestone. *6:45.* Kath would be out jogging. His wife jogged daily, faithfully, rain or shine. You could set your clock by her. It was one of the little quirks that endeared her to him. And to the neighbors, who had long since stopped gossiping about the crazy Yankee lady and had found somebody else to talk about.

He parked beside her faded Plymouth. When they'd bought the old Chandler place, it had been deserted for years. The yard had been a jungle, and vermin had taken over the house. But Kath had fallen in love with the high ceilings, with the carved woodwork and the marble fireplace mantels. All the systems had been in working order, and they'd gotten it for a song. They'd tamed the jungle undergrowth and begun restoring the house, one room at a time, as their budget allowed.

The oppressive heat followed him indoors, for they hadn't yet installed central air conditioning. A massive bouquet of magnolia blossoms dominated the center of the kitchen table. Michael hung his necktie over the back of a chair and took a pitcher of lemonade out of the refrigerator. The tinkling of the crystal stirrer woke Moses, who hopped down from the rocking chair, stretched, and began rubbing against Michael's legs. "Hey, buddy," Michael said, going down on one knee to rub the cat's belly. "How's it going?"

He was still on his knee when he heard the thud. It sounded like somebody had dropped a heavy object on the hardwood floor above his head. Moses pricked up his ears and they both looked in the direction of the stairs. Michael rose and set down the stirrer. "Kath?" he said. "Is that you?"

There was no answer.

A rivulet of sweat trickled down his spine. He walked to the foot of the stairs and peered up into the gloom of the upstairs hall. "Kathryn?"

Above his head, a floorboard creaked. And then silenced.

And the hair on the back of Michael McAllister's neck stood up.

* * *

Above her head, thunder growled, and the air had that greenish sheen that presaged a thunderstorm. Back home, a storm would cool the air. Here, cool was little more than an abstract concept. Kathryn stripped off her sweatband and mopped her face. If she hurried, she could get a cold shower before the storm hit. Michael was due home tonight, and she didn't want to greet him smelling like a quarterback.

But when she turned into the driveway, past the yuccas and the blooming magnolia, Michael's car was already there. So much for greeting him smelling like *Jean Nate*. Her scent would more closely resemble *eau de Namath*. She couldn't wait to see him. He'd been gone for three days, the longest they'd ever been apart, and she was dying to hear how his meeting with Walston Associates had gone.

Michael McAllister was a creative genius. Kathryn had recognized it the first day they met, in a life drawing class at Boston University. While Kathryn and the rest of the class had struggled to follow the demands of the instructor, Michael had managed, with a determination bordering on grimness, to capture the essence of the model in a few deft strokes. His tremendous creative energy was one of the things that had drawn Kathryn to him. That and the utter sincerity with which he conducted his life. Michael was an anachronism, a throwback to a gentler age, a true Southern gentleman.

He had left the kitchen door ajar, and Kathryn closed it behind her. The lemonade pitcher sat in a puddle of condensation on the counter. Kathryn returned it to the refrigerator and wiped up the puddle. "Michael?" she said.

There was no answer, but if he'd driven all the way from Richmond without air conditioning, she'd be willing to bet he was in the shower. He'd been talking for weeks about taking the car into Rollie's and having it fixed, but he hadn't gotten around to it yet. Maybe it wouldn't matter that she smelled like a card-carrying member of the NFL. If she joined Michael in the shower, he would never notice.

Outside, thunder grumbled, louder than before, and somewhere upstairs, Moses was yowling. Kathryn took the stairs at a trot, expecting to find Michael in the bathroom. But the shower was silent, the room empty. Down the hall, behind her closed bedroom door, Moses howled loud enough to wake the dead. No wonder they called it caterwauling. "Poor Mose," she said. "You got shut in."

She turned the doorknob and Moses shot past her, all fourteen pounds of him, and thundered down the stairs. He raced behind the couch and stayed there, staring out at her, his eyes wild and huge. Kathryn gaped at him in amazement and turned back to the bedroom. "Michael?" she said, opening the door wider. "Are you—"

The white bedroom carpet was dotted with crimson feline footprints.

Blood. A lot of blood.

Fear slammed into her. "Michael?" she cried, hearing the panic in her own voice. "Michael!" Chest aching, she edged into the room on legs that suddenly weighed a hundred pounds each. Michael McAllister lay face down on the white shag carpet, one arm flung over his head, the carpet beneath him saturated with blood. The telephone receiver dangled beside him, bleating indignantly. With a cry of despair, Kathryn dropped to her knees on the bloodstained carpet. Michael was a big man, and it took all her strength to roll him over. His head lolled at a crazy angle when she turned him, and his left arm flopped onto the carpet with a soft thud.

Her twelve-inch wallpapering shears were embedded in his chest.

Bile rose in her throat. Kathryn swayed, nearly fainted, unaware of the soft animal sounds that were coming from her throat. She grasped the handle to the shears and pulled them from his chest. For a moment, she just looked at them stupidly, and then she flung them across the room, where they slammed into a Hummel figurine and smashed it. She picked up his wrist, frantically sought a pulse. There was none. Overhead, a deafening clap of thunder shook the house. Her hands and her clothes smeared with blood, Kathryn dropped her husband's arm and struggled to her feet. With a sob, she backed slowly away from him, then turned and ran, stumbling on the stairs, gasping for breath, numb with shock and terror. She shoved open the screen door and it slapped shut behind her as rain hammered down on the tile roof of the porch.

She tripped on the steps and fell on her knees in the mud. For a moment she stayed there, pelted by rain, too stunned to move. Then she was up and running again, she didn't know where, just running. She had to get away from what she'd seen. Away, away, away....

Until she slammed up against an immovable object with so much force it temporarily knocked the breath from her. Arms reached out to catch her and the object turned into a man. Pure, visceral terror took over. Blinded by the rain and her tears, she fought him like an enraged grizzly, snarling like the wild animal she had become, kicking and gouging and biting. "Hey!" said a voice. "Take it easy, little lady!" She drove an elbow into his ribcage, and he grunted. "Earl!" he roared. "Get your ass over here and help me!"

In the distance, a siren began to wail, faint at first, then louder. A second pair of arms wrapped themselves around her from behind, lifting her off her feet and rendering her helpless as a turned turtle. "No!" she screamed. "Let me go!" Her captor bent her arm backward, painfully, and clamped her wrists together in his massive fists. She kicked frantically at the other man, aiming for his crotch and missing.

The shrieking of the siren grew unbearable, then squawked to a halt as a county rescue vehicle barreled into her driveway, skidding the last twenty feet on the wet limestone, missing by inches the police cruiser that was parked there.

For the first time, she realized that her captors wore uniforms and badges. They were friends, not foes.

All the starch went out of her. "Oh, God," she said weakly, appealing to the stocky one, the one whose badge identified him as the chief of police. "Oh, thank God. My husband's dead. You have to help me. Please!"

The two officers looked at each other and then they looked back at her. "Ma'am," the chief said, "maybe you'd best wait in the car."

Drenched to the bone, Kathryn sat in the back seat of the patrol car, rubbing the circulation back into her wrists as the red sweep of the ambulance's revolving light reflected off the wet hood of the cruiser. The two police officers entered the house, guns drawn. Too drained to cry, Kathryn wrapped her arms around herself for warmth and listened to the indecipherable crackle and static of the police radio.

The men emerged from the house with grim faces. They held a huddled conference on the porch with a yellow-slickered ambulance attendant, and then the chief of police ambled back to the cruiser. He slid into the driver's seat and spoke into his two-way radio. "Ro, honey," he said, "looks like we got us a nice little homicide out here. Want to round up Blake and Parker and send 'em out to back us up? Ten-oh-five Ridgewood Road. Oh, and call the coroner for me, will you, sugar?"

He opened a notebook, took a pen from his pocket, and clicked it. "I'm afraid I'm gonna have to ask you some questions, Miz—?"

It took her a moment to realize he was speaking to her. "McAllister," she said. "Kathryn McAllister."

"And the name of the deceased?"

"Michael," she said dully. Her voice broke as the pictures came flooding back, pictures that would haunt her dreams for the rest of her life. "Michael McAllister."

His eyes, already too small for his face, narrowed. "Judge McAllister's boy?"

Kathryn bit her upper lip. "Yes," she said.

He snapped the notebook shut and regarded her with keen interest. "Well, well," he said. "Now ain't that interesting? Well, Miz McAllister, I sure hope you got yourself a good lawyer."

She looked at him stupidly. "A lawyer," she said. "Why would I need a lawyer?"

He lifted his hat from his head, smoothed down what was left of his hair, and replaced the hat. "Well," he said, "I don't imagine Judge McAllister's gonna take too kindly to you killing his only son."

chapter one

Wilmington, North Carolina
Four Years Later

The Carolina Women's Penitentiary sat squat and ugly in the midday sun, high on a bluff overlooking the Cape Fear River. Behind its drab concrete walls, four hundred women counted down the days of their penance. Before the massive iron gate, a lone figure stood, suitcase in hand, a slender woman dressed in stiff jeans, a clean white tee shirt, and cheap loafers. She held her shoulders back and her head high as she waited. There was a loud click and a buzz, and the gate swung open. Gripping the handle of her suitcase, Kathryn McAllister stepped through the opening to freedom.

The gate slammed shut behind her, and Kathryn flinched, her reaction automatic after four years of doors closing behind her. But this time, she was on the outside. She set down the suitcase and took a deep breath of sweet, steamy air, holding it in until her lungs ached as she attempted to cleanse them of the stench of prison. But it was still there, would always be there, gnawing at the edges of memory long after it was gone from her lungs.

Kathryn stepped out of the loafers, peeled off her socks, and wriggled her bare toes in the dry, red dust of the roadside. She tugged at the elastic band that held her hair back. It snapped, releasing the fall of honey-colored curls to her shoulders. Kathryn combed her hair back with the fingers of both hands and raised her face to the sun.

After four years inside a damp, dark cell, its heat felt wonderful. She closed her eyes and reveled in the sunshine, replenishing her senses with the rich, earthy scent of summer, the buzzing of insects and the sweet trilling of birdsong.

Presently, she became aware of another sound, this one mechanical. An automobile was racing down the road toward her, a cloud of dust billowing out behind it. The electric blue Mustang convertible approached at a velocity roughly comparable to that of the moon shuttle. With admirable precision, the driver swerved and halted the car neatly beside her. "Honey, I am so sorry," Raelynn said in that sugared drawl. "We should have been in and out of the courtroom in ten minutes. An open-and-shut divorce case. Instead, that old buzzard Connolly had to pick this morning to rake my client over the coals. Took me a half-hour afterward to calm her down." Eyeing Kathryn through mirrored sunglasses, she shook her head in righteous indignation. "And here you are, left standing in the street."

Kathryn bent and picked up her suitcase. "At least," she said wryly, "I'm on the right side of the fence." She opened the passenger door, tossed the suitcase and her loafers in the back, and sank gratefully into the white vinyl bucket seat.

Raelynn talked the way she drove, eighty miles an hour and with more verve than Kathryn had ever seen in another living soul. Freed of any necessity to attempt conversation, she leaned back in the seat and let the wind sweep through her hair as Raelynn's monologue floated in one ear and out the other.

They traveled inland, leaving behind the coastal plain and entering the Piedmont, where each crumbling plantation house, each tin-roofed shanty on stilts, had its own cotton patch, often growing side by side with endless green fields of broadleaf tobacco. They drove through villages that were little more than a handful of shotgun houses gathered around a weathered Baptist church and a defunct gas station whose rusted pumps still displayed the Flying A.

Raelynn finally ran down, and they traveled for a time in silence. A sign painted in blood red and tacked on a telephone pole warned sinners that Jesus was coming. "Are you sure you're doing the right thing," Raelynn said, tapping red-lacquered nails against the steering wheel, "coming back to Elba?"

Kathryn's spine stiffened. "We've been over this before," she said.

"And frankly, I still don't get it. If I were you, I'd be on the first bus headed north of the Mason-Dixon line."

They passed another sign, warning them to repent or burn. "Somebody killed my husband," Kathryn said, "and framed me for murder. I'm not going anywhere until I find out who." She paused. "And why."

Raelynn tossed her thick, black hair away from her face. "As your attorney, I'm advising you against that course of action."

Kathryn turned her head and looked at Raelynn. "And as my friend?"

Raelynn punched the accelerator and raced around a curve. "And as your friend," she said, "I'm advising you to listen to your attorney."

Kathryn squared her jaw. "I can't."

"Hell's bells, Kat, you just got out of prison! Do you want to go back there?"

Quietly, Kathryn said, "I'll never go back there."

"Then give up this ridiculous obsession of yours and move on with your life. It's too late to do Michael any good, and it's not about to change anybody's feelings toward you. The public has already crucified you. They're not going to appreciate you rising like Lazarus to proclaim your innocence."

Kathryn's mouth narrowed into a grim line. "The conviction was overturned," she said.

"And the Yankees won the Civil War. But you couldn't prove it by anybody around these parts."

Of their own accord, Kathryn's fists clenched. "I spent four years rotting away in that concrete tomb, while the monster who killed Michael walked away a free man. I'm going to find him, and he's going to fry for what he did."

Raelynn pursed her lips and said nothing. After Kathryn's conviction, it had taken four grueling years of appeals before they got the break they needed in the form of an elderly widow named Clara Hughes, who had seen Kathryn jog past her home on Old County Road at the precise time that Michael McAllister, mortally wounded, had made his ill-fated call to 911. Clara's razor-sharp memory was corroborated by the journal she kept, in which she chronicled the daily activities of a large segment of the population of Elba.

Armed with this new evidence, Raelynn had returned to court. One steamy June morning, a week before the court date, a second miracle occurred: old Judge Harper, affectionately known in some circles as the hanging judge, and declared by his detractors to be too ornery to die, keeled over right there on the bench, smack in the middle of a rape trial. Three days later, Judge Harper was buried with the pomp and circumstance that befitted a man of his stature, and a new judge was assigned to overhear Kathryn's case.

Judge Graves took a week to mull over the evidence, but in the end, he ruled in their favor, declaring that the old lady's testimony was sufficient to establish reasonable doubt. The conviction was overturned, and Kathryn became a free woman. One who had been tried and found guilty in the eyes of the upright and outraged citizens of Elba, North Carolina, who weren't gullible enough to believe an overturned conviction meant a tinker's damn. Kathryn McAllister would be watched and feared, talked about and despised, for the rest of her life. Or until the real killer was unmasked.

"Listen," Raelynn said, her normally buoyant voice uncharacteristically somber, "whoever killed Michael wasn't fooling around. What if he comes after you? If you end up dead, sugar, all my hard work will be for nothing."

Kathryn's tension slowly dissipated, and her heart rate returned to normal. Raelynn was a dear friend, and she was genuinely concerned. Bitterly, Kathryn said, "I'm not quite the innocent I was four years ago. Prison has a way of doing that to you. I can take care of myself."

"Honey," Raelynn said, "I sure as hell hope you know what you're doing."

They reached the outskirts of Elba, and Kathryn intently studied the sleepy little town, pondering the secrets it held and making mental note of the changes that had taken place since she'd seen it last. Rollie's Auto Emporium and Repair Shop had disappeared, and a sleek, modern convenience store had sprung up in its place. Two kids sat on the curb drinking Slush Puppies and wiggling their toes in the dust. Next door, in front of Carlyle's Barber Shop, an ugly yellow dog lazed in the shade of Hobie Carlyle's green striped awning. The municipal building, circa 1880, was built from burnished red brick with freshly-painted white wooden trim. Oblong planters brimming with red geraniums lined the walkway. Parked out front, nose in to the curb, sat Elba's two police cruisers.

Somewhere in this picture-postcard town, she would find the answers she sought. Somehow, she would uncover the secret to Michael's murder.

A shiver skittered down her spine and she quickly turned away. Across the street, in the parking lot of the Dixie Market, her mother-in-law was climbing out of a new bottle-green Cadillac. The last time she'd seen Michael's mother had been at the trial. Neely McAllister had sat directly behind the prosecution table, dressed in a beige silk dress and her grandmomma's pearls, weeping copiously into a lace hanky.

Neely had never liked Kathryn, had never approved of Michael's marriage to the slender Yankee upstart who was absolutely nobody. As she was fond of telling anybody who'd sit still long enough to listen, Kathryn hadn't even had the common decency to come to Elba and meet Michael's family before dragging him off to get married in some stranger's living room. Neely might have been able to forgive Kathryn for her common beginnings. She might have been able to forgive her for any number of inadequacies. But she had never forgiven her daughter-in-law for depriving her of the chance to attend the wedding of her only son.

Halfway across the parking lot, Neely looked up and saw her. The older woman stiffened as she recognized her daughter-in-law. Chin thrust high, she deliberately turned her back on Kathryn and stormed toward the entrance of the market.

Kathryn squared her jaw and focused her gaze directly ahead of her. She couldn't fathom why she always allowed Neely McAllister to get to her. The woman simply had a way about her, like an itching powder that burrowed just beneath the top layer of skin and refused to budge.

Raelynn crossed the railroad tracks and turned down a side street, pulling up in front of a modest white frame house. It was set back from the street behind a tidy lawn, and shaded on one side by a tall oak tree draped with Spanish moss. "Here we are," she said. "Welcome home."

Kathryn followed her into the house. It was small, but homey, and after four years in a cell, she found it more than adequate for her needs. Abundant sunlight poured in on the hardwood floors. There was plenty of fresh air, plenty of space, a half-dozen window sills where she could grow her beloved African violets. "This is perfect," she told her friend. "I don't know how to thank you."

Raelynn blew it off with a wave of her slender hand. "Since Momma died, nobody's been using the place anyway. You need a place to stay, and the house—" She paused to run a finger along the fireplace mantel. "—the house," she continued, "needs somebody to love it."

"I'll pay you back," Kathryn vowed. "Every penny I owe you."

Raelynn patted her arm. "I know you will, darlin'. Hell, it's only a few thousand dollars. Just enough to keep you going until you can get back on your feet. I want you to think of all this as a temporary setback. Your life'll get better soon enough, it's just going to take some time." Her face softened. "You're strong, Kat. I don't think you know how strong. If I'd gone through what you have, I'm not sure I would've made it."

"Don't be ridiculous. We all do what we have to do to survive."

Raelynn dimpled. "Listen, sugar, there's food in the fridge and fresh linens on the bed. I have a client coming in at three, so I have to scoot. Think you'll be okay on your own?"

Freedom. Glorious, blessed freedom. After four years of being told when to get up, when to go to bed, when to go to the bathroom, she wasn't sure she remembered how to handle being in charge of her own life. But after all she'd survived, she was certain she could re-learn the art of independence. "I'll be fine," she said. "Just as soon as I figure out where to start."

Raelynn eyed her tee shirt and jeans, and grimaced. "Well," she said, "far be it from me to tell you what to do. But if I were you, I'd start with some new clothes."

* * *

Police Chief Nicholas DiSalvo sat in his swivel chair, feet up on his desk, doing his best to perform his sworn duty to protect the good citizens of Elba, North Carolina, by tearing sheets of paper off a legal pad, crumpling them up, and free-throwing them into his office wastebasket.

He'd seen Michael Jordan play once, when the Bulls went up against the Knicks at the Garden. Now, that was something truly

13

beautiful: Jordan and Ewing, head to head. He paused a moment to savor the memory before he wadded up another sheet, aimed, and sank it with deadly accuracy.

Outside, on the street, traffic moved lazily. Inside the municipal building, with its twelve-foot ceilings built long before the days of central air conditioning, the clock ticked indolently in the sultry heat. Crime in Elba, North Carolina, population 2,703, ran primarily to barking dogs and kids shoplifting jujubes at the Bijou. Hardly worth writing home about. But for a man who had nothing left to live for, Elba was as good a place as any to bury himself.

He crumpled another sheet of paper, took aim, and raised his arm. From the open doorway, Rowena Hathaway pointedly cleared her throat. The sound did double duty, serving as both salutation and criticism, for there was no love lost between Chief DiSalvo and the secretary he'd inherited from his predecessor. Rowena had made it abundantly clear, when Shep Henley retired and Nick took over the job of Chief, just where her loyalties lay.

With a sigh of regret, he lowered his arm and swiveled around in his chair. "Rowena, my sweet," he said with a wolfish grin. "What can I do for you this fine morning?"

She refused to rise to the bait. Sternly, she said, "There's somebody here to see you. I swear, I never thought the day would come when I'd see the likes of that woman here at city hall. Leastways, not on this side of a cell door."

His curiosity was piqued. Score one for his visitor. If Rowena didn't like her, she had to be doing something right. "By all means," he said, "send her in."

With a sniff of disdain, she turned and stalked away, her spike heels *tap-tapping* in the cavernous corridor. He heard the murmur of voices, Rowena's scorn obvious even though her words were indecipherable. Footsteps approached his door, and a young woman paused at the threshold.

She wore a short-sleeved white blouse over a splashy flowered cotton skirt and white high-heeled sandals. Beneath the clothing, she had the long, lean body of a runner. Spectacular legs, he noted, before his eyes moved northward past a slender waist and softly rounded breasts to the blonde hair she'd pulled back into some kind of convoluted affair. The hairdo was obviously intended to play down her looks, but in reality, it had just the opposite effect.

"Thank you for seeing me on such short notice," she said in a soft voice that carried the broadened vowels of New England. Massachusetts, he thought, or maybe New Hampshire. "I'm Kathryn McAllister."

She paused, as though expecting that the name would have meaning for him. Nick quickly ran through his mental files, but drew a blank. "Nick DiSalvo," he said, standing to shake her hand. He indicated the chair opposite his desk. "Have a seat."

Reclaiming his own chair, he leaned back, propped his feet on the desk drawer that refused to close, and folded his arms across his middle. "So, Ms. McAllister," he said, "what can I do for you?"

He knew the instant she recognized Brooklyn in his voice. In this Southern paradise, he'd grown accustomed to heads swiveling the minute he opened his mouth. Her chin snapped up and her eyes narrowed, holding his in a lengthy stare. They were blue, those eyes, a cool, distant blue, like the Hudson River on an overcast winter day. "You're from New York," she said.

"That's right," he said. "Damn accent gives me away every time."

Still looking at him, she said, "I'm here about a murder."

After sixteen years as a cop, he'd become adept at hiding his feelings. Nick dropped his feet to the floor, straightened his spine, and wheeled his chair closer to the desk. In a deliberately neutral voice, he said, "A murder."

"My husband's murder. Michael McAllister."

The name clicked, and it all fell into place. After four years, the locals still talked about the biggest scandal in the town's history. A rising young architect, the son of one of Elba's most prominent families, brutally stabbed to death in his own home by his pretty young wife. Nick picked up a pen and began idly tapping it against a pile of papers atop his desk. "I thought there'd been a conviction in that case," he said, and met those cool blue eyes head on. "His wife."

She gripped the arms of the chair so hard her knuckles went white. "Last week," she said, "the conviction was overturned."

He kept his expression politely professional. "I'm afraid I'm not following you."

She leaned forward, determination etched in every line of her body. "I spent four years in prison for a crime I didn't commit," she said. "I lost everything, Mr. DiSalvo. My husband, my freedom, my reputation, my self-respect. And the person who stole my life from me is still walking around free. One way or another, I intend to see that he pays."

"I see." He didn't see, but he was willing to play along for a while until he figured out what she was really after. "And how do I fit into that scenario?"

She recrossed her legs, demurely smoothed the flowered skirt over her knees. "I want you to reopen the investigation."

He dropped the pen and leaned back in his chair. "I can't do that," he said.

The fire in those blue eyes banked itself and cooled. "I see," she said, and stood up. "Well, I certainly do want to thank you for your time, Chief DiSalvo. I'm so sorry to have troubled you." She glanced around the office and set her lips in a thin line. "I can see what a busy man you are."

"Ms. McAllister. Sit back down, and listen to me. You have to know that the case isn't in my hands any more. And even if we were in a position to reopen a four-year-old homicide investigation, I can't spare the manpower to waste time looking behind every bush and under every rock when the only suspect in the case is standing right in front of me."

The mask dropped, for just a moment, allowing him a glimpse of the fury behind it. "I didn't do it!"

"And you're walking free right now. Why don't you just count your blessings and go on back to New Hampshire or wherever it is you come from, find yourself some nice guy, and start making babies?"

"Somebody killed my husband," she said bitterly. "Do you understand that? We'd just bought our dream home. Michael's career was finally taking off. In another year or two, we were going to start a family. And now that's gone. All of it, just like it never existed. Do you have any inkling of how I feel?"

He picked the pen back up and slapped it against his open palm. Cleared his throat. "I'm sorry," he said. "But I can't help you."

"Fine," she said. "But remember one thing. With or without your help, I'll find this monster, and I'll put him away."

"Fine," he said. "Now I'd like you to remember one thing. If, in the process of putting him away, you step an inch beyond the line of the law, I'll nail your ass. *Capisce?*"

Rowena's disdain was nothing compared to the contempt he saw on Kathryn McAllister's face. "Good-bye, Chief DiSalvo," she said. "Don't bother to get up. I know where the door is."

After she was gone, he leaned back in his chair and pondered the situation. The chances that she was innocent were slim to none. The D.A. couldn't have convicted without substantial evidence. So why the hell was she back out on the street? No judge would overturn a murder conviction without a damn good reason.

In the flowered skirt and the virginal white blouse, Kathryn McAllister looked soft and feminine, but beneath the surface, she was one tough lady. Still, Nick knew enough about pain to recognize it when he saw it. The lady was hurting. But did that pain come from grief or remorse? It was hard to say.

Idle curiosity. That was all he was feeling. Since he had nothing better to do, he wandered out to the front desk, where Rowena was busily knitting a crib blanket for her newest grandchild, due in September. The needles raced, clicking softly as the monstrosity in her lap doubled in size almost daily. He paused by her desk, and she shoved harlequin glasses, the height of fashion back in 1962, up her bony nose. "Yes?" she said, as though he were interrupting something of vital importance.

He jingled a fistful of change in his pocket. Casually, he said, "I'd like you to pull the file on the McAllister homicide."

Rowena's mouth fell open, and Nick continued on down the hall to the soda machine. He dropped in three quarters and made his selection. He'd lived for thirty-five years without tasting RC Cola, but after just four months in Elba, he was hooked. He returned with the can of RC, already beading up with condensation. "Jesus," he said, "it's hotter than a bastard in here." He popped the top on the RC and added, "Where's the file?"

Rowena's eyebrows drew together in disapproval at his flagrant abuse of the Lord's name. One more thing she'd made abundantly clear. "It's not there," she said.

He paused with the can of RC halfway to his mouth. "What?" he said.

"The McAllister file. It's not in the drawer."

He lowered the can. "Well, where is it?"

She looked at him as though he were a very small, very stupid child. "If I knew where it was," she said, "we wouldn't be havin' this conversation, now, would we?"

If she'd been an officer, he would have been tempted to charge her with insubordination. "You're sure it's not there?" he said. "It's not misfiled or something?"

The knitting needles paused mid-click. "Chief DiSalvo," she said, her voice cold enough to induce frostbite, "I've been workin' here for thirty-two years, and I have yet to misfile anything. If it's not there, it's because somebody took it out of the drawer and didn't return it."

"But there was a file—I mean, this department did conduct an investigation into the McAllister homicide, correct?"

"There most certainly was," she said. "Chief Henley himself headed the investigation." She pursed her lips. "It was a terrible thing. A handsome young man like that, cut down in his prime. His Momma and I attend the same church, you know. First Baptist, down on Wabash Street." Lips still pursed, she resumed her knitting. "Poor Neely just went to pieces when Michael died. He was her only child, you know. She hemorrhaged when he was born, and they had to take out half her insides. She couldn't have any more babies."

Nick closed his eyes at the vivid picture her words evoked. "Thank you," he said, and retreated to the safety of his office.

He sat at his desk for a while, idly rotating the can of RC in his hands while he reminded himself of all the reasons he shouldn't get involved. He didn't give a rat's ass about Kathryn McAllister. He'd come to Elba four months ago to bury himself in a place where life was sluggish, a place where there'd be no life-and-death decisions to make, a place where he could pretend he'd been born the day he drove into town. He'd been doing a damn good job of fooling himself until Kathryn McAllister walked through his door.

He might have been able to maintain the illusion a while longer if it hadn't been for the tickle at the back of his neck, just beneath the hair he kept an inch or two longer than was approved by Elba's city fathers. He tried to ignore that tickle, but it wouldn't go away, and he was too good a cop to ignore it. It wasn't just Kathryn McAllister's protestations of innocence that had his wheels turning. In sixteen years, he'd met only a handful of criminals who'd admitted their guilt. It was always somebody else's fault, somebody else who'd pulled that trigger or held up that liquor store. But logic said that the McAllister woman had been turned loose for some reason. And there was still the matter of the missing file.

It probably didn't mean a thing. Somebody had misfiled it when the dragon lady wasn't on guard duty. When you added it all together, you came up with a big, fat zero. It was probably nothing more than his overactive imagination that had given birth to the gut feeling that something, somehow, wasn't quite right here.

He called Dora Hastings at the county clerk's office and arranged to have a transcript of the McAllister trial sent over by courier. "While you're at it," he told Dora, "you might as well give me a copy of the judge's ruling to overturn the conviction."

It took him another five minutes to get her off the phone. He still hadn't adjusted to this Southern preoccupation with small talk. In New York, where people barely spoke to each other, it wasn't uncommon to live next door to someone for twenty years and never have more than a nodding acquaintance. But here in Elba, five minutes after you met somebody, you knew their entire history, back at least four generations, whether you wanted to or not.

Rowena was still knitting, and he could have sworn the blanket had grown by several inches in the last twenty minutes. "Anybody's looking for me," he told her, "I'll be over at the *Gazette*."

The *Dixie Gazette* was located in a modern brick building a block south of downtown. He parked out front and went in search of Shanice Williams, the efficient young black woman who was in charge of the *Gazette*'s back files. Within minutes, Shanice had him settled at a microfiche viewer with several rolls of microfilm stacked beside him and a dire warning to treat them gently or else.

He started at the beginning, on the morning of May seventeenth, when the *Gazette*'s front-page headline had screamed: PROMINENT LOCAL MAN BRUTALLY SLAIN; WIFE ARRESTED. He paged slowly through the newspaper accounts of the murder, the arrest, the subsequent trial. In sleepy little Elba, murder had been big news, and the *Gazette*'s coverage of it had bordered on obsession.

There was a picture of Michael McAllister, most likely his high school portrait. He'd been a big bear of a man, a good-looking guy with a grin a mile wide. Another picture, this one an informal snapshot, showed Michael and Kathryn McAllister together at the seashore, arm in arm, looking young and tanned and preposterously happy.

Numerous other photos followed. But the photos were only the tip of a very large iceberg. During the months preceding the trial, the city fathers had renamed a small park after Elba's fallen son. Letters had poured in to the *Gazette*'s editor from citizens urging the State to seek the death penalty. Editorials had painted Kathryn McAllister as a gold-digger, a ruthless daughter of Polish immigrants who had latched onto Michael McAllister because his family had money. The *Gazette* interviewed neighbors, Kathryn's co-workers, the parents of her students. Every one of them expressed shock at the savagery of the crime. As one neighbor put it, "Miz McAllister seemed to be such a caring lady."

Nobody argued for her innocence.

Her attorney had been granted a change of venue, so the trial had taken place in neighboring Stetson County. The *Gazette* had published numerous photos of Kathryn entering and leaving the Stetson County Courthouse, her shoulders back and her chin raised, her face blank and expressionless. Because of the lack of emotion she displayed, the press had dubbed her the Black Widow, after the female spider that kills and devours its spouse after mating. NO REMORSE FOR BLACK WIDOW, one headline said, while another claimed: BLACK WIDOW BRAZEN AS EVIDENCE AGAINST HER PILES UP.

The trial had taken eight days, but the outcome was never really in doubt. Guilty or innocent, Kathryn McAllister had been convicted by the media long before the jury of eight men and four women had reached a verdict.

Nick removed the last microfilm and turned off the viewer. In the course of the past two hours, he'd learned a great deal about the McAllisters and about Elba, North Carolina. Like any small town, when something this gruesome happened, the citizens banded together to fight the evil in their midst. And that evil had been Kathryn McAllister.

He felt a twinge of empathy, somewhere in his belly, mingled with a grudging respect. Right or wrong, it took guts to come back and face that kind of animosity. And unless he missed his bet, he was going to have his hands full with Kathryn McAllister.

chapter two

Dressed in sweat pants and a tank top, Kathryn sat cross-legged on the living room floor and dragged the first box over to the coffee table. Rising to her knees, she blew a layer of dust off the top and opened the flaps. This job would be a nightmare, but she had to start somewhere, and the household records that Raelynn had been storing for her seemed as logical a place as any to begin.

She had no idea what she was looking for. Something unusual, something suspicious, something out of place or time. She could only hope that she would recognize it when she saw it. Taking a deep breath, she pulled out the first folder and opened it.

Michael McAllister had been meticulously organized. Each sub-category of recordkeeping had its own folder, and the folders were precisely organized in alphabetical order. It was amazing, the volume of paperwork two people could accumulate in four years of marriage. Insurance policies, canceled checks, income tax forms, old utility bills. She glanced at a bank statement, thumbed slowly through the canceled checks, but found nothing suspicious. Ditto for the income taxes. Until they'd bought the house, they hadn't even filed a long form.

After three hours of searching through a sea of paper, her vision was blurry and her head was pounding. And she still had two boxes left. Kathryn closed the box, changed into jogging shorts and headed out for a run.

After four years of jogging around an enclosed track in full view of leering prison guards, being able to run free was exhilarating. She chose a route where she was unlikely to meet anybody, and settled into the simple pleasure of running, of pushing her muscles to perform, the way a virtuoso aims for perfection on his chosen instrument. She'd worked hard to keep herself in shape while in prison, running three times a week, hefting eighty-pound bags of linens in the prison laundry daily. She'd built up biceps that were as strong as any man's. Her one failure, and the lone female vanity she'd tried unsuccessfully to overcome, was her hands.

She'd always had lovely hands, slender and delicate, with soft, perfumed skin and gently rounded nails. Michael had been fond of holding those hands in his much larger ones and tracing the delicate lines with his fingertips, marveling at her daintiness next to his oversized masculinity. But after four years in the prison laundry, her hands were red and chapped and wrinkled, her nails blunt-tipped and ragged. They looked like the hands of an old woman, and although she'd told herself, time and again, that the condition of her hands was inconsequential compared to the bigger problems in her life, still she couldn't help the petty vanity that made her furious because this had happened to her.

She turned off the main highway onto the narrow, gravel-topped road that circled around Lake Alberta. Bathed in solitude and shaded by towering pines, it had always been one of her favorite places to run. The sun glinting off the surface of the lake was dazzling, and she was slowing to admire it when she heard the car.

It approached her from behind at a moderate rate of speed, and she edged closer to the shoulder to give it room to pass. A dozen yards behind her, the car halted, its engine still idling, and uneasiness slithered up her spine. The first thing she'd learned in prison had been how to scent danger. Kathryn quickened her pace in sync with her suddenly rapid heartbeat. Without warning, the driver punched the accelerator, and the car raced toward her.

She had no more than a couple of seconds to react. Throwing her entire body into the motion, she twisted away, lost her footing in the loose gravel and fell hard on her hip on the grassy shoulder. The car roared past, so close she could feel the heat from its engine, and sped off in a cloud of dust.

Kathryn lay there gasping, her heart racing as she tried to take in the stunning reality that somebody had just tried to kill her. Her arrival in Elba hadn't exactly been celebrated with a parade and a brass band. But she hadn't even started snooping around yet, and already somebody wanted her out of the way.

The truth was, a lot of people wanted her out of the way. This might have been simply one more upright citizen who'd decided do the town a favor by ridding it of an unwanted pest. She should report the incident to the police, but she'd already found out just how helpful the police were going to be. She wanted to laugh at the irony of it. She'd been safer in prison, where she at least knew her enemy, than she was here, walking the streets of the town where she'd spent four years of her life, a town where everybody hated her, and at least one of those people was a killer.

Kathryn picked herself up and brushed the gravel from her bare legs. Her hip was aching from the force of her landing, and she'd twisted her ankle somehow when she fell. It hurt like the blue blazes when she rested her weight on it. Tears blurred her eyes, but she furiously brushed them away. She'd survived four years of prison. She could survive this.

By the time she reached her house, her ankle had started swelling. A strange vehicle was parked in the driveway, a black Chevy Blazer. And sitting casually on the front porch swing, looking for all the world as though he owned the place, was Police Chief Nick DiSalvo.

Trying to hide the pain she felt with every step, Kathryn marched resolutely up to him. "It didn't take you long to find out where I live, did it, Chief? I suppose you're here to arrest me for violating some archaic law. Like the one that says women can only show their legs in Elba on alternate Tuesdays."

"You're limping," he said.

"Congratulations," she snapped. "You can go to the head of the class."

"What happened?"

She used the key that hung around her neck to unlock the door. "Nothing much," she said, and stepped inside. "Somebody tried to kill me, that's all."

He grabbed her arm and yanked her around, causing her to wince at the sudden movement. "What?"

"I was nearly run down by a car." She looked down at the hand that gripped her arm. His skin was several shades darker than hers, the back of his wrist dusted with black hairs that disappeared into the cuff of his blue shirt. "Let go of me," she said.

Ignoring her, he said, "Sit down before you fall on your face."

In too much pain to argue, she sank gratefully onto the couch. DiSalvo knelt before her and carefully removed her sneaker. He wiggled her foot around to make sure there were no broken bones, and she flinched. "Sorry," he said, and rocked back on his heels. "That's some sprain you got there, kid. Want to tell me what happened?"

"Some maniac tried to run me down. If my reflexes had been a little slower, I'd be dead right now."

Those mournful Italian eyes were sharp with interest, along with something else she couldn't identify. "What kind of car?" he said. "Make, model, color?"

"Some kind of dark-colored sedan. It all happened so quickly."

"I don't suppose you got a look at the license plate?"

Her head snapped up. "I was on my ass in the ditch," she said. "I'm sorry I didn't get a better description of my assailant."

"You'd better put some ice on that ankle. You stay put. I'll get it."

She waited impatiently while he rattled around in her kitchen. He returned with a half-dozen ice cubes wrapped in a dish towel. "Sometimes," he said, "you just have to improvise. Hold still now."

Kathryn winced when he applied the ice to her swollen ankle, but the cold immediately eased the red-hot pain. "I can do that," she said, shoving his hand away. She moved the ice pack around a little, trying to cover all her bases. "What are you doing here?"

Instead of answering her, he walked around the room, pausing to study with great interest the boxes she'd left stacked beside the couch. "What's this?" he said.

She wondered just how far she could trust him. After all, he was a cop. And he still hadn't told her why he was here. "Old household records," she said, "that Raelynn was storing for me."

"Old household records."

"I thought if I went through them, maybe I'd stumble across a clue that would lead me to Michael's killer."

He lifted the flaps on one of the boxes and thumbed through the neatly labeled and color-coded tabs. "This your work, or your husband's?"

"Michael's. He was very organized."

"You can say that again." Absently, he added, "The file's missing, by the way."

She wasn't following him. "What file?" she said.

"The departmental file on the McAllister homicide. It's not in the drawer."

Her heart began to thud again, this time for a different reason. "Meaning?"

"Hell of a coincidence," he said, still looking at the files. "First, you're freed because a new witness appears out of the blue. And then—" He looked up, and those chocolate eyes bored directly into hers. "—the department's file disappears, too."

So he'd been checking up on her. She wasn't sure how she felt about that. "Are you saying you think I had something to do with it?"

"I haven't decided yet. It could mean you have a friend with access to confidential materials who decided to help you out. Or—" He paused, closed the cover on the box of household records. "Or," he said, "it could mean that somebody's trying real hard to hide something. You want to file a complaint?"

"What?"

"The car," he said. "You want to file an official complaint?"

"What good will it do me?"

"Most likely none. Without a description, without a license number, we've got squat to go on. It was probably nothing. Kids, trying to scare you."

"You weren't there."

His level gaze studied her face. "No," he said. "I wasn't."

Was he implying that she might have made up the whole incident? "You can leave now," she said. "The door's right over there."

She hadn't thought he knew how to smile. It changed his entire face, brought light to the shadows that lurked there. "Make sure you keep putting ice to that ankle," he said as he opened the door. "If the swelling doesn't go down in a couple of days, you might want to consider seeing a doctor. Oh, and be sure to keep your doors and windows locked."

"Thank you, Chief DiSalvo, for that pithy advice."

"Watch yourself," he said sternly, and closed the door behind him.

* * *

Wanita Crumley lived in a little brick ranch house on the outskirts of town. The front lawn was sparse, most of the grass yellowed by the hot Carolina sun and the lack of a sprinkler. As Kathryn climbed out of the secondhand blue Toyota she'd bought the day before, she could hear the shrill laughter of small children coming from around the back. She smoothed the wrinkles from her skirt, fortified herself with a deep breath, and strode toward the door.

There was no bell, so she opened the screen and knocked on the inside door. When there was no answer, she stretched up on her toes and peered through the tiny oval window at the top. She knocked again, harder this time, and then she heard footsteps approaching. "Just a minute!" a peevish voice said. The door was flung open, and she was face to face with the woman whose testimony had helped put her behind bars.

The years had not been kind to Wanita. She must have put on forty pounds since Kathryn had last seen her. Her blond hair was teased and sprayed in a vain attempt to look fashionable. She must have been napping, because her mascara was smeared and a red ridge scarred one cheek.

When she recognized Kathryn, her eyes went wide and her mouth formed a perfect o. "I'd like to talk to you," Kathryn said.

Wanita closed her gaping mouth. "Get out of here," she said. "I got nothing to say to you."

She moved to close the door, but Kathryn was quicker. She crammed her foot between the door and the jamb and threw her entire weight into pushing it open. Wanita might outweigh her, but Wanita hadn't spent the last four years toting eighty-pound bags of laundry. Kathryn shut the door behind her and leaned on it. "Now," she said, "you and I are going to have a talk."

Wanita walked away from her, picked up a pack of cigarettes from an end table, and lit one. "You got no right to be coming here," she said, "pushing your way into my house like this." She sat on the couch and crossed her legs. "I ought to call the cops and have you removed from my property."

Kathryn smiled. "And perhaps while they're here removing me, you'd like to tell them why you perjured yourself in court."

Beneath the heavy makeup, Wanita paled visibly. She sucked

hard on the cigarette, brazenly met Kathryn's gaze, and blew out the smoke. "I have no idea what you're talking about."

"You lied in court, Wanita. You testified that you believed I killed Michael after I found out the two of you were having an affair. I want to know why."

Wanita tossed her honey-colored mane. "That's right, sweetcakes, I did tell 'em that. Because it was the truth."

"Bullshit. Even if he'd been cheating on me, which he wasn't, Michael would never have gone near someone like you. He had more taste than that."

"Michael came to me," Wanita said, "to give him what his stuck-up, tight-ass Yankee wife wouldn't. You were always so damn proper. Michael liked a good time, so he came to me." She exhaled a cloud of smoke and smiled cruelly. "Who would have guessed we'd fall in love?"

"I don't believe you."

Wanita drew deeply on the cigarette. Exhaled. "Well," she said, "that's my story. I say it happened that way, there's nobody alive who can prove it didn't. Michael sure as hell isn't talking."

"Fine. Now I'm going to tell you my version of the story. Somebody wanted me out of the way. Wanted me out of the way very badly. Maybe he had something on you, something you were trying to hide. Or maybe he just paid you to lie in court. Dangled a carrot in front of your nose." She looked around the cluttered living room. "I doubt you bought this house on the salary you make clerking at Winn-Dixie."

Something sparked in the depths of Wanita's eyes. "Interesting story. Now I'd like you to leave."

"Who paid you, Wanita? Who paid you to lie in court?"

"Nobody! I'm tellin' you, nobody paid me!"

"Look," Kathryn said softly. "You and I both know that I didn't kill Michael. Which means that whoever did kill him is still out there somewhere. We're both in this mess up to our necks. If we don't bring him down, we could both end up losing our heads."

The fear that flickered across Wanita's face was genuine. "Get out!" she shouted. "Goddamn crazy meddling bitch. Just get out!"

Her shouting brought two preschool-age children in from the back yard to see what all the ruckus was about. They stood in the archway to the dining room, eyes wide with curiosity and fear.

Kathryn smiled reassuringly at them. "I lost my husband, and four years of my life," she said softly. "And I will keep right on meddling until I find out why." She reached into her purse and pulled out a pen and paper. "Here's my phone number," she said. "You can call me any time, day or night."

She held out the slip of paper, but Wanita refused to take it. "You'll end up dead," the woman said. "If you don't let it be, you'll end up dead."

Kathryn's mouth drew into a grim line. "I guess that's my problem, isn't it?" she said, and set the slip of paper on the end table.

On her way home, she took a detour past the old Chandler place. To her surprise, the house was empty, deserted, the windows boarded up, the grass unmowed, and the garden, which had once been her pride and joy, overrun with weeds.

She parked the car in the driveway and sat there for a time, looking at the house. The last time she'd seen it had been the day Michael died, when she'd looked back at their home from the rear seat of a police cruiser. She'd expected that the memories, and the pain, would be unbearable.

But to her surprise, the pain she'd expected to feel wasn't there. The memories would be with her always, but the pain had eased. She'd loved Michael dearly, but she'd stopped mourning him a long time ago. Perhaps because of the passage of time, perhaps because it all looked so different now, their home was only a house to her. A beautiful house that was slowly succumbing to time and the elements.

She wondered why the place was still empty. The bank had foreclosed a few months after Michael's death because she'd been unable to keep up with the payments. But they'd put so much into the house, so much work, so much money, so much love, that she'd expected somebody would snatch it up the instant it went on the market.

Some people, she supposed, would have been frightened off by the fact that the house had been the site of a grisly murder. But other houses with violent histories were bought and sold every day. Michael's murder might have slowed down the sale of the house, but it shouldn't have prevented it.

Still pondering, she drove through town slowly, enjoying the summer afternoon, the shady, tree-lined side streets, the old houses set back behind broad green lawns. The ladies of the Elba Historical Society were holding a tag sale on the front lawn of the Methodist Church, and out in front of the five-and-ten, the Good Humor man was peddling his wares.

Kathryn pulled into her driveway and parked, gathered her mail from the box and meandered up the walk, riffling through the advertisements addressed to Occupant that were her only mail. She'd reached the porch before she realized something wasn't right. The front door she'd left locked was ajar. She came to an abrupt halt when she realized that somebody had kicked it in. The lock dangled at an awkward angle, and splintered wood littered the floor.

Cautiously, she pushed open the door and stepped through. The living room looked like a tornado had torn through it. The three boxes of files had been emptied on the floor and the papers scattered everywhere. The coffee table had been bashed repeatedly against the stone fireplace until it was nothing but a pile of kindling. Plants had been overturned, the potting soil ground into the scatter rugs she'd bought just yesterday. The couch cushions had slashed, their stuffing pulled out and strewn about the room.

Her breath a red-hot fire in her chest, she stepped gingerly around a broken Depression glass vase and walked into the kitchen. The cupboards had been emptied, dishes smashed, china that had belonged to Raelynn's mother lying in shards on the floor. Kathryn put her fist to her mouth to stifle a sob, then spun around and marched directly to the telephone.

While she waited for the police to arrive, she sat on the front steps in the sunshine, quaking with fury. Somebody hated her, and that was one thing. But this house, this furniture, these damn dishes, belonged to Raelynn. Whoever had done this hadn't cared, and that was what made her furious. They'd taken what should have been a personal grudge and aimed it at an innocent party.

She heard the siren as it turned the corner from Myrtle Street. Blue lights flashing on the dash, Nick DiSalvo's Blazer came to a stop at the curb, followed closely by a police cruiser in full regalia. DiSalvo ambled across the lawn toward her, taking his time, in no particular hurry on this fine day. "Afternoon," he said.

Kathryn was in no mood for his game playing. "Inside," she said, and buried her face in her hands.

The uniformed officer who'd been driving the cruiser followed

DiSalvo inside. She heard them talking quietly, indistinctly, heard the crunch of glass beneath their shoes. A short time later, DiSalvo came out alone and sat down on the step beside her. "How's the ankle?" he said.

"Fine!" she snapped.

He took a pack of Juicy Fruit out of his pocket and removed a stick of gum. Held the packet out to her. "Gum?" he said.

"No," she said. "Thank you."

He returned the packet to his breast pocket. "I quit smoking six months ago," he said, unwrapping the gum. "It keeps me from losing my mind." He popped the gum into his mouth, rolled the foil into a ball and dropped it in his pocket. "You do have a way of drawing trouble to you."

She didn't know whether to cry or laugh at the absurdity of the situation. "It must be my magnetic personality."

He leaned back on both elbows and gazed up through the lacy foliage above them to the sky beyond. "I've been a cop since I was eighteen," he said. "I spent nine years walking a beat for the NYPD before I made detective. Just about anything that one human being can do to another, I've seen. And I have to say that somebody out there has really taken a dislike to you."

"Bravo, DiSalvo. You are one sharp detective."

An electric-blue Mustang convertible pulled up in front of DiSalvo's Blazer, and Raelynn climbed out. DiSalvo glanced at her out of the corner of his eye. "Any particular reason," he said, "that you called your lawyer?"

"She also happens to be my landlady," Kathryn said. "Most of the furniture and the dishes in this place, what's left of them, belong to her."

Raelynn clicked up the walkway in bright red shoes that would have been at home on a cocktail waitress yet looked smashing with her navy Donna Karan suit. "Afternoon, Chief," she said, dimpling and holding out her hand.

In a courtly gesture that left Kathryn's mouth agape, Nick DiSalvo bent and kissed the proffered fingers. "Ms. Wilbur," he said. "I hear that some of the property destroyed belonged to you. My condolences."

Raelynn waved him off and held out her arms to Kathryn. "Sugar, I'm so sorry. I can't believe they'd do this to you."

"I'm the one who should apologize," Kathryn said. "Those dishes were family heirlooms."

"Better to lose a family heirloom," Raelynn said, "than a friend." She straightened her spine and sighed. "I suppose I might as well go in and survey the damage."

"Better brace yourself," DiSalvo said.

They both stood there, watching her go, and then Kathryn said quietly, "This wasn't kids."

"No," DiSalvo said. "I don't think it was. This wasn't just random vandalism. It's too savage. There's a rage behind this, so strong you can feel it."

So she wasn't the only one who sensed the malevolence behind this act. She was absurdly relieved to know that he felt it, too.

"I'm assuming," he said, "that this time you want to file a complaint."

"You'd better believe I do!"

"Why don't you come on down to the station? We can do it there."

She hesitated, looked back questioningly at the house.

"Earl will be here for a while. And then you'll be needing one hell of a clean-up crew. You might as well avoid it as long as you can."

At the station, he gave her coffee that would probably grow hair on her chest, and ushered her into his office. His secretary looked up from her knitting long enough to glare at them, and then he shut the door in her face. "Sometimes I wonder if she has the place bugged," he said, and Kathryn smiled politely over the rim of her cup.

He opened a drawer, pulled out a sheet of notebook paper, and picked up a pen. "Okay," he said. "What time did you leave the house?"

"Around noon. Maybe quarter past."

"And you got back when?"

"Two-ish."

He wrote something on the piece of paper. "And where were you during that time?"

"Look," she said, setting down the coffee cup, "is this really necessary?"

"These are standard questions, Kathryn. You can answer 'em

for me, or I can turn you over to Bucky Stimpson. It's up to you."

His use of her given name unnerved her. Perhaps that was his intent. "I suppose the devil you know," she said acidly, "is preferable to the one you don't."

"Exactly. Now, where were you?"

She raised her chin. "I went to see Wanita Crumley."

She could tell from his face that he knew who Wanita was. "I see," he said, and steepled his fingers together on the desk. "Friend of yours?"

"Hardly. If you've read much about the trial, you'll know what she did to me."

"She testified against you in court."

"She lied in court! She committed perjury."

"Why did you go to see her, Kathryn?"

"To find out why she lied. I think somebody paid her. Somebody who wanted to put me away someplace where I wouldn't be able to look too closely at what happened to Michael."

He leaned back in his chair with a deep sigh and a pained expression. "Tell me you didn't threaten her."

"Of course I didn't threaten her! Do I look like a complete fool? I gave her my phone number and told her to call me if anything of significance should occur to her."

He looked up at the ceiling and said something in Italian that sounded suspiciously like a curse. "What the hell am I supposed do with you, McAllister? You've been in town for what—three days? Already, you've come within inches of being run down by a car, and now somebody's trashed your house. What do you do for an encore?"

"For my encore," she said, "I'm going to bag a killer."

He gripped the edge of his desk. "I didn't come to Elba, North Carolina, so I could spend my time baby-sitting some damn woman who's too stupid to leave well enough alone!"

Incensed, she sprang to her feet. Swinging her purse strap over her shoulder, she said, "This interview, Chief DiSalvo, is over."

"Sit down," he said, "and shut up. It would be a damn shame if I had to go down to the morgue to identify your body, lying there on a cold slab like a piece of meat. I'm trying to prevent that from happening. But you're making it damn difficult!"

She leaned over his desk. "What that woman did to me," she

said, "was unconscionable. In the midst of a media circus, she painted me as a cold, unfeeling harpy who drove her husband into another woman's arms. It was a lie. It was all a pack of lies. Michael never touched her. He loved me." She stabbed the tip of her index finger into her chest. "He loved *me!*"

Mildly, he said, "Nobody's claiming he didn't."

"Wanita Crumley did. And the jury bought it. Hook, line, and sinker. The only possible reason she could have had for perjuring herself was if somebody put her up to it. And I intend to find out who that somebody was."

"Even if it means putting yourself in jeopardy?"

"I'm on a mission, DiSalvo. They're not going to scare me off."

A half-hour later, he drove her home. The police had finished with the scene, and DiSalvo lingered until the locksmith arrived. "While you're at it," he said, "change the lock on the back door, too. I checked it earlier, and it's a joke."

He turned to Raelynn, who was standing with her arm around Kathryn's waist. "Will you try to talk some sense into this crazy woman?" he said.

"Believe me, sugar, I've tried. But our little Kat is not a good listener."

"I'll try to step up patrols in the area for a while," he told Kathryn. "In the meantime, don't open your door for anybody you don't know. Or trust. Whoever did this has a mad on, and a mean streak a mile wide."

He spent a few minutes giving instructions to the locksmith, whose head bobbed up and down as he nodded assent. Kathryn stood at the picture window, gnawing absently on her bottom lip, and watched as he climbed into the Blazer and drove away.

"Whoo-ee," Raelynn said behind her, "do we have a mess to clean."

Still looking out the window, she said, "What do you know about him?"

"DiSalvo? I know I've been trying since April to get him into bed, but so far, he hasn't shown a glimmer of interest."

"Maybe he doesn't like women."

Raelynn threw back her head and laughed. "Trust me on this one, sugar. There ain't nothing wrong with that man. Everything is in the right place, and in working order."

"How fortunate for him."

Raelynn grinned wickedly. "Or whoever gets to him first."

"What else do you know about him? Professionally?"

"The rumor mill says that our boy Nick is squeaky clean. A straight arrow. A good cop. Easygoing, until you cross him, and then watch out. Italian temper."

Kathryn fingered the window drape. "Can I trust him?"

"According to the rumor mill? Probably."

"I know better than to trust the rumor mill. What does Raelynn Wilbur have to say?"

Her friend's face tightened. "Raelynn Wilbur says that there are two people in this town you can trust. One of them's me, sugar. The other one just walked out that door."

chapter three

There were certain things in life a man needed in order to survive. A cold beer, a sirloin on the grill, and a little cool Metheny on the stereo could go a long way toward helping a guy maintain his sanity. Dressed in faded jeans and the loudest Hawaiian shirt he'd been able to score during a long weekend last month in Myrtle Beach, Nick turned the steak and listened to the satisfying sizzle of raw meat hitting a hot grill. He uncorked the barbecue sauce and poured on a generous dollop, then returned to his lounge chair and his John Grisham novel.

He made it through maybe half a page before the phone rang. With a sigh, he earmarked the page and picked up his cordless phone. "DiSalvo," he said.

"Nicky? I didn't expect to get you. You never used to come home this early. Isn't it ironic that men always wait until after the divorce to reform?"

A headache sprang to life behind his left temple. "Lenore," he said. "What do you want?"

"Your mother asked me to call. She's worried about you." His ex-wife hesitated. "She says you don't return her calls."

A twinge of guilt passed through him. "So she sicced the family bloodhound on me. Remind me to thank her the next time I see her."

"You don't have to be nasty. She just asked me to talk to you. She thought maybe you'd listen to me." Her voice grew coy. "There was a time when I had more than a little influence over you, Nicky."

The headache increased in intensity. Nick closed his eyes. "How's Walter?" he asked pointedly. Her new husband was a pharmacist at one of those nationwide chains that was part drugstore, part grocery, part department store. One-stop shopping for all your household needs.

"Walter," she said, "is just fine. And *he's* home every night by 5:30."

It had been a bone of contention between them, would always be a bone of contention between them, that when he'd been working a case, he had put in twenty-hour days, had canceled family vacations, had basically absented himself from the home. Lenore had always resented what it meant to be a cop's wife. So she'd gone out and found herself a new husband. "What should I tell your mother?" she said.

He rubbed absently at his temple. "Tell her I've been busy. My new job's a headache. Tremendous responsibility. You know how it is."

Her bark of laughter was brittle. "Crime running rampant down there in Mayberry, is it, Nicky?"

"Knock it off, Lenore. Tell Mom I'll call her." He hesitated. "Is Janine there?"

"Yeah. I'll put her on. It's been great talking to you, Nicky."

A moment later, his thirteen-year-old daughter picked up the extension. "Daddy!" she exclaimed.

His heart squeezed in his chest. "Hi, baby," he said.

"Jenny Giulio's having a Fourth of July bash at her Gram's place in Syosset, with a live band and everything. Robbie Morrison invited me, and Mom said I could go!"

Since when had Janine been old enough to go out with boys? "Who the hell is Robbie Morrison?" he said.

"He's this totally awesome boy in my class, Daddy."

He didn't know how to respond. He hadn't expected this so soon. Gruffly, he said, "You be careful, you hear?"

"Oh, Dad, don't be a dork." Janine paused. "I miss you," she said.

"I miss you, too, lambchop."

"How come you don't ever call?"

Guilt twisted inside him. "I'm sorry, baby. I've just been so damn busy. I'll try to call more often, okay?"

Janine sighed. "Okay," she said.

"Hey, kiddo, maybe you could fly down and visit me sometime."

"Right. Mom would probably have a bird."

The steak was burning. He could smell it. "We'll work around Mom," he said. "Listen, sweetheart, I have to go, I'm in the middle of cooking supper."

"Okay. I love you, Daddy."

"I love you, too, baby."

He managed to salvage the steak, but his mood, and his appetite, had taken a nosedive. He ate his supper halfheartedly, left the dirty dishes in the sink, then showered and changed and drove out to Dewey Webb's.

Dewey's was a roadhouse just outside of town, with a reputation for loud music, free-flowing liquor, and fast women. It was the kind of place the pastors of Elba's two dozen churches vilified from their respective pulpits on Sunday mornings. Folks went to Dewey's to sin, and tonight, Police Chief Nick DiSalvo was in a sinning mood.

He ordered a beer and wandered out to the back room. A few of the locals eyed him warily. Most people still weren't quite sure how to take him, so they greeted him with uneasy formality. "Evening, Chief," one of the men said, and the others, not to be outdone, chimed in with lukewarm greetings.

He played a couple rounds of pool, and the atmosphere relaxed a little. Afterward, he drank a few beers with Linc Stempel and Gus Hoyt, two old-timers who spent most of their days sitting outside Carlyle's Barber Shop, chewing tobacco and talking about the old days. But tonight, there was just one topic of conversation. He couldn't escape the woman, no matter where he went.

"I hear that McAllister woman's back in town," Gus said. He raised his bottle to his mouth and glugged down half of it, then let out a loud belch. "She's gonna be a thorn in your side, boy."

"We'll see," Nick said.

"Folks around here," Linc said, "don't cotton to the idea of some murderess running around loose."

"Her conviction was overturned," Nick said amiably.

Gus snorted. "On a technicality's what I hear. Don't mean diddly 'cept them lawyers screwed up somehow, and now she's walking free."

"It was new evidence," Nick said. "A new witness came forward."

"And she's come back to rub our faces in it."

Nick tore at the label on his bottle of Bud. "You guys think she did it?"

"Don't matter what we think," Linc said laconically. "The jury said she did it. That's what matters."

"Somebody trashed her house this afternoon," Nick said.

Gus leaned forward, always eager to hear a new sliver of gossip. "Do tell?"

"Stove up the furniture, broke dishes, upended plants, emptied the kitchen cupboards all over the floor."

Linc shook his head. "People hereabouts ain't gonna make it easy on her. She'd be better off going back where she come from. 'Round here, we take care of our own. And Michael McAllister was one of our own."

Nick clapped him on the shoulder. "Right you are, my man. Listen, if either one of you hears anything, I'd appreciate a call."

He bought both of the boys a round of beer before he went out into the muggy night. The air was thick and heavy and hard to breathe. He drove through the streets of Elba slowly, with meticulous care. It wouldn't do for the new police chief to be arrested for driving while intoxicated.

He'd already pulled up in front of Kathryn McAllister's house before he realized it was where he'd been headed all along. Her living room light was on, and soft music drifted out the open windows to mingle with the night air. Classical. It all sounded alike to him, but it was nice. Pretty. Soothing.

He rang the bell and tucked his hands in his pockets like some high school kid on a first date. Footsteps approached the door, and then her voice, cautious, asked, "Who is it?"

"Nick," he said. "Nick DiSalvo."

There was a moment's hesitation, and then she unlocked the door and opened it. Her hair was damp, and she was wearing a white terry cloth wraparound robe that tied around the middle. The front of it plunged in a shadowy vee, and as far as he could tell, she wasn't wearing anything under it. "What do you want?" she said.

He wasn't really sure what he was doing here. Christ, he must be drunker than he thought. He struggled to bring her into focus. "Coffee," he said.

She eyed him long and hard. And then she stepped back to let him in. "I think that's probably a good idea."

There was virtually no evidence of this afternoon's devastation. She'd covered the torn furniture with blankets, repotted the houseplants that were salvageable, swept up the glass and the potting soil and the Corn Flakes. He followed her to the kitchen, watched as she stretched up on bare toes to reach the cupboard. "It'll have to be instant," she said. "It's all I have."

He cleared his throat. "Fine. Whatever you got."

She filled the teakettle, turned on the burner beneath. "Been to Dewey's, have you, DiSalvo?"

"Great detective work, McAllister."

"It isn't hard," she said, turning and leaning against the stove with her arms crossed, "in a town that has twenty-three churches and one bar. I doubt that the First Methodist has taken to serving boilermakers at its Wednesday-night prayer service."

He wondered what her hair would feel like if he ran his hands through it. Soft, like a burnished cloud, tangled and damp from the shower she'd just come from. He already knew what it smelled like, sweet and tangy, like the scent of a fresh-peeled orange, and he wondered if her skin would taste that same way if he touched the tip of his tongue to the soft hollow at the base of her throat.

The kettle wailed, and she busied herself making coffee for both of them. It must be Lenore that had him so edgy tonight. Until his ex-wife called, he'd forgotten how long it had been since he'd been with a woman.

Kathryn turned to look at him. "Cream and sugar?" she said.

In the background, soft piano music played. "I think I better go," he said.

She just stood there, saying nothing, her face expressionless. And then she nodded. "Yes. I think you probably should."

"I'm sorry. I don't belong here. Not tonight."

He wove his way to the front door and fumbled with the lock. "Nick?" she said softly, behind him.

He looked over his shoulder. Swaying slightly, he said, "Yeah?"

"Let me get dressed and drive you home."

He swung the door back and forth a couple of times. "Nah. I'll
be all right. I don't live far."

The corners of her mouth settled into a frown. "You won't be
all right if you wrap your truck around a tree."

"I won't wrap it around a tree." He stepped through the door,
paused on the porch to look back at her. "Remember what I said
about keeping your doors locked. Don't let anybody in."

One slender hand went to her hair and tucked it behind her ear.
"I let you in," she said.

"Yeah, well, I'm not exactly your garden-variety rapist."

"Good-night, DiSalvo," she said. "Drive carefully."

And she shut the door in his face.

* * *

The clerk at the Rowley County Courthouse was helpful and
efficient, pulling out all the property map books for Elba and
stacking them on the table next to Kathryn's chair. The books were
musty from disuse, and some of the pages had yellowed with age.
She paged through them slowly until she found the map that showed
Wanita Crumley's property. It was bordered on the north by the pig
farm of Ellis Jenkins, whose two children had both been in Kathryn's
fifth-grade class a few years back. To the south and east, Wanita's
property butted up against that of Neely and Kevin McAllister.

No surprises here. Both the Crumley and the Jenkins properties
had been carved out of acreage that had belonged to the McAllister
family since before the Civil War, when the antebellum plantation
had supported several thousand acres of cotton and tobacco, worked
by a small army of slaves. Subsequent to President Lincoln's 1863
emancipation mandate and The Late Unpleasantness, as the war was
known to many in these parts, the family had begun selling off
chunks of the land which had once been an asset but had now
become a liability. Without all those slaves to work the land, a
number of families suddenly found themselves land-rich but money-
poor, and had been forced to sell off pieces of their once-glorious
plantations in order to put food on the dinner table.

Kathryn closed the heavy book and set it aside. As an
afterthought, she drew it back across the table, opened it back up,
and began paging through it in search of the Chandler place, curious

about the identity of the property owner who was letting the place disintegrate. She found it on page 83, and began scanning the fine print. *Two-acre lot bordered on the south by Francis Trimble, on the east by Ridgewood Road, on the north and west by Harriet Slocum. Property owners Kevin and Neely McAllister.*

She stopped abruptly. Backed up to re-read it, certain she was wrong about what she thought she'd read. But there it was, in black and white. Kevin and Neely McAllister owned the house where Michael had been murdered. They were the absentee owners who were allowing their son's home to go to ruin.

It made no sense at all. Why would the Judge have bought the Chandler place after his son had died there under violent circumstances? Why would they want the constant reminder? If Kathryn had been the one whose child was brutally murdered, she would have wanted to burn the place down. Instead, the Judge and Neely were letting the house die a slow and ugly death.

She drove back into town and parked in front of the First National Bank of Elba. Wendy Sue Mortimer, John Chamberlain's buxom young secretary, looked up from her typewriter and her eyes went wide with recognition. "I'd like to see Mr. Chamberlain," Kathryn told her.

"I'm afraid he's busy right now."

"Fine. I'll wait."

Without waiting for an invitation, she made herself comfortable in one of the padded oak captain's chairs the bank supplied for its customers. Everything about the place, from the plush mauve carpeting to the rich mahogany wainscoting, shouted out that Serious Business took place here, beneath the watchful eyes of a gallery of former bank presidents going back more than a century. The South, Kathryn had quickly learned, took its history seriously.

She waited thirty-seven minutes for her audience with the bank president, countering the curious and angry stares of passing customers with a bland and impersonal smile. John Chamberlain finally emerged from his office, glanced quickly right and left, and ushered her inside. He sat in a plush leather chair behind a massive desk of polished walnut and folded his hands over his ample girth. With false joviality, he said, "And what may I do for you on this fine day, Miz McAllister?"

"I just learned something that I find curious, Mr. Chamberlain. And I thought perhaps you could enlighten me."

"And what might that be?"

"After Michael's death," she said, "while I was in prison, you foreclosed on our mortgage."

He straightened in his chair. "That's correct. Since you were unable to make the payments, Miz McAllister, we were forced to take back the house and sell it."

"To my father-in-law."

The joviality disappeared. "I'm afraid," he said, "that I'm not followin' you."

"Don't you find it odd, Mr. Chamberlain, that a couple like the McAllisters would buy the house where their only son had been brutally murdered just a few months earlier?"

"I don't find it anything, Miz McAllister, except none of my business." He smiled thinly. "Or yours."

"It just seems a rather gruesome reminder of their loss. I can't imagine why they'd do such a thing. Can you?"

"I really cannot continue this discussion any further. These are questions that should be directed to your former in-laws. Now, is there anything else I can do for you today, Miz McAllister?"

"Not a thing."

"Good. Then I suggest you leave, quietly and promptly."

Her hand was on the door knob when he spoke again. "Oh, by the way—"

"Yes?" She turned to look at him, sitting there behind his huge desk, looking for all the world like a walrus.

"If you're thinking of opening a bank account," he said, "First Federal Savings is right down the street."

* * *

On the sidewalk in front of the bank, she came face-to-face with her mother-in-law.

Even on the hottest summer day, Neely McAllister wore silk and pearls. Today her dress was a soft coral shirtwaist, with tiny pearl buttons down the front. Thanks to the miracle of Lady Clairol, her hair was still a soft ash blonde, and it was drawn up in an elegant chignon that was the envy of all the younger members of the Ladies

Aid Society.

Her eyes were a glacial blue that somehow managed to cool by several degrees the instant she saw Kathryn. Her mouth narrowed and her face drew into a hard mask that emphasized every wrinkle accumulated in her fifty-seven years.

"Good morning, Neely," Kathryn said evenly.

"How dare you come back here," her mother-in-law said in a voice that managed to be harsh without losing the even modulation all finely-bred young Southern ladies learned in finishing school. "After all you put us through, how dare you show your face in this town?"

"After all *I* put *you* though? You may have lost a son, but I lost a husband. I loved him, and you didn't even stand by me. You threw me to the wolves and watched while they licked my bones clean. And you have the nerve to criticize me?"

A muscle twitching in Neely's cheek was the only indication of her emotional state. "You're nothing but a tramp," she said. "I told Michael that the day he brought you home. I begged him to reconsider the marriage. I offered to pay any price you asked to have it annulled. But he laughed at me. His own mother." She stiffened her spine and raised her head. At that angle, in the bright light of midday, the wattles beneath her chin were plainly visible. "You had him bewitched. You, a nothing little tramp who got him to do your bidding by spreadin' your legs whenever he asked."

Of their own accord, her fists clenched. "That's enough," she said.

"He never loved you," Neely went on, as though she hadn't spoken. "He was just highly sexed, like his father. And he had a weakness for long-legged, trashy women." She pursed her mouth in distaste. "Also like his father."

"What do you know about love? You've never loved anybody but yourself."

"I love this town. And I know that it breaks my heart to see white trash like you dirtying up our fair streets." Her face hardened, and so did her voice. "I want you out of my town."

"The last time I looked," Kathryn said dryly, "I didn't see your name written down the center of Main Street."

"Well, then, Kathryn, perhaps you should consider looking a little more closely." And with her shoulders back and her head raised, Neely walked away without looking back.

For a single instant, Kathryn seriously considered picking up a large rock and bashing in the back of that perfectly-coifed head. Rage could drive people to do things that were light years beyond their normal ethical boundaries. She'd seen it more than once during those four years she spent in prison. But this was the first time she'd experienced it firsthand.

Her hands were shaking when she climbed into her car and slammed the door. She tore out of the parking space, shifted gears with a vengeance, and the little car shot forward, past the old men who were smoking and chawing outside Carlyle's Barber Shop. Like trained dogs, they all looked up as she passed, watching her with keen interest, probably already laying odds on the outcome of the contest between the two McAllister women.

She was still steaming an hour later when the telephone rang. She picked it up, balanced it against her shoulder. "Hello?" she said.

Silence. Dead silence.

"Hello?" she said, louder this time.

"If you know what's good for you," the voice whispered, "you'll get out of town now."

"What? Oh, for Christ's sake. Who is this?"

At the other end, the phone was quietly hung up. Kathryn looked at the receiver in disbelief, then slammed it back into place on the kitchen wall.

A moment later, it rang again. She gritted her teeth and picked it up. "Hello?" she said.

Again, silence.

"Look," she said, "don't you think you're being a tad melodramatic?"

"Bitch," the caller said, and hung up the phone.

When it rang a third time, she snatched it up. "What the hell do you want?" she shouted.

"Mother of mercy, McAllister," Nick DiSalvo drawled, "remind me not to get you riled up any time soon."

She went limp. She hadn't realized how hard she'd been trembling. "DiSalvo," she said weakly. "I wasn't expecting you."

"That's a relief. I'm glad to hear that greeting wasn't meant for me."

She ran a hand through her hair. "I'm sorry," she said. "I've been getting some interesting calls."

"Congratulations. I hear you managed to piss off quite a few people today. I'm sorry I missed your little *tète-a-tète* with your mother-in-law. I would have paid money to see it."

"My," she said dryly, "word does travel quickly around here."

"Welcome to Elba."

"Is there a reason you called, DiSalvo, other than to mock my public humiliation?"

At his end, there was a brief silence. "I called to apologize for last night," he said. "I had too much to drink and I was acting stupid."

It was the last thing she'd expected, and something softened inside her. "Apology accepted," she said. "And I didn't witness any stupid behavior. Of course, I can't vouch for what you did before or after you came to my house."

"Listen..." He paused, and her fingers tightened on the telephone receiver. "Do you have plans for dinner?"

Her stomach took a hard kick. She cleared her throat. "DiSalvo?" she said. "Are you asking me for a date?"

"I'm asking you to have dinner with me, McAllister. I have to eat dinner, you have to eat dinner. I just thought we might consider eating dinner together."

It was stupid. He was a cop, and she was a convicted felon. To hell with the fact that the conviction had been overturned. It was still the most monumentally stupid thing she'd ever done. "Yes," she said. "I'll have dinner with you."

"You like barbecue?"

"Everybody likes barbecue, DiSalvo. It's a prerequisite for living in this place. That, and knowing all the verses to *Dixie*."

"Is that a note of cynicism I hear in your voice, McAllister?"

"Why, Mr. DiSalvo," she said in an exaggerated Southern belle voice, "whatever possible reason could I have for being cynical?"

"I'll pick you up at six. That'll give me time to shower and change first."

The picture his words painted in her mind was best left untouched. Gruffly, she said, "Don't keep me waiting, DiSalvo. It's been a busy day, and I've worked up a powerful appetite."

chapter four

Buzzy's Bar-B-Q was located twenty miles east of Elba, just over the Stetson County line. Political correctness had not yet reached this section of the Bible belt, where tobacco was king, so a haze of blue smoke hung thick as kudzu over their heads, and well-oiled laughter lubricated the room. They were served humongous portions of barbecued ribs, swimming in Buzzy's own secret sauce, with a generous helping of potato salad on the side. They washed it down with long-necked bottles of Bud. "Do you have any idea," Kathryn said, licking a drop of barbecue sauce off her thumb, "how long it's been since I've eaten in a restaurant?"

DiSalvo raised his head and looked around the noisy, crowded room. "This is a restaurant? I thought we'd just been dropped into the middle of Dante's Inferno."

"I just got out of prison, DiSalvo. This place is heaven."

He smiled just a little. "You have barbecue sauce on your chin."

She rubbed briskly with her fingertips. "Better?"

He picked up a paper napkin and dipped it into his water glass, then leaned over the table and scrubbed at her face. "Better."

She rested her chin on her palm and studied him. "So tell me, DiSalvo. Why'd you become a cop?"

He leaned back in his seat and stretched out his long legs. "My dad was a cop. And both of my uncles. I guess it's in the blood."

She toyed with her beer bottle. "No burning desire to save the world?"

"More a burning desire to put food on the table. I got married when I was nineteen. That pretty much put an end to any save-the-world fantasies I might have had. I was too busy paying for the pediatrician and the new washer and dryer."

"You have kids," she said in surprise. Somehow, she hadn't pictured him as a father.

"A daughter. She's thirteen. They grow so fast, you know? One day they're wearing Pampers, the next day they're going out on dates." He looked at her in bewilderment. "Where the hell does the time go?"

"Is she in New York?"

"Yeah. With her mother. Want to see a picture?"

He reached for his wallet, opened it, pulled out a photo of a slender, dark-haired girl with his melted-chocolate eyes. "She's pretty," Kathryn said.

Nick took the photo back and studied it. "Yeah," he said, "she is. She looks just like her mother."

"So what happened? How did Mrs. DiSalvo become the ex-Mrs. DiSalvo?"

He slipped the picture back into his wallet and returned it to his pocket. "She wanted a husband who was home every night for supper. I was married to my job. After a while, she found somebody who wasn't."

"Ouch."

He raised his beer bottle. "Ouch," he said.

"How in the world did you get from New York City to Elba, North Carolina?"

"You want the truth, or the gussied-up version?"

She took a sip of beer. "I've always been partial to truth."

With his thumbnail, he tore at the label on his beer bottle. "I worked Vice out of Midtown Manhattan," he said. "Lenore and I had just split up, and I was a mess. Drinking too much. Distracted. Careless. One night, my partner and I went out on a routine call. Something went wrong, and Jimmy ended up dead. The next day, I turned in my badge."

"And?" she said softly.

"And—" He raised his beer bottle and looked at her through its amber light. "After six months or so, when I finally got tired of feeling sorry for myself, I answered a classified ad, and I ended up here."

"The grapevine says you're a good cop, Nick."

"Yeah? Tell that to Jimmy. Tell that to his pregnant wife and his three-year-old kid. I screwed up, and my best friend ended up dead."

"We're all human. We all make mistakes."

"I don't want to talk about it any more. It's your turn to bare your soul. Tell me about Kathryn."

"There's not much to tell, really. I grew up in a Boston suburb. Blue-collar. Probably a lot like the neighborhood where you grew up. My mom died when I was eleven, so it was just Pop and me after that. He never made it past the eighth grade, but he always told me I could be anything I wanted to be." She smiled wistfully at the memory. "He was the most incredible human being I've ever known."

Quietly, DiSalvo said, "He's gone now?"

"He died while I was in prison. They wouldn't even let me go to his funeral."

His face hardened. "Bastards," he said.

She raised her shoulders. "Anyway," she said, "I met Michael my junior year of college. I needed an art elective for my teaching degree, so I signed up for life drawing, thinking it would be easy. I couldn't draw worth beans, but there was this guy in my class who was just so intense, and—God, so talented! We got to talking after class, and he invited me for coffee. He was planning to be an architect, and he was the most charming, most genuine guy I'd ever met. I brought him home to meet Pop, and they hit it off like old chums. After he left that night, I told Pop I was going to marry him. And I did, two years later, the night before graduation."

"And he brought you home to Elba."

"And he brought me home to Elba. Michael loved this town, and everybody in it. And they all loved him. Or so I thought." She busied herself folding her napkin. "Obviously, I was wrong. Somebody hated him enough to want him dead."

"And now," he said dryly, "you're on a one-woman suicide mission."

"I was so much in love with him," she said. "In love with that kind of wide-eyed intensity you feel at twenty, when you have the whole of life ahead of you, and forever's real, and nothing can get in your way. We had it all planned out. The careers, the house, the kids. Two, maybe three. We both grew up without siblings, and we both swore we wouldn't do that to our own kids. He'd be the major breadwinner, once his architecture practice got off the ground. I'd teach school, which meant I'd be home when the kids needed me. We were young and idealistic, and we knew we had plenty of time to make it all happen. But you see, we ran out of time. Somebody did get in the way, and I can't just let it go. Michael was a good man. He didn't deserve to die that way. He won't be at peace until the person responsible for his death is punished. And I won't be at peace until I clear my name."

"Whoever killed him isn't going to stop at one, Kathryn. If you keep nosing around in the wrong places, you're going to wind up in a ditch somewhere with your throat slit. It's not worth it."

"And that, Chief DiSalvo, is where we disagree."

The camaraderie between them had abruptly fizzled out. They drove the twenty miles back to Elba in a strained silence. Nick pulled the Blazer into her driveway and left the engine running. "I'll come in with you," he said, "to make sure the house is empty."

"I can take care of myself. Thank you for dinner."

"I'm not leaving," he said gruffly, "until you're in the house."

She wasn't sure why she was so angry. She slammed the door of the Blazer and stalked indignantly toward the house and up onto the porch. She reached into her purse to pull out the key, and that was when she saw the box. Roughly three feet square, it was an ordinary cardboard box, the kind anybody could pick up from the pile out back of the Dixie Market, and it had been intentionally left where she would have to move it to open the front door. With a sigh of resignation, Kathryn walked over to it and peered inside.

The snake was coiled like a garden hose, sleek and shiny, the diamondback pattern clearly visible in the moonlight. He was probably five feet long, and as thick as a man's arm.

Her breath left her in a single, mighty rush. Adrenaline shot through her veins as she stood frozen, rooted to the spot, unable to move, unable to take her eyes off the hideous creature that watched her from less than a yard away.

Her mouth moved, but no sound came out. Her chest ached as she struggled for breath, and then oxygen filled her lungs and she began screaming, screaming hysterically, screaming DiSalvo's name over and over again.

She heard his truck door open, heard his footsteps running toward her, and still she continued to scream. In the box, the snake raised its head, its tail, and began that distinctive rattling sound.

DiSalvo came to an abrupt halt behind her. "Holy mother of Moses," he said. "For Christ's sake, don't move."

"Nick. Oh, God, Nick, please do something."

"I'm thinking. Christ, I left my weapon at home. Let me think. Shit. Whatever you do, don't move—"

"Don't leave me!"

"I'm not going anywhere. Look, I'm going to get a good grip on the back of your pants. You with me so far?"

She wet her lips. "Yes."

His warm hand burrowed down inside the waistband of her jeans. In spite of the hot, steamy night, her body, her blood, had turned to ice, and the contact with his warm flesh was reassuring. "Okay," he said quietly. "I'm going to count to three. When we get to three, I'm going to yank as hard as I can, as quick as I can. And we're both going to run like hell. Got that?"

The snake continued to watch her. "Yes," she said.

"One more thing."

"Yes?"

"I don't know if you're a particularly religious person, but if you were ever going to be, now's as good a time as any to start. Count with me. One. Two. Three—" He yanked so hard she lost her footing. The snake reared, and Nick caught her around the waist by one arm and vaulted over the porch railing.

They landed in the flower bed, a tangled, writhing mass of arms and legs and bodies. "Up!" he said, struggling to free himself from the brambles of the wild rose bush that climbed the trellis to the roof. She peeled a thorny branch away from his shirt, and then they were both on their feet and running toward the Blazer.

They climbed in and slammed the doors and sat there panting, cold with sweat and fear. His shirt was ripped from the brambles, and her hand was bleeding. While her heart thundered in her chest, he reached into the glove compartment, pulled out a clean tissue, and tucked it into the palm of her hand. "You okay?" he said, dabbing at the blood.

"I don't think...I'll know...for a while."

"You're okay. You haven't lost your sense of humor." He reached for the radio mike. "This is DiSalvo," he said into it. "Radio Bucky Stimpson and tell him to drop whatever he's doing and come over to Kathryn McAllister's place as fast as he can get here. I don't have my weapon with me, and somebody left a gift on Ms. McAllister's front porch tonight."

The scratchy voice at the other end said dubiously, "A gift?"

"That's what I said. Tell Bucky we have ourselves a full-sized rattler here, and Kathryn and I are not leaving this vehicle again until somebody comes over and blows his damn ugly head off."

* * *

The atmosphere was almost carnival-like. It was the biggest event Elba had seen since Alvin Deverell had gotten likkered up at Dewey's last May and shot out all the lights on Main Street. While Kathryn hovered inside Nick's Blazer, half the male population of the town stood on her front lawn, admiring the dead snake and testifying as to how he was the biggest rattler they'd seen since the one that bit the Crosley kid back in '83. Kid damn near died. Would have, too, what with the hospital being forty-five minutes away, if his Pa hadn't remembered that Dewey Webb kept a snakebite kit on the shelf in his supply room.

Kathryn closed her eyes and tuned out their voices. When the Blazer's door squawked open, she jumped. DiSalvo stood there in the dim glow of the dome light. "You okay?" he said gruffly.

"I've lost ten years off my life, but I'm okay."

"Yeah. You and me both. Listen, maybe you shouldn't stay alone here tonight."

"This is my home. I won't let them drive me from it."

"Whoever put that snake here wasn't fooling around, Kathryn. This isn't like emptying out your cupboards and tipping over your plants. If that damn thing had bitten you—"

"It didn't. And I'm not going anywhere."

"Then at least call Raelynn or somebody to stay with you."

Ignoring him, she said, "How much longer are they going to be here?"

"I'll chase 'em away. Why don't you go on in the house? You look beat."

Because she didn't know what else to do, she went inside and put on the teakettle. She stood in the kitchen, gripping the edge of the countertop and trying to shake off the panic that still hovered just beneath the surface. It wasn't a stranger who'd left that creature on her porch tonight. Whoever put it there had known about her irrational fear of snakes.

She squeezed her eyes shut and stood there trembling. Behind her, DiSalvo said softly, "Kathryn?"

She hadn't even heard him come in. She bit her lip. "Are they gone?"

"They're gone."

"And the snake?"

"Bucky carted it off, all excited, like it was the greatest archeological find since T. Rex." He came up behind her, rested both hands on hers and hooked his thumbs around her wrists. "You're cold," he said.

"Nick..."

Still holding her wrists, he folded his arms around her from behind and pulled her into him. He was warm, so warm, and for a moment, she allowed herself to relax against him, allowed herself to savor the wild mix of emotions that swirled up inside her. "Nick," she said again.

His breath was hot on the back of her neck, and if she turned in his arms, she would be lost. "What?" he said.

"Before you go...would you...check the house for me?"

Her words had the intended effect. He released her, stepped away, and the coldness rushed back in to blanket her. Beside them, the teakettle whistled. She cleared her throat. "Coffee?" she said, still not looking at him.

Stiffly, he said, "Sorry. I don't have time."

Hurt by his tone of voice, she turned to look at him. "Nick," she said softly. "Don't. Please."

"I have to go," he said. "I'll check the closets and look under the bed."

"Damn it, DiSalvo, don't be this way."

"Don't bother to see me out. I know where the door is."

* * *

When he got to work the next morning, there was a note on his desk requesting his immediate presence in the mayor's office. He poured himself a cup of coffee and went upstairs. Marilu Kelso, the mayor's secretary, smiled at him in a way that, had he been fifteen years younger, might have tempted him. But she was only five years older than his daughter, for Christ's sake. "Mayor says to go right in, Chief DiSalvo," she said, batting luxurious lashes, assisted no doubt by Maybelline, as he passed.

Mayor Wayne Stevens was the only black elected official in Elba. When longtime mayor John Chamberlain had retired, Stevens had run against Dewey Webb and had won by a landslide. He was now halfway through his second term, and he held the enviable position of being liked by the majority of his constituents, both black and white.

Stevens was busy writing something on a sheet of paper. "Be with you in a minute," he said. "Sit down."

Nick sat and waited, listening to the scratch of pen against paper. Stevens crossed a final t and scrawled his signature across the bottom of the page, capped the pen and set it down. He shoved the paper aside. "Chief DiSalvo," he said.

"Mayor Stevens."

Nick waited. The mayor steepled his fingers on the desk top. "I heard about last night's little episode at Kathryn McAllister's residence."

He smiled thinly. "Word does get around in this town, doesn't it?"

"I don't like to see this kind of thing going on in my town. Ever since that woman got here, she's done nothing but stir up trouble."

Nick raised an eyebrow. "She's not the one who left a five-foot rattlesnake in a box on her porch."

"No. But she obviously provoked somebody else into doing it. Do you have any leads?"

"Not yet. But we're working on it."

"Chief DiSalvo, I realize this is a delicate issue, but I feel I have to ask. What in hell were you doing at her home in the first place?"

He felt the jolt all the way to his stomach. Sitting up straighter, he said carefully, "We'd just had dinner together. I was escorting the lady home."

The mayor looked pained. "Do you really think it's appropriate," he said, "for you to be having a relationship with this woman?"

"I had dinner with her, Mayor. That hardly constitutes a relationship."

"Nevertheless, Mr. DiSalvo, it's not quite seemly for the chief of police to be seen squiring around a convicted felon."

Nick leaned forward in his chair. "I have a couple of problems with that, Mayor. Number one, her conviction was overturned—"

"In the eyes of the court, Nick. Certainly not in the eyes of the three thousand people who live in this town."

"—and second, it's none of anybody's business who I have dinner with when I'm off duty. My private life is my own business."

"Wrong again, Chief. I speak from experience when I say that as a public official in this town, you don't have a private life." The mayor leaned back in his chair and sighed. "Look, Nick, this town has eyes and ears, and every move you make, in or out of uniform, is meticulously scrutinized. If you look bad, the town looks bad, and our citizens won't stand for it."

The fury rose so quickly he shot to his feet. "As chief of police," he said, "I was hired to maintain peace in this town. To protect its citizens. Am I correct?"

Stevens sighed. "Yes," he said, "but—"

"Do you have a problem with the way I'm performing my duties?"

The mayor's mouth thinned. "No," he said.

"Good." Nick slung his cup of coffee into the wastebasket and stalked to the door. "When you have any complaints about my job performance, you let me know."

And he slammed the door behind him.

Downstairs, things weren't much better. "Earl called in sick," Rowena said as he passed her desk. "Lumbago's actin' up again."

"Lovely. Has the lab called back with anything on those prints yet?"

"Not yet."

"What the hell is taking those idiots so long?"

"Well, they are all the way up to Raleigh, Chief. It takes time, you know. This isn't New York."

"No shit. Listen, give 'em a call, rattle their cage a little. Hey,

Betty?"

Across the corridor, the town clerk looked up from her copy of *True Romance*. "Chief?"

"You know anything about snakes?"

"Snakes?"

"Rattlesnakes in particular."

Her eyes widened in curiosity. "Any particular reason?"

"Somebody left Kathryn McAllister a little calling card last night. A five-foot rattlesnake, in a box on her porch. How the hell would somebody get it there without getting bit?"

Telephone receiver in hand, Rowena paused in the middle of dialing. "My Lord and Savior," she breathed. "Did she get bit?"

"No."

"Well, what happened?"

"Bucky came over and filled it full of lead."

"I read somewhere," Rowena said with ghoulish good cheer, "that the mortality rate for rattlesnake bite is somewhere around forty percent. That's forty out of a hundred people who don't survive being bit."

"Thank you, Rowena, for sharing that information."

Betty tried, unsuccessfully, to hide a smile, and then her phone rang and she picked it up and was all business. A moment later, she said, "Hey, Nick, what about Dwight Ingram? He lives out on Old Raleigh Road. He's retired from the wildlife biology department at UNC. Maybe he can help you out."

He found Ingram's number in the phone book. Called and left a message on his machine. He pushed the disconnect button, waited for the dial tone, and dialed Kathryn's number. It rang and rang, and in a fit of temper, he slammed down the receiver. The woman was becoming increasingly difficult to keep track of, and the more people she pissed off, the worse it was going to get. It was obvious that somebody disliked her in a big way, but trying to find that somebody was like looking for the proverbial needle in a haystack. The back of his neck was itching like crazy, and if he ever found out who had left that snake there, he would arrest them on an attempted murder charge. If he didn't beat them to death first.

It was the first satisfying thought he'd had all morning.

chapter five

Surrounded by a sea of paperwork, Kathryn rocked back on her heels and gazed with distaste at the unopened bank statement in her hand, postmarked six days prior to Michael's death. She'd found it in a file folder with several other pieces of unopened mail, secured with a rubber band, most likely tucked away by Michael in his haste to leave for Richmond.

The phone rang. Grateful for the reprieve, she sprang up and headed for the kitchen. Given the events of the past few days, she wasn't even sure she wanted to answer it. But at this particular moment, it was the lesser of two evils. There was something highly distasteful about opening mail addressed to a dead man, even though that dead man had been her husband. Besides, the athletic whistle she'd bought at the Sears store in Fayetteville would capably handle the next fool who had the audacity to make a crank call.

She tucked the stack of unopened mail in a cubbyhole next to the microwave and cautiously picked up the phone. She needn't have worried. "I just heard," Raelynn said. "Are you all right?"

"I am today. Last night I wasn't so sure."

"If I had come home and found that loathsome creature on my doorstep—*ugh!* I can't even think about it without getting the heebie-jeebies. I think I would probably fall dead on the spot. Was it as horrible as I imagine?"

"Worse. I thought I might wake up this morning with snow-white hair, but when I checked in the mirror, I didn't look any different than I did yesterday afternoon."

"An experience like that is bound to leave a mark on you, sugar. Just not where you can see it. I can't imagine what anybody could be thinking, pulling a stunt like that. Are the police trying to find out who did it?"

"They took the box as evidence, but unless somebody comes forward as a witness, I don't think there's much chance of finding out who it was." She paused, debated whether to continue, then plunged ahead. "You know, Raelynn, I have the funniest feeling about this. I'm petrified of snakes. It's a totally irrational fear. I go white, I shake all over, I'm paralyzed with fear at the smallest grass snake. I think whoever did this knows about that fear."

"Meanin' it's somebody who knows you well."

"Exactly."

"Have you given any thought as to who it might be?"

"I've racked my brain, but I'm not coming up with anything. I lived in this town for four years, Raelynn. I knew a lot of people. Neighbors, my students, their parents, Michael's clients—"

"And his relatives," Raelynn said pointedly.

Kathryn sighed. "And his relatives."

"Neely McAllister is a hard woman, Kat, but I can hardly see her carrying over a snake surprise and leaving it on your doorstep as a small token of her esteem."

"Neither can I."

"Nor can I picture her communing with the Great Unwashed in order to hire some commoner to do her dirty work for her. She might get those lily-white hands soiled. Which leaves the Judge."

She considered the fair-haired and genteel Kevin McAllister, who spent most of his spare time on the fairway with a five-iron in his hand. "The Judge always treated me with respect," she said, "until he thought I'd killed his son. And that kind of behavior seems childish in the extreme for someone of his stature."

"Well, somebody certainly wanted to give you one dilly of a fright. If it hadn't been for Nick DiSalvo, you and I would probably not be having this conversation right now. Which reminds me. I hear that you and our revered chief of police were seen having a romantic dinner together at Buzzy's last night, prior to all hell breaking loose. Is there something you'd like to be telling me, sugar?"

"No."

"He's an exceedingly attractive man."

"I hadn't noticed."

"There's not a female on the planet who could fail to notice that man's outstanding qualities."

"He's not all that good-looking," she said irritably. "Nice eyes, I suppose, if you like that dark, ethnic look. I think his nose has been broken at least once, maybe twice. And—"

"For somebody who hasn't noticed, you seem to be rather well acquainted with various aspects of his appearance."

"Oh, shut up."

Raelynn sighed dramatically. "Four months," she said. "Four months I spend being my most charming self every time I encounter the gentleman, and what do I get for all my labors? Nothing. You, on the other hand, are in town for five days, and already you have him sniffing around you like a blue-tick hound sniffs around a—"

"Raelynn!"

"I was about to say a prime cut of sirloin. Nothing salacious had even crossed my mind. You, my dear, are the one with your mind in the gutter."

Through gritted teeth, she spat out, "We had dinner. Period. End of story."

"Ouch. I do believe I have located a sore spot. And on that auspicious note, I shall take my leave, before Rowley County ices over. Y'all take care of yourself, you hear? If anything happened to you, I'd never forgive myself."

* * *

Dwight Ingram was tall and lean, with a shock of white hair beneath a Charlotte Hornets cap perched at a jaunty angle on his head. "Chief DiSalvo," he boomed in a hearty voice, and shook Nick's hand with a bone-crunching grip. "Can I offer you a drink?"

"Thanks," Nick said, "but I'm on duty."

"Of course. Iced tea, then?"

Nick shrugged agreeably. "Iced tea'll be fine."

While Ingram busied himself in the kitchen, Nick stood at the open window of the sun porch and admired the panoramic view of the greens at the Rowley County Golf Club. Ingram returned with two tall glasses on a serving tray, long-handled spoons laid out neatly, a lemon wedge balanced on the rim of each glass. "Let's sit on the patio," he said, and Nick followed him to a wrought-iron table shaded by a green and white striped umbrella.

"Sun tea," Ingram said. "Ever had it before?"

"Can't say that I have." He'd never been much of a tea drinker, but he took a sip and was pleasantly surprised. "It's not bad," he said.

"Easiest thing on earth. Fill a gallon jar with water, toss in your teabags, and leave it sitting on the steps in the sun for a few hours. Brews by itself, and it comes out perfect every time. All you need is a little lemon and some sweetener." Ingram emptied half his glass in one long swig. "So," he said, leaning back in his chair and crossing his legs, "you want to know about snakes."

"Yes, sir. Rattlesnakes in particular."

"Ah, yes. *Crotalus adamanteus*. The Eastern Diamondback Rattlesnake. A member of the family *Viperidae*, the pit vipers, so called because of the depression between the eye and the nostril that serves as a heat sensor to help them locate prey. Quite deadly when provoked. They grow to enormous size, you know."

"Yes," Nick said dryly, "we're acquainted."

"What do you want to know, Mr. DiSalvo?"

Nick rested his glass on his knee. "If you were going to leave one of these things as a little calling card in a box on somebody's porch, how would you get it there without being bit?"

Ingram's thick white eyebrows drew together as he considered. "How big?" he said.

"Five, maybe six feet. As big around as my arm."

"What kind of box?"

"An ordinary cardboard box, the kind you get at the supermarket. Uncovered."

"Hmn...a snake that big, and that deadly, you'd probably want some help. Let's say I wouldn't attempt it by myself."

Nick leaned forward. "So you're saying there must have been two of them?"

"That would be my guess, if only for safety's sake. If you were alone, the bite could easily incapacitate you before you could drive yourself to the hospital."

"How would you pick it up?"

"With a tool called a snake hook. You'd hook the snake about halfway down its body. Evenly distribute the animal's weight, which could be considerable in a snake that large."

"Could it be moved right in the box?"

Ingram considered it. "Possibly. If you kept it refrigerated somewhere for a few hours, it would probably be relatively docile. Snakes are cold-blooded animals. Their body temperature and their activity level change according to the temperature of the environment. They grow lethargic when they're exposed to cold for lengthy periods."

"You think that's what they did? Cooled it off first to make it more manageable?"

"It's possible." Ingram paused. "Of course," he said as an afterthought, "there is one other possibility."

"What's that?"

"Are you familiar with snake handling churches, Chief DiSalvo?"

"Excuse me. I thought I heard you say churches."

Ingram smiled. "In parts of the South," he said, "primarily in rural Appalachian areas, there are fundamentalist Christian sects who use snake handling as a religious ritual. Pentecostal splinter groups, for the most part. They believe in a literal interpretation of some biblical verse that portrays the handling of serpents as evidence of their faith."

Nick whistled. "Holy mother of Moses," he said.

"It's not a common phenomenon," Ingram said. "There are probably only a handful of them left. But if your visitor happened to be a member of one of these sects, chances are he'd have had considerable experience handling large snakes."

"And they don't get bit?"

"Of course they do. But they're relatively proficient with the creatures, and not too many of them die of snakebite."

"Are there any of these churches in Rowley County?"

"It's hard to say. They don't exactly take out advertisements in the local newspaper. Wait here a minute. I have something that might interest you."

Ingram disappeared into the house, returning a few minutes later with a book and a small wooden box. "I thought you might want to borrow this," he said, handing Nick the book. "It details the story of the Appalachian snake handlers. It's fascinating reading."

"Thanks. I'll be sure to return it when I'm done."

Ingram slid open the box, upended it, and shook out its

contents into his palm. "Rattlesnake fangs," he said, holding out his hand so Nick could see them. "Quite amazing, really."

"Amazing," Nick said, without moving to take them from him.

Ingram grinned and dropped the inch-long fangs back into the box. "The rattlesnake," he said, "has suffered mightily because of the ignorance of man. When left alone, they're not particularly aggressive."

Nick held out his hand. "Professor Ingram, thank you for the information. It's been enlightening."

"One more thing," Ingram said. "Leaving a five-foot rattlesnake for an unsuspecting and inexperienced person to stumble over is a little like handing a baby a loaded gun. If I were you, I'd warn the recipient of this little gift to watch his back."

* * *

Since he was already in the neighborhood, he decided it was high time to pay the Judge and Neely McAllister a friendly little visit.

The paved drive cut a knife-sharp line through fields that were green with broadleaf tobacco. Its pungent scent hovered on the heavy air, bringing with it a longing Nick thought he'd left behind him after six months without a cigarette. But it was still there, insidious and seductive, waiting to sneak up and grab him at a vulnerable moment.

The house itself was brick, with a two-story front porch whose roof was supported by mammoth white columns. Surrounded by rolling green lawns and shaded by towering elms that must have been well over a century old, it bespoke a gentler era, when men were men and ladies were ladies and the South had been a place of culture and refinement.

The door was opened by a rawboned black woman wearing a crisp white apron. "Afternoon," she said.

"Good afternoon," Nick said. "I was wondering if Mr. and Mrs. McAllister might be home?"

"Do come inside, Chief DiSalvo. I'll tell them you're here."

She left him waiting in a massive entry hall that smelled pleasantly of old-fashioned paste floor wax not quite concealed by the scent of the yellow roses that sat in a vase on a cherrywood table, beneath an oval mirror that was probably as old as the house. The ceiling rose thirty feet to accommodate the magnificent mahogany staircase that ascended gracefully to the second floor. Somewhere in the murky bowels of the house, he heard voices, indistinct, but plainly those of a man and a woman.

On the wall opposite the mirror hung an oil painting of a young man he recognized as Michael McAllister. He stepped closer to study it, wondering just who he had been, this handsome and affable young man who had swept young Kathryn Sipowicz off her feet and carried her away from home and hearth to this town, this house, these people who had ultimately condemned her.

The rapid *click-click* of a woman's heels echoed down the corridor. He turned as Neely McAllister entered the room. "Chief DiSalvo," she said. "What a surprise."

She was dressed in pale blue silk and a double strand of pearls. She held out a diamond-encrusted hand, and he stopped himself just short of bowing to kiss it. Instead, he shook the proffered hand, noting the small *mouè* of displeasure around her mouth at his obvious ignorance of what constituted proper manners. "Mrs. McAllister," he said. "I thought maybe I might have a few words with you and the Judge."

"Certainly. My husband is in the sunroom. Why don't we join him there? It's so much nicer than the parlor."

He followed her in a circuitous route through the house, past a small fortune in antiques, to a sunny room off the kitchen. "Kevin and I had this room added on about ten years ago," Neely said. "The kitchen was just so gloomy. May I offer you something? Iced tea, perhaps?"

"Thanks," he said, "but I'm all set." He nodded toward the man across the room. "Judge."

Kevin McAllister was seated at an easel near the window, applying delicate brush strokes to an oil painting of the orchids that grew in wild profusion just beyond the windowsill. Without looking up from his work, he said, "Chief DiSalvo."

"My husband," Neely said dryly, "as you can see, is a painter."

"And a damn good one," Nick said, edging closer for a better look.

"He painted the portrait of our son that hangs in the front hall. Perhaps you noticed it as you came in?"

"As a matter of fact, I did. Your son was a handsome man, Mrs. McAllister."

"Yes, well, he of course took a great deal of his looks from his father." Her mouth thinned. "Among other attributes."

Still looking at the painting, he said, "I bet the girls flocked around him like ants at a Sunday school picnic."

"Oh, yes. Right from the time he was a boy. Michael was such a charmer, you know. He loved the girls, and the girls loved him."

"But once he met Kathryn," Nick said casually, "that was it, right? The end of his roving days." He peered critically over the Judge's shoulder. "Nice use of that viridian," he said.

"Kathryn Sipowicz," she said coldly, "was never good enough for my son. She was nothing more than a little Polack tramp who undoubtedly slept with every boy she dated. She wasn't quality people, Mr. DiSalvo. Most certainly not of a caliber to have earned the right to call herself a McAllister."

"Now, Neely," the Judge said evenly.

"Well, it's the truth, Kevin, and you know it. She had Michael mesmerized. Did you know, Mr. DiSalvo, that the entire four years they were married, Michael refused to take a penny from us? That boy had grown up with every advantage a young man could ever hope for. But he preferred livin' in poverty with that little slut. It was a disgrace."

"You'll have to excuse my wife, sir," the Judge said genially. "She and Kathryn never did quite hit it off."

"Obviously," Nick said. "Tell me, Judge, have you been painting for a long time?"

"Years and years," Neely said petulantly. "Not always to the benefit of his family, I might add."

"Mrs. McAllister," Nick said, "did you know that Kathryn is deathly afraid of snakes?"

There was a sudden and deafening silence before Neely said, "May I ask why on earth you are badgering us with these ridiculous questions, Mr. DiSalvo?"

"Chief," he said.

"I beg your pardon?"

"It's Chief DiSalvo. Did you know that she suffers from a pathological phobia when it comes to snakes?"

"I can't say as I recall, *Chief* DiSalvo. Now, if you don't tell us where you're heading with this line of questioning, I'm going to have to ask you to leave."

Watching her eyes, he said, "Somebody left a five-foot rattlesnake in a box on her porch last night."

Behind him, the Judge said, "Good Lord!"

Neely stared at him without blinking. "Are you suggesting," she said, "that the Judge or I might have had something to do with this incident?"

Nick shrugged. "It's not an illogical conclusion. Especially considering that you publicly denounced her during her trial. At this point, I'd have to say that you're at the top of my list of suspects."

"I see. And precisely how long is that list, Mr. DiSalvo?"

He smiled thinly. "Right now," he said, "there are exactly two people on it."

She raised her chin imperiously. "Let me tell you one more thing, Mr. DiSalvo, before Althea shows you the door. Neither Kevin nor I had anything to do with putting a snake on Kathryn's doorstep." She paused, and then she smiled. "But I do bitterly regret that I wasn't the one who thought of it first."

* * *

He paid for the damn dog himself.

It was a mixed breed, part Rottweiler, part something that nobody but its mother would ever know, and the lady in question wasn't about to divulge the details of her indiscretion. Three-quarters grown, it already weighed seventy-five pounds, and had teeth sharp enough to rip out the throat of a grown man. It sat upright in the passenger seat of the Blazer, tongue lolling out the open window, on its face a look of such idiotic delight that he wondered how it could possibly have passed training school. Maybe, like the illiterates being turned out by high schools these days, the dog had just been passed along from class to class, his grades rubber-stamped in order to graduate him with an age-appropriate group of his peers.

"You're getting hair all over my upholstery," he said irritably.

The dog looked at him, decided he was a person of no importance, and turned back to the open window.

"You probably eat your weight in raw meat every day."

The dog's ears pricked in interest. He pulled the Blazer into

Kathryn's driveway behind the pathetic excuse for a car that Forrest Whitley had bilked her out of nearly eight hundred dollars for, when everybody in town knew he'd bought it from Dewey Webb a month ago for less than half of that.

The dog followed him up onto the porch and sat obediently at his feet while he knocked. "Who is it?" Kathryn said from behind the door.

"It's me," he said. "I brought you something."

The door opened and she stood there looking out at him. Her gaze dropped, and she stared. "What's that?" she said.

"It's a watch dog. I thought, since you're too stubborn to listen to anything I have to say, you might consider—"

"What am I supposed to do with a dog that big? He'll break what's left of the furniture."

"Wait. He's not done growing yet."

"He'll eat me out of house and home."

"He'll rip the throat out of anybody who tries to lay a finger on you."

"I suppose," she said, "that would be an advantage." She opened the screen door and knelt. Gingerly, she said, "Nice doggie."

"His name's Elvis."

Those blue eyes looked at him in disbelief. "Elvis?" she said. "You're kidding, right?"

"Come on, McAllister. Could this face lie to you?"

Warmth replaced the skepticism in her eyes. "I hope not," she said.

Over Elvis' head, he said casually, "I paid a visit to your in-laws today."

Her hand, busy scratching the dog's neck, paused. "Did you?" she said. "I'll bet they were anxious to inquire about the state of my health."

"That's some spread they have there, isn't it? Nope, they didn't ask about the state of your health, but we did have a nice little chat about snakes."

She returned her attention, and her eyes, to Elvis. "Learn anything useful, DiSalvo?"

"I learned enough."

Her fingers toyed with the dog's ear, stroking, smoothing the fur. Still looking at Elvis, she said, "I'm sorry about last night."

He got the distinct impression that Kathryn McAllister wasn't comfortable with apologies. He opened his mouth to respond, and his pager went off. He muttered a quick curse. "Can I use your phone?" he said.

"In the kitchen." She sprang to her feet and stepped back out of range so he could pass without touching her.

"This is DiSalvo," he said, when Rowena answered. "What you got?"

"Bucky's got a bad wreck out on Highway 1 near Shoney's. Couple of DOA's. He's requesting backup."

"Great," he said. "Just what I needed to complete my day. Anything from the lab yet?"

"I'd tell you what they said, but considering the kind of day you're having, I dare say we'd both be a lot happier if I waited until tomorrow."

"You're right. I don't want to know. Tell Bucky I'm on my way."

"Ten-four. By the way, Chief, I hear you bought a dog."

"Where the hell did you hear that?"

"My sister-in-law, Marjorie Clemens, lives next door to Sylvia Fellowes, who heard it from her cousin Lottie, who cleans house for Edie Hastings, who runs the K-9 training school where you acquired that mean-tempered beast."

"Jesus Christ. Can a man take a leak in this town without the entire population knowing about it before it hits the ground?"

"I dare say, Chief DiSalvo, that any man who had the audacity to attempt doin' it on the ground in this town would find himself locked up in your jail a good half-hour before it hit."

He coughed to cover the laugh he couldn't quite choke back. Damned if the old bat wasn't starting to grow on him.

chapter six

The Magnolia House was Elba's finest restaurant, the kind of place where ladies of quality met for iced tea and pecan pie on lazy summer afternoons. Raelynn Wilbur was already waiting for him when he sat down across from her. "Sorry I'm late," he said. "We just got back the lab results on those prints we lifted from Kathryn's house the day it was vandalized."

"Anything?" she said.

"Nah. Everything we got was hers. The perpetrator must have worn gloves."

"Damn. I don't like this. I don't like it a bit."

"Neither do I. Listen, thanks for meeting me today. I know how busy you are."

"Don't be absurd. I want to get to the bottom of this mess, just like you. I'll do whatever I can to help."

The waiter came and took their order, and then Nick leaned back in his chair, water goblet in hand, and studied Raelynn Wilbur. She was an extremely attractive woman. A bit flamboyant, but that only added to her attractiveness. "You grew up in this town," he said. "You must have known Michael McAllister."

She took a sip of water. "Everybody knew Michael McAllister," she said.

"According to everything I've heard, he was as pure of heart as Dudley Do-Right. Somehow, I find that hard to believe."

"Oh, Michael was all that, and more. Handsome, intelligent, charming, rich—and a Boy Scout at heart. What more could any girl ask for?"

"Did he date a lot of girls?"

"Like a revolving door, sugar. Michael had a girl for every day of the week. At one point or another, he broke the heart of most all of Elba's debutantes."

The waiter returned, bringing coffee in fine china cups. "Thank you," Nick said, and stirred sugar into his. Trying to figure out how to grip the delicate handle with his oversized male hand, he said, "Did you date Michael?"

Raelynn smiled wryly. "My family, Chief DiSalvo, wasn't in quite the same social class as the McAllisters. I grew up in a one-room shanty out by Persimmon Creek. Due to the unfortunate circumstances of my birth, I was forced to admire young men like Michael McAllister from afar." She took a sip of sparkling water. "My mother took in laundry for folks like the McAllisters."

"How'd you end up in law school?"

"By the grace of God, who made poor little Raelynn Wilbur from the wrong side of the tracks the beneficiary of the razor-sharp brain that lies beneath these ebony curls."

"What about the house Kathryn's living in? I thought it was your mother's."

"This business of lawyering being rather profitable, I was able to provide for Momma in the last years of her life. She lived in the house, Chief DiSalvo. The deed has my name on it."

"I see. He studied her over the rim of his teacup. "Did Michael screw around on Kathryn?"

"My, you certainly do go right to the heart of the matter. I like a man who knows what he wants and goes after it." She ran a finger along the rim of her water glass. "Now, you must understand, for the first three years that Kathryn and Michael were married, I was away at Columbia University."

"Ah," he said. "New York." It explained a great deal.

"That's right. But from all I saw, all I heard, Michael McAllister was totally besotted with his lovely Yankee wife."

"So you don't think he was sleeping with Wanita Crumley?"

Raelynn threw back her head and laughed. Several proper matrons swiveled their perfectly coifed heads to frown in disapproval of her flagrant breach of etiquette. "Have you met Wanita Crumley?" she said.

"I'm afraid I haven't had the pleasure."

"That's what I suspected. If you had, you wouldn't have asked such a ridiculous question. Beside Kathryn, the woman's a sow. Michael wouldn't have touched her if his pecker had been on fire and she'd been carrying a bucket of water."

Their meal arrived, poached salmon for Raelynn, a club sandwich for him. Nick removed the top slice of bread and glopped on a thick layer of mustard. He took a huge bite and closed his eyes in ecstasy.

"Whenever I watch a man take such great pleasure from eating," Raelynn said, "it always makes me believe he likely finds other pleasures most enjoyable, too."

He almost choked on his sandwich. He set it down and busied himself dabbing at his mouth with a snowy linen napkin. Cleared his throat and took a drink of ice water. "So tell me," he said, "who *did* Michael date?"

"If you're lookin' for a list of names, sugar, you'd be better off asking who he didn't date." Raelynn picked up a forkful of poached salmon. "The list would be shorter."

Nick took a bite of his sandwich, chewed and swallowed. "Then let me rephrase the question. Did he date anybody who might still be carrying a torch? Somebody who might have killed him in a jealous rage? Somebody who might be jealous enough, even after all this time, to leave that snake on Kathryn's porch?"

Chewing thoughtfully, Raelynn considered his question. "Well," she said, " now that you mention it, I do recall that the summer before he met Kathryn, he and Georgia Pruett were quite an item. The way I heard it, they were goin' at it hot and heavy every chance they got. A lot of folks expected they'd get married." She took a tiny nibble of asparagus. "In the eyes of certain segments of society, it would have been an ideal match, what with Michael's daddy being on the bench, and Georgia's daddy being a state senator."

He wiped his mouth with the napkin. "Do tell," he said.

"Georgia," she said, leaning over the table, "apparently had her heart set on being the next Mrs. McAllister. It didn't set too well with her when Michael came home from college with a wife trailing along behind him. And a Yankee wife to boot."

"I can imagine."

For a time, they both concentrated on eating. "So," Nick said, polishing off the remains of his sandwich, "where's Georgia now?"

"Oh, she's still right here in Elba. A respected member of the Junior League. Married and divorced several times. She's now with husband number three. Eugene Pepperel, Junior. But everybody just calls him Junior. Richer than Midas. It's a pure shame he has the body of a troll." She pursed her mouth in distaste. "Some women," she said, "really sell themselves short. You know what I mean, Chief DiSalvo?"

He cleared his throat. "I believe I do, Ms. Wilbur."

"You know—" She paused with her fork in midair, a tiny sliver of asparagus perched on the tip. "Not that it has any bearing on the case, but with all these questions you're asking about Michael's catting around, I thought you should know you're barking up the wrong tree. You're looking at the wrong McAllister." She brought the fork to her mouth and delicately nibbled at the asparagus.

"What?" he said. "What do you mean? Are you saying Kathryn was fooling around?"

She dabbed at her mouth with her napkin. "Not Kathryn," she said. "The Judge."

He leaned forward with a great deal of interest. "Judge McAllister cheats on his wife?"

Her laugh was low and husky. "Kevin McAllister," she said, "is one of the biggest whoremasters in Rowley County. He even hit on me once. Although, according to rumor, he prefers dark meat." She lifted her glass. "Young dark meat."

"Son of a gun." He remembered the vague missiles that Neely McAllister had launched in the direction of her husband, and suddenly they made sense. "I imagine his wife probably doesn't care much for his indiscretions."

"Let's just say she likely prefers that he keep them discreet. Beyond that, I doubt she cares much what the Judge does. The way I hear it, Neely McAllister hasn't opened her legs to Kevin for nigh onto twenty years."

"Yet they've stayed married."

"Because they're both gettin' what they need out of the marriage, sugar. It looks good on the outside. Kevin has an attractive wife to manage his household and accompany him to social affairs. Neely has the McAllister name, not to mention the money, and a solid place in society. She turns a blind eye to Kevin's whoring, and in turn, he leaves her alone. It's a marriage made in heaven."

"I guess that depends on your definition of heaven."

She glanced at the slender gold watch on her wrist. "Oh, Lord, look at the time. I'm sorry to rush off, but I'm due in court in forty minutes." She dabbed at her mouth with her napkin and rose from her chair. "Thank you, Chief, for lunch."

He dropped his own napkin and stood. "Thank you," he said. "It's been a most enlightening conversation."

She opened her purse, pulled out a compact, and opened it to check her makeup. "By the way," she said casually, studying her reflection, "if Kathryn finds out I told you this, I'll swear on a stack of Bibles that you're a liar. But—" She snapped the compact closed and slipped it back into her purse. And smiled at him like a cat about to dive into a bowl of cream. "I do believe, Mr. DiSalvo, that our little friend has a major case of the hots for you. What I want to know, sugar, is what you plan to do about it?"

When she exited the room, amid whispers and stares, his mouth was still hanging open.

* * *

He was at his desk, thumbing through the snake book Ingram had given him, when the phone rang. He picked it up absently. "DiSalvo," he said.

"Nick, it's Lenore."

His attention sharpened instantly. Something in her voice. And she never called him at work. Not since the divorce. "What's wrong?" he said.

"Janine's run away from home."

His backbone straightened like a steel rod. "*What?* Why the hell would she do that? Have the two of you been going at it again?"

"Go ahead," she said, "blame it on me. Blame everything on me, Nick. If Janine had a father who was there for her, maybe this kind of thing wouldn't be happening."

A ball of fire ignited in the pit of his stomach. He leaned back in his chair and stared at the ceiling. "I'm not the one who went whoring around," he said, "so you'd better be careful where you're tossing blame, Lenore."

"This has nothing to do with you and me, Nick. This has to do with your relationship with your daughter. You've never been there for her. All you cared about was your damn job."

The ball of fire expanded to volcanic proportions. "Look," he said, "we can sit here all day and sling mud at each other, but it's not getting us anywhere. If you'd just calm down, maybe we could—"

"My baby's out there somewhere, and I don't even know where she is! Maybe you can stay calm, buster, but I sure as hell can't!"

He reminded himself that no matter how much he wanted to reach through the phone and wring Lenore's scrawny neck, Janine was her daughter, too. "I know you're upset," he said. "I'm not exactly jumping with joy myself." He tried not to think about the runaways he'd seen on the streets of New York, or how most of them ended up. "What happened?" he said.

"She left sometime during the night. When I went in to wake her up this morning, she was gone. Along with my suitcase, and most of her clothes. No note, no nothing."

"Did you try her friends?"

"That was the first thing I did. I called everybody I could think of. Nobody's seen her. Walter's been out all morning, driving around the neighborhood, looking for her."

"What about this boy she was talking about? obbie somebody?"

"He's in Vermont with his parents. They left three days ago."

"She wouldn't have gone up there, would she?"

"I don't think so. I talked to Jenny Giulio, and she said Janine told her Robbie Morrison was a dork."

He drew a notepad across the desk and began doodling on it. "Have you called the cops?"

"Of course I've called the cops!" she snapped. "You know what they told me?"

He sighed. "That there are thousands of runaways every year in New York City alone, and they'll call you if she turns up."

"Damn it, Nicky, isn't there something you can do? You're a goddamn cop, for Christ's sake!"

"Not much," he said. "Especially from six hundred miles away. Who'd you talk to?"

He wrote down the name and number she gave him. "I know the guy," he said. "I'll give him a call. Look, she's probably hiding out at a friend's house. Try not to panic yet. I'll see what I can do from this end. And for Christ's sake, let me know if you hear anything."

He hung up the phone and sat there with his head bowed, running his fingers through his hair. From the doorway, Rowena said, "Everything okay?"

"It's my daughter," he said. "She's run away from home."

"Oh, Lord. How old is she?"

"Thirteen. Goddamn kids think they're invincible, you know?"

She let his vulgarity pass unnoticed. "That's a very difficult age," she said. "I imagine her mother's about fit to be tied. I would be, if it was my daughter."

"She's probably just at a friend's house," he said, "but it's still enough to scare the living daylights out of you. Kids don't realize what can happen to them out there. I was a New York cop for sixteen years. I've seen what happens to kids on the street, and it isn't pretty. But they don't think about that. They don't think it can happen to them. And they sure as hell don't understand the fear we parents go through, every damn day of our lives. I guess you have to be a parent yourself before you really understand."

"She'll show up, Chief. Tired and hungry and most likely more than a little sheepish."

"I hope to God you're right."

"I'm right. Can I fetch you a cup of coffee?"

"Thanks, but I'm already wired so high I'm about to take off for the moon. I have to call this guy Ramirez in New York. If anything comes through, interrupt me."

The NYPD wasn't much help. "You know how it works, Nick," Ramirez said. "We don't have the resources to be combing the streets of Manhattan, looking for teenage runaways. I wish I could help you out, but you know as well as I do that she could be anywhere. We've followed standard procedure here. She shows up somewhere, we'll hear about it, and so will you."

It was the best he was going to get. He broke the connection, called Lenore back and made soothing noises. When he finally got rid of her, he swiveled around in his chair and stared out the window, wondering where Janine had gone, who she was with, what she was doing. But that kind of thinking made him crazy. When he got his hands on her, he was going to—

Going to what? he thought gloomily. At thirteen, she was a little old for him to be taking her over his knee and whaling the tar out of her. He couldn't very well ground her. He'd abdicated that right the day he walked out the door and left her with Lenore. To all intents and purposes, Walter the friendly pharmacist was her father now.

Furious at that thought and all it implied, he shoved his chair back from his desk so hard it hit the wall and bounced off. His face was set in grim lines when he stalked past Rowena's desk. "You hear anything," he said curtly, "you page me."

"Chief?" she said. "Where are you headed?"

"Out," he said, and left her shaking her head in dismay at his dearth of proper manners.

* * *

Georgia Pruett Pepperell had obviously tried hard, but neither the matronly hairdo nor the severe cut of the gray linen suit were capable of camouflaging the exotic beauty that must have made her the object of many a young man's fantasy. She walked the corridors of the Cumberland Convalescent Center like a queen inspecting her kingdom, pausing to touch a shoulder here, whisper a word of encouragement there. Reaching an elderly colored lady in a wheelchair, Pepperell knelt to take her bony hand. Pressing it between both of hers, she said, "And how are we doing today, Marion? Is the rheumatism any better?"

"Oh, yes," the old lady said, beaming. "And my son's coming to see me on Saturday, you know, all the way from Raleigh."

"Why, that's wonderful, Marion. You give him my best, you hear?"

She worked the room like Wayne Newton working the crowd at Caesar's Palace. Everywhere she went, eyes brightened and faces lit with smiles where vacant stares had been a moment before. Straightening, she beckoned for Nick to follow her.

They passed through a glass door into an atrium where potted palms shaded sturdy redwood patio furniture. In the center, beneath a thirty-foot palm, stood a marble statue of a cherub, his dimpled smile intended to distract the viewer from the fact that he was continuously peeing into a shallow pool. "Classy," Nick said.

"Isn't it, though?"

He sat on the edge of the pool. "How often do you come here?" he said.

She perched, legs crossed with circumspect refinement, on the opposite corner. "Three afternoons a week," she said in dulcet tones. "My grandmother died in this place. Alzheimer's. That was when I became determined to devote my free time to comforting the elderly. These people, Mr. DiSalvo, are at their final stop on the road of life, and I do my utmost to see that their last days are spent in comfort."

"That must be a very satisfying calling, Mrs. Pepperell."

"Certainly preferable to sitting around drinking tea and playing bridge," she said dryly. "Now, what can I do for you?"

"What can you tell me about Michael McAllister?"

Her sweet expression never altered. "Michael McAllister," she said.

"I expect you've heard that his wife is back in town."

"This is Elba, Mr. DiSalvo. The whole town knew a half-hour before she arrived."

"Somebody left a five-foot rattlesnake on her porch a couple nights ago."

"Something else that I've heard. What possible reason could anybody have for doing that?"

"I was hoping," he said, "that you might be able to tell me."

"I can't imagine," she said.

"What was your relationship with Michael McAllister?"

She reached up to brush an invisible strand of hair away from her face. She had the most perfect skin he'd ever seen outside the pages of a fashion magazine. "We were lovers," she said.

"Before or after his marriage to Kathryn?"

Her smile was distant, cool. "I was very young, Mr. DiSalvo. Very immature. I'd just been jilted by my lover, a man I'd expected to marry. A young girl in love like that does things she wishes later she could take back." She shrugged philosophically. "I pleaded. I begged. I cried. I threatened. But it was all for nothing. The day Michael set eyes on Kathryn, as far as he was concerned, all other women ceased to exist."

"How did you feel about that?"

Casually, she said, "I wanted to kill her."

Behind them, the smiling cherub continued to urinate into the pool. "And now?" he said.

"Michael was the most incredible lover I ever knew," she said. "He knew—perhaps by instinct, perhaps from experience—exactly how to turn a woman inside out with need. And then how to satisfy that need. Losing him was the most devastating thing that ever happened to me. I can only begin to imagine how much worse it was for Kathryn. She had an added advantage, you see, Mr. DiSalvo. Michael loved her."

"You don't believe she killed him?"

"Kathryn was a convenient scapegoat. Of course she didn't kill him."

"Any idea who did? An old girlfriend? A jealous husband? A pissed-off business associate?"

Pepperell uncrossed and then recrossed her spectacular legs. "It was no business associate," she said. "You and I both know that Michael's killing was personal. Whoever plunged those shears into him was nursing a powerful rage. If I were Kathryn McAllister, I'd get as far from Elba as I could get, as fast as I could get there." Her mouth thinned. "And I would never, ever look back."

* * *

An hour later, he was back in the office, thinking about what she'd said, when the phone rang, jumping him out of his sullen reverie. He snatched it up. "Yeah?" he barked into the receiver.

A very small voice said, hesitantly, "Daddy?"

His stomach went through the floor. "Janine," he said. "Where the hell are you?"

"I'm at the airport," she said, her voice growing more querulous by the minute. "In Raleigh."

Dumbfounded, he said, "Raleigh, North Carolina?"

"Will you come get me?"

His hands started shaking, with relief or anger, he wasn't sure. "Do you have any idea," he bellowed, "how much you scared your mother and me? Any idea at all?"

"I just wanted to be with you."

"Damn it all to hell!"

His daughter sniffled. "Don't you want me?" she said.

"Of course I want you! But that was damn irresponsible of you, taking off like that without telling anyone. Your mother's been frantic!"

"I didn't mean to upset anybody."

"Well, you did. A lot. I want you to sit yourself down, and you're not to move an inch until I get there. Do you understand?"

"Yes," she said pitifully.

"I'll be there in an hour or so. And then I'll decide what to do with you."

"Daddy? You're not going to send me back, are you?"

"Right now, I'm too mad to know what to do. What I'd really like is take you over my knee and spank you so hard you won't be able to sit down for a week."

He hung up the phone and called his ex-wife. "Janine's okay," he said. "She just called me."

"Oh, thank God! Where is she?"

"Seems she decided to pay me a little visit. She's at the airport in Raleigh, waiting for me to pick her up."

"I'm gonna kill her, Nicky! I'm gonna ground her until she's forty. That damn kid just took ten years off my life. I've been sitting here all day, imagining all the awful things that could have happened to her!"

Unexpectedly, he softened. Lenore might not be at the top of his list of favorite people these days, but they had made this child together, and for better or for worse, that bond would remain between them until death. "Yeah," he said, "me too. Look, I'll have her call you as soon as we get in, okay?"

Rowena looked up expectantly when he blew through the door of his office. Smugly, she said, "Told you she'd turn up."

"Damn kid's in Raleigh," he said. "Can you believe she got on a plane and flew all the way from New York to North Carolina, all by herself? Thirteen years old."

"Gutsy little thing," Betty said.

"Yeah." He laughed humorlessly. "Gutsy. What on God's green earth am I going to do with her?"

"Well, Chief," Rowena said, sliding those hideously outdated harlequin glasses up her nose, "not that I believe in telling people how to run their lives, but you could try loving her. In my experience, it seems to work quite well."

* * *

He promised he'd give himself time to cool off before he lit into her, so they drove for nearly an hour in an awkward, pregnant silence. It wasn't until he reached the outskirts of Elba that he trusted himself to speak without blowing the roof off the car. "What on earth were you thinking?" he said grimly.

Janine, no bigger than a peanut to begin with, shrank even smaller as she burrowed into the Blazer's seat. "I just wanted to be with you," she said.

He muttered a few choice words under his breath. "Where'd you get the money to buy a plane ticket? That must have cost two, three hundred bucks."

Incredibly, she seemed to shrink more. "I used Mom's credit card."

His mouth fell open, and the pain in his stomach exploded with volcanic intensity. "Great," he said. "That's just great. Guess who's gonna take the heat for that one?"

"I'm sorry, Daddy."

"You should be. Christ, Janine, I'm living in a one-bedroom apartment. Where am I supposed to put you?"

"I'll sleep on the couch. I won't take up much room. And I'll wash the dishes and do the laundry and keep the apartment clean. I'll be so quiet, you won't even notice I'm there."

He gaped at her in amazement, this slender teenager who couldn't even keep her own room clean. "Look," he said, softening, "first we call Mom. See what she says. Then we take it from there. Okay?"

She sniffled. "Okay."

Because it was past suppertime and his stomach was gnawing, he pulled into the drive-thru of the only fast food joint in town and bought them both burgers, fries, and shakes. The apartment smelled musty when he unlocked the door. Janine carried their meal to the kitchen table, set it down, and looked around at the oatmeal-colored wallpaper, the matching priscillas that covered the bay window. "Home, sweet home," he said wryly. "This is as good as it gets."

Chocolate shake in hand, she left him in the kitchen while she explored the rest of the apartment. It didn't take long. "This is where you live?" she said when she came back.

He drew his eyebrows together. "You got a problem with it?"

"How long have you been living here?"

"Four months. I told you not to expect much."

"It looks like a motel room, Daddy. You haven't even hung any pictures on the walls!"

"What do I need pictures for?"

She looked at him as though he suffered from profound retardation. "To make it into a home. There's nothing personal here at all. It just looks...blank."

"I have a picture of you on the dresser in the bedroom," he said defensively.

"And except for the CD player, that's the only personal item in the place."

"Bullsh—baloney. I have a TV I bought on sale at Circuit City in Raleigh."

Janine rolled her eyes. "Do you have to be such a *man*, Daddy?" She crossed the hardwood floor to the television and drew her fingertip across the screen. Holding it up so he could see the grayish accumulation of dust, she said, "And when was the last time you watched it?"

"I watched the news," he said, "just last week."

Janine shook her head in pity. "It's a good thing I'm here," she said. "Mom was right. You do need to get yourself a life."

They ate cold burgers together, phoned his ex-wife, and then they spent five minutes moving his clothes from the bedroom to the hall closet. He wiped off the TV screen and put the framed picture of Janine beside the TV. "Are you sure you don't mind sleeping on the couch, Daddy?" she said as she hauled Lenore's massive suitcase into the bedroom. "It really doesn't matter to me where I sleep."

"You take the bedroom. A young lady needs privacy."

She disappeared into the bedroom to get settled, leaving him alone to consider the situation he'd unexpectedly been thrown into. Lenore hadn't been thrilled, but she had consented to let Janine stay, at least for the rest of the summer. After that, they'd reassess and regroup. The local high school was just around the corner. She could easily walk to school in five or ten minutes. Maybe he should move into a larger place before September. Maybe he could buy a house somewhere nearby. He liked living here. It was close to work, close to everything. Easy to swing by Kathryn's house several times a day to keep an eye on her.

Janine's voice startled him out of his reverie. "Daddy? Do you have any tape?"

"Tape," he said blankly. "What for?"

"I have to put up my posters."

"Posters? Posters of what?"

"You know. *Posters.* Leonardo DiCaprio and Mariah Carey and a whole bunch of other people." She stood in the doorway, hand on hip, her expression of impatience so like her mother's that it threw him for a minute.

"Oh," he said. "I don't think I have any tape."

"Then we'll just have to go out and buy some, because I have to put up my posters, and I can't do it without tape."

He drove past Kathryn's house on his way to Wal-Mart. The Toyota was in the driveway, but there was no sign of life anywhere. No Kathryn. No Elvis. He sighed with irritation and pressed a little harder on the gas.

"Dad? Aren't we taking a roundabout route to get to Wal-Mart?"

She'd been in town for two hours, and already she knew her way around better than he did. "What are you talking about?" he said.

"Well, we were on Route 1 North before, but then you took a couple of turns and drove around for a while, and now here we are, back on Route 1 North again. Why didn't you just go straight?"

A muscle twitched in his eyelid. "I was just checking something out," he said.

She brushed her dark hair back from her face. "What?"

"Business," he said. "I can't really talk about it."

Interest lit her face like a high-powered spotlight. "Cop business?" she said.

"Yeah," he said, silently cussing himself for his misstep. "Cop business."

"Everybody at school is so jealous because my dad's a cop."

Nick turned to look at her. "Jealous?" he said in surprise. "Why?"

"You do important things. You protect people. You put bad guys in jail, where they belong."

He thought about the four months he'd spent in Elba, scolding prepubescent shoplifters and issuing parking tickets, and he felt guilty. His daughter's admiration was undeserved. He was no hero, just an ordinary guy who'd run away from the problems in his life. "You know what?" he said.

"What?"

"I love you a whole lot."

His little girl broke into a heart-stopping grin. "Aw, Daddy," she said, "I love you, too."

chapter seven

Kathryn lingered in the produce section, debating whether to buy okra or fresh spinach. After four years of eating the bland and flavorless institutional food served to the inmates at Carolina Women's, she was awestruck every time she visited the grocery store. So much variety, so many choices. It was a joy, relearning the simple pleasure of being able to choose what she wanted to eat.

It was worth the twenty-mile drive to the Mechanicsville Food Lion. The selection was vastly superior to that of Elba's Dixie Market, the prices considerably lower. And the one time she'd attempted to shop at the Dixie, the looks she'd received from both customers and employees alike had made her feel like a leper on a crowded city bus. Here in Mechanicsville, she was slightly less notorious, more able to blend into the crowd and be treated like any other customer.

She chose the okra, placed it carefully in her cart next to the fresh string beans and the basket of strawberries. Gaping in wonderment at a six-foot-high pyramid of grapefruit, she wheeled her shopping cart around a corner and slammed unceremoniously into a loaded cart that somebody had left sitting directly in the center of the aisle.

Irritated, she tried in vain to disentangle the two carts. And then a voice said, "Hey, kid," and she looked up in disbelief.

"DiSalvo," she said. "What the hell are you doing here?"

He stood there tossing a can of pork and beans from one hand to the other. "Same thing you are," he said. "You know, McAllister, we really have to stop meeting like this."

He was wearing jeans and a madras plaid shirt with the sleeves rolled up, revealing tanned forearms sprinkled with dark hair. Heat shot through her, and unbelievably, she felt herself blushing. Several awkward moments ensued as they both tried to pretend they weren't scoping out the contents of the other's shopping cart. Frozen pizza, she noted. Pop Tarts. Popsicles. *Count Chocula?* She stared at him in amazement. Did the man actually eat this stuff?

"Dog working out?" he said, nodding toward the fifty-pound bag of dog food that took up most of her cart space.

"Nobody's threatened my life in at least three days."

He gave her that smile, the one that always chased the shadows from his face and turned her inside out. "Sounds like my definition of success." He tossed the can of pork and beans into his cart and moved closer to survey the damage. "Looks like your wheel's caught on mine." He knelt beside the two carts and manually redirected the position of the front wheels. "There. That ought to do it." He stood back up, wiped his hand against his thigh. "So how've you been? Everything going okay?"

"I can't get anybody to talk to me, DiSalvo. It's like I'm wearing this huge scarlet M for Murderess."

"I tried to tell you. You need to forget this damn obsession you have with—"

"I found it, Daddy! It's only $3.95. Can I get it?"

They both looked up in surprise at the young girl who had joined them. She wore her dark hair parted in the middle, and she had that slender, beanpole look that young teenage girls sometimes get just before they begin to develop hips and breasts. "Kathryn," Nick said, "this is my daughter, Janine. Janine, this is Kathryn McAllister."

Janine looked at her father, at Kathryn, back at her father. "Hi," she said carefully.

"Hello, Janine." She smiled at the girl and raised an eyebrow in DiSalvo's direction.

"Long story," he said. "Janine's visiting me for a while."

"I see. What do you think of North Carolina so far, Janine?"

Janine stepped closer to her father, threaded her arm through his. "It's okay," she said.

Over the top of his daughter's head, DiSalvo shot her a wink.

They stood there arm in arm, father and daughter, looking
remarkably alike with the same coloring, the same soulful dark eyes.
"Well," Kathryn said briskly, "I should be going. It was nice meeting
you, Janine."

"Sure," Janine said sullenly, still clinging to her father.

Kathryn looked at DiSalvo, hesitated a moment, then steered
her cart out around his. "Good-bye," she said.

"Yeah," he said, and his voice followed her. "I'll be seeing
you."

* * *

They were halfway home when Janine said, "Who is she?"

His mind a million miles away, he had to force himself to
concentrate on what she'd said. "Who's who?"

"That woman in the grocery store." Her tone grew accusatory.
"Is she your girlfriend?"

At thirteen, she was already trying to legislate his love life. She
was every inch her mother's daughter. "No," he said, irritated, "she is
not my girlfriend."

"She'd like to be, then. I saw the way she was looking at you."

"She wasn't looking at me any way," he said.

"Yes, she was. She was looking at you the same way you were
looking at her. Are you sleeping with her, Daddy? Because if you
are, I think that's really gross and disgusting."

His fingers tightened on the steering wheel. "I will remind
you," he said, "that I didn't invite you here. You're more than
welcome to stay with me for as long as you want. But you will not
pry into my private life. Is that understood?"

Those huge, dark eyes filled with tears. She turned away from
him, toward the window. "Yes."

"Fine. And for your information, no, I am not sleeping with
her."

They drove in silence for a time. "She's pretty," Janine said.

He kept his eyes on the road. "Yeah," he said. "She is."

"Do you like her? As a girlfriend, I mean? You could ask her
out on a date or something. I bet she wouldn't say no."

"Jesus Christ, Janine, I hardly know the woman."

"Well, then, what about Mrs. Belmont, upstairs? She likes you a lot. I've seen her watching you."

His landlady, Caroline Belmont, was an attractive, dark-haired divorcee who wore tailored suits in floral pastel colors. Another transplanted Northerner, she sold real estate for a living, and had twice tried to lure him upstairs for a drink. "Fine," he snapped. "You want me to ask Caroline Belmont out for a date, I'll ask her out for a date. Are you happy now?"

With typical female logic, she said in genuine bewilderment, "It doesn't matter what I want, Daddy. I want whatever makes you happy."

* * *

She was putting away the groceries when the phone rang. Elvis sat patiently beside the refrigerator, waiting for a doggie treat, his eyes following her every move. "Hang in there," she told him, snatching the phone off the wall. "Hello?"

"Miz McAllister?"

Kathryn froze. She knew that voice. "Yes," she said carefully, trying to conceal her excitement.

"This is Wanita. Look, I can't talk right now, but I got some information that you'd probably find interesting. About your husband's murder."

Adrenaline gushed through her veins, and she forced herself to be low-key. "What?" she said.

Wanita cleared her throat and lowered her voice. "What's it worth to you?" she said.

In the background, she could hear children playing. Her pulse hammered as she considered her options. "How much are you asking?" she said.

"Fifty bucks," Wanita whispered.

"It's yours. Shall I meet you somewhere?"

"Tomorrow night. Eight o'clock. You know that turnout by the lake, where all the coon hunters park their trucks?"

"On the Swanville Road?"

"Right. Meet me there at eight tomorrow night. You give me the cash, and I'll give you the information."

When she hung up the phone, her hands were shaking. This was the first break she'd had since she arrived in town. Could it be possible that the tide was turning in her direction?

She went to the cupboard and took out a doggie biscuit. Tossed it to Elvis. "Elvis, my man," she said to the dog, "it looks like you and I have a hot date tomorrow night with Wanita Crumley."

* * *

For her evening attire, Caroline Belmont had foregone the tailored suit in favor of a soft mint green chiffon dress that swirled around her legs and clung in all the right places. Over her shoulders, she wore a matching silk wrap. Caroline was attractive, intelligent and vivacious, had graduated *summa cum laude* from Penn State, and had been to Europe half a dozen times. Her voice was soft and well-modulated, she could speak on any topic with ease, and she managed to ask questions designed to draw him out without prying too deeply into his personal life. On the arm of any man, president or pauper, she would have been considered an asset.

Nick had never been so bored in his life.

After numerous attempts at snagging his attention, Caroline set down her fork. "Nick," she said.

"Hmn?"

"Nicholas?"

He started, looked up guiltily. "What? I'm sorry, did I miss something?"

"You haven't heard a word I've said tonight, have you?"

He couldn't tell her that while she'd been talking about the MBA she'd recently completed, he'd been thinking about the book Ingram had given him. He couldn't tell her that while she was savoring the escargot and the cherries jubilee and the Debussy, he'd been remembering the barbecued ribs he'd shared with Kathryn McAllister in a smoke-filled, dirty hole-in-the-wall where Garth Brooks played on the jukebox, and none of Elba's Junior League matrons would have deigned to show their faces.

"This wasn't such a good idea, was it?" Caroline said.

"I'm sorry," he said. "I've been distracted lately. Work."

She raised a single elegant eyebrow. "I wouldn't think that the police chief in a town like Elba would have too taxing a job."

"Do you know anything," he said, "about snake handling churches?"

"Only what I've seen on the television news magazines." She studied him quizzically. "Why do you ask?"

He shook his head. "Something about a case I'm working on."

"You're a dedicated cop, aren't you?"

"I'm a cop," he said. "There's no other kind."

It was barely ten o'clock when he brought her home. He followed her up the stairs to her apartment, admiring the sway of her derriere in the chiffon dress and the shapely calves that showed beneath its hem. At her door, they paused. "Would you like to come in for a drink?" she said.

He nearly turned her down, but she was an attractive woman, and he'd been celibate for a long time. "One drink," he said, and she smiled warmly.

While she busied herself in the kitchen, he wandered around the living room, examining the family photos on the credenza, inspecting the bric-a-brac tastefully displayed here and there, studying the titles of the books on her built-in shelves. In the background, Harry Connick, Jr., crooned about flying to the moon.

"Nick?" she said softly, from the doorway.

He turned and took the drink she held out to him. Instead of drinking, he set it down on the table beside him and took Caroline Belmont in his arms. She was as willing as he'd expected her to be, soft and feminine and fragrant, and he kissed her open-mouthed, his knee thrust between her thighs, one hand pressed hard against the small of her back. For a full thirty seconds, he kissed her. And then he drew back and examined her lovely face. Those long-lashed eyes stared back at him, and he thought he saw amusement in them. "Well," she said, "I guess we can't say we didn't give it a try, can we?"

"I'm sorry," he said, and released her.

While he paced, hands in pockets, she smoothed her hair, her skirt. "Why'd you ask me out tonight, Nick?" she said.

He stopped pacing, shrugged sheepishly. "My daughter pushed me into it. She thinks I need to get a life."

Her smile was genuine. "Look, Nick, you're a very nice man. It's not your fault the chemistry isn't there."

At the door, he gave her a brotherly peck on the cheek, and then he went downstairs and checked in on Janine. She was curled up on the couch, wearing her yellow flannel pajamas, his pillow

cradled in her arms, watching *Caddyshack* for the umpteenth time.
"Hi, Daddy," she said, giving him that smile that never failed to
squeeze his heart right there inside his chest.

"Hi, baby. Listen, I have to go out for a little while. Will you
be okay?"

"Of course." She waggled her eyebrows. "How'd it go with
Mrs. Belmont?"

"It was okay. She's one sharp cookie. She likes you a lot."

"I like her, too. Go ahead and take your time, Daddy, I'll be
fine."

"I won't be too late, I promise. Keep the doors locked, okay?"

Janine rolled her eyes. "Yes, Dad."

He locked the door behind him, double-checked it and went out
into the hot summer night.

* * *

She waited ninety minutes at the turnout on the shore of Lake
Alberta, but Wanita Crumley never showed.

At 9:30, she finally gave up, and drove back into town, past
Carlyle's Barber Shop and the Dixie Market, past the police station,
eerily quiet at this time of day. Up Oak Street and past the quaint old
house where Nick DiSalvo rented the downstairs apartment from
Caroline Belmont. Blue light flickered behind the bay window, but
the Blazer wasn't in the yard, and she wondered where he was at this
time of night while his daughter sat home alone with the TV.

Restless, she drove out to the east end of town, past Wanita
Crumley's little ranch house, but the place was dark, the driveway
empty. She turned her car around at the end of Judge McAllister's
driveway and headed home, drowning in disappointment. She'd been
in town for ten days, and so far, she was no closer to solving
Michael's murder than she'd been the day she arrived. Kathryn
clenched her fists in frustration and banged them against the steering
wheel.

Elvis looked at her with mild curiosity. With a sigh, she
reached out to rub behind his ear. "It's all right, partner," she said.
"When we get home, you'll get an extra doggie biscuit for being so
patient."

Drawn like the proverbial moth to the flame, she drove past

DiSalvo's house again. This time, the Blazer sat in the yard, and upstairs, in Caroline Belmont's apartment, several lights were on. But DiSalvo's apartment remained dark, illuminated only by the flickering light of the television.

Her own little house was cozy and welcoming. She double-checked the locks, gave Elvis his promised doggie biscuits, then stripped off her clothes and climbed into the shower.

The hot water rejuvenated her, and as it trickled down her body, she wondered what could have happened to Wanita. Perhaps it had all been a ruse. Maybe the woman had never really known anything. It hadn't occurred to her until now that somebody might have used Wanita to lure her out to a place where she'd be vulnerable and highly unlikely to garner protection from Elba's finest.

Cursing, she shut off the water and briskly dried off with a thick towel. She put on her terrycloth robe and tied it around her waist, then brushed her hair with quick, angry strokes. Tossing the brush on the counter, she headed barefoot down the hall to get a drink before she went to bed.

She was pouring herself a glass of iced tea when she heard the muted purr of an automobile crawling down the street. It turned into her driveway, and her heart rate took a sharp jump. The driver turned out the lights and sat there with the engine idling, and she had her hand on the phone to call the police when she recognized the sound as DiSalvo's Blazer.

She went limp with a combination of relief and fury. It was past ten-thirty. How dare he frighten her like that? What kind of idiot would sit there in her driveway with the engine running, instead of shutting off the truck and coming inside?

She strode to the front door, undid the locks, and flung it open. Barefoot, she marched across the grass and stopped at his open window. "What the hell are you doing?" she said.

He just looked at her. "I wish to Christ I knew."

She folded her arms over her breasts. "A civilized person would come to the door."

"Nobody ever accused me of being civilized."

"Well? Are you coming in or not? Because I'm going back inside, and I'm locking that door behind me. And once it's locked, nobody gets in. Not you, not Jesus Christ Almighty. So it's up to you."

Without another word, she turned and marched back across the grass.

Behind her, the Blazer's door screeked open. She stomped up onto the porch and into the house, past Elvis, who stood with ears pricked, his watchful gaze following DiSalvo's approach. Kathryn picked up her glass of iced tea and took a long, slow swallow, then set it down and leaned against the kitchen counter with her arms crossed.

"Hey, dog. How goes the battle?"

Elvis sniffed DiSalvo's outstretched hand and wiggled his rump. Nick stood fiddling with the lock on the door while she tapped a foot in impatience. "You have precisely five minutes," she said, "to tell me why you're here. And then I'm booting your ass out the door."

He looked at her with those melted-chocolate eyes. "You're a hard woman, Kathryn McAllister. Did prison do that to you?"

"Five minutes, DiSalvo. You're wasting time."

He moved slowly toward her, so slowly that her heart rate, already too rapid, doubled. He stopped a half-inch away from her, so close his body heat tangled with hers and battled for supremacy. She tried to back away, but the counter held her fast. With his gaze locked on hers, he picked up her glass of iced tea and downed it in a single long draught. She watched in fascination as his Adam's apple moved up and down. He set down the empty glass and rested his hands on the counter, one on either side of her. "I came here tonight," he said, "to find out just what it is that's going on between us."

She wet her lips. "Nothing," she said. "Nothing's going on between us."

"The hell it isn't! Because of you, I've been running around for the last ten days with my head up my ass. Before you showed up, my life was simple. Uncomplicated. Boring as hell. *And I liked it that way!*"

"Sounds like a personal problem to me."

He towered over her, so close she could feel him, could taste him, was inhaling him with every breath. "It's damn personal," he said.

She thrust her chin forward. "Are you trying to intimidate me, DiSalvo?"

Impossible as it seemed, he moved closer. "Yeah," he said. "I am."

"It's working," she said, wondering if that was really a tremor she heard in her own voice.

"I don't want you," he said, leaning over her, forcing her to bend backward over the sink. "Do you hear me?"

"I hear you. But maybe we should record it. For posterity."

"You're nothing but trouble, do you understand? You're a goddamn pain in the ass, and *I don't want you!*"

She had a microsecond to wonder how long she'd been clinging with both fists to his cotton shirt before his mouth came down on hers and she disintegrated. Heat, raging, roaring, sucked all the oxygen from her lungs. Her hands twisted and tangled involuntarily, destroying the material of his shirt as his kiss destroyed her, their tongues fighting a sinuous and glorious battle at the molten center of the universe. She'd waited ten days for him, a lifetime, and now she wanted all of him. She tugged at the shirt, yanked it free from his belt, sought the hot, damp flesh beneath. His stomach was rock-hard, his chest a forest of crisp hair that she explored with frantic and curious fingers.

His mouth left hers, and she gasped for air. Hands tangled in her hair, he tugged her head back, baring her neck to him, and ran his tongue down the long column of flesh to the vee of her robe. "Nick," she gasped as he continued along the curve of one breast. Her fingers fumbled clumsily with his belt buckle. She found the thick swelling beneath his zipper and stroked it. He groaned and drove his hips hard against hers. Trembling, she arched against him, cradled him, her hips restless in their desire to find that remembered rhythm.

And his pager went off.

They both froze. He raised his head to look at her, and his eyes were wild. Cursing violently, he released her to turn off the incessant shrilling of the pager. Running a hand through his hair, he picked up the telephone and viciously punched in a series of numbers. "DiSalvo," he barked.

Her stomach was still somewhere in the vicinity of her tonsils, her body aflame, her breath coming in hard, racking gasps. *"What?"* he said. Then, "Jesus Christ al-fucking-mighty."

It was amazing to watch, his instantaneous transformation from man to cop. He began frantically checking his pockets for a pen and paper. She produced one from the kitchen drawer and he took it without speaking and began writing. "Yeah. Uh huh. Where? Yeah. Have you called the coroner yet? Good. Give me fifteen minutes. I have to make a couple of calls first."

He hung up the phone. With his back to her, he unzipped his pants, tucked in his shirt, and zipped them back up. Buckled the belt she'd unbuckled just moments earlier. "Nick?" she said.

When he turned back around, his face was blank, emotionless, professional. The face of a stranger. "Two kids out coon hunting just found Wanita Crumley's body in a cornfield. Somebody put a bullet in the back of her head."

The cold was like being dunked into a vat of ice water. She began trembling violently. "Oh, God," she said. 'Oh god oh god oh god."

He grasped her by both arms and shook her. "Stop it!" he said. "Don't you dare to go to pieces on me now!"

"It's my fault!" she said. "It's because of me. She called me yesterday and said she had some information for me about Michael's murder. We were supposed to meet tonight out at the lake. She never showed up. Christ, DiSalvo, somebody killed her because of me!"

He closed both eyes. "When are you going to listen to me?" he said violently. "You have to stop playing detective! That's my job!"

"She had little kids, Nick."

"She was a stupid woman who got mixed up in something she had no business being mixed up in, and she paid for it with her life." His voice softened. "It's not your fault."

Kathryn closed her eyes and sighed. "I know," she said softly.

He brushed his knuckles against the back of her cheek. "You okay?"

"I've been better."

He drew her into his arms, and she lay her head against his chest. Still holding her, he dialed the phone. "Caroline," he said, "it's Nick. Look, I have an emergency. I don't know how long I'll be. It could be all night. Do you think you could go downstairs and stay with Janine? Thanks, kid, you're a peach."

He broke the connection and dialed again. She clung to him, soothed by the steady beating of his heart. "Hi, sweetheart," he said, "it's Daddy. I just got an emergency call. I don't know when I'll be able to get home, so I called Caroline and asked her to come down and stay with you tonight. I'm really sorry. Yeah. Yeah, I love you, too, baby."

He hung up the phone, released her, and began moving toward the door. "You're to lock your doors," he said, digging in his pocket for his car keys, "and keep 'em locked. Do you understand?"

"Yes."

Still moving, still not looking at her, he said, "You don't open the damn door for anybody but me. I don't care if it's your freaking grandmother. Only me. Understand?"

"Only you," she said.

He paused, hand on the doorknob, to look at her. "You see anything suspicious, I'm talking a goddamn squirrel running across your lawn, you call and have me paged."

She nodded silently. He opened the door and stepped through it. "Nick," she said.

He paused, looked back at her. "Be careful," she said.

He came back through the door, swept her into his arms, and kissed her hard and long. "I'll come back," he said, "afterward. If that's what you want."

Her fingers tightened on his shirt sleeve. "Yes," she said. "Come back."

He kissed her again, gently this time. "Lock the door behind me," he said.

And he was gone.

* * *

Both of Elba's police cruisers were at the scene, as well as the county ambulance and the coroner's private vehicle, all of them with lights flashing. He pulled up behind the coroner, left his blue dash light running, and climbed out of his vehicle.

He passed a group of wide-eyed gawkers, nodded to a couple of pasty-faced teenage boys accompanied by a brace of hunting dogs that were surprisingly silent. He stepped over the crime scene tape that Bucky had put up and edged closer to where the county coroner, David Ellsworth, still in his flannel pajamas and robe, was hunched over the body. "Doc," he said.

"DiSalvo," Ellsworth acknowledged.

Nick looked up at the sky. Above his head, the Milky Way was clearly visible. "Nice night for a murder," he said pleasantly.

"I was all settled down in my easy chair," Ellsworth said, "getting ready to watch *Casablanca* on one of those fancy satellite stations. They don't make movies like that anymore."

"Nope." Nick knelt in the red Carolina soil and examined the body. Wanita was lying on her face, her hands tied behind her back, a single neat little hole drilled in the back of her head. ".38," he said, and Ellsworth grunted. "Hands tied together behind her back," he observed, more to himself than to anyone else. "Single bullet wound to the back of the head. Execution style. Somebody wanted to teach her a lesson."

"That would be my guess."

"Any estimate yet on the time of death?"

"Two, three hours, tops. Probably closer to three. Rigor mortis is already advancing quite nicely."

"Not much blood."

"Mmn. My guess is he did her somewhere else, then dumped her here."

"He?"

Doc Ellsworth smiled. "Wanita's no lightweight. It would take a strong man to heft her all the way out here and dump her in the middle of this cornfield."

"Official cause of death?"

"We'll save that for the autopsy. Preliminary cause of death, single bullet wound to the head, most likely a .38 caliber. Now can I go home?"

"Thanks, Doc." Nick patted the older man on the shoulder and went in search of Bucky.

He found him stringing out more yellow crime scene tape. "Anything?" he asked his second-in-command. "Tire tracks, footprints, a piece of fucking lint someplace it doesn't belong?"

"We got a couple of good footprints, but they'll most likely match up to the boots the kids are wearing. They were all over the crime scene. And the dogs, too."

"Peachy." He looked past Bucky to where Officer Earl Martin was being reamed out by an older gentleman in faded jeans and a torn tee shirt. "Who's the old guy giving Earl the business?"

"That's Wilford Austin, sir. He wants to know when we'll be

done tramplin' his corn all to hell."

"Did you get a statement from him?"

Bucky grinned. "I do believe that's what Earl is attempting, even as we speak."

"What about the kids?"

"This just might turn out to be their last coon hunting experience, Chief. Looks like they might've lost their taste for it."

"Where's the photog?"

"Drew Logan usually does it, but he's gone to Talladega, to a family reunion, so Eddie Sheldon from the *Gazette*'s coming over, soon's he can get his film loaded."

Nick ran both hands over his face. "Christ," he said, "is there anybody around here who doesn't do two or three different jobs?"

"Small town, Chief. A man's gotta eat. You might want to talk to the kids, sir. They're looking like they'd rather be somewhere else."

He spent fifteen minutes with Freddie Floyd and Billy Jo Wright, asking them to repeat again the stories they'd already told four or five times. "This is the last time," he promised. "Then you can go home."

So they ran through their disjointed story again, both of them obviously repelled by the details but nevertheless excited by their status. Finding a dead body, especially one that had been recently murdered, was a rare event indeed in a town the size of Elba. People would be tossing their names about for the next twenty years, remembering them as *those two boys that stumbled over Wanita Crumley's body.*

"I lost my supper," Freddie Floyd admitted. "I ain't never seen no dead person before."

Nick patted the boy's slender shoulders. "It's normal. Nothing to be ashamed of. My first time, I tossed my cookies all over the sidewalk."

"Chief," Bucky said, as the boys and their dogs headed for home, "we found this in her pocket. Looks like she was supposed to meet somebody. There's a phone number. Think it might mean something?"

Sixteen years as a cop had perfected his poker face. On the slip of paper Bucky held between gloved hands, next to Kathryn's phone number, somebody had scribbled, *Lake Alberta, 8:00 Friday.*

For the long moment in which he studied it, his entire history as a good cop passed in front of his eyes. One tiny slip of paper. One very tiny slip of paper that could easily disappear. And who would know the difference?

Nick closed his eyes. Took a deep breath. "Bag it," he said.

chapter eight

She was napping, but she awakened instantly when Nick pulled into the driveway with just his parking lights on. She glanced at her bedside clock and saw that it was nearly 2:30 in the morning. He shut off the Blazer and squawked open his door, and she hastily pulled on her robe and went downstairs to let him in.

Even in the darkness, she could see the exhaustion on his face. He locked the door behind him and without speaking, she stepped into his arms.

Warm. He felt so warm. They stood intertwined, heat melding with heat, bodies swaying gently in rhythm with their breathing. Nick buried his face in her hair and murmured, "You smell good."

He skimmed his mouth down her cheek, her jaw, the length of her neck, his hot breath raising goosebumps on sensitive flesh. She knotted her fists in his hair and let her head fall back in limp acquiescence as he loosened the belt to her robe and peeled it back. He sank gentle teeth into her shoulder, and white-hot desire shot through her. "Nick," she said hoarsely. "Oh, Christ, Nick."

And the robe dropped to the floor.

Tomorrow, she might regret this, but tonight there was no regret, no coherent thought at all, only sensation, only the touch, the taste, the scent of this man she'd been waiting to touch since the day she first walked into his office. There was a wildness in him that called to a corresponding wildness in her, a wildness she'd never known existed before today. As his mouth worried the soft flesh of her shoulder, she unbuttoned his shirt and tugged it free of his belt.

He shrugged out of it, and it fell to the floor. Beneath it he was sleek and hard and muscled, exquisitely male. She inhaled his scent, tasted the tang of salt on his skin, knowing she'd never wanted anything in her life as much as she wanted Nick DiSalvo.

"I didn't intend to do this," he said harshly. "I kept telling myself I had to stay away from you. But I couldn't." He ran his tongue down the swell of her breast, took the hard little peak into his mouth, and exquisite pleasure tore through her as his tongue circled and teased. Just when she was certain she would implode, he changed tactics, working his way back upward, toward her mouth. Hoarsely, he said, "I'm not an easy man, Kathryn."

Her heart thundered in her chest. Trembling violently, she said, "And I'm a hard woman."

"You can say that again." He ran a hand down her back, slipped a single finger between her buttocks, advanced it until he reached the hot, wet center of her. When he slipped it inside her, she nearly detonated. Near her ear, he rasped, "I've wanted you naked like this, McAllister, since the first day you walked into my office."

Her body no longer belonged to her. He had total control as she moved involuntarily against his hand. "DiSalvo," she whispered. "Oh, God, Nick, don't make me wait."

His kiss was savage, his tongue sleek against hers, sending shudders to the pit of her stomach. With his free hand, he fumbled with his belt buckle. Still riding the glorious pleasure of that finger sliding in and out of her, she helped him, loosening his belt and shoving his clothing aside. Then he was free and she took him, thick and heavy and pendulous, in her hands.

"Kat," he said raggedly. "Jesus, Kat, it seems like I've been waiting forever for you to touch me like this."

This time, the kiss they shared was gentle, delicate. A surge of tenderness swelled inside her, frightening in its intensity, confusing in its significance. After four years in prison, tenderness wasn't something she'd thought herself capable of. She could accept herself as a sexual creature, wanting, desiring, even needing. But caring for Nick DiSalvo was something else entirely.

He knelt on the floor and hastily arranged her robe beneath him. Rocking back on his heels, he held out his hand. "Come here, Kat," he said. "Come to me, baby."

Kathryn looked into those melted-chocolate eyes and forgot all uncertainty. Hooking both arms around his neck, she wrapped her legs around him, and his fingertips dug into her buttocks as he lowered her to his lap and drove that hot hardness up inside her.

She cried out, locked her thighs around his waist, and rode him. He whispered hoarse and muffled words into her ear, but she couldn't answer him, couldn't draw in enough oxygen to speak. She clung to him, her face buried in his shoulder, lost in the white-hot heat that fused them together, gasping with each thrust of that rock-hard body. "Hang on," he rasped, and took her to the floor beneath him.

He was heavy on top of her, heavy and wet and shuddering and thoroughly, unequivocally male. She twined her fists in his hair and kissed him as they rocked together, both of them shuddering, both uttering harsh, breathy sounds of pleasure. Gasping to fill her overheated lungs with oxygen, she rolled and tumbled with him across the floor, slamming into an end table and sending it skidding across polished hardwood.

"Kathryn," he said hoarsely. "Tell me when, baby. Tell me when."

"Now. Oh, Nick. Now!"

He drove into her, hot and hard and slick, and together they tumbled over the edge into paradise.

When it was over, they lay dazed and gasping, glued together by their own dampness. The clock on the fireplace mantel ticked in the silence. In the kitchen, Elvis yawned long and loud, then thunked his head back down onto his paws. "I think I'm dead," Nick said hoarsely. "I think you killed me."

"You started it, DiSalvo."

"You don't hear me complaining, do you, McAllister?"

She stroked the smooth slope of his shoulder. "Do you have to go home?"

"Caroline said she'd stay all night."

"Then come to bed. You need some sleep."

He was asleep the instant his head hit the pillow. She nestled close against his warmth and lay there watching the rise and fall of his chest. Since the day she'd come home and found Michael dead on the floor, she'd never felt safe. Not anywhere, not until she met Nick DiSalvo. He was inordinately bossy, and frequently infuriating. But he made her feel safe, and she trusted him in a way she trusted no other living soul.

She hadn't counted on this. Hell, after four years in prison, she'd stopped hoping for anything more satisfying than a hot meal and a hard bed. And as long as Michael's killer was still running around loose, she couldn't indulge herself in the luxury of any romantic entanglements. She couldn't afford to be distracted. There was too much at stake.

Yet there was a part of her, some soft woman-place hidden beneath the hard-edged veneer she showed the world, that still dared to hope prison hadn't succeeded in stamping out her ability to love. In four years, she'd never let anybody through that veneer to touch the woman beneath. Until Nick DiSalvo.

As he slept peacefully beside her, moonlight spilling through the window and turning his dark hair to silver, Kathryn realized she wanted to run. But did she want to run toward Nick, or away from him?

She honestly didn't know.

* * *

It was the pager that woke him, insistent and annoying, and he rolled over in bed and reached out to shut it off before he realized he wasn't in his own bed. Beside him, Kathryn lay sleeping, and on the bedside table, the clock read 7:02. He sat up on the side of the bed and rubbed his eyes, and then he went naked to the living room to find the pager in the heap of clothing they'd left in a haphazard tangle on the floor.

He shut it off and went back upstairs. Kathryn sat up in bed with the sheet tucked demurely around her breasts, her blue eyes still soft with sleep. "Morning," he said.

"Yes," she said. "It is, isn't it?"

There was a phone next to the bed. He sat down beside her and dialed the station. "Hear you had quite a night," Rowena said cheerfully, and it took him a minute to realize she meant the murder and not his heated entanglement with Kathryn.

"What's up?" he said.

"There's some fella from the SBI waiting in your office. Seems extremely anxious to see you."

"What the hell is he doing here? Wanita's been dead less than twelve hours, and already the State's sticking their nose in?"

"I made him a cup of our finest coffee and told him you'd be along in a bit."

"It won't hurt him to cool his heels for a while. Use some of your innate charm to keep him occupied. I'm running on three hours of sleep and I haven't had my morning caffeine yet. Or a shower. I'll be there when I get there."

He hung up the phone and turned to Kathryn. She was still sitting there holding the covers to her bosom like a fifteen-year-old virgin. He caught the bedding in his hand and tugged, peeling it down and tossing it over the foot of the bed. "That's more like it," he said.

Her body was just as he'd imagined it a thousand times, lean and willowy, her belly flat, her waist tiny, her breasts ample and firm. He ran an exploratory hand down that smooth, flat belly and cupped the soft mound between her legs. "Pheromones," he said.

"Excuse me?"

"I've finally figured it out. That's what keeps me coming around here, again and again. Pheromones."

"That's certainly flattering, DiSalvo."

"I'm desperate for a shower," he said. "You game?"

They made hot, wet, soapy love in the shower while Elvis whined and scratched at the closed door. Afterward, while he dressed and combed his hair, she brewed coffee. He followed his nose to the kitchen and found her bustling around, pulling things from the refrigerator. Eggs, milk, butter. "I don't have time for breakfast," he said as he poured himself a cup of coffee.

She wasn't quite quick enough to hide the disappointment in her eyes. "Oh," she said.

"I have to go home and change. And check on Janine." Christ, he'd forgotten all about Janine. "And this State guy's waiting in my office." Why did he feel as though he owed her an explanation? He'd only slept with her, for Christ's sake. It wasn't as though he'd offered her a goddamn engagement ring. "Look," he said, "there's something I want you to do for me."

She leaned against the counter, spatula in hand, and tossed those blonde curls back from her face. "What?" she said.

"I want you to get dressed and pack a suitcase," he said, pouring milk into his coffee. He capped the milk and returned it to the refrigerator. Took a sip. Her coffee was weak and insubstantial. He was going to have to teach her how to make it right. "I'm sending Bucky over, and he's driving you someplace where you'll be safe until this is all over."

"You're kidding, right?"

"I don't care where you go—Fayetteville, Raleigh, Charlotte—I just want you out of Elba."

He'd seen that stubborn look before, and it didn't bode well for him. "I see," she said. "Is that a direct order, Chief DiSalvo, to get out of your picturesque little town before sundown?"

He slammed down the cup of coffee, and hot liquid sloshed over the side. "Goddamn it, Kat," he said, "I'm not talking to you as a cop, I'm talking to you as a man." He crossed the room, removed the spatula from her hand, and took her in his arms. "The man," he said pointedly, "who just spent the night in your bed."

She studied his face, and for a moment he thought she was going to give in. "There's just one problem with that, Nick," she said. "You can't separate the cop from the man. They're one and the same."

He brushed the back of his knuckles across her cheek. "Why do you have to fight me at every turn?"

"I told you already. I'm not letting them scare me off."

"You're a goddamn stubborn woman, Kathryn. And I can't watch over you every single hour of every single day."

She reached up and straightened his collar, and that simple gesture turned him inside out. "Kiss me, DiSalvo," she said, "and then go to work. They need you more than I do right now."

He buried his face in her hair and lost himself. She smelled so damn good. "I don't know when I'll be able to come back," he said, running the pad of his thumb along the line of her jaw. "With Janine, and now this homicide investigation—"

"It's all right. I understand."

He turned her face up to his and studied those clear blue eyes. "I *will* be back," he said.

She tightened her fingers on the fabric of his shirt. "I know," she said.

He kissed her gently, sweetly. "I have to go now," he said, "but—"

"I know," she said with resignation. "Keep the doors locked."

It was a fine Carolina morning, and he drove with his window down, surprised at how good a man could feel with three hours of sleep, a lousy cup of coffee, and an unsolved homicide hanging over him. He wheeled into his driveway and sprang up the steps to the apartment. Janine and Caroline Belmont were having breakfast together at his kitchen table. "Morning," he said, and Janine shot up from her chair.

"Daddy!" she said. "You're home!"

He returned her hug. "Just for a few minutes, squirt. I have somebody waiting for me in my office."

"That's not fair, for them to make you work so hard." She looked wildly indignant. "When are you supposed to sleep?"

"I, uh, caught a couple hours of sleep," he said, and Caroline raised a single, elegant eyebrow.

"Where?" Janine demanded.

"At the station. Look, sweetheart, I have to change and get back. Maybe tonight I can take you out for pizza. Would you like that?"

"I'm always up for pizza," she said. "But I'd rather have you."

Her words soured his mood considerably. He changed into his uniform, checked his gun and holstered it, rubbed at a smudge on his shoes. He felt guilty all the way to work, guilty for leaving her alone, guilty for being a cop when everybody else's father was home every night at 5:30. Guilty for screwing his brains out with the prime suspect in a homicide investigation.

He poured himself a huge cup of Rowena's hi-test coffee before he went in. Nodding toward his office, he whispered, "Name?"

"Melcher," Rowena said. "Special Agent Richard Melcher. And if I were you, Chief, I'd consider taking two cups instead of one. Our friend Melcher's gettin' a little testy."

He poured a second cup for Melcher and carried them both into his office. "Thought you could use a refill," he said, and set it down in front of his visitor.

"Mr. DiSalvo," Melcher said. "So nice that you could drop in and join us this morning."

Melcher was the kind of cop Nick hated on sight. Somewhere around twenty-five years old, he was one of those buzz-cut, spit-and-polish, by-the-book assholes who thought he had all the answers.

Young, desperately earnest, and green as fresh-mown grass. Nick sat down in his chair, rolled it back against the wall, and propped his feet up on his desk. While Melcher waited, he took a long, satisfying sip of coffee. Rowena knew how to make a cup of coffee. Maybe she could give Kathryn a few pointers.

"Now that we have the amenities taken care of," he said, "why don't you tell me what's your interest in the case?"

"A convicted killer is turned loose and comes back to the sleepy little hamlet where the only murder in the last thirty years was her husband's. Ten days later, the State's prime witness in her conviction turns up dead, conveniently carrying the lady's phone number in her pocket." Melcher leaned back in his chair and adjusted his perfectly creased pants. "You tell me what our interest is."

Nick smiled agreeably. "Maybe you'd like to tell me just how you happened to come by that little piece of information."

Melcher returned the smile. "Let's just say a little bird told me."

"The conviction in that case," he said over the rim of his coffee cup, "was overturned."

"Following the testimony of some little old lady who probably can't tell her ass from her elbow."

"Come on, Melcher. Do you really think Kathryn McAllister is stupid enough to kill Wanita Crumley and leave her own phone number in the victim's pocket?"

"You and I, DiSalvo, have both been around long enough to know that anybody is capable of doing anything, given the right motive and the right opportunity. We have motive, and we have opportunity. Now all we need is physical evidence, and we can nail her ass to the wall."

A muscle twitched in his eyelid. "This is my town," he said quietly. "This is my investigation. I don't need your help. I don't want your help. Now, why don't you toddle on back to Raleigh, or wherever the hell you came from, tell your boss that we're doing just fine on our own here in Elba, and let me get on with the business of solving this homicide?"

"Sorry, DiSalvo. No can do. I'm not budging until I get some answers from Kathryn McAllister."

He dropped his feet to the floor so suddenly that the kid jumped. In a deadly quiet voice he said, "She had nothing to do with it."

"Fine. Then she has nothing to be afraid of, does she?"

* * *

She was getting ready to take Elvis for a run when the police cruiser pulled into her driveway and Bucky Stimpson climbed out. He took a moment to hike up his pants and adjust his gun belt before he walked gingerly up the driveway. Furious, she flung open the front door and glared at him. "I told DiSalvo I wasn't going anywhere," she said, "and I'm not!"

"Ma'am?" Bucky stood there on her porch, bouncing on the balls of his feet and throwing nervous glances at Elvis, who stood rigidly by her side. "The Chief asked me to come down and pick you up, escort you down to the station."

"Down to the station?" she said. "Why does he want me at the station?"

Bucky tucked his hands into his pockets and squirmed. "Well, ma'am," he said, "there's a fellow down there from the SBI—" He paused and adjusted his hat. "That's the State Bureau of Investigation," he clarified.

"I know what it is!" she snapped.

Bucky cleared his throat. "Seems this fellow wants to question you regarding the killin' of Wanita Crumley."

She didn't bother to change out of her running clothes. It didn't really make any difference, anyway. She sat stiff and silent in the back seat of Bucky's patrol car, her purse clasped tightly in her hands, her knuckles white. The last time she'd ridden in the back seat of a police cruiser, she'd been covered with Michael's blood, and numb with fear. At least this time, there was no blood. The irony wasn't lost on her, though. She'd been wearing running clothes that time, too.

She followed Bucky wordlessly up the walk of the municipal building, past the blooming geraniums, up the front steps and through the door. Rowena looked up as she passed, gave her the evil eye, and returned to her knitting. Her breath was a fiery pain in her chest as Bucky knocked on the door and opened it. "Chief?" he said. "Miz McAllister's here."

She walked through the door like a woman walking to her

execution. Nick sat behind the desk, long legs sprawled, wearing his cop face, the one that would have identified him as a cop anywhere, even if he hadn't been wearing a gun and a badge. The SBI agent was young, clean-cut, and wore a gray suit with a red power tie. "Ms. McAllister," he said wryly, "do come in."

She stubbornly refused to take her eyes off DiSalvo, refused to hide the hurt, and he just as stubbornly refused to acknowledge it. The man who'd made passionate love to her just hours earlier was gone, replaced by a stone-faced stranger whose eyes looked at her with an indifference that was far more painful than the act of being hauled in for questioning.

"Go ahead, Melcher," he said to the agent, "it's your party." And without even glancing in her direction, he got up from the chair, turned his back on her, and walked over to the window.

She stared at him for a moment in disbelief, and then she turned to the eager young agent. He reminded her of a half-grown pit bull. "Richard Melcher," he said briskly, "SBI. I'd like to ask you a few questions concerning the Crumley homicide."

Her stomach had gone sour, and for a moment she was afraid she might vomit. She sat down heavily in the chair and folded her arms across her stomach. "I don't know anything about the Crumley homicide," she said.

"What was your relationship with the victim?"

"I didn't have a relationship with her. Shouldn't my lawyer be present, Mr. Melcher?"

"There's no need for that, Ms. McAllister. We're just having a friendly little Q&A here. Did you or did you not know Wanita Crumley?"

"I knew her. So did everybody else in Elba."

"Did you hate her?"

"I don't like what you're implying by that question—"

"Because I would sure as hell hate anybody who did to me what that woman did to you. She aired your dirty laundry in public, Kathryn. She let the whole world know that you couldn't keep your husband satisfied. That must have made you very angry."

"My husband," she said, "never touched that little tramp. And you may not call me Kathryn."

"Maybe you'd like to explain to me why we found a slip of paper in the victim's pocket with your phone number on it, along with the words *Lake Alberta, 8:00 Friday*."

She glanced at Nick. He must have known. He must have known last night, when he came back to her house. But he'd come anyway. He'd made love to her anyway. She silently begged him to turn around, but he never moved a muscle, just stood there rigidly at the window, his back ramrod straight. "I have no idea," she said.

"Come on, Kathryn. We're all intelligent people here. Did you or did you not have a meeting with Wanita Crumley at 8:00 last night?"

She debated how to answer, decided on the truth. "We'd scheduled a meeting. Wanita never showed up. And my name, Mr. Melcher, is *Ms. McAllister*."

He got up from his chair and began walking around the room. She followed him with her eyes, not trusting the little worm as far as she could throw him. "Why did you schedule a meeting with her?" he said.

"She phoned me two nights ago and told me she had information that might prove useful to me. I agreed to meet her and pay her fifty dollars for the information. That's the kind of woman she was, Mr. Melcher. She would have sold her own grandmother for a fifty-dollar bill."

He sat on the edge of Nick's desk and adjusted the crease in his pant leg. "What information?" he said.

"About who killed my husband. It seemed rather important at the time."

Nick turned away from the window, leaned against the wall, and crossed his arms. She glared at him, but those chocolate eyes never flickered, never softened.

Melcher tapped his hand against the edge of the desk. "Why did you come back to Elba?" he said.

"Mr. Melcher, am I being charged with anything?"

"I told you, this is just a friendly little—"

"Q&A, yes, I remember. In that case, I'm leaving now."

"You're free to go at any time. Chief DiSalvo? Is there anything you'd like to ask Ms. McAllister while she's here?"

Nick gazed steadily at her. "No," he said, his voice as flinty-hard as his eyes.

"Fine," she said, her eyes locked with his. "Then good-bye, gentlemen."

Her hand was on the doorknob when Melcher stopped her. "Ms. McAllister?" he said. "If I were you, I wouldn't plan any sudden trips out of town."

She paused with the door half open to look back at him. He was sitting on the edge of Nick's desk, one leg swinging in midair, a look of supreme satisfaction on his face. She looked at DiSalvo in disbelief. "Is this guy for real?" she said.

And she slammed the door behind her.

chapter nine

She came close to kicking the dog, thought better of it and hurled a water glass across the room instead. The act was childish, petulant, and thoroughly satisfying as she watched it shatter and imagined it slamming into Nick DiSalvo's head and bursting it like a watermelon. "That son of a bitch," she told Elvis, who sat watching her with his ears pricked and his ugly face radiating curiosity. "I trusted him," she ranted. "*I trusted him*! And he's no different than the rest of them!" For emphasis, she slammed her fist against the side of the microwave.

Pain shot through her knuckles, and the stack of mail she'd tucked into the cubbyhole a few days earlier fell to the floor. Tears flooded her eyes as she brought her knuckles to her mouth and bent to pick up the forgotten mail. A four-year-old electric bill. A couple of flyers. And the damn bank statement.

She glared at the envelope. The way this day had started out, it couldn't possibly get any worse. "Screw it," she said, and tore the envelope open. She set the statement on the counter and, still sucking on her injured knuckles, began thumbing through the checks.

She found it near the bottom of the stack, stopped riffling to backtrack and take a second look. It wasn't a big thing, just slightly odd, a check made out to Francis Willoughby for $250, and signed in Michael's neat, elegant handwriting. The name sounded vaguely familiar, but she couldn't place it. She flipped over the check. It had been endorsed with one of those personalized stamps that said

Willoughby Contracting — For Deposit Only.

Why on earth would Michael have paid a contractor two hundred and fifty dollars?

She opened the drawer and took out the phone book, opened it to the yellow pages, riffled through them until she found Willoughby Contracting. She dialed the number, then stood at the sink, running cold water over her bruised and bloody knuckles, while it rang. "Willoughby Contracting," a soft female voice said.

Kathryn turned off the water. "Francis Willoughby, please."

"Just a minute, hon. Fran, it's for you!"

Obviously a highly professional setup. Kathryn tapped her toe as she waited, and then Francis Willoughby came on the line. "Mr. Willoughby," she said, "this is Kathryn McAllister."

The silence at the other end told her he knew who she was. She took a deep breath and made her voice as pleasant as possible. "I'm looking for some information. I just came across a check that Michael wrote you two weeks before he died. It was for two hundred and fifty dollars. I was wondering if you could tell me what it was for?"

There was a long silence. And then he blurted out, "I would've paid the money back, but you was in jail, and—"

"No, no," she said, "I don't want the money. I just want to know why he gave it to you."

"It was a retainer. He hired me to rip out the kitchen in the Chandler place and build a new one."

Blankly, she said, "He was going to renovate the kitchen?"

"He said you'd been wanting a new kitchen ever since you bought the house. I came over and checked it out one day while you was at work. It was in sorry shape, Miz McAllister. We decided the best thing to do was to gut it out and start over. Your husband wanted me to tear down the wall by the dining room, put in an archway, install new flooring, new ceiling, new appliances and countertop. New everything."

"Why would he have done that without telling me?"

"He was gonna surprise you. It was supposed to be an anniversary present."

She thanked him and hung up the phone. Went slowly to the open back door and stood there, looking out through the screen, her eyes slowly filling with tears. "Oh, shit," she said, and leaned her head against the screen. Elvis walked over to her, nudged her thigh with his nose, and she reached down absently and scratched his head. If Michael hadn't died, her life would be so different now. The house that was sitting empty out on Ridgewood Road would be the showplace they'd always intended it to become. They'd have a couple of toddlers playing in the yard, sunny and blond, with their father's laughing eyes. And she would still be Mrs. Michael McAllister. Still young, still innocent, still in love.

Not the greedy, grasping woman who'd rolled wantonly around the living room floor with Nick DiSalvo.

The phone rang. Ignoring it, she bent to pick up the shards of broken glass. She walked to the wastebasket and dropped them in, ran cold water over her hands. Her knuckles were throbbing, and the phone continued to ring. Woodenly, she went to it and picked it up. "What?" she said.

"I'm sorry," DiSalvo said softly.

Her stomach turned inside out. His voice was low and intimate, like they were pals or something. "I have nothing to say to you," she said, and hung up the phone.

It rang again almost immediately. The man was nothing if not persistent. She took out the broom and dustpan and finished cleaning up the broken glass, then turned Elvis loose into the back yard, where he immediately lifted his leg on Raelynn's mother's peony bush.

After a while, the phone stopped ringing. She brought Elvis back in and tossed the bank statement into the trash. There was no sense in wallowing in the past. Michael was dead, those beautiful blond babies would never be born, and last night with Nick DiSalvo had been the biggest mistake of her life.

Five minutes later, the Blazer came roaring down the street and sailed into her driveway. He stomped on the parking brake and opened his screeking door and stalked up the walkway and onto the porch.

"That hinge could use a little WD-40, DiSalvo," she said through the locked screen door.

His dark eyes were wild. "Why'd you hang up on me?" he demanded.

"I told you, I have nothing to say to you."

"Damn it all, Kathryn, it wasn't my fault. He insisted on talking to you."

"And just when were you planning on letting me know I was a suspect in another murder? Christmas? Arbor Day?"

"Look," he said, "I have a teenage daughter who's hounding hell out of me to be a proper father. I have an unsolved homicide hanging over my head and the mayor breathing down my neck to get it solved. I have a twelve-year-old hotshot who thinks he's Efrem Fucking Zimbalist sniffing around in my investigation. I don't need this shit from you!"

Her fingers tightened on the door frame. "You knew, Nick! You knew last night, but you didn't bother to let me in on it. You used me!"

"Oh, for Christ's sake. I didn't do anything you didn't want as much as I did!"

"Are you familiar with the word betrayal?"

His face hardened. "Let me in."

"No."

"I'm not standing out here on the damn doorstep and telling everybody in Elba our business. Let me in the damn house."

"Your truck spent the night in my driveway, Nick. Everybody in Elba already knows our business!"

"I just want to talk to you. Alone. In private. That means without the whole neighborhood listening in."

"No."

"McAllister, you are the stubbornest damn woman I ever met! Why the hell won't you let me in?"

"Because if I open this door, in five minutes we'll be rolling around on the floor! I can't do this, DiSalvo!"

"Oh, for Christ's sake! I won't touch you. Just open the goddamn door and let me in."

She grasped Elvis's collar and held it tight. From somewhere deep in his throat, the dog made a low, growling sound.

Nick gaped at him in disbelief. "Call off the dog," he said.

"No."

Elvis growled again, and Nick scowled at him. "Call off the frigging dog, Kathryn."

"If you try to touch me," she said, "he'll rip your throat out. He has very large teeth. He could kill you in fifteen seconds."

"And I'm carrying a loaded .38 that could kill him in one shot."

Appalled, she said, "You would *shoot* my *dog*?"

He clenched his fists, and a vein stood out on the side of his neck. "I AM NOT GOING TO SHOOT YOUR DAMN DOG!"

"And I'm not letting you in, DiSalvo. You seem to have this warped idea that you can come slinking up to my doorstep every time you have a hard-on, and then refuse to acknowledge me in public. I won't be treated that way."

"I'm trying to keep your ass out of the slammer!" he shouted. "What was I supposed to do? Tell Melcher I'd just finished rolling in the bedsheets with you?"

"Yes! And then walk down Main Street beside me, right in the light of day!"

"I could lose my job, Kathryn. I'm the goddamn chief of police, in case you've forgotten."

"Right. I forgot you're a cop. The job always comes first with you, doesn't it, Nick?"

"You're missing the point, McAllister. If I lose my job over this, I can't protect you. And that's the goddamn bottom line!"

Her anger dissipated, leaving her feeling strangely deflated. "Jesus, DiSalvo," she said. "Are you really naïve enough to believe you can protect me?"

"Nobody's touching you," he said grimly. "I won't let them."

"If the State really wants me," she said, "they'll have me. And there's not a thing on God's green earth you can do about it."

"Kat," he said, and his voice was silken, seductive, reaching into every soft, feminine place inside her. "Open the door. Please."

It took every ounce of strength she possessed to turn him down. "Not until you're willing to acknowledge me in public," she said. "Go away, DiSalvo." And she shut the door in his face.

* * *

Rowena was knitting again, and he was just steamed enough to call her on it. "I'd appreciate it," he said, "if you wouldn't do that during working hours. It makes us look like a bunch of backwoods hicks."

Her mouth fell open and she nearly dropped her knitting needles. "Why, ah—whatever you say, Chief."

"Thank you. I'm calling a staff meeting in my office in a half-hour. See that everybody's notified."

She hastily tucked her knitting into a bag beside her chair. "Everybody?" she said.

"Everybody who's employed by this department. Make it crystal clear that if they want a job tomorrow, they'd best show up."

A half-hour later, they assembled in his office, curious, silent, and nervous. He sat down in his chair and without speaking a word, looked at each of them in turn. Rowena. Bucky. Earl. Teddy Crane, the night dispatcher. Linda Barden, who filled in on a part-time basis nights and weekends.

His little kingdom. His little army. One of whom was a rat. "I want to know," he said grimly, "which one of you tipped off the SBI about the note that was in Wanita Crumley's pocket."

They looked at him, looked around at each other. Bucky cleared his throat nervously, but nobody spoke. Nick stood up and walked around the corner of his desk. "The information didn't just up and walk its way to Raleigh," he said. "It had to be one of you. Nobody else knew about it. Did they?"

Bucky cleared his throat again. "Not as far as I know, Chief."

"Well, then?"

The silence grew uncomfortable. "Bucky?" he said.

"Sir? Uh, no, sir, of course I didn't tell anyone. I'd never do that."

"Earl?"

"Twern't me, Chief. I went home the same time you did and fell into bed."

"Teddy?"

Teddy shifted his weight to rest on the other leg. "The only person I told," he said nervously, "was my wife. But she wouldn't tell nobody. She's never even heard of the SBI."

"Rowena," he snapped.

"Sorry, Chief. I slept like a baby last night. Didn't know anything about it until I read it in the *Gazette* this morning. Agent Melcher was already here when I got to work."

The exhaustion was catching up to him. He ran both hands down his face, rubbed his eyes. "Linda?" he said.

"I wasn't even on duty last night, Nick. My kid was sick."

Nick walked slowly to the window and gazed out at the street. Turned around and looked at them again. "Somebody's lying," he said. "And when I find out which one of you it is, I'm going to wrap my fingers around your throat and squeeze as hard as I can."

Rowena and Bucky exchanged glances. "You feeling all right, Chief?" she said.

"Ladies and gentlemen," he said, "we are running a police department here. This is not a craft club or a meeting of the Ladies Aid Society. Nor is it a gambling hall, a flea market, or a kaffeeklatsch." He looked at them again, one after the other. "It's a fucking police department!" he bellowed. "And we are going to start acting like one! Is that understood?"

For the third time, Bucky cleared his throat. "Yes, sir," he said quietly.

"Fine. You can leave."

In unison, they turned like rats escaping a sinking ship. "Not the rest of you!" he yelled. "Just Bucky!"

Rowena paused with her hand on the doorknob. Earl stopped dead in his tracks. Teddy and Linda looked uncertain. "I want to hear it from your own lips," he said. "Each of you. *Do. You. Understand?*"

His response was a chorus of *yes sirs* in varying tones. "Good," he said. "Now get the hell out of my office."

Linda was the last to go. She paused to look back at him. "Should I close the door, Chief?"

He looked at her for a moment without saying anything. "You're a cop," he said. "You figure it out."

Her eyes widened, and she hastily shut the door behind her. Nick drew off and kicked the wastebasket as hard as he could. It rolled across the floor and slammed into the wall opposite his desk.

And then he sat down at the desk and put his head in his hands.

chapter ten

He heard the baying as soon as he got out of the truck. It sounded like the hounds of hell had descended. Nick strode up to the front door of the house and knocked. When there was no answer, he walked around the side and followed the yapping past a couple of outbuildings and into the field behind the house.

There were several of them, black and tan hunting dogs, yelping with frenzied excitement and leaping in a vain attempt to reach something hanging from an outflung branch of an ancient oak tree. Shep Henley stood nearby, watching them with no expression on his weathered face. Nick's predecessor was tall and squarely built, with a noticeable paunch and a permanently sour expression. They'd met just once, when Nick had flown to Elba to interview for the position of police chief. A week later, Henley had called to offer him the job.

As he drew nearer, he saw that it was some kind of animal carcass the dogs were trying to get at. It had been skinned and hung just beyond their reach. Henley turned and watched his approach. "DiSalvo," he boomed, when Nick was within hailing distance.

"Chief Henley," he said, over the baying of the dogs. He leaned his weight on one hip and stood watching their frenzied efforts.

Henley pulled a pack of Camels from his pocket and lit one. "Hear you had a bit of excitement last night," he said, dropping his lighter back into the pocket of his plaid shirt.

"That's one way of putting it." As always, the smoke drew him in, made his mouth water. "Mind if I ask what you're doing with the dogs?"

Henley flicked an ash and studied his dogs. "I suppose they don't do much coon huntin' up in New York City."

The way he said the words *New York City* set Nick's teeth on edge. "No," he said flatly. "In New York, we only hunt two-legged prey."

Henley drew on the cigarette, then flicked it to the ground and stepped on it. "Trying to quit," he said. "But I'll be damned if I can do it."

"I hear you," Nick said.

"See, to train a huntin' dog," Henley said, "you skin a coon carcass and tie it up in a tree. Gets 'em all excited, used to the scent of coon. You can tell a good coon dog early on, by the sound he makes when he sniffs that carcass and thinks he's treed something mighty important. If the dog don't get excited, best thing you can do with him is put a for sale sign 'round his neck and turn him into somebody else's problem."

"I see. So what are these, some kind of hound?"

"These here are genuine, AKC-registered Walkers. Best coon dog there is. Good one'll go you fifteen, sixteen hundred."

Nick raised an eyebrow. "Dollars?" he said.

"Well, you see, DiSalvo, around these parts, coon hunting's been elevated almost to the status of a religion. There ain't much, not even the love of a good woman—" He paused suggestively, giving Nick the distinct impression that he knew a great deal more than he was telling. "— that's gonna come between a man and his dogs." Henley eyed him speculatively. "Maybe you'd like to come along some night, see what the excitement's all about. If you don't have other, ah—obligations."

"Maybe," he said.

"I don't imagine you came here to talk about dogs. What's on your mind?"

"I'd like to ask you some questions about the McAllister case. I have this feeling. Call it a hunch, call it whatever. I think the two murders are related."

It was Henley's turn to raise an eyebrow. "McAllister and Crumley?"

"That's right. I think whoever killed McAllister did Crumley, too. To shut her up."

Henley considered it in silence. "What's the connection?" he said.

"I'm working on that. McAllister's widow believes that Crumley lied on the witness stand. If that's true, she must have had a reason."

"You think somebody put her up to it."

"It stands to reason. Why else perjure herself?"

"Well," Henley said, "I suppose we'll never know now, will we? Seeing as how she and Michael McAllister have both gone on to their eternal rewards."

The dogs continued their cacophony. "What can you tell me," he said, almost shouting to be heard above the uproar, "about the day McAllister died?"

"Open and shut case, far as I was concerned. She found out he'd been whoring around, and she stuck him with the scissors. Who'd have thought a pretty little thing like that could hold so much of a grudge? Anyway, by the time we got there, she was in shock. Couldn't believe what she'd done."

His pulse quickened. "You were there?"

"Earl and I. She come running out of that house like a bat out of hell. Blood everywhere. And she fought like a wildcat." Henley's eyes grew glassy, as if he were enjoying the memory. "You ask me," he said, "there's your killer. I don't give a rat's ass that Clara Hughes claims the McAllister woman couldn't have done it because she was somewhere else at the time of the killing. That woman was guilty as sin. I knew it then, and I know it now. You really believe the two killings are related, you'd best be checking out McAllister. She's your damn killer."

"Maybe," he said. "Maybe not. Listen, while I think of it, mind if I ask you another question?"

Henley had already lost interest in him and was watching the dogs again. "What's that?" he said.

"You familiar with snake handling churches?"

Henley looked at him. "That kind of thing's illegal in North Carolina," he said.

"Uh huh. I was just wondering. Do you know if there are any around here?"

* * *

It was nearly eight o'clock when he got home, drained and running on half his cylinders. He went to the refrigerator for a beer, and paused in puzzlement at the kitchen doorway. There was a new lace tablecloth on his kitchen table, a vase of fresh-cut flowers sitting dead-center. "Janine?" he said.

She came up behind him like a wraith. "What do you think, Daddy? Doesn't it look pretty?"

Those dark eyes begged him to be pleased with the results of her handiwork. He cupped her cheek. "Sure, baby. It looks real nice."

"Come see what I did in the living room!" She caught him by the hand and drew him along behind her. His head was throbbing, and all he wanted was to kick off his shoes and decompress with a cold one. Instead, propelled by guilt, he followed her. She switched on the overhead light. "What do you think?"

The plain but serviceable couch had been disguised by a new throw in a soft shade of peach. Miniature pillows in splashy colors were scattered about its length. In the corner by the window, a wicker basket held a six-foot palm tree, and on the wall, a framed picture of the New York City skyline dominated the room. "Wow," he said.

"Do you like it?" She looked eager and breathless.

"It's beautiful," he said. "Where'd you get all this stuff?"

"Caroline took me shopping. Isn't it great, Daddy? I thought the New York picture would make you feel more at home."

"Sure, sweetheart. That was really thoughtful of you."

She beamed at the compliment. "Are you ready to go for pizza?"

Christ. He'd totally forgotten. This morning had been a lifetime ago, back when he'd still been strutting like a rooster, back before Kathryn had disemboweled him with one fell swoop. His face must have given away his feelings. "Daddy?" his daughter said, looking crestfallen. "We are going, aren't we?"

No matter how tired he was, he just couldn't do it to her. "Hey," he said, "would I disappoint a face as gorgeous as yours? Give your old man ten minutes to shower and change, and then we'll track us down some pizza."

They ended up at the bowling alley, where they ate pepperoni and anchovy pizza and bowled a few strings. Janine was a fair-to-middling bowler, beating him by a spread of more than a dozen points. She was also tactful enough to overlook the gutter balls he threw due to lack of sleep and a churning brain. It didn't really matter anyway. What mattered was that they were together, and his little girl was glowing in a way he hadn't seen since before the divorce.

She chattered all the while, told him about her friends and her school, about joining the yearbook club and playing field hockey, about making the Honor Roll every single semester of her seventh-grade year, and he realized how little he really knew about this child he and Lenore had created. For the first time, it struck him that Lenore had been right all along. He hadn't been there for Janine. He'd thought that working his ass off and being a good provider was enough. But he'd been wrong. His marriage had disintegrated, and his daughter was growing up a stranger right in front of his eyes.

He wondered if it was too late to make it up to her.

They finally called it quits around eleven. He was so tired he could barely see straight, and he couldn't wait to fall into bed. As they were taking off their bowling shoes, he said, "I was wondering. Are you afraid of snakes?"

She rolled her eyes and gave him a look that clearly said he was an idiot. "Oh," he said. "One of those things I should already know, right?"

"Geez, Daddy. For years and *years* I wanted to be a veterinarian. Don't you even remember?"

"I'm sorry. I have a lot on my mind right now. I was thinking about going to church tomorrow. Want to go with me?"

"*You* want to go to *church*?"

"Well," he said, bending to tie his shoelaces, "this isn't just any ordinary church. They have snakes there. Big, poisonous ones."

"Are you serious? You mean like rattlesnakes and stuff?"

"Yeah. I guess so."

"Oh, wow. I'd love to!"

"It's a long drive," he said. "It'll take us a while to get there."

"I don't care. This is too good to pass up."

They left the air-conditioned comfort of the bowling alley, and the hot, steamy night hit him in the face with almost physical force. His truck was one of the few left in the parking lot, a dark, hulking shape turned orangey by the sodium-arc light above it. They were halfway across the parking lot when he saw the lettering, a good eighteen inches tall, spray-painted in white down the driver's side of his Blazer.

FORNICATOR.

The word was ugly, turning something that had been meaningful into something dirty, indecent. Beside him, Janine stopped dead. "Daddy?" she said.

He swore. "Stay here," he said, and stalked off toward the truck. He unlocked the passenger door, yanked it open. Checked out the front seat, then opened the glove compartment and took out his high-powered flashlight. He walked all around the vehicle, aiming the beam of light at it. The paint had run, giving the lettering a slightly eerie appearance. Nick got down on his knees with the flashlight and checked the underside of the Blazer. Brushed off his hands and pointed the beam of light at the vehicle's interior, slowly scanning it for anything that might be out of place. Or that shouldn't be there. A rattlesnake, for instance.

He popped the hood and checked beneath it. There was nothing. "It's all right," he said, turning off the flashlight. "Just somebody being a wise-ass. Let's go home."

Janine climbed reluctantly into the truck, but she wouldn't let it rest. "Who would do something like that?" she said indignantly.

He gripped the steering wheel so hard his knuckles turned white. "Probably just kids with nothing better to do."

"Dad? Are there people here who don't like you?"

"I'm a cop, sweetheart. There are always people who don't like cops."

After a time, she said, "I know what that word means."

"Yeah," he said grimly. "So do I."

"Why did they say it? Why did they call you that?"

He didn't know what to tell her. At thirteen, was she ready to handle the truth, that her father had the same sexual needs as everybody else? Would he run the risk of alienating her if he admitted that he was human?

He cleared his throat. "Somebody," he said, "apparently doesn't approve of the company I keep."

She looked at him for a long time without speaking. "You didn't sleep at the station last night, did you?"

He gnawed at the inside of his cheek. "No," he said.

"I knew you didn't. Rowena called the house this morning, looking for you."

He turned into his driveway and shut off the engine, and they sat there in the darkness for a while, listening to the chirping of crickets and the drawn-out whine of a tractor trailer out on Route 1. "Is it the lady from the grocery store?" she said.

Nick let out a long sigh and leaned back against the headrest. "I'm sorry if you're disappointed in me, Janine, but I'm not any kind of hero. I'm just a guy, just a goddamn ordinary guy, and—"

"Do you love her?" she said.

He toyed with the blinker switch. "It's complicated."

"Does she love you?"

He thought about last night. There had been tenderness, and passion, and the fulfilling of a blinding need. But had there been love? "I don't know," he said honestly. "Right now, she's pretty upset with me. I guess there's a lot of that going around."

"I wish you'd told me the truth in the first place. I'm thirteen years old, not a baby. But I'm not mad at you, Dad. I told you, I just want you to be happy."

After Janine had gone to bed, he took the cordless into the kitchen and called Kathryn. She answered the phone sounding sleepy and disoriented, and his stomach knotted from the need to lie down beside her in the heart of those cool, crisp sheets. "Please don't hang up on me," he said. "This is important."

There was a moment of silence before she said softly, groggily, "Nick."

"I'll be tied up for a few hours tomorrow," he said, "so I won't be here if you need me. I want you to be careful. Somebody decided to paint my truck a new color tonight."

"What?" Her voice sharpened, and he imagined her sitting up with the covers falling down around her. "What are you talking about?"

"Janine and I went bowling. When we came out, some joker had painted 'fornicator' down the side of my Blazer."

"Oh, Christ. Poor Janine. How did she react?"

"She asked a few questions I wasn't expecting to have to answer. I told her the truth. What else could I do?"

"You told her about us? About last night?"

"Hell, Kat, she knew about us before I did. That night we bumped into each other at the grocery store, she was already asking questions."

"I don't like this," she said. "This hatred, overflowing onto you. And now your daughter. I don't want you involved."

"I'm the goddamn chief of police. I can't help being involved."

"It's not because you're the chief of police," she said bitterly. "It's because you made the mistake of fornicating with the town pariah."

"Damn it, Kathryn, don't let them turn what happened between us into something dirty. It wasn't like that, and you know it."

"No? Just what was it like, Nick?"

He heaved a mighty sigh. "What do you want me to say, Kathryn? You tell me what you're expecting, because I can't read you any more."

"I have to go now." There was an almost inaudible tremor in her voice. "Talking with you just confuses me."

"Promise me you'll be careful."

There was a moment of silence. "You, too," she said. "Take care of that beautiful daughter of yours. Good-night, DiSalvo."

And she hung up the phone.

* * *

The autopsy report was waiting on his desk the next morning. While Janine played with Rowena's typewriter, he skimmed through it. He didn't find any surprises. Official cause of death was a single gunshot wound to the head. Ellsworth had removed a .38 slug, and it had been shipped off to the state crime lab for examination. The angle of the bullet indicated the gun had probably been fired by a right-handed person, from a distance of about five feet. Only minute traces of gunpowder had been found.

Nick set down the report, sighed, and ran his fingers through his hair. Now all he needed to do was check out every right-handed person in Rowley County. Shouldn't take more than a year or two. They'd spent most of yesterday taking statements from everybody who'd been even peripherally involved. Bucky and Earl had canvassed the neighborhood where they'd found the body, talking to everybody they could find, but nobody had seen a thing. There was nothing to link anybody to the crime. Except for that damning piece of paper with Kathryn's phone number on it.

The NCIC report on Wanita Crumley that he'd asked Rowena to run before he left yesterday was far more interesting. Apparently Crumley had spent some time in Baltimore since the McAllister trial. She had a lengthy arrest record with the Baltimore PD. Solicitation. Shoplifting. Possession of a controlled substance. Attempting to solicit sexual favors from an undercover police officer. "Well, well," he said. "Our little friend Wanita was a busy girl."

He phoned Baltimore, and was connected with a Vice cop named Houston. Nick introduced himself, then said, "We got us a DOA down here by the name of Wanita Crumley. I understand you boys might be acquainted with her."

"Ah, yes, the lovely Wanita. One of my all-time favorites. What happened to her?"

"She took a .38 slug in the back of the head, night before last."

"Aw, geez. Hang on while I look for my crying towel. Shit happens, don't it?"

"Yeah," he said, thinking of the white lettering he'd attempted to cover with black spray paint this morning. "Shit happens, all right. Anything you can tell me about her?"

"She peddled her ass on the street to keep herself and her boyfriend rolling in powder. Got any idea who did her?"

"That's what I'm trying to find out. What's the scoop on the boyfriend?"

"Sorry, DiSalvo, you just missed him. He checked out a couple of months ago. Got into some bad shit that somebody cut with strychnine. By the time we found him, the rats had been at him for a while."

"What a picturesque vision on this lovely Sunday morning. Anything else you can tell me? Anybody who might've wanted her out of the way?"

"Crowd she ran with, who could say? Any one of 'em would probably sell their grandmother for a couple of snorts."

He thanked Houston and went into the outer office to check the files. Chances were slim to none that Crumley had discontinued her extracurricular activities when she returned home to Elba. If so, there had to be an arrest record somewhere.

The file cabinets were locked. "Damnation," he said, and

Janine looked up from her typing.

"Are we going soon, Daddy? I'm bored."

"Soon," he said. He opened the desk drawer and rummaged through it, hoping to find a key for the files, but there was none.

Cursing, he flipped through the Rolodex, found Rowena's number, and called her. "I'm sorry to call you at home on your day off," he said, "but I need the key to the file cabinet. Where is it?"

There was a silence, and then Rowena cleared her throat. "Well, Chief," she said, "if you really need it, I suppose I could prob'ly drop it off on my way to church."

He leaned against the desk and closed his eyes. "Why am I not surprised? There isn't one here, is there?"

"I keep it on my key ring," she said defensively. "For safekeeping. Chief Henley always had one of his own. I assumed he gave it to you when you took over."

"The only thing Chief Henley gave me when I took over was his headaches."

"Well, then," she said cheerfully, "looks like we'll just have to get one made up for you. Shall I drop mine off to you this morning?"

Nick sighed. "Never mind," he said. "It can wait until tomorrow. Sorry to bother you, Rowena."

He hung up the phone and rubbed his knuckles on the top of Janine's head. "Come on, squirt," he said. "Let's go hunt us up some snakes."

* * *

"There's sin in this world, brothers and sisters. The devil is mighty powerful, and he tempts us all!" Dressed in his Sunday finest suit, outdated by about fifteen years, Brother Leroy looked out over his congregation.

"Amen!" said a man in the first row.

"Hallelujah!" said somebody just behind Nick.

The wispy thatch of sandy hair that Brother Leroy had combed over his bald spot fell to one side. "But them that's got a strong faith," he said, "them that believes in the Lord Jesus with all they got in 'em, that faith is gonna make 'em strong, help 'em to fight Satan."

"Hallelujah, brother!"

"And the Bible tells us, brothers and sisters, that if our faith is strong, we can do mighty things. Like healin' the sick."

There were fervent amens scattered around the room.

"And raisin' the dead."

"Praise the Lord Jesus!"

"And drinkin' strong poisons."

"Thank you, Jesus!"

"And the takin' up of serpents in his name!"

Around Brother Leroy's neck hung a four-foot copperhead. The snake writhed and squirmed, clearly uncomfortable, clearly wishing to be somewhere else. Brother Leroy closed his eyes and raised his beatific face to the Lord. "My faith is strong," he said. "And I know that my Lord won't let this serpent, this tool of Satan, hurt me. Long as my faith never wavers, I won't be hurt by followin' the signs."

"Yes!" a woman shouted. "Thank you, Jesus!"

Nick shot a glance at Janine. She looked back at him from the corner of her eye, raised both eyebrows, and inched closer to him on the hard wooden pew. Across the aisle, a woman stood up and began babbling a stream of nonsensical syllables. "Yes, Sister!" Brother Leroy shouted. "Thank you, Jesus, for giving our dear sister Beulah the gift of tongues. A sign of her purity and unwavering faith in the Lord!"

"Amen!"

All around them, people were weeping, wailing, crying out the name of their Lord and Savior. A man in patched overalls got up and stood in the aisle. "Thank you, Jesus," he said. "I got a powerful love for you, Jesus." And he fell into a dead faint.

"Daddy?" Janine whispered.

"Shh. It's okay." He took her hand in his and squeezed it.

A second man approached the podium, carrying a small rattlesnake. He wrapped it lovingly around Brother Leroy's arm, and the snake raised its head and hissed.

"Thank you, brother. Tell me, brothers and sisters, do you have a strong faith in the Lord? Do you believe with all your might? Is your faith in Jesus, our Lord and Savior, strong enough, pure enough, to keep you safe in His name?"

Around the room, there were soft murmurs of assent. While Brother Leroy stood by, beaming, members of the congregation began coming forward, one by one, and handling the serpents. "Can you feel the love?" Brother Leroy asked. "Can you feel it, brothers and sisters? Don't it feel good, now?"

"Amen!"

"Thank you, Jesus!"

The service went on for another forty-five minutes, quite possibly the most bizarre forty-five minutes Nick DiSalvo had ever experienced. When it was finally over and the snakes had been returned to the wooden box from which they'd come, he relaxed his shoulder muscles and realized how tense he'd been throughout the entire service. "You okay?" he asked Janine.

"It gave me the creepy-crawlies," she whispered back.

"I thought you weren't afraid of snakes."

She glanced around to make sure nobody was listening. "It wasn't the snakes that creeped me out."

He caught her by the back of the neck and squeezed affectionately. "Come on, squirt," he said. "I have to talk to somebody."

Janine rolled her eyes. "More cop business," she said with resignation.

Brother Leroy was beaming and shaking hands. Nick stood by patiently, until he was done glad-handing the members of his congregation. "I don't believe I know you, sir," Brother Leroy said.

"Nick DiSalvo," he said, shaking Leroy's hand. "This is my daughter, Janine."

"The Lord and I are very happy to have you with us this fine Sunday, Janine."

She hooked her arm through Nick's. "Thank you," she said.

"Actually," Nick said, "I was wondering if I could ask you some questions."

Brother Leroy eyed him levelly. Some of the welcome left his face, and Nick knew he'd been made as a cop. "I will continue to fight the State of North Carolina," Brother Leroy said curtly, "for my right to worship as I see fit."

"And I'm behind you one hundred percent," Nick said. "That's not why I'm here. I'm the police chief in Elba, and I'm conducting an investigation into a recent incident we had with a big rattler. I thought maybe you could give me some information on snake handling."

Brother Leroy continued to study him. And then his face eased a bit. "Why don't we go next door," he said, "to the parsonage? We can talk there."

The parsonage was a small house trailer parked out back of the church. The linoleum was worn through in places, the tablecloth was threadbare, the curtains at the window limp and faded. Brother Leroy's wife stood by nervously, her face as pale and limp as the kitchen curtains. "Can I fix you some iced tea, Mr. DiSalvo?" she said.

"Thank you," he said. "we'd like that, wouldn't we, squirt?"

Janine, who'd probably never ingested a non-carbonated liquid since she lost her milk teeth, nodded assent.

"Now," Brother Leroy said, "how can I help you?"

"I'm not really sure. I'm flying by the seat of my pants here, so bear with me. Last week, a local woman came home and found a five-foot rattlesnake in a cardboard box on her front porch. I'm trying to figure out how it could have gotten there. How do you people handle snakes without getting bit?"

"By the power of the Lord, Mr. DiSalvo. There's no big secret. If your faith is strong enough, you can do anything."

"So, you don't, like, train people how to do this or anything?"

"It's a God-given power, a sign of purity in our faith."

"And nobody ever gets bit?"

"Oh, lots of us get bit. But if our faith is strong enough, God don't let that bite hurt us. He takes care of us, you see."

Brother Leroy's wife set tall glasses of iced tea in front of both of them. "Thank you," he said. "Now let me be sure I have this right. The members of your congregation don't die if they get bit by a rattlesnake?"

"If their faith is pure, Mr. DiSalvo. I've seen it with my own eyes, over and over again. Folks gettin' bit, and the Lord just cleansin' that venom out of their bodies."

He took a drink of tea and considered Brother Leroy's words. "And if their faith isn't pure?"

Leroy lowered his eyes. "Sometimes, Mr. DiSalvo, our faith falters. Yours, mine, your pretty little girl's, here. If that happens, and one of us gets bit, that poison'll kill us as quick as it'll kill anybody."

"So if somebody had a strong enough faith in God," he said, thinking aloud, "they could have left that snake on the doorstep without fear of being bit."

"Our faith in the Lord enables us to do good works," Leroy said. "Anybody who'd leave a dangerous snake for a non-believer isn't doin' good works. His faith has faltered. Satan has won the battle for his soul."

"Right. Listen, do any of the members of your congregation live in Elba?"

"We're a poor rural church, Mr. DiSalvo. Our people live nearby, here in the foothills of the Appalachians. Most of 'em never been no further than High Point."

He'd reached a dead end. Nick finished his tea, got up from the table and held out his hand. "Thank you for your time, Brother Leroy. And thank you for the refreshments, Mrs—" He paused, realizing he'd never asked their last name.

"Dawson," she said, smiling through thin, bluish lips.

"Mrs. Dawson."

They were already out the door and on the dirt path that led back to the church when Brother Leroy said, "You're from Elba, you said?"

"That's right."

"I got me a cousin that lives in Elba. Or did, last I knew. Haven't heard from her in years and years. She moved away from here when we was just kids. We used to play together, out back of the church. Perhaps you know her."

"Could be. What's her name?"

"Raelynn," he said. "Raelynn Wilbur."

chapter eleven

He swung by Kathryn's house on the way to work the next morning. Her car was in the driveway, but when he knocked on the door, there was no response. Nick walked around to the back door and peered through the glass. The dog's leash wasn't hanging on the hook beside the refrigerator where he'd seen her leave it. That meant she was probably out jogging. He'd advised her to vary her daily schedule. It made him antsy, the knowledge that somebody out there was watching her every move. And his. At least she was taking the dog everywhere she went. It was little comfort, but it was all he had for now.

When he walked into the station, Rowena held up a small silver key on a brass ring. "Morning, Chief," she said. "I stopped by Galway's Hardware after church and had this made up for you."

"Great," he said. "Thanks." He pocketed the key, made a beeline for the coffeepot, and poured himself a cup of strong, black coffee. "Listen," he said, tearing open a sugar packet and stirring it in, "do you know if there's any kind of arrest record on Wanita Crumley?"

She was uncharacteristically silent, and he swung around to look at her. Raised his eyebrows at her pious expression. "I don't like to speak ill of the dead," she said. "But that woman had problems. She wasn't precisely known for her charitable works."

"Find the file," he said, setting down his spoon, "and bring it in my office."

Richard Melcher was sitting at his desk, feet propped up on the bottom drawer, reading the autopsy report and eating a jelly doughnut. "Excuse me for interrupting," Nick said.

"DiSalvo!" Melcher said, almost trembling in his enthusiasm, like an eager pup ready to show off his newest trick. "I've been out doing a little investigating on my own, and I've come up with some information you might find interesting."

"You have powdered sugar all over you," Nick said amiably.

"What? Oh, shit!" Melcher dropped his feet to the floor and hastened to brush the white powder off his expensive suit. The harder he brushed, the deeper the sugar went into the fabric.

"Up," Nick said. "Take your damn doughnut and get out of here, before everything on my desk is covered with jelly."

Melcher paused in his rubbing. "You really ought to hear this, DiSalvo—"

"Later. Right now, I have a phone call to make."

Melcher reluctantly gave up his seat. "Where the hell am I supposed to sit? How can I run an investigation without the proper equipment? You don't even have a spare desk here in this godforsaken place!"

"Call your friends in Raleigh. I'm sure they'd be more than happy to requisition one for you. Maybe you can get one of those little gold-trimmed name plates to go with it." Nick picked up the phone, dialed Raelynn Wilbur's office, and leaned back in his chair. He scowled fiercely at Melcher. "And I'm running the investigation," he said.

Cindy Hawkins, Raelynn's bubbly and capable secretary, informed him that Ms. Wilbur was at a convention in Atlanta and wouldn't be back until Thursday afternoon. "I hear your daughter's visiting you," she said.

Nick rolled his eyes, then sat through a ten-minute discourse on the joys of parenthood. Cindy's oldest daughter, it seemed, had walked at twelve months and had started school at the age of four. Now, she was fifteen and very rebellious, and wasn't it just the hardest job there ever could be, tryin' to raise a teenager in these troubled times?

When he finally succeeded in getting rid of her without resorting to deadly force, he dialed Kathryn's house. The phone rang eight times before he gave up. Melcher was still eating the doughnut, still hovering like an impatient child. "What?" Nick barked. "What the hell do you want?"

Melcher drew himself up to his full height and looked down his aristocratic nose. "That's very unprofessional behavior, DiSalvo. We're supposed to be working together on this case. But you're determined to work against me."

Nick put his feet up on the desk and folded his hands together in his lap. "I'm determined," he said pleasantly, "to ignore you."

"I might have to report this to my superiors," Melcher said. "It won't look good on your record, the fact that you've been belligerent and uncooperative with the SBI."

"Melcher," he said, "if it makes you feel better, you can go ahead and tattle to whoever you please, up to and including the President of the United States. Just get your sorry ass out of my office while you're doing it."

The SBI agent paled and spun on his heel, nearly mowing down Rowena, who stood in the doorway holding a file folder. "Think he'll be back?" she said cheerfully as she handed Nick the file.

"Wild horses couldn't keep him away. This everything we got on Crumley?"

"This is it, Chief."

The file wasn't very thick. It dated back to a year or two before Michael McAllister's death, when Wanita had first been arrested for shoplifting. The charges had ultimately been dropped. Eight months later, she'd been hauled in on a drunk & disorderly. Again, the charges had been dropped. Following that second charge, there had been a gap of several years, during which time she'd plied her trade in Baltimore. Since her return a year ago, Wanita had been arrested three times for solicitation.

Each time, the charges had been dropped.

The back of his neck began itching. He closed the file and sat there, thinking, as he rotated his Styrofoam coffee cup in his hand. Leaning over the desk to push the button on the intercom, he said, "Rowena? Would you come back in here a minute?"

She edged into his office, looking as if she were about to face a firing squad. "Shut the door," he said, "and sit down."

Rowena sat on the wooden chair across from him, her hands folded primly in her lap. "I'd like you to tell me," he said, "how it can possibly be that every time Wanita Crumley was arrested in the past five years, the charges were dropped?"

She crossed and re-crossed her ankles. "I'm not the person to be addressing that question to, Chief."

He leaned over the desk. "You know every goddamn move that goes on in this town, Rowena, so don't play dumb with me. Why were the charges dropped?"

"Well," she said, "you see, Chief Henley—" Her voice changed when she spoke his name, as though it were synonymous with that of Jesus Christ. "His wife, Maybelle, she's such a kind-hearted lady. Always givin' and givin' to the church, and to the community. Why, just last year, she donated five hand-pieced quilts for the raffle to benefit those poor colored orphans who lost their folks in that terrible fire—"

"Do you think we could get to the point before lunch?"

She leveled a barbed glance at him. "Maybelle's younger sister Alice had a hard row to hoe," she said. "Their mother died when she was a teenager, and she lived in a foster home over to Wakefield for years. Maybelle always felt guilty about it, because she and Shep had just gotten married, and it was his first year on the force, and they weren't making any money, not to speak of. They really couldn't afford to take in her younger sister. Well, to make a long story short, Alice had real poor taste in men, you see, and her first husband—"

"Rowena!"

"I might just get to the point, Chief DiSalvo, if you'd stop interrupting me! After Alice's first husband left, she had to raise those two little girls all by herself. They was on welfare for the longest time, and it close to broke Maybelle's heart. The oldest one, June, was a dear girl. After high school, she worked her way through secretarial school and married a fine young man. Oh, he didn't have any money, but he takes good care of her. But the other one, Wanita, she was wild and rebellious right from the start. And Maybelle's still so protective towards her sister, knowing that Alice's lot in life would have been different if she could've done more for her. I didn't really approve of it myself, and I told Chief Henley that. I told him that girl would never learn to take responsibility for her own life until somebody made her accountable for her actions, but Maybelle was real insistent, and—"

"Hold it," he said, dumbfounded. "Stop. Are you telling me that Wanita Crumley was Shep Henley's niece?"

"By marriage," she said. "His niece by marriage."

He thought about the man who had so casually discussed Wanita Crumley's murder while his dogs struggled to reach the dead animal carcass he'd stuck up in a tree. "And he dropped the charges," Nick said, "to keep his wife happy?"

"I guess you could put it that way, yes. Because of the way she worried so about poor Alice."

"I'll be damned," he said.

* * *

Wanita Crumley's funeral was held at the Third Methodist Church, down on Coleman Avenue. The eulogy was brief and impersonal. There were few mourners. Wanita's sister, June, walked arm in arm with her husband, leading Wanita's two little boys, who looked somber in their navy suits and bow ties. Her mother, Alice Buford, sat in the front row beside her third husband, Buck, who reeked of gin. On her other side sat a matronly woman in a navy silk dress, her short gray hair done up in tasteful curls. Maybelle Henley. Beside her sat Shep Henley himself. He didn't look too brokenhearted.

There were a few friends, all of them women, none of them candidates for the Junior League. And near the back, sitting alone, looking desolate and thunderstruck, sat Dewey Webb.

When it was over, and the family and friends filed past the casket for a last look at the dearly departed, Dewey got up from the pew and stormed out the door of the church. Nick stood up, nodded to a dour-faced deacon, and followed him.

Dewey was halfway to his pickup truck, his size thirteen boots eating up ground, rawhide laces flapping in the wind. "Hey, Dew!" Nick said. "Wait up!"

Dewey continued moving, ignoring him. He opened the door of his truck and hoisted his considerable bulk up into the cab. He turned on the ignition and was revving the engine when Nick caught up to him. Using the oversized side mirror for leverage, Nick pulled himself up onto the running board. "Dewey?" he said. "Can I talk to you for a minute?"

"I'm busy, man. Some other time." Dewey's eyes, normally bloodshot anyway, were red-rimmed, the whites lined with broken veins and damp with unshed tears.

"I'm sorry, Dew," he said. "I didn't realize you knew Wanita."

"Ah, shit, Nick. What am I gonna do now?" With a snort of anguish, the beefy man who stood six-six in his stocking feet broke down and cried.

Nick walked around the truck and climbed up into the cab beside him. The man's grief was hard to watch. Who would have thought that this easygoing, hard-drinking good ole boy would fall for a woman who was, among other things, a prostitute and a junkie? Nick sat there silently and let him get it out of his system, and then he pulled a crumpled handkerchief from his pocket and handed it to him. Dewey took it, blew his massive red nose, and handed it back.

"Keep it," Nick said. "No knowing when it might come in handy."

Dewey nodded and tucked it into the pocket of the suit that was a couple sizes too small. "Ready to talk about it?" Nick said.

"I loved her," Dewey said. "She was the best thing in my life, and now she's gone."

Nick patted Dewey's shoulder. It was a lot like patting a stone wall. "I know this is a bad time," he said, "but I need to ask you a few questions."

"Go ahead," Dewey said despondently. "My life is over, anyway."

"How long did you know Wanita?"

"Since we were kids. We grew up together. I asked her to marry me when we finished high school, but she didn't want to settle down. Then she got mixed up in that McAllister mess, and after that, she left town. But I never stopped loving her." Dewey's red, bearded face was fierce. "I never stopped lovin' her, man. When she came back, a year ago, we got back together. We been together ever since."

"Do you know of anyone who might've wanted her dead?"

"No! Why the hell would anybody want her dead?"

He decided now wasn't the time to bring up Wanita's sordid past. If Dewey didn't know about it, there was no sense in telling him today. It could wait. "Who'd she have for friends, Dew? Besides you?"

The big man sniffed. "Mary Lou Elkson was her best friend since kindergarten. Like two peas in a pod."

He made note of the name. "Dewey," he said, "I have to ask you this. Do you own a gun?"

"Of course I do. This is coon hunting territory, Nick. Everybody owns guns. Why?" His face darkened as the realization hit him. "You can't mean to say you think I had anything to do with killing Wanita?"

"It's routine, Dew. I have to check out everybody who was close to her. Do you own any handguns?"

"Just the one I keep on the shelf under the cash register. Once in a while, things get rowdy. I gotta protect my investment."

He had a hunch he wasn't going to like what he was about to hear. "What caliber?"

"It's a sweet little .38 that I picked up in Raleigh a couple years ago. Why?"

Nick sighed. "You got a permit for it?"

Dewey looked blankly at him, then reached into his wallet and pulled out a piece of paper. Nick looked it over silently, then handed it back to him. "Dewey," he said, "I hate like hell to do this to you, but we're going to have to take your gun, run a few tests on it."

Dewey's face hardened. "Go ahead," he said bitterly. "I got nothing to hide."

"What do you say we go pick it up now?" Nick said. "I'll follow you in my truck."

This early in the day, Dewey's place wasn't doing much business. Skip Sullivan was hunched over the bar, nursing a scotch and soda, and in a shadowy corner, a young couple Nick didn't recognize was playing footsie beneath the table. Behind the bar, Luther Murdock, the emaciated black man who'd tended bar here since the day Dewey opened for business, was polishing glasses with a clean white towel. "What you doin' back here, Dew?" he said. "You need to take some time for yourself, son. You in no condition to be working today."

"I ain't working," Dewey said. "Chief DiSalvo here wants to get a look at my pistol. He seems to have the crazy idea that I might've been the one that killed Wanita."

Still polishing, Luther silently assessed Nick. "Routine procedure," Nick said. "That's all."

"That boy din't kill nobody, Mr. DiSalvo."

"I'm sure you're right, Luther. But I'd be remiss in my duties if

I didn't investigate."

"Jesus Christ," Dewey said, rummaging frantically beneath the cash register, "where the hell is it?"

Luther set down the glass he was polishing and turned to his employer. "It ain't there?"

"Hell, no." Dewey swept the shelf clean with one massive arm, and its contents landed in a pile on the floor. He began digging through it like a dog digging for a bone. There were dozens of register tapes, new and used, a money bag full of change, various pieces of paper. A broken pencil, a couple of dirty rubber bands.

But no gun.

Dewey looked at him in bewilderment. "I swear to Christ, Nick, it was here the last time I looked."

The back of his neck was itching like crazy. Either Dewey was one hell of a liar, or there was something damn smelly about this. "Who knows you keep the gun here?" he said.

"Hell, I don't know. Probably half my reg'lars. It's not exactly a secret."

Nick said something foul under his breath. "I think you'd better come on down to the station," he told Dewey.

The man looked thunderstruck. "You're not gonna arrest me, are you, Nick?"

"No," he said grimly. "You're going to fill out a robbery report."

* * *

The note came in the mail on Monday morning. Written in a spidery hand on creamy violet-scented stationery, it was an invitation to meet with Clara Hughes at two o'clock that afternoon. Because she hadn't yet thanked the woman who was responsible for her freedom, Kathryn called and said she'd be delighted to meet with the bright-eyed octogenarian.

Quite certain that Clara was not the kind of woman who wanted to be kept waiting, she arrived at precisely two o'clock. "I'm so glad you could come," the old lady said in a quavery voice. "I don't get much company any more."

"I've been meaning to come ever since I got back," she said, "to thank you for what you did. You can't know what it means to me."

"Fiddle-faddle," the old lady said, shoving a strand of white
hair behind her ear as she waddled to the kitchen. "They had no
business leavin' you there to rot away in that place when even the
village idiot could have seen that you were innocent. Iced tea or
lemonade, dearie?"

They settled on iced tea, and sat on the front porch swing to
drink it. "I picked two o'clock," Clara explained, "because it falls
right after my nap and right before my stories come on channel
seven. I never miss my stories." She put a bony hand on Kathryn's
arm. "You know," she said, "I tried to tell the police that you
couldn't have killed Michael. But they weren't interesting in hearing
the truth. If it hadn't been for that nice Raelynn Wilbur comin' to my
door, you'd still be sitting in that terrible place down to
Wilmington."

She felt a tightness in her chest. Lowering her glass from her
lips, she said, "You tried to tell them?"

"Oh, my, yes. More than once, I called Shep Henley and told
him that you'd come jogging by here that night, right on schedule,
nowhere near Ridgewood Road at the time the coroner said your
husband suffered the fatal wounds. But Chief Henley always told me
that justice had been done, the jury had found you guilty, and it was
too late to do anything about it now. I feel more than a little
responsible for the length of your incarceration. I was stupid enough
to believe him."

Kathryn patted her hand. "It doesn't matter now," she said.
"What matters is that somebody finally believed you. And because
of you, I'm free."

"It reminds me a great deal of Victoria," the old woman said.
"Do you know Victoria?"

Kathryn smoothed her skirt over her knees. "No," she said.
"Why don't you tell me about her?"

"Well, Victoria was in the very same situation. It was obvious
to anybody with a brain in their head that she couldn't possibly have
killed Stefan. I know she was furious with him for sleeping with her
sister, but she's a gentle soul, and besides, she loved him something
fierce. She would have forgiven him eventually. And I'm sure she'd
never even held a firearm, let alone fired one! It was that wicked
Deidre, the one who embezzled all the money from Stefan's father's

bank. She was the one that killed him. Not poor, dear Victoria."

Completely lost, Kathryn just stared at her in bafflement. Clara beamed at her. "Do you know what time it is, sugar plum?"

"Uh, yes." She glanced at her watch. "It's two-fifteen."

"Oh, good. We still have plenty of time to visit. My story comes on at three o'clock. Today the verdict is going to be read. I do hope that Victoria isn't convicted."

It took her a moment to realize that Clara was talking about the characters in a soap opera. She coughed to hide the laugh that threatened to bubble up out of her. "I'm sure," she said soothingly, "that if Victoria is as nice as you say, the jury will realize she's not guilty."

"Oh, I surely do hope you're right. Tell me, how is that nice Mr. DiSalvo? He's always so pleasant when I see him. Not like Shep Henley." Her forehead drew together in a fierce scowl. "Now, there is one unhappy man. But Nick DiSalvo is the best thing that ever happened to this town. Elba needed new blood, it was getting stale. And he's so attractive and charming to boot. Why, if I were forty years younger, I'd be chasing after him myself. Tell me—" She leaned toward Kathryn and lowered her voice. "Is he as good in the sack as he looks?"

Heat rushed up Kathryn's face as she stared, dumbfounded, at the old woman. Clara patted her hand. "Don't be embarrassed, chickie," she said. "There's nothing wrong with a little heat between a man and a woman. The hotter the better, far as I'm concerned. Enjoy it while you can. Once you reach my age, you'll be lucky if you can remember what's supposed to go where. But that's not why I asked you here today."

Kathryn cleared her throat, exceedingly grateful for the change of subject. "Why did you ask me here?"

"To warn you, sugar plum. Somebody out there doesn't like you. I don't want to see you get hurt."

"A lot of people out there don't like me," she said. "What's one more?"

"I know, baby. But there's one in particular who wants you gone."

Her interest sharpened. "Do you know who?" she said.

Clara shook her head. "I sit here, day after day," she said, "and I watch what goes on around me. Some of it's good, and a whole lot of it's bad. I can't quite figure out who it is. There's a piece missing somewhere. If I could just find it, I'd know." She sighed, closed paper-thin lids over her bright blue eyes. "It was that damn house started it all," she said. "I knew nothing good would ever come of it."

"House?" Kathryn said. "What house?"

Clara opened her eyes. "Why, the Chandler place," she said. "With such a notorious past, nothing good could ever come out of that place."

Intrigued, Kathryn leaned forward. "The Chandler place has a notorious past?"

"Indeed it does. That's where they used to meet. The Businessmen's Benevolent Association."

"Who?"

"They called themselves a civic organization. You know, like the Elks or the Jaycees. It was for gentlemen only. The *crème de la crème* of Elba's society. Men like John Chamberlain, Kevin McAllister, Manley Pruett, and Eugene Pepperell, Senior. Ladies, of course, weren't allowed in."

"And what did they do?"

"Oh, they did charitable works. Raised money to build a new school. Organized Fourth of July parades. Took dinner baskets to the poor folk out by Persimmon Creek on Thanksgiving."

"And they met in the Chandler place?"

"It was their headquarters. When Hilton Chandler died, he left the place to them. It became a clubhouse of sorts. And there was always stories circulating about what went on in that place behind closed doors. Especially with the women."

"I don't understand. I thought you said women weren't allowed in?"

"You weren't listening carefully enough, sugar. What I said was that *ladies* weren't allowed in. There are other kinds of women."

"You mean that while their wives were home alone, the men were entertaining their, ah...female friends?"

"So the story goes. I never saw it with my own eyes, mind you. But the way I've heard it, there was a couple of prerequisites that had to be met before a woman could walk through those doors."

Fascinated, she leaned forward again. "Which were?"

"They had to be young. Very young. Nineteen, twenty, thereabouts."

In the oak tree above their heads, a mockingbird sang. Kathryn nodded. "And what was the other?" she said.

Clara fanned her face with a bony hand. "They had to be colored."

Kathryn sat up straight, let out a long, low whistle. "Do tell," she said.

"It's not such an unusual thing, you know. Been going on for centuries, rich white men taking their pleasures with brown sugar. People that knew what was goin' on, well, they just looked the other way."

"What happened?" she said. "The house had been empty for years and years when Michael and I bought it. What happened to the Businessmen's Benevolent Association?"

"Well, the way folks tell it, some of the wives upped and figured out what was going on. Neely McAllister and a couple of the others, and they put an end to it. The Businessmen's Benevolent Association disbanded, and the house just sat there empty until you folks bought it."

"Unbelievable," she said. "I don't remember Michael ever mentioning anything about any organization his father belonged to."

"He probably never even knew about it. It all ended about the time he was three or four years old." The old woman felt for her cane. "It's almost three o'clock," she said. "Would you be kind enough to assist me? I didn't mean to get off on a tangent like this. My sister always used to tell me that I talked too much."

"No! No, really, it was fascinating. Amazing."

She helped the old lady back into the house, got her settled in front of the television. "Y'all come back and visit again," Clara said.

"I most certainly will come back," she said. "It's been lovely."

"And next time," Clara said, "you're to bring young Nicholas DiSalvo with you. You hear?"

It wasn't a request, it was an order. Kathryn held back a smile. "Next time," she said, "I'll bring Mr. DiSalvo with me."

"All right. Now y'all scoot on out of here. My story's beginning, and I need to know what happens to Victoria."

* * *

Mary Lou Elkson was a scrawny little thing with bleached-blond hair and a pockmarked face. Her eyes were red and puffy, and she fidgeted nervously while she talked. "Wanita didn't have no fear," she said, folding and unfolding an empty matchbook. "She'd take on anybody or anything. That's what killed her in the end, you know. She met up with somebody she couldn't bullshit her way around."

Nick leaned back in his chair. "Were you aware of her, ah, extracurricular activities, Mrs. Elkson?"

"You mean the hooking? Yeah. I tried not to be judgmental, you know? I mean, it's not my cup of tea, but, hey, you gotta put food on the table somehow." Mary Lou glanced at the clock over his head and played with the strap to her handbag. "You mind if I have a cigarette?"

"Go ahead."

She pulled a disposable lighter from her purse and lit up a Virginia Slim. Blew out the smoke in a thick cloud. "Jesus," she said, "I've needed that for about three hours."

The smoke swirled around his head and filled his lungs. "Did you know her boyfriend in Baltimore?" he said.

"Chuckie? Yeah, he was a real trip." Mary Lou tossed a stringy lock of yellow hair back from her forehead. "I went down to visit a couple of times, but he was such an asshole that I only stayed a few days. I woulda booted his ass out the door a long time ago."

"But Wanita stayed with him."

"For almost three years. Go figure. Well, they had a couple of kids. She tried to stick it out for their sake, I guess."

"Was it an amicable split?"

Mary Lou snorted. "Amicable. That's a great word. She come home one day and caught him screwing some floozy in her bed. She packed up both the kids and caught the next bus back to Elba. Best thing that ever happened to her."

Nick rested his feet on the desk drawer. "Why's that?" he said.

"Because she got back with Dewey. That man just loved her so much, Mr. DiSalvo. He wanted to marry her, adopt her kids. And she kept tellin' him no." She looked around for an ashtray, found it on the corner of his desk, and flicked the ash from her cigarette.

"Did she love Dewey?" he said. "Or was it one-sided?"

"Who wouldn't love Dewey? I mean, he's a big ole cuddly teddy bear." Her eyes, hard and glassy until now, softened. "But

Wanita," she said, "had somethin' else going on."

His interest sharpened, and he dropped his feet to the floor. "Something else?"

Mary Lou eyed him steadily. "She had herself a sugar daddy."

It explained the house. It explained a lot of things. "Who?" he said.

"She wouldn't tell me. Somebody important. Somebody with money to burn and an upstanding reputation in the community. Not to mention a wife."

"What did she tell you about him?"

"That he treated her good. That he paid for her house. Bought her little trinkets. Took care of her."

"And you have no idea who he was? Not even a guess?"

"Well," she said, "and remember, this is just my own opinion. But she used to drop little hints every so often, just to drive me crazy, you know? About how his wife was such a gracious lady, but a real cold fish in the sack, if you know what I mean. And I got the impression that maybe she was talking about Judge Kevin McAllister."

"Ah, yes, the infamous Judge McAllister. He does get around, doesn't he?"

There was a knock on the door. "Yes?" he said.

Bucky Stimpson opened the door and stuck his head through the crack. "Sorry to interrupt, Chief, but I thought you'd probably want to know about this right away. Wilford Austin called a few minutes ago, said he found a gun in his cornfield, not far from the crime scene. I went out and picked it up. It's a .38, and I don't know how we could've missed it. I swear, Chief, we went over that whole area with a fine-tooth comb, and there was no gun there Friday night."

The back of his neck began itching again. "Mrs. Elkson," he said, standing and coming around the desk to shake Mary Lou's hand. "Thanks for coming in. If you think of anything else, anything at all that you think might help us, give me a call."

She shuffled out, eyeing Bucky nervously. Bucky shut the door behind her and sat down in the chair across from Nick. For a long moment, they just looked at each other. "Well?" Nick said softly.

Bucky's youthful face darkened. He sighed. "The gun," he said, "belongs to Dewey Webb."

"Dust it for prints," he said, "and send somebody out to print Austin. He probably had his hands all over the damn thing."

"I already thought of it, sir. Also pulled a copy of Dewey's prints from when he was arrested a couple years back for DWI. We got us a couple of real clear prints, Chief. They both belong to Dewey."

"Shit."

"My sentiments exactly. I called the ballistics folks in Raleigh. Got me a cousin that works up there. He says if we're willing to tote the gun up there, he'll check it out right away, see if it matches up to the slug Doc Ellsworth pulled out of Wanita."

Nick eyed him carefully, from the shock of red hair atop his head to the toes of his polished black shoes. "Officer," he said, "what's your salary?"

"A little over twenty thousand, sir. Why?"

"I think it's about time I talked to the city council about giving you a raise."

He drove the gun to Raleigh himself, cooled his heels drinking the State's pathetic excuse for coffee while Bucky's cousin Lester checked out the gun. He was thumbing through a dog-eared copy of *Soldier of Fortune* magazine when Lester Stimpson emerged from the lab, holding two bullets. "See how this one's scored on the top?" Stimpson said, holding up the first one. He held up the second bullet. "Same pattern here. And this funny little mark's on both of them. Same distance from the tip, measured precisely."

Nick rubbed his chin. "Both fired from the same gun," he said.

Lester's grin was identical to Bucky's. "Piece of cake," he said, and snapped his fingers.

He used the phone in Lester's office to call the station. Rowena answered on the first ring. "Why are you still there?" he said.

"You don't really think I could sleep tonight without knowing what the lab said?"

"Rowena, you never fail to astound me. Bucky still around?"

"He's right here, waiting with me."

"Good. Tell him to go on out and pick up Dewey. Bring him in and book him."

"Oh, my Lord and Savior. What are we charging him with?"

"Murder one," he said grimly, and hung up the phone.

chapter twelve

When the first thwack hit the screen, she was sleeping deeply, engrossed in a crazy dream where she and Michael grappled with her wallpapering shears. Then, in the way of dreams, Michael's face changed and he became Nick DiSalvo, and he took the shears from her hand and shoved her hard onto the bed and away from the body on the floor.

The second thwack took a few moments to sink into her subconscious. And then, slowly, reluctantly, she eased out of sleep.

The third time, she realized that somebody had tossed a hard object against her window screen. On the floor at the foot of the bed, Elvis raised his head, pricked his ears, and growled menacingly. She got up from the bed, wrapped her robe around her, and padded cautiously to the window.

"Hey, McAllister," Nick DiSalvo said from the shadows at the edge of the lawn. "You snore loud enough to wake the dead."

Her stomach turned inside out. A bittersweet joy went ricocheting through her, and she quickly tamed it into submission. She knelt in front of the sill and raised the window screen. "It wasn't me snoring," she said, "it was Elvis. What in hell are you doing here, DiSalvo?"

"I thought it was time we had a talk."

Standing there in the shadows beneath her window, hands in his pockets, face turned skyward and moonlight illuminating his badge, he looked like a twelve-year-old playing dress-up. "It's the middle of the night," she said.

He leaned back to see her better. "It's eleven-thirty," he said. "Hardly the middle of the night."

"What do you want?"

"I told you, McAllister. I want to talk to you."

She glanced toward the driveway, saw that her Toyota was the only vehicle parked there. "How'd you get here?" she said.

"I walked. I am capable of walking, you know."

She raised her eyebrows. "You must be a desperate man."

"I have information that you might find interesting, McAllister. "But I'm not standing here and yelling up at your window all night. The neighbors'll call the cops. And how would we explain that?"

"I can just imagine the headline. *Police Chief Arrested for Violating Peeping Tom Ordinance.* Have you been drinking again, DiSalvo?"

"I'm as sober as the day I was born. Are you going to let me in, McAllister, or do I have to wake the neighbors and cause an embarrassing scene?"

She glanced across the street, where Minnie Rawlings still had a lamp burning in her living room window. "Come around the back," she said.

Elvis followed her downstairs, where she let DiSalvo in through the kitchen door. "You're insane," she said, locking the door behind him and snapping shut the blind. "Skulking around in the bushes like a common criminal. Where's Janine?"

"She's not home tonight. She's staying over with Caroline's niece."

Kathryn snapped on the light over the sink. "What did you throw against the screen, anyway?"

"Acorns," he said. "I picked 'em up off your front lawn. Listen, we need to talk."

"Fine," she said, crossing her arms. "You talk, and I'll listen."

"I thought you might be interested in hearing that your status as our number-one suspect just changed. You've been dropped to number two. We just arrested Dewey Webb for Wanita Crumley's murder."

It took a moment for the significance of his words to sink in. Swiping her hair back from her face with one hand, she said, "Dewey Webb? *Dewey Webb*?"

"They'd been seeing each other. The gun that killed her

belonged to Dewey. So did the only set of prints on it."

"But—" She tried to take this in, tried to reconcile it with what she knew in her gut. "Damn it, Nick, I'm not crazy. I know that whoever killed Wanita killed Michael, too. What possible reason could Dewey have for wanting Michael dead?"

"I know you don't want to hear this," he said, "but it could be that he found out Michael had been fooling around with his woman, and he killed him in a jealous rage."

"That's preposterous. Michael was not fooling around with Wanita Crumley. Besides, the timing's all wrong. Michael's been dead for four years."

"Wanita wasn't exactly known for her fidelity. If he caught her once, he could have caught her again. Only this time, he decided to get rid of the source of all his troubles."

"I don't buy it, DiSalvo."

"I'm just playing devil's advocate," he said. "I don't really think Dewey killed Wanita, any more than you do. But the evidence all points to him. His prints were on the damn gun that killed her. I had to arrest him. I didn't have a choice."

She considered it. "Do you think somebody set him up? The way I was set up?"

"I don't have thing one to go on," he said. "Except—" He stepped closer, caught her hand in his and brought it to his mouth. Kissed her fingers. "I have this spot," he said, "at the back of my neck. Right about—" He touched her fingers to the warm place where his hair grew down to meet his collar. "—there. It itches like crazy whenever I'm on to something. When something's not what it seems to be. And this whole mess has it itching like a dog at a flea circus."

Of their own volition, her fingers played in his hair. "So," she said softly, "do you have any suspects in mind?"

He nudged her cheek with his nose. His breath warm against her ear, he said, "One or two."

Breathlessly, she said, "I swore I wouldn't let you in the house again."

"I remember," he said against the side of her neck. "I was there."

"All you do is complicate my life. I don't have time for an affair."

"Mmn. A woman on a mission."

"Besides," she added, "you confuse the hell out of me."

He touched his tongue to the pulse point at the base of her throat, sending her vital signs skyrocketing. "And you've done wonders for my image," he said, "since you landed here in Elba."

"See what I'm saying?"

"Mmn." His mouth, leisurely and erotic, skimmed over her flesh, making its presence felt in every erogenous zone she possessed. "The mayor's ready to fire me," he said, "and the rest of the town wants to lynch me."

"So the best possible thing for both of us," she said, leaning back to give him easier access, "is to forget all about each other. Move on with our lives."

He drew the tip of his tongue down into the hollow between her breasts, and she gasped. "You're probably right," he said.

"Nick?"

He traced a damp path up her jaw to the spot just beneath her ear. "Yeah?"

"I've never kissed a man wearing a gun and a badge."

He drew his head back and looked at her with those melted chocolate eyes. And smiled. "This must be your lucky day," he said.

* * *

He sprawled naked across her bed, moonlight illuminating the blurred lines of his body. She lay beneath him, supremely content, his face buried in her hair, his breath warm on her neck, her fingers tracing continuous patterns on the sleek flesh of his shoulders. Their clothes were tossed haphazardly around the room. His pager lay on the bedside table, beside his gun in its holster. Beyond the closed door, Elvis snored softly in the hallway. "What are we going to do?" she said.

"Hmn?"

"You and me. This is crazy. A cop and a convicted felon."

"The conviction was overturned," he mumbled. "Christ, I'm starting to sound like a broken record."

She ran both hands down his back, past his shoulder blades. "Rub," he said.

"What?"

"My back. Rub."

She worked at his smooth, warm flesh with her palms, her fingertips, her knuckles, while he groaned in pleasure. "Magic hands," he said.

She nibbled at his shoulder. "You think that's good," she said, "wait 'till you see what else I can do."

He turned his head and their eyes met. They studied each other at length, and then he drew her mouth to his and he kissed her, his lips warm and damp and pliable. The kiss deepened, and she wrapped a leg around his thigh and drew him, already hard, deep inside her.

"Kat," he whispered. "Oh, Christ, Kat."

She cupped her hands around his rock-hard biceps, stroked the smooth flesh with the pads of her thumbs, drew her fingers through the thick pelt of hair on his chest. "Tell me," he said near her ear. "Tell me you like this as much as I do."

He was hot and slick inside her, and she gasped aloud in delight. Her hands found his face, and she ran her fingertips over his cheeks. "There were times," she said, her voice husky, "when I thought I'd never do this again. Never feel this way again."

A fine sheen of sweat slickened their bodies and glued them together. She arched her back and he moaned softly, and she went liquid inside. "Nick," she breathed. "Oh, Nick."

He lowered his head and ran his tongue down her neck, past her collarbone, to her breast. Greedy for more, she arched against him, wrapped herself around him in a frantic attempt to swallow him whole.

"Kathryn," he said hoarsely.

"What?" she said.

"I'm about ready to explode here, baby."

"Just a little longer. Just a little—"

The sound of glass shattering ripped through them, giving a whole new meaning to the term *coitus interruptus*. Still gasping, still connected, they looked at each other as Elvis began frantically barking. "What the hell was that?" he said.

"I don't know. A window. I—"

"Stay here." He rolled away from her and out of bed, removed his gun from its holster, and edged to the bedroom door.

"Nick," she whispered.

"Quiet." He opened the door silently, stood there listening for a moment, and stepped through it.

"Nick!" she hissed.

"If you move one step out of that bed," he said, "I'll take you over my knee and whale the tar out of you."

He disappeared down the hall, and she picked up the phone and dialed 911. "This is Kathryn McAllister," she said. "Somebody just broke into my house."

She threw on her robe and went after him. Elvis had stopped barking, and she found Nick on his knees in the living room. She stepped on a squeaky floorboard, and he spun around, gun pointed directly at her heart. "Jesus Christ, woman!" he said, lowering the gun. "Do you ever do anything you're told?"

"What is it?" she said. "What happened?"

"It's another gift. This one came through your living room window. Watch the glass, it's everywhere." He stood up and held it out to her, an old chimney brick with a piece of paper wrapped around it with a rubber band. In blood-red letters, it said SINNER REPENT.

"Charming," she said.

"Quite. You'd better shut the dog in the kitchen before he gets cut."

In the distance, a siren began to wail. DiSalvo looked at her suspiciously. "Tell me you didn't call the cops," he said.

"Of course I called the cops!"

"Damn it, McAllister! When are you going to get it through your head that I *am* the cops?"

Lights flashing, siren screaming, a patrol car barreled into her driveway. "I don't know how to tell you this," she said, "but unless you're into exhibitionism, you might want to consider putting some pants on."

He looked down at himself, realized he was still naked, and cursed. He stormed off upstairs to get dressed, and Kathryn flicked on the porch light and opened the door for the police.

Linda Barden was a real professional, a cop right to the marrow in her bones. When Nick returned, carrying his shirt in his hand, she didn't bat an eye. "Evening, boss," she said.

The man had a ferocious scowl. "You didn't see me here tonight. That's a direct order."

"I never saw a thing. What happened?"

"Some joker decided to send us a message. Tossed a brick through the window with a little note attached."

Linda read the note and nodded slowly. "That would probably be the same joker," she said, "who painted WHORE OF BABYLON down the front of the house."

"What?" Forgetting his earlier order, Nick yanked open the door and stalked outside, barefoot and shirtless. "Damn," he said. "Damn, damn, damn!"

The lettering was crude and spidery, spray painted in blood red on the white wooden siding. "Do you think this was the same person who sprayed your Blazer?" Kathryn said.

Linda raised her eyebrows. "Somebody vandalized your Blazer?"

"You don't need to know about it," he snapped.

Linda met Kathryn's eyes and winked. "Yes, sir," she said. "By the way, Chief—"

"What?" he barked.

Linda grinned. "Nice pecs," she said.

* * *

They got the glass picked up, and he patched the window with a sheet of newspaper until she could get it repaired in the morning. When the patrol car left, he felt curiously deflated. "Well," Kathryn said, "that certainly spoiled the mood, wouldn't you say?"

"No kidding. Listen, you got any decaf in the house?"

"I could probably find some."

He put on his shirt and his shoes and got a flashlight from the kitchen drawer, and he retraced the route around the house and the yard that he'd already searched once with Linda Barden. He didn't expect to find anything, but he had to check it just one more time. Somebody was toying with him, yanking his chain, and he didn't like it. The yard didn't look any different than it had twenty minutes ago, when he'd checked it with Linda's high-powered flashlight. Whoever had thrown the brick had disappeared without leaving behind so much as a broken blade of grass.

When he came back in the house, Kathryn handed him a mug of coffee. He took a sip and grimaced. "What's wrong with my coffee?" she said.

"Nothing," he hastened to assure her. "Nothing at all."

She crossed her arms and tossed those blond curls back over her shoulder. "Nothing?" she said.

"Well," he said, "it's just a little, uh...insubstantial."

Her eyes narrowed. "It's better than that sewer sludge you drink down at the station."

Referring to Rowena's coffee as sewer sludge was nothing short of sacrilege, but he knew there was no way he'd win this battle. He was getting in deeper by the minute, and it wasn't looking good. In the interest of self-preservation, he decided diversion was the most promising tactic. "How much do you know," he said, "about Raelynn Wilbur?"

Kathryn blinked, obviously startled by his abrupt change of subject. "Why?" she said.

"Do you know where she comes from?"

"She comes from here, DiSalvo. Elba, North Carolina."

"Wrong," he said.

Those blue eyes widened appreciably. "Wrong?" she said.

"She comes from a little place in the foothills of the Appalachians. It's called Hickory Crossing. Not much more than a wide place in the road. A few houses, a gas station, and a church."

"And your point is?"

"Her cousin Leroy is the minister there. Probably not ordained. I doubt that kind of church cares too much about those pesky little details. Anyway, this church is different. Special. They bring snakes to their worship services. Big snakes. Wrap 'em around their necks, hold 'em up in the air, and sing hallelujah to Jesus."

She whitened. "Please," she said, and closed her eyes.

"Sorry," he said.

It took her a moment to compose herself. "Are you suggesting," she said, "that it might have been Raelynn who put the snake on my porch?"

His eyes never leaving hers, he raised his mug to his mouth and took a sip of coffee.

Kathryn ran a hand through her hair. "That's preposterous," she said. "Raelynn is my attorney. She worked for four years to get my conviction overturned. She's my friend. She wouldn't do something like that. She wouldn't—"

"You've done time," he said softly. "You of all people should know that given the right motivation, anybody is capable of doing anything."

"But—"

"I'm not saying she did it. I just wanted to point out the astounding coincidence." He took another sip of her watered-down coffee. "I've been a cop for sixteen years," he said. "Frankly, I don't believe in coincidences."

"What earthly motivation could she have?"

He shrugged. "You tell me."

"Oh, Nick."

The despair in her voice got to him. He set down his coffee and took her in his arms. "It's all right," he said. "No matter what happens, I'm here. I won't let you down."

Her arms went around him and she rested her forehead against his chin. "I asked Raelynn once if I could trust you."

He stroked her hair, fascinated by its varying shades of blond, all of them beautiful, all of them natural. "What did she say?"

"She said there were only two people in this town I could trust. She was one, and you were the other."

"Well," he said, "she was at least half right."

They held each other for a while, and then she straightened her spine and stepped back, out of his arms. "I almost forgot," she said. "Have you ever heard of a local organization called the Businessmen's Benevolent Association?"

"The Businessmen's Benevolent Association?" He thought about it, but it didn't ring any bells. "Not that I recall. Why?"

"According to Clara Hughes, it was a civic organization here in Elba, thirty or so years ago. They raised money for worthwhile causes, helped out with community projects, that kind of thing. But apparently the organization had a dark underbelly. According to Clara, it was a front for an exclusive private men's club. While their wives played bridge at home, the men were at the club, entertaining their young black mistresses."

Both his eyebrows went sky-high. "You don't say."

"And I bet even a Yankee newcomer like you can come up with a list of members without having to think too hard."

"Let's see. How about Chamberlain and Pepperell and McAllister, just for starters?"

"Bingo, DiSalvo. You win a gold star. What's even more interesting is that they used to meet in my house."

He frowned and looked around him. "This house?"

"No, no. The Chandler place. Where Michael and I used to live. That was their headquarters."

The back of his neck began to itch again, and he turned the information over and over in his head, but damned if he could see what possible connection it could have to either of the murders. With the obvious exception of Kevin McAllister, who kept showing up in the damnedest places. "Did you know," he said, "that Wanita had a sugar daddy?"

"I'm not surprised. I knew damn well she wasn't paying for that house on her own. Who was it?"

"I don't know yet. But her girlfriend seemed to think it might be Kevin McAllister." He took a sip of coffee. "Funny, isn't it, how that name keeps popping up?"

"And wouldn't that be convenient," she said, "considering that he lives right next door."

"That's what I was thinking. He could hold his liaisons right in his own back yard. The little woman wouldn't be interrogating him about how much time he spent away from home. He could pop in for a quickie just about any time he wanted, and the wifey would never know the difference."

"It makes sense."

"Except," he said, thinking aloud, "it breaks his pattern."

"What pattern is that?"

"According to my sources, Wanita's the wrong color. A bit long in the tooth, too. Our boy likes 'em young." He eyed her speculatively. "He ever hit on you?"

"Judge McAllister? Christ, no. Why?"

"Just wondering about his code of ethics. If he has one. Would it keep him from hitting on his lovely young daughter-in-law?"

"You just said yourself, I'm not his type. As Clara would put it, he prefers brown sugar."

"Not necessarily. Raelynn told me he hit on her once."

She yawned, and he emptied his cup in the sink. "It's late," she said. "We should try to get some sleep. Although I'm not sure I can, after this little episode."

"I'll give you a massage. That'll do the trick."

She drew her hair back from her face and rubbed the back of her neck. "That sounds wonderful," she said.

"Oh, and there is one other thing," he said. "One other little unresolved issue."

She dropped the heavy fall of hair and looked at him. "What's that?" she said.

"You didn't follow orders. I still owe you that spanking."

* * *

By morning, everyone in Elba knew that Dewey Webb had been arrested for killing Wanita Crumley. The people who knew Dewey, who'd known him all their lives, shook their heads in bewilderment and said that it couldn't be true. Those who knew him only by his reputation shook their heads in righteous piety and said that any man who made his living selling sin to sinners was bound to get his comeback sooner or later. The police station was a madhouse, the phone ringing off the hook, news reporters from Raleigh and Charlotte hovering like spiders, waiting to pounce on Nick DiSalvo the instant he walked through the door.

With the phone receiver attached to her ear, Rowena waved a stack of pink message slips as he passed. Nick poured himself a cup of ambrosia. Like a pack of wolves, the reporters followed him to the door of his office. He slammed it in their faces and leaned on it to catch his breath.

Richard Melcher was sitting at his desk again. "Melcher," he said, "you really are a slow learner, aren't you?"

"Awfully convenient for you, DiSalvo, that Dewey Webb's prints turned up on that gun. Considering that until last night, your personal piece of tail was the prime suspect."

He dropped his cup of coffee and grabbed Melcher by the front of his shirt, yanking him up out of the chair and onto his feet. "If you ever refer to her that way again," he said quietly, "I'll kill you. Do you understand?"

Melcher's eyes met his coolly. "You," he said, "are an animal. An uncivilized, boorish heathen. How the hell you ever ended up with this job, I can't—"

Nick shook him so hard Melcher's teeth snapped together. "You didn't answer my question," he said. "*Do you understand?*"

The younger man's eyes narrowed. "I understand," he said.

Nick released him so suddenly that Melcher lost his footing and nearly fell. "Get the hell out of here," he snapped. "We have our suspect in custody. Now you can go back to Raleigh and tell your boss what a stupendous job you did here. Maybe you'll get a corner office out of it."

Melcher smoothed his tie and returned Nick's scowl. "Just remember, DiSalvo, this will go down as a black mark on your record."

"Get out of here!"

When Melcher was gone, he fished a fistful of napkins out of his desk and mopped up the spilled coffee. To steady his hands, he drank what was left of it while he paged through his messages. The mayor was requesting an audience with him first thing. Wanita Crumley's sister, June, wanted to talk to him. Celeste Geary, the anchorwoman from channel seven in Raleigh, wanted an exclusive interview before the noon news report.

He tossed Geary's message in the trash, set aside the one from the mayor, and phoned Crumley's sister and made an appointment to meet with her later in the day. And then, reluctantly, he went upstairs to meet with the mayor.

Marilu looked like an ice cream soda this morning, all pink and white froth. She raised her tanned shoulders and thrust out her impressive chest and smiled at him. "Good morning, Chief," she said. "Mayor's waiting for you right inside. Congratulations on catching your killer so quickly."

He grunted a response and stepped up to the open door and knocked.

"Nick! Come in, come in." Wayne Stevens leaned back in his chair, his hands clasped over his flat abdomen, a smile on his face. "Fast work," he said. "I'm impressed."

Nick shut the door behind him and sat down. "I wouldn't get too impressed just yet," he said.

The mayor's smile faltered a little. "What do you mean?"

"I'm not thoroughly convinced that Dewey Webb killed Wanita Crumley."

This time, the smile disappeared altogether. "I don't understand," Stevens said. "You have the man in custody, and his prints all over the murder weapon. How much more will it take to convince you?"

He debated whether or not Stevens could be trusted. "I think," he said slowly, carefully, "that there's something really smelly going on around here."

Stevens drew his bushy eyebrows together. "Smelly in what way?"

"I think somebody set up Dewey Webb. Just like they set up Kathryn McAllister four years ago. I think the two murders are related. There's a killer walking our streets, Mayor, and I intend to find out who it is and put him away."

He could see that Stevens was considering his suggestion. "How many people have you told?"

"Just you, sir. And Kathryn McAllister."

"Many a good man has had his head turned by a pretty face, DiSalvo."

"She's innocent," he said, "and I intend to prove it."

"Are you sleeping with her?"

The truth was bound to come out, sooner or later. Too many people already knew. Better that the mayor should hear it from his own mouth. "Yes," he said.

"Goddamn it, Nick!"

"I'm a good cop, sir. I know what the hell I'm doing."

Stevens sighed. "Damn it all to hell! Why can't anything be uncomplicated? What about Dewey Webb?"

"Right now," Nick said, "he's the only suspect we've got. It'll never make it to trial. We'll find the real killer, and Dewey'll be released."

"In the meantime, DiSalvo, I'm expecting you to keep this little conversation between us. Our official line remains the same. Dewey Webb is our killer. Am I making myself clear?"

"Crystal," he said. "By the way, have you ever heard of an organization called the Businessmen's Benevolent Association?"

It was subtle, the change in Stevens, but it was very real. "I'm not the person to ask," the mayor said stiffly.

"Any idea who might be?" Nick said casually.

"I'd suggest you drop it," Stevens said. "Now, if you'll excuse me, I have a meeting in five minutes."

* * *

It ate at him for the rest of the morning, the mayor's reaction when he'd asked about the Businessmen's Benevolent Association. There was something there, of that he was certain. Whether or not it had any connection with the murders he had no idea. But what he'd seen in Stevens' eyes had looked remarkably like fear, and he couldn't help wondering what Mayor Wayne Stevens had to fear.

At nine o'clock, he issued a brief statement to the waiting reporters. Celeste Geary called again, and he was on the phone with her when his door burst open and Janine flew in, her face thunderous. "Excuse me," he told Geary. "I'll have to call you back." He hung up the phone and leaned over his desk. "Hi, baby," he said to his daughter.

"Why didn't you tell me?" She crossed her arms over her chest, and he realized that she'd begun developing breasts, this womanchild of his. Where had the years gone?

"Why didn't I tell you what?" he said.

"That she killed someone, Daddy! How could you not tell me something that important?"

He'd known it was coming, had postponed it as long as possible, but here it was, and he had to face it. "Shut the door," he said, "and sit down."

Sitting there in all her righteous fury, she was a miniature version of her mother. How many times had Lenore met him at the door with this kind of anger because he'd worked late again and missed some crucial family function? "First of all," he said, "Kathryn didn't kill anybody."

"That's not what Sylvie says. She says that Kathryn killed her husband with a knife and went to prison for it!"

"It wasn't a knife," he said, "it was a pair of wallpapering shears. And yes, she did go to prison. But she's not the one who killed him. That's why she's not in prison any more. A judge overturned her conviction."

"I don't understand, Daddy. You're a cop. How could you involve yourself with somebody like that?"

"I thought your mom and I taught you not to judge people until you got to know them? You don't know anything about her."

"Because you've conveniently kept us apart. I think you're embarrassed about being involved with her, and you don't want anybody to know. You're a hypocrite, Daddy, that's what you are."

Her words went through him like a knife, at least in part because there was some truth in them. What was it Kathryn had tried to tell him the other day? Something about walking down the street beside her in the broad light of day?

Janine tapped her foot. "Well, Daddy?"

With a sigh, he picked up the telephone and called Kathryn. "Would you do me the honor," he said, "of having dinner with me tonight? You, me, and Janine. In public. In broad daylight. Right here in River City."

"Nick?"

"Just say yes, McAllister, and don't ask questions."

"Yes," she said.

"Thank you. My day is now complete. I'll pick you up around six. Try to leave the evil twin at home, okay? Janine's been listening to rumors, and she's convinced I'm keeping company with Lizzie Borden."

"Ah. I see. I'll try to be on my best behavior, then."

"Kat?"

"DiSalvo?"

He realized his daughter was listening to every word, and besides, he wasn't sure what it was he wanted to say. Wasn't sure he could put it into words. Not yet, anyway. "Nothing," he said. "I'll see you tonight."

He hung up the phone and faced his daughter. "There," he said. "Are you happy now?"

* * *

Luther Murdock looked older than his sixty-seven years. His face was drawn, the wrinkles more pronounced than they'd been the last time she'd seen him, some five years ago. "Dewey din't kill nobody," he told her, wiping absently at the counter with a wet rag. "I've known that boy since he was no bigger'n a flea. He loved that woman, Miz McAllister. He wouldn't of done anything to hurt her."

She leaned forward over the bar, glanced around, and lowered her voice. "I think Dewey was set up," she said. "Just like I was. I think whoever killed Michael also killed Wanita. I'm looking for proof."

"Who'd want to do that to Mister Dewey?"

"I doubt that it was personal. Dewey just happened to be the most likely suspect. Just like I was, with Michael."

"I don't see how I can help, Miz McAllister."

"You might know something you don't even realize you know. Some piece of the puzzle that I haven't been able to fit together."

"This is a job for the police, ma'am. You're liable to get hurt if you go messing around in stuff that ain't your business."

"It *is* my business," she said. "It's my business to find out who killed my husband. It's my business to clear my name. And now," she added, "it looks like it's up to me to clear Dewey."

"You're a right fine lady," he said. "I never believed you killed Mr. McAllister. You was always nice to my grandkids. You was their favorite teacher."

She remembered them fondly, Denise and Della Murdock, a pair of sweet-faced pre-teens who were being raised by their grandparents after their mother left town with her latest boyfriend and never bothered to come back. "They were beautiful little girls," she said. "They must be almost grown now. Young ladies."

His grin took years off his face. "They surely are, Miz McAllister. They surely are."

"Luther," she said, "what do you know about an organization called the Businessmen's Benevolent Association?"

His face went still, except for the twitch in his eyelid. "Nothing," he said blankly. "Never heard of 'em."

He was lying. She knew it. "Come on, Luther. You've lived in this town all your life. Why won't you talk about them?"

"That was thirty years ago, ma'am. It don't matter now."

"And what if it does?"

He picked up a glass and began polishing it with a clean towel. Glanced nervously past her shoulder. On the television above his head, *Days of Our Lives* was playing. "They's things goes on in this town," he said, "that decent folk don't talk about."

"Such as?"

"I'm an old man, Miz McAllister. I keep my mouth shut, and everything goes along right smooth. I says the wrong thing to the wrong person, and who knows what might happen? My baby girls are fifteen and sixteen. I gotta take care of 'em."

"I swear to you on a stack of Bibles that what you tell me will never leave this room."

"I don't see what the Benevolent Association got to do with Dewey bein' in jail."

"Neither do I. But there's a connection. I feel it in my bones."

"What went on in that house," he said softly, "was shameful. Place ought to be burned down and the ground sowed with salt. Young women of color—beautiful young women—being paraded in and out like they was a revolving door on the place. White men using 'em for their own perverted pleasures. And not giving 'em a choice."

"Do you mean to say that the women weren't willing? They were raped?"

He glanced out at the nearly empty room. "You gotta understand," he said, "what it was like. They was all rich white men. They owned the town, and everybody in it. If one of 'em decided he wanted a particular colored girl, there warn't nothing she could do about it. Not if she didn't want her daddy being fired from his job when he had six or seven mouths to feed."

"My God," she said, outraged. "And they got away with that?"

"All the colored people knowed about it. Some of the white folks, too, I imagine. But the white folks turned their heads the other way. And we was all in the same position as the girls. Nobody darin' to step forward and put a stop to it. They owned us, Miz McAllister. Lincoln might of freed the slaves a hunnerd years ago, but around here, it din't make no difference. We still in chains. We still owned by the rich white folks who can do anything they want and get away with it."

"What happened, Luther? What happened to bring an end to it all?"

He glanced around again, set down the towel. "I don't dare to say no more. They could burn my house down tonight while my babies sleep."

"Luther, don't quit on me now. I need this from you! Dewey needs it from you! You're the only one who can help us!"

He looked at her for a very long time. Sighed. Picked up a napkin and a stubby pencil from behind the bar. He wrote something on the napkin, folded it, and shoved it across the bar. "This is all I'm givin' you," he said. "You gotta figure out the rest on your own. Now git on out of here, girl, before somebody sees you that shouldn't."

She was trembling with excitement when she left the bar. The steamy summer heat hit her the moment she left the air conditioned building, and the bright sunlight blinded her. She unlocked the Toyota and sat down behind the wheel, started the engine and turned on the air conditioning. She gave her eyes a moment to adjust to the brightness, and then she opened the napkin.

Ruby Jackson, it said. *December, 1972.*

chapter thirteen

Shanice Williams showed her how to load and unload the microfiche and then left her alone. With agonizing concentration, Kathryn began paging through the December, 1972 daily editions of the *Gazette*. On page two of the December third edition, she found a picture of a much younger Kevin McAllister and several other men she didn't recognize, shaking hands with a young and surprisingly handsome Mayor John Chamberlain. The caption read *Benevolent Association donates $1000 to Christmas Fund for Needy Children.*

In fascination, she paged through the advertisements. Rollie's Emporium was having a twenty-nine-cent special on gasoline. Ground chuck was selling for forty-nine cents a pound, and ABC Textiles, long since defunct, was advertising for experienced stitchers at two dollars per hour.

She was so caught up in the nostalgic look back that she almost missed it, buried on page nine of the December fourteenth edition. *Police Puzzled By Disappearance of Local Woman.* Kathryn paused, her heart in her throat, pulse hammering as she read the brief news article.

> Elba, NC - In a case that has local law enforcement officials stumped, a young colored woman disappeared late Tuesday afternoon. Nineteen-year-old Ruby Jackson left her

place of employment, the Dixie
Diner, where she worked as a
waitress, around 3:00 p.m.
Tuesday. The young woman
never arrived home.
Subsequent investigations by
Elba police have failed to
unearth any clues regarding her
disappearance. Jackson, the
daughter of Raymond and
Beulah Jackson of Persimmon
Creek, is a 1971 graduate of
Elba High School. She stands
five-foot-five and weighs 120
pounds, and has brown hair and
brown eyes. Anyone having
information concerning her
whereabouts is asked to call
Chief Wallace Hayes of the
Elba Police Department.

The article was accompanied by a grainy black-and-white
photo of a young black woman. Kathryn studied it carefully, but the
quality of the newspaper photo, reproduced on microfiche, was so
poor that it was almost impossible to discern features. She pulled out
a notebook from her purse and took quick notes, read the article
through again, then began paging forward, looking for a follow-up
article. It took her nearly an hour to page through to the end of
January, but there was no further mention of Ruby Jackson. Which
could mean anything. She'd returned home. Had been located, safe
and sound, in Atlanta or Charleston or Richmond or some other
place young girls fled to when they left stifling hometowns like Elba.
Or she had never been seen again, and had subsequently been
forgotten by everyone except those who loved her.

She carefully rewound the microfiche and returned it to its
case, then went in search of Shanice Williams. "Where do you keep
the obituaries?" she said.

"Nowadays," the woman said, "they're all on computer."

"You mean, you can just punch in a name and bring it up on

the screen?"

"That's right," Shanice said. "The last fifty years' worth."

"Can you look up a name for me? Ruby Jackson."

The name obviously meant nothing to Shanice, who swiveled in her chair and efficiently typed the name into her computer. A moment later, a blue screen popped up with the words NO MATCHING ENTRY. "She's not here," Shanice said.

"And if she'd died, and her obit had been printed in the *Gazette*, it would be here?"

"That's right," Shanice said.

Her next stop was the Elba Public Library, located on the corner of Elm and Persimmon. The librarian looked up, recognized her, and pursed her lips in disapproval. "Good afternoon," Kathryn said. "Do you keep copies of high school yearbooks?"

"Row five, left side, near the end."

She found it on the second shelf from the top, the 1971 Elba High School yearbook. She carried it to an oak table and opened it up, flipping through the senior portraits until she found Ruby Jackson. Ruby had been a pretty girl, with a slightly exotic tilt to her eyes, as though she'd had a trace of Asian ancestry. She'd been a junior varsity cheerleader as well as a member of the yearbook club, and she'd sung in the school choir.

Kathryn took the yearbook to the photocopier, paid a quarter and made a copy of the page. "Phone book?" she said to the librarian with the permanently sour expression.

The woman reached beneath the counter and handed the book to her, and she opened it and turned to the J's. Twenty-six years ago, Ruby Jackson had disappeared at the age of nineteen. That would make her forty-five now. Her parents could easily still be living out on Persimmon Creek.

But there was no listing for either Raymond or Beulah Jackson. Frustrated, she handed the phone book back to the librarian. "Where would I find voter registration records?" she said.

"Municipal building, town clerk's office."

"Thank you," she said. "You've been very helpful."

Betty Watson, the town clerk, eyed her with open curiosity. "So you're the lady who's got our boy Nick all wrapped up in knots," she said.

"Christ," Kathryn said, "are there any secrets at all in this town?"

"None worth talking about," Betty said. "How can I help you?"

"I'm trying to locate a Raymond or Beulah Jackson, who lived out on Persimmon Creek back in 1972. I couldn't find a telephone listing, but I thought they might be listed in voter registration records."

"Well," Watson said, "let's have a look-see." She opened a wooden card file and began thumbing through cards. "Jackson," she said. "Hmm...we have Jackson, Abel, Jackson, Arthur. Jackson, Beulah. Bingo!" She pulled the card and checked the address. "Looks like her last known address was Cumberland Convalescent Center. Know where that is?"

"Old Raleigh Road?"

"You got it."

The drive out Old Raleigh Road was lovely at this time of year, past majestic plantation homes surrounded by tobacco fields wearing a rich, deep green. The Cumberland Convalescent Center had been built in a field where acres of cotton had once grown. She parked near the entrance and went inside and up to the front desk. The receptionist was a middle-aged black woman. "Hello," Kathryn said. "I'm looking for a Beulah Jackson. According to voter registration records, this was her last known address."

The woman eyed her silently. "You a bill collector?" she said.

Taken aback, she said, "No, no, nothing like that."

"Good thing," the woman said, "because if you was, you wouldn't be getting much out of old Beulah, seeing as how she up and died last spring."

"She's dead?" She hadn't expected this depth of disappointment. After all this searching, she'd reached a brick wall.

"Sorry, lady. What'd you want to see her about?"

"Nothing," she said. "It doesn't matter. Thank you."

She was halfway out the door when the woman shouted, "You might try her daughter."

Her heart stumbled in her chest. She forced herself to turn slowly. "She has a daughter?"

"Sure, hon. Her name's Eloise Fitzgerald. You want to hang on a minute, I'll find her address for you."

* * *

Eloise Fitzgerald lived in a trailer park on the banks of Persimmon Creek. Small children in varying shades played in the red dust beside a '67 Chevy Impala with the hood up and its engine missing. Kathryn knocked on the door, and it was opened by a fiftyish black woman with reddish hair done up in dreadlocks. "Yeah?" the woman said.

"My name is Kathryn McAllister," she said, "and I'm trying to track down a woman named Ruby Jackson."

The woman eyed her for a very long time. "I know who you are," she said. "What I want to know is what a classy white lady like you would be wanting with Ruby Jackson?"

"I was given her name by a confidential source. I'm trying to find out who murdered my husband. I think there may be a connection somewhere."

Again, the woman looked at her. "Ruby Jackson was my sister," she said, and opened the door farther. "Come in."

* * *

Wanita Crumley's sister June wore a navy blue dress with a white collar, and sat primly on the couch with her dress carefully covering her knees. "I didn't always approve of what my sister did," she said in a soft drawl, looking at Nick with pale blue eyes. "But Wanita was still my sister, and I loved her."

"Of course you did," he said, "and I'm sorry for your loss."

"Now I got her boys to raise, and I'm just praying to Jesus that we can do it right, Wally and me. We're all they got in the world now that Wanita's gone." With a white lace handkerchief, she dabbed at the corner of her eye.

"Mrs. Roberts," he said gently, "why'd you ask to see me today?"

"I'm just so distraught over Dewey's arrest," she said, those blue eyes warming. "I mean, I certainly don't approve of what he does for a living, selling hard liquor to foolish men who ought to know better—but Dewey's a gentle soul, and I can't believe he would have harmed a single hair on my sister's head."

"I know this is a terrible question to ask you after such a recent loss, but please understand that I have to ask. Were you aware that your sister was a prostitute?"

"Jesus loves us all, Mr. DiSalvo, saints and sinners alike. Yes, I was aware of Wanita's weaknesses. She sold her body on the street for drug money. That's why I thought Dewey was such a good influence on her. He wasn't the kind of man who'd put up with that nonsense for long."

"Did Dewey know about Wanita's ah—extracurricular activities?"

"I don't think so, no. If he had, he would have carried her off on his shoulder to the nearest preacher and that would've been that. Lord knows, he tried. But Wanita was stubborn and defiant right up until she breathed her last. She wouldn't let the other one go."

His interest sharpened. "What other one?" he said.

"The one who helped her pay the bills and stuff. He was an older man who could afford to throw money around, I guess. She called him her honey bun. Isn't that just nauseating?"

His pulse quickened. "I don't suppose you know his name?"

"No. But I think he fathered her oldest boy."

He raised an eyebrow. "I assumed the boyfriend in Baltimore was the father of her kids."

"Only the youngest. Joey. She was already pregnant with Timmy when she left town."

"So this relationship's been going on for a while?"

"Oh, sure. Off and on since she was nineteen or twenty."

"I'll be damned. Is the father's name listed on the boy's birth certificate?"

She looked thoughtful. "I don't know. I've never seen it."

"Born in Baltimore?"

"That's right."

He pulled out a pen and paper. Clicked the pen. "Date of birth?"

"January 16, 1995."

"Full name?"

"Timothy Ward Crumley."

He slapped shut the notebook. "It's something to go on," he said. "Thank you."

"What about Dewey? Do you think he'll be convicted?"

"Mrs. Roberts," he said, "right now, Dewey's the only suspect we've got. Unless or until somebody better comes along, he's our man, no matter how many well-meaning friends pop up to attest to his sterling character. If it goes to trial, it'll be up to the judge to decide what happens to him. It's out of my hands now."

* * *

Kathryn sat on the couch in Eloise Fitzgerald's living room. "My grandkids," Fitzgerald said, nodding toward the children who played outside. "I take care of 'em while my daughter works." She walked across the room to the television and picked up a framed photo of a young woman, carried it over so Kathryn could see it. "This here's my sister Ruby."

Kathryn recognized the face, the faint tilt of the eyes, the fresh young smile. So much joy in that smile. So much anticipation of what life held in store for her. "She was a lovely girl," she said softly.

"Two weeks before Christmas," Fitzgerald said. "That's when she disappeared. Poor Momma never did get over it. Every Christmas until the day she died, she lit a candle for Ruby and prayed that God would bring her baby back home to her. But God wasn't listening. She died of a broken heart."

Kathryn swallowed, and leaned forward. "Eloise," she said, "what happened to Ruby?"

The older woman sat down across from her. "You tell me," she said.

"She never came back, then?"

"Never came back, never wrote. Ruby would've come home if she could." Fitzgerald's mouth thinned. "But she never did."

"You think somebody killed her."

"I know somebody did. I just ain't got no proof."

"And the police never had any leads?"

"The police," Fitzgerald said, "didn't exactly look too hard. You got no corpse, you got no evidence, you got no crime. Besides—" Fitzgerald spread her hands wide on her knees. "If you don't want to see something, it's pretty easy to not see it."

"And the police didn't want to look too closely at what happened to Ruby."

"Nobody gives a damn what happened to some nineteen-year-old colored girl. Specially if it ain't convenient for them to give a damn."

Kathryn frowned. "Tell me about the Businessmen's
Benevolent Association."

Fitzgerald's smile was cynical. "Didn't take you too long to get
around to them boys, now, did it?"

"I know a little," she said. "Tell me the rest."

"The Businessmen's Benevolent Association," Fitzgerald said.
"Yes, ma'am, they were a bunch of pistols, them boys. Liked to play
God, they did. Liked to play God with young girls."

"Were you one of them?"

"No," she said flatly. "I wasn't eligible for their little private
parties."

Kathryn raised an eyebrow. "Not eligible?" she said. "Why?"

"They went for the sweet young meat. Untouched. The girls
that did what momma done told them and kept their legs crossed. I
was used goods. Tainted. Not their style a-tall."

"You mean they only wanted virgins?"

"Young," Fitzgerald said. "Innocent, pretty, and pure as the
driven snow. Wouldn't want to take no chances that some colored
boy'd been there first. Might get somethin' dirty, don't you know?
They treated them girls some special, I tell you. Had a special
initiation rite for a girl making her debut into their oh-so-polite
society. First, they'd gag her so nobody'd hear her scream. Then
whoever'd issued the formal invitation got to do the deflowering
while the rest of 'em watched. And then they all got their turns, one
after the other."

Her stomach soured. "Those monsters," she whispered.

"Of course, after the third or fourth man, the girl usually
stopped fighting. And once the fun and games was over, she never
dared to say a word to nobody. Those men ran the town, sister, and
they was mean as rattlesnakes."

"And what happened then? After the first time, I mean?"

"Oh, the men all had their favorites, their reg'lars. They'd keep
a girl comin' back with threats and promises. They'd threaten her
family, her livelihood. Threaten to burn down her house if she didn't
cooperate. Sometimes, the old goats would get sweet on one o' their
girls. Buy her little trinkets, make empty promises 'bout how they
were gonna leave their sorry-ass rich white wives. As if any one of
'em would've jeopardized their status in the community by giving up

a white woman for a black whore. That's what they turned them into. Whores."

"I don't understand," she said, "how they got away with this."

"Miz McAllister, you're a Yankee, you gotta understand what the South was like then. This was only a few years after young black protestors was getting arrested for sitting at a white lunch counter at Woolworth's. They might've passed laws, but discrimination was still going strong. Hell, public buildings still had three bathrooms when I was a girl. Men, women, and colored. The boys of the Benevolent Association weren't doing anything new. That kind of thing's been going on since slave days. They just took an old sport and gave it a new twist. Sorta unionized it, that's all."

"And Ruby," she said softly. "She was part of this?"

"Ruby was a good girl," she said. "Got good grades in school, always did what Momma said. She wasn't like me. Hell, I got myself into trouble when I was just fifteen. I got a daughter older'n you. But Ruby, she wasn't having none of that. She wasn't getting mixed up with no men. She was going on to college, soon as she could come up with the money. So she started working at the Dixie Diner, and that's where she met up with that no-good son of a bitch. He used to come in for coffee, flirt with her over his morning paper. Up-and-coming young white man, handsome as sin, loaded with money, headed for a fine and glorious future. Silver-tongued devil, he was, evil incarnate. And he ruined my sister. She fell in love with him. Actually fell in love with the bastard, after all he did to her. After all these years, it still makes me mad enough to want to kill the son of a bitch."

Kathryn wet her lips. "He," she said, leaning forward. "Who was he?"

Fitzgerald gave her a long, level look. "I imagine you already know."

Her hands began shaking. "Kevin McAllister," she said.

"That's right, honey. Your esteemed father-in-law. And there's one other fact that nobody else knows except me. And maybe one other person. The one who knows what happened to my sister."

"What?" she whispered.

"When Ruby disappeared, she was carrying Kevin McAllister's child."

chapter fourteen

He showed up at her house at five minutes to six, showered and shaved and nervous as a schoolboy. Janine sat silent in the passenger seat beside him, hands folded primly in her lap, as he pulled the Blazer to a stop in front of Kathryn's house. He turned to his daughter. "You will be polite," he said sternly. "You will not ask impertinent questions. You will act like a young lady, not a shrew. Is that understood?"

She eyed him at length. "Yes," she said sullenly.

"Good. Now, like civilized people, we can get out of the car."

Kathryn met them at the door, wearing the same flowered skirt she'd worn the day they met, topped by a short-sleeved fuschia-colored blouse with a scoop neck. Above it, dangling against that sweet flesh he couldn't seem to get enough of, was a heart-shaped locket on a gold chain. Her eyes met his, warmed, and stayed there for a long moment before she looked down at his daughter and smiled. "Hello, Janine," she said.

Janine said nothing, and he nudged her with his hand at the small of her back. "Hi," she said.

He gave Kathryn an apologetic smile and they exchanged a look that clearly said, *So this is the way it's going to be.* "Ready?" he said. "We wouldn't want to miss our reservation."

Once they were in the Blazer, nobody said anything. He stopped at the end of the street, where Wilson Harkness was watering his lawn. Nick waved a hand at the white-haired gentleman, turned left onto Myrtle Street, and cleared his throat. "House looks better," he said.

"Thank you," Kathryn said stiffly, "for sending Bucky over with that can of paint."

"No problem. He felt it was his civic duty. You got the glass replaced?"

"Emmet Crosley," she said. "He came over first thing this morning and took care of it."

There was another long silence, broken only by the soft jazz that played on the radio. "Where are we going?" she said.

"You'll see," he said cryptically.

When he pulled into the parking lot of the First Baptist Church, past a white sign advertising CHURCH SUPPER TONIGHT, her head swiveled around and she regarded him with eyes that hadn't made up their mind yet whether to be startled or amused. "You're not serious," she said.

He wheeled the Blazer into a parking spot next to Neely McAllister's new Cadillac. "I thought we'd set a few asses on fire tonight. You game?"

"You've lost your mind, DiSalvo. They'll eat us alive."

"Oh," he said, "I think we can hold our own. Janine's a tough kid. These people don't scare me a bit. And the only thing you're afraid of is snakes."

"I rest my case. They're a pit of vipers. With fangs."

"You're the one who wanted to be seen together in public. It doesn't get much more public than this."

"Well," she said dryly, "we certainly will make a splash, won't we?"

"Look at it this way, McAllister. It'll be the wildest coming-out party this town has ever seen."

He patted her cheek and turned to Janine. "Welcome to Elba," he said. "You're about to get an education. Roll with it, and try to enjoy the show." He squawked open his door. "Shall we, ladies?"

Kathryn alighted from the Blazer, then lingered to allow Janine time to get out of hearing range. "I need to talk to you," she whispered to Nick. "In private."

His face changed subtly. "Everything okay?" he said.

"I'm not sure. I uncovered something today that might be significant."

Janine turned on the path ahead of them, rolled her eyes and put her hands on her hips. "Are you coming or not?" she said.

"The boss has spoken," Kathryn said.

"We'll talk later," he said. "For now, let's go set off some fireworks."

Mildred Evans, dressed in a flowered muumuu, manned the front door. She gaped at him, at Kathryn, then back at him, and her mouth dropped open. "Why, Mr. DiSalvo," she said, "I never expected to see you here."

He gave her a twenty-dollar bill and a wolfish grin. "I told you I'd show up one of these days for a taste of your pecan pie. And I know the church will use my donation wisely."

"Oh, my, yes," she said, fumbling in her awkward rush to make change for him. "The money we're raising goes to support our missionaries in Guatemala."

"And a fine cause it is, Mrs. Evans. By the way—" He laid a hand on each of Janine's shoulders. "This is my daughter, Janine."

Mildred shoved her glasses up her nose and peered at Janine through bottle-thick lenses. "Why, hello, dear. So nice you could come here tonight."

He dragged Kathryn forward. "And I believe you already know my date, Kathryn McAllister."

"Yes, of course," she said, dropping her eyes to the cash box, obviously uncertain of how to proceed in this awkward social situation. "We're acquainted."

"It's so nice to see you again, Mildred," Kathryn said.

"Likewise," she squeaked, before turning, red-faced, to her next customer.

The church basement, normally used for Sunday School classes, had been converted to a dining room for the occasion. Long trestle tables had been covered with paper tablecloths, and a few husbands who had been drafted into helping—among them Shep Henley and Kevin McAllister—were lining up wooden folding chairs at each table.

At the far end of the room, amid mouth-watering and heavenly smells, Neely McAllister reigned over the buffet table, queen of the casseroles, her silvery laughter cascading over the room like a celestial waterfall. At the next table, standing guard over a huge keg of lemonade, was Georgia Pepperell. Her eyes met his and a catlike smile curled her lips. He nodded in greeting, and propelled Kathryn forward.

As they worked their way deeper into the room, conversation came to an abrupt halt and mouths dropped. Ignoring the stares and the furtive whispers, he told Janine, "Tonight, you're going to experience old-fashioned Southern cooking at its very best. Right, Kat?"

"Right," she said dryly. "If they don't draw and quarter us first."

"They wouldn't dare," he said. "I'm the chief of police. If they make a scene, I'll haul their pompous asses off to jail, and they know it."

"Now there's a picture."

They took their place in line, and he handed a plate to Janine, another to Kathryn. The feast was incredible. Fried chicken, baked beans, a dozen or more different casseroles. Macaroni and potato salad, home-baked yeast rolls, and of course Mildred's pecan pie. Several pecan pies. The first face he saw was Rowena's, her mouth pursed but her eyes bright with merriment. "Rowena, my sweet," he said. "Did you make this wonderful meatloaf?"

"I most certainly did," she said, serving him a huge helping. "Won first prize at the Rowley County Fair two years in a row. By the way, Chief, what is it they say about a thin line between a brave man and a fool? I do believe you may have crossed it tonight. And how are you this fine evening, Janine?"

"Hungry," Janine said.

"Well, of course you are. A growing girl like you needs to eat." She gave Janine an extra-large serving. "Keep an eye on your father," she said. "I'm beginning to think the man needs a keeper."

She and Kathryn exchanged weighty glances. "Meatloaf?" she said.

"Thank you, I believe I will. It looks delicious."

With a graciousness befitting a queen, Rowena served her a generous helping. "If you like it," she said, "I'll give you the recipe." And then, seemingly horrified at what she'd said, she quickly turned to the next person in line.

"Mrs. Clark!" Nick greeted the next stunned chef. Lowering his voice, he said, "I hear you make the best fried chicken in Rowley County."

"Why—why—thank you, Mr. DiSalvo," the matronly woman

stammered. She turned her attention to Janine, and beamed in a grandmotherly sort of way. "I understand this lovely young lady is your daughter."

"This is Janine," he said. "Can you believe this kid hopped a plane all by herself and flew down here from New York? Fearless, that's what she is. Hey, Kat, make sure you get some of Mrs. Clark's fried chicken. I hear it's worth killing for."

Standing behind him in line, Kathryn poked her thumb and forefinger into a fold in his shirt and pinched him soundly.

He ignored her. "And Mrs. Miner," he said, "these must be the yams I've heard so much about. I can't wait to try 'em. How about you, Kathryn?"

"I hate yams," she said.

His eyes reprimanded her. "You have a piece of lint on your blouse," he said, and lowered his head toward hers as he pretended to pick it off. "Work with me," he murmured near her ear. "There's a method to my madness."

"Daddy?" Janine said. "What's this stuff?"

He turned around to see what she was talking about. It looked like a giant biscuit-covered chicken casserole. "I have to admit," he said, "I'm not sure. Mrs. Pruett, what are these biscuit things?"

"You New Yorkers," she said, shaking her head gleefully at his woeful ignorance. "They're dumplings, Mr. DiSalvo. You should try one, they're mighty fine."

"Try one," he instructed Kathryn. "Mrs. Pruett says they're delicious."

"There's nothing wrong with my hearing," she said.

"And Mrs. McAllister," he said, moving ahead. "Did you make this elegant lemon meringue pie?"

Neely McAllister, as usual, was in silk and pearls. Pearls at her throat, pearls at her ears. If her expression had been any colder, his genitals would have withered and fallen off. "Mr. DiSalvo," she said, "I'm not certain what you're up to here, but you will not be playing me for a fool."

"What I'm up to?" he said in blatant bewilderment. "What I'm up to is the same thing everybody else is. I'm eating supper with all you fine people."

Those glacial blue eyes bored into him. "At whose invitation?"

"I believe yours, if I recall correctly. Just last month, you told me I really should stop by one of your church suppers and see what real Southern cooking was all about. And here I am. By the way, this is my daughter, Janine." He rested a hand on Janine's shoulder and squeezed. "Janine," he said, "this is Mrs. McAllister. She baked the lemon meringue pie."

"Hello," Janine said. "I really love lemon meringue."

"Well, then," Neely said with reptilian warmth, "in that case, be sure you take two slices."

"Thank you," Janine said. "McAllister," she added thoughtfully. "Are you any relation to Kathryn?"

"Neely is Kathryn's mother-in-law," Nick said heartily.

"*Former* mother-in-law," Neely clarified, her voice dripping with venom. "Now I suggest you take your little circus sideshow somewhere else, Mr. DiSalvo."

"*Chief* DiSalvo," he said. "How many times do I have to remind you of that?"

The barb hit its mark. Her face turned a gratifying shade of red. "Listen, baby," he told Janine, "there's room at that table over there. Take my plate and head on over. I'll get us something to drink."

"Thanks for the pie, Mrs. McAllister," his daughter said. It was very nice meeting you."

"I believe I'll go with her," Kathryn said. "Neely, you're looking particularly lovely tonight. That shade of pink goes so well with your complexion."

He stood there and watched them go, proud as hell of both of them, the one that was his by blood, and the one that was his by choice. "Damn," he said. "They're something, aren't they?"

"Mr. DiSalvo? I'm afraid you're not hearing me."

"Oh, I hear you, Neely. I'm just not one of the people you can wrap around your little finger. I'll decide for myself where I eat and with whom."

"Perhaps," she said in a voice whose silk didn't quite hide its cruelty, "it's time I did a little persuading of the city fathers to reconsider your suitability for the position for which you were hired."

"I'm not going anywhere," he said casually, "until I solve this homicide case."

"Dewey Webb killed Wanita Crumley, Mr. DiSalvo. You've solved the crime. Your job is done."

"Maybe," he said, "I wasn't talking about Wanita Crumley. Have a nice evening, Mrs. McAllister."

He ambled over to the lemonade keg and poured three glasses. Georgia Pepperell smiled wryly. "My, my, my, Chief DiSalvo, you are just full of surprises, aren't you?"

"Aren't I, though?"

"I applaud your audacity. I must admit I can't recall the last time I saw Neely wearing that particular shade of red. Quite becoming on her, isn't it?"

"Quite," he said, and carried the glasses over to the table where Janine and Kathryn had seated themselves.

"What in hell do you think you're doing?" Kathryn whispered when he sat down beside her.

"I thought I'd poke a stick at 'em, stir 'em up a bit. Worked pretty good, didn't it? Just listen to that hissing and rattling. Especially your revered mother-in-law."

"She's a mean woman," Janine said.

"The Lucretia Borgia of Elba, North Carolina," Nick agreed. "I rattled her cage a bit. I can't help it. She brings out the worst in me."

"I think it's universal," Kathryn said.

In one corner of the room, a handsome and smiling Judge Kevin McAllister was holding court over a bevy of young matrons who giggled and poked at each other in delighted embarrassment each time he opened his mouth. Behind the serving table, his wife was talking to Shep Henley, going a mile a minute, her composure severely damaged. Henley turned around, his gaze scanning the room, stopping when it reached their table. The fury in his eyes was a living, breathing thing. Nick raised his glass in greeting, and Henley turned back to Neely McAllister. He took her hand in his and patted it soothingly, while she continued to talk rapidly and with obvious distress.

Nick narrowed his eyes. "Hey, Kat?"

She looked up from her meatloaf. "What?"

"Take a quick gander at the serving table. Henley and McAllister. Tell me what you see."

She and Janine both discreetly glanced toward the buffet table. "He's holding her hand," Kathryn said dryly. "Comforting her. Telling her that she's right, that Nick DiSalvo really is the spawn of Satan."

"Is that all you see?" he said, disappointed. "There's something else, but I can't put my finger on it."

"It's the way he's looking at her," Janine said.

Kathryn swiveled her head around and looked at his daughter. "What?" she said.

"The way he's looking at her," Janine repeated. "And the way she's looking back at him. It's the same way you and Daddy look at each other."

Kathryn and Nick stared at each other, stunned, and then they both looked back at the couple who stood at the serving table. Henley was still holding Neely's hand, still hanging on her every word, still gazing at her with obvious adoration.

"I'll be a son of a bitch," Nick said.

* * *

"Ubiquitous," Janine said gleefully as she arranged the letters on the Scrabble board. "That gives me—what? Twenty-seven points."

"And the championship," Kathryn said. "This kid is good, DiSalvo. You should have warned me."

"Just one of her many talents," he said. "Right, squirt?" Balancing his coffee on his knee with one hand, he ruffled his daughter's hair with the other.

"I used to play with Mom all the time," Janine said as she gathered up pieces and dumped them back into the box, "when you were working late."

His gaze met Kathryn's, and the stricken look in his eyes made her heart contract. "Is your mom a good player?" she asked, picking up a stray letter and tossing it into the box.

"She's okay. Not as good as me." Janine covered the box and rested her elbows on her splayed knees, long dark hair falling all around her. "But Walter—" She said the name with exaggerated disdain and a roll of the eyes. "He's really good. He's a wimp, but he's really good at Scrabble."

"Janine," Nick said in mild reprimand. "That's not a very nice thing to say."

"Well, it's true, Daddy. Walter is a dork."

"Your mom seems to like him," he said flatly.

"She liked you better," Janine said.

With his left hand, Nick rubbed at the knuckles that were clenched tight around the handle of his coffee cup. "Yeah, well, that was a long time ago."

"Not that long ago," Janine said.

Kathryn looked from father to daughter and back. "I think," she said briskly, "it's time for me to be getting home. It's late, and I need to let the dog out."

Janine looked at her with renewed interest. "What kind of dog do you have?"

"A Rottweiler. Your dad gave him to me."

"Really, Daddy? You gave her a dog? How come we don't have a dog?"

"We don't need a dog," he said curtly. "I'll drive you home."

"That's not necessary," Kathryn said. "It's a beautiful night, I can walk. I am capable of walking, you know."

He gave her a look fraught with meaning. "Then I'll *walk* you home."

"Fine," she said. "I'll get my purse."

"I'll be home in an hour or so," he told Janine. "Don't open the door to anybody you don't know. Basically that means nobody but me or Caroline."

Janine sighed. "I'm thirteen years old, Daddy. I grew up in the city. I'm not stupid."

"I want you to remember," he said, "that just because you're in a small town, that doesn't mean there's no danger. There are bad people in small towns, too."

"Like Kathryn's mother-in-law?"

He met Kathryn's eyes. "She's the queen of mean," he told his daughter. "But that doesn't necessarily mean she's bad. Not in the sense I'm talking, anyway. But there are dangerous people around. We had a murder just the other day, and we still don't know for sure who did it. And that scares the hell out of me."

"I don't understand," Janine said. "I thought you arrested somebody. Dewey something-or-other."

Again, his eyes met Kathryn's, helpless and beseeching.

"Shall I tell her?" she said.

"Go ahead. It's really your story to tell."

"Come on, sweetheart," she said to Janine. "Let's sit on the couch while I tell you all about it."

Janine looked from Kathryn to her father. "Okay," she said.

"Four years ago," Kathryn said, settling onto the cushion beside her, "I came home one day and found my husband dead. He'd been murdered, stabbed to death with my wallpapering shears. I was young, and I was ignorant, and I was scared. I made the mistake of pulling the shears out of his body. By the time the police got there, I had his blood all over me and my prints on the murder weapon. They said I killed him, but I didn't." She leaned forward and took Janine's hands in hers. "It's important to me that you believe that. I was so scared. I loved Michael so much, and I couldn't understand why they thought I would have killed him. It took me a while to figure out that I'd been set up. I took the fall for somebody else, somebody who made sure I was put away someplace where I couldn't ask too many questions about what happened to Michael. I spent four years in prison, Janine. If you've never been there, you can't imagine what that's like. The kind of things that go on. The kind of people you're forced to be with, day after day after day."

"It must have been scary," Janine said.

"It was very scary. But finally, my lawyer found new evidence and brought it to trial, and a judge released me. He overturned my conviction. And I came back to Elba to find out who really killed Michael."

"Why would anybody want to kill him?" she said. Her eyes narrowed in concentration, making her look so much like her father that it was startling. "Was he like that awful woman? His mother?"

Kathryn closed her eyes at the poignancy of her memories. "No, honey," she said, opening them again. "Michael was the kindest, sweetest man I'd ever known. He was nothing like his mother. I can't imagine why anybody would have wanted to kill him. But I intend to find out. Now, Wanita Crumley is dead, and I think the two murders are related. I think that whoever killed Michael is the same person who killed Wanita. So does your dad. We don't believe that Dewey killed her. But people around here have long memories, and they don't believe I'm innocent. So I'm not exactly winning any popularity contests these days. Things have happened."

"Like the spray paint on Daddy's Blazer?" Janine said.

She decided it would be a good idea to skip over the snake incident. And the driver who'd nearly run her down. "Yes," she said.

"Like that. Which is why your dad wants you to be very careful. People know we're—" She looked up at Nick, at a loss for words, uncertain of what their relationship really was. "—seeing each other," she finished. "In their eyes, that makes him guilty by association. Neither one of us," she said pointedly, "wants anything to happen to you as a result of this mess."

Janine spent a long time considering her words. Then she patted Kathryn's hand. "It's okay," she said. "I believe you." She turned to her father. "Daddy," she said gravely, "I think it would be safer for you to drive Kathryn home."

When they were alone in the Blazer, she said, "That's quite a kid you have there, DiSalvo."

"You're telling me." He shifted gears, threw an arm over the back of the seat and backed out of the driveway. Shifted again, and the truck lurched forward. "Okay," he said, "now that we're alone, you can tell me what's got you so wired up."

So she told him, told him about Ruby Jackson, about the Businessmen's Benevolent Association, about Ruby's rich and handsome white lover. "I'm on to something," she said. "I know it. There's some connection here. Four people, four different lives. Ruby, Kevin, Michael, and Wanita. But I'll be damned if I can figure out what connects the four of them."

He rubbed absently at his chin while he deliberated. "If there's a connection," he said at last, "we'll find it. We're too deep into this now to back off."

"Is that the reason behind tonight's little performance?"

He pulled up to the curb in front of her house and shut off the engine. "Tonight," he said, stretching out his long legs, "I wanted to deliberately provoke somebody. I just wish to Christ I knew who it was."

"All signs," she said, "point to my erstwhile father-in-law. The scumbag."

Still rubbing his chin, he said, "Mmph."

"What's that supposed to mean?"

"I don't know exactly."

She turned, folded a leg beneath her, and studied him. "You don't think Kevin's the one?"

"I honestly don't know. A father killing his only son. A crime of passion, committed in a moment of rage? What possible motive could he have?"

She thought about it. Except for the blood that ran in their veins, what did Michael and Kevin McAllister really have in common? Michael knew exactly what his father was, and had been determined not to turn out like him. Or like Neely, for that matter. He might have inherited his father's looks, but the resemblance had ended there. Michael McAllister had been his own man, determined to make his way in this world not because of the McAllister name, but in spite of it.

"What do you make of Neely and Shep?" he said.

"It gives me the creepy-crawlies just to think about it. Do you suppose they're doing it? Or just yearning after each other, committing the sin of lust in their hearts, like Jimmy Carter?"

"I don't know," he said. "I can't imagine Neely messing up that perfect hair."

"Or taking off the pearls. I bet she wears them in the shower."

Dryly, he said, "Now there's a picture worth a thousand words."

"You know," she said, "Clara says she tried several times to tell Shep Henley that I was innocent, but he refused to listen. Couldn't that be construed as obstruction of justice?"

"He's a cop. As far as he was concerned, he already had his killer, tried and convicted and sent up the river. Who's going to listen to a batty old broad like Clara? Besides, can you imagine the headache he'd have gotten if he'd believed her, and started snooping around in a case that was already settled? It was a hell of a lot easier to just leave it alone."

She pursed her lips. "And leave me in prison," she said.

"Welcome to the American justice system."

"How can you sleep at night, DiSalvo, knowing you're a part of something so corrupt?"

"I'm one of the good guys," he said. "I put the bad guys in jail. Simple, first-grade logic." He moved across the bench seat toward her, resting his arm on the back of the seat, near her shoulder. "By the way," he said, his voice low and intimate and silken, "I meant to tell you earlier." He toyed with the locket at her throat. "You're looking pretty damn spectacular tonight, McAllister."

It was astonishing, the way just a few words from him, spoken in that particular tone of voice, could send goosebumps racing up her arms and down her belly. In a husky voice, she said, "You think so?"

He reached out a hand to cup her cheek. His thumb, whisper-soft against her skin, moved sensually against her bottom lip, and she went limp in all those dark, fluid woman-places that only he could touch. "Nick," she whispered.

His mouth was soft on hers, and she kissed him with fierce eagerness, hands tangled in his dark hair as his tongue slithered against hers with exquisite delight, sparking a fire that burned, dark and throbbing, inside her. His hand slid beneath her skirt and his knuckles brushed the tender flesh at the inside of her thigh. She moaned softly and bit at her bottom lip. "Stop," she gasped. "We're right on the street where people can see us."

"They can't see a thing," he said. "Besides, the whole town knows we're sleeping together. We might as well give 'em something to talk about."

"Minnie Rawlings," she said, "probably has her infrared binoculars...trained on us...even as we speak."

He skimmed fingertips up and down her inner thigh, causing her stomach to convulse in excitement. "You have the most spectacular legs," he whispered against her throat, "that I've ever seen."

"Oh, Christ, Nick," she breathed, "don't."

Beneath the flowered skirt, his hand reached the warm spot between her thighs. Knuckles brushing against the crotch of her panties, he said, "You don't like it?"

"You know I like it."

"Yeah. Me, too."

He slipped a finger inside the panties, inside the place where she was already hot and wet and ready for him, and she moaned in ecstasy. "How much time do we have," she said hoarsely, "before Janine sends out the bloodhounds?"

His mouth grazed the flesh left bare by the scoop neck of her blouse. "Enough," he said.

"Let's go in the house."

"I was just about to suggest that."

The instant the door shut behind them, he shoved her up against it, his mouth hungry on hers as he pressed his rock-hard pelvis against the soft, yearning hollow between her legs. Still kissing, he peeled off her blouse while she unbuckled his belt and tugged free the tails of his shirt. Across the living room floor and up the stairs, their clothes blazed a random trail of unorthodox pairings. Her panties and one of his socks in a puddle near the door. The other sock tangled with her bra, dangling from the fireplace screen. His belt coiled on the stairs next to the flowered skirt that huddled perilously close to the edge.

He crawled onto the bed and pulled her down with him. Her blood running dark and sultry, she knelt over him and took him inside her, thick and hot and exquisitely hard. He groaned in utter defenselessness. Fluid and boneless, she closed her eyes and let her body lead her through the firestorm.

His hands found her hips and his fingers sank into her tender flesh as he guided her movements, matched them to his own rhythm. Wave after wave of pleasure slammed into her, buoyed her up and took her higher and ever closer to the jagged edge of madness. "Look at me, Kat," he demanded. "Open your eyes."

His eyes had gone soft and blurry with passion. Kathryn tilted forward and he cupped her face in his hands, and they watched each other, witnessed each other's vulnerabilities, each other's strengths, each other's emotions. She'd never trusted a man this completely before, but Nick DiSalvo was no ordinary man. "Let it take you," he said in a hoarse whisper. "Let it take you while I watch."

When her body splintered, she cried out his name as fire raged upward from her core, stole away all her oxygen, tore through her from the center outward, leaving her limp and bruised and gasping. She fell onto him, spent and shuddering, and watched his face as he followed her over the edge. Nick looped his arms around her and buried his face in her hair. Her heart was beating so hard she thought it might explode, and her breasts were squashed unceremoniously against that solid chest.

Time passed. Eventually, she cleared her throat. Cleared it again. "Well," she said.

"Shut up, McAllister," he said gruffly. "Don't spoil it for me with your mouth."

Hiding a smile, she closed her eyes. After a while, she said, "Nick?"

"Mmph."

"Do you think the Judge had something going with Wanita?"

"Holy mother of Moses, McAllister. We just shared the most

incredible sex that I've ever experienced in my entire thirty-five years, and you're already thinking about Wanita? I must be losing my touch." He sighed dramatically. "At least it was good for me."

"Fishing for compliments, are you, DiSalvo?"

He lifted a strand of her hair and played with it. "A man likes to know when he's done his job well."

She took his face between her hands, looked into those dark eyes. "You have done your job," she said, "very, very well."

"Does that mean I can quit the day job now?"

She raised both eyebrows. "So you can become a gigolo?"

"It's a dirty job," he said, "but somebody has to do it."

"Sorry," she said, "but I'm not sharing you, DiSalvo. Not until I'm good and done with you, anyway."

He rolled her onto her back and kissed her. "You're a royal pain in the ass," he said with a tenderness that was at odds with his words.

She ran her fingertips up the back of his neck and into his hair. "You've already told me," she reminded him. "I complicate your life."

He flicked aside the gold locket, kissed the spot where it had lain. "I shouldn't even be here," he said. "I have a daughter waiting for me at home."

Her hand paused in its stroking. "You're free to leave," she said, "any time you want to."

"That's the problem, McAllister. I don't want to."

For four years, finding Michael's killer had been the only thing she thought about, the only thing she cared about, the only thing that mattered in her life. The need for justice had burned in her with obsessive fury. Now that she was so close, she couldn't allow anything, not even her feelings for Nick DiSalvo, to get in her way. "You have to go home, Nick," she said. "You can't leave Janine alone."

"What the hell is this between us, Kathryn? Because it's not just sex. We both know that. There's something happening here, something that quite frankly scares the bejesus out of me. I'm coming damn close to saying something I can't take back."

Her stomach turned over. "Don't say it," she begged. "Please don't say it."

"You're inside me, Kat, like an itch I just can't scratch. But what happens after this is all over with? What then?"

"I don't know," she said.

His mouth thinned. "You're a hard woman."

"Not hard. Just determined."

His eyes stayed on hers, searching deep, gauging, assessing. And then he rolled away from her. "I have to go."

She threw on a pair of sweatpants and a tee shirt and followed him downstairs. In the living room, in the dark, she stood by while he dressed silently, swiftly, every harsh, angry movement tearing holes in her heart. "Nick," she pleaded. "Don't be mad."

Curtly, he said, "I'm not."

"Look," she said, "you have your job to do, and I have mine. You've known that right from the start."

He sat on the couch and yanked viciously at his shoe laces. "I don't need this," he said. "I don't need any of this."

"And you think I do?"

"I think you're deep into something that's over your head, Kat, and you don't know how to handle it."

Furious, she said, "I think I've done quite nicely at handling it. I tracked down Ruby Jackson, didn't I? And nobody's killed me yet."

He got up from the couch, stood there looking at her. "I wasn't talking about the murders," he said. "I was talking about us."

And without even reminding her to lock up, he slammed out the door.

In disbelief, she stared at the closed door. And then, propelled by fury, she stormed across the room and flung it open. "Damn you, Nick DiSalvo!" she shouted. And then she froze as the shadowy figure who crouched on the ground beside the rear wheel of her Toyota looked up. Moonlight illuminated his face and flashed off the blade of the knife he'd just used to slash her tire. "Son of a bitch," Nick said.

The intruder dropped the knife. Like a bullet, he sprang to his feet and took off, with Nick in hot pursuit. In the kitchen, Elvis began barking. Kathryn grabbed her flashlight from the hall closet, stepped into her shoes, and sprinted after them. Footsteps pounded in the darkness ahead of her as they ran into the shadows beneath the trees. "Come back here, you little son of a bitch!" Nick said, and then they crashed into the underbrush. She followed them, flashlight beam bobbing crazily, kudzu vines slapping at her face, her heart thundering as she heard a grunt and then saw the two of them rolling, flattening underbrush, grunting and cussing as they struggled.

"Let me go, you motherfucker!" the intruder said. "Let me go!"

"You sleazy little punk!" Chest heaving with the effort, Nick pinned the intruder's arms to the ground and straddled his chest, grabbed him by the shoulders and began shaking him.

She finally reached them. "Nick!" she said, training the flashlight beam on the pair. "Nick, stop it!"

He ignored her, just kept shaking. "Nick!" she shouted, grabbing at his shoulder and yanking him around. "Stop it! He's just a boy!"

Her words finally got through to him. He looked at her, his eyes glassy with fury. She stared back, then pointed the flashlight beam downward and got her first look at the intruder's face. "Tommy?" she said in disbelief. "Tommy Russell?"

Nick's chest heaved as he struggled for breath. His shirt was drenched with sweat. "You know this piece of shit?" he said.

"He was one of my students, five or six years ago." She knelt on the ground beside the terrified, gasping boy. "He can't be more than fifteen or sixteen."

"It weren't my fault," Tommy said. "Honest. She paid me! She paid me to slash your tires and put the snake on your porch. It weren't my idea!"

Kathryn went cold inside. "What?" she said.

"She said she wanted to scare you, and I remembered that time Kenny Babcock brung that little bitty grass snake to school and you almost swooned. So I told her a snake would do it, and she paid me a hunnerd bucks to get one and put it there. A big one, she said. She give me another fifty to slash your tires. It weren't my fault. I ain't crazy enough to pass up easy money like that."

Nick rocked back on his heels, and Tommy scrambled to his feet, his clothes torn and dirty. With the flashlight still trained on Tommy, Kathryn rested her free hand on Nick's shoulder. He reached up and took her fingers in his much larger ones, and together they swayed back and forth in rhythm with his breathing. "She," Nick said hoarsely. "She who?"

Tommy's eyes grew wild, darted here and there as though he were looking for an escape route. And then he seemed to wilt. "Mrs. Pepperell," he said. "Mrs. Georgia Pepperell."

chapter fifteen

The house wasn't quite as elegant as the McAllister place, but it ran a close second. There was a forest green Mercedes sports coupe parked in the circular drive, and when he rang the bell, the door was answered by a pasty-faced maid. She took one look at their uniforms and turned paler. "Good morning," he said. "Is Mrs. Pepperell at home?"

The maid looked from him to Bucky and back again. "Come in," she said in a stiff British accent. "I'll locate the Missus."

The entry hall boasted a massive crystal chandelier. Bucky gaped in awe at its thousands of winking crystals. "Hell of a dump, eh?" Nick said, looking around him.

"I never saw anythin' like it," Bucky said.

"You think this is something, you should see the McAllister place. Ah, here comes our lovely hostess now."

Georgia Pepperell was dressed in tennis whites, and carried a racket in her hand. "Mr. DiSalvo," she said in her genteel voice, "how nice of you to drop by." She turned to Bucky and bestowed that siren's smile upon him. "And Mr. Stimpson, I do believe?"

Bucky reddened. "Yes, ma'am. This sure is a lovely house you got here."

"My husband's great-great-grandfather built it in 1852, shortly before the start of the War. It's on the National Register of Historic Places. What can I do for you gentlemen today?"

"We'd like to ask you some questions," Nick said.

Her eyes warmed, and he thought he saw a flash of humor in

their emerald depths. "Why, of course, Mr. DiSalvo. Anything I can do to assist Elba's finest."

"Do you know a boy named Tommy Russell?"

Something flickered in her eyes, but her cool never fluttered. She was a Southern lady, true to her genteel upbringing, a steel magnolia all the way to the marrow in her bones. "Is there some reason why I should know him?"

"According to him, you paid him a hundred bucks to leave that rattlesnake on Kathryn McAllister's porch. And another fifty last night to slash her tires."

"Well, then," she said, "I guess that means it's his word against mine, doesn't it?"

"Tell me again about Michael McAllister."

A muscle twitched in her jaw. "What on earth does Tommy Russell and his lies have to do with Michael?"

"You filled me full of bullshit the first time," he said. "This time, I thought you might want to take a stab at the truth."

The warmth in her eyes cooled with amazing rapidity. "I'm busy, gentlemen. I have a tennis date with Neely in a half-hour. I don't have time to stand here and listen to your preposterous accusations."

"I'm afraid you do, Mrs. Pepperell. You see, Bucky here's gonna put his handcuffs on you, and then he's gonna drive you down to the station and book you." He eyed her attire. "You might want to change first. No knowing what kind of mess you might meet up with in a jail cell."

She thrust her chin forward, and again he noticed how lovely her skin was. Like an airbrushed Cover Girl model. "And what, pray tell, are the charges?"

"Vandalism. Malicious mischief. Terrorizing. And that's just for starters. We're thinking about tossing in a little attempted murder charge to go along with the rest. A rattlesnake's a pretty dangerous weapon to be playing games with."

"Oh, for pity's sake," she said, "I wasn't trying to kill her. I just wanted to frighten her a little. Put the fear of God into her. Make her life a tad more difficult than it already was. I had high hopes that she might take the hint and leave town, but I obviously underestimated her."

"Obviously. Care to tell me why you wanted her to leave Elba,

Mrs. Pepperell?"

"You're the detective," she said. "You figure it out."

"She married Michael," he said, "and you didn't."

Her eyes narrowed with fury. "He was mine," she snapped. "Do you understand that? *Mine!* We were going to be married. Everybody thought I was marrying him for his money and his name, but that wasn't it at all. I was crazy, absolutely *crazy* in love with Michael. And my daddy actually approved of the match. Oh, I knew that Michael'd had his days of catting around, but I had my own methods for dealing with that. I knew I'd tame his wild ways once I got that gold band on his finger." Her voice flattened. "And then *she* came along. Kathryn. That bitch stole him right out from under my nose. I was all set for a June wedding, and he came home from college wearing a wedding ring. Have you ever been betrayed, Mr. DiSalvo? Have you ever been hurt so bad it liked to rip the heart out of your chest?"

Thinking of Lenore, he said truthfully, "Once."

"Then you understand how I felt. I wanted to die. I wanted her to die. I used to drive by their house every night, park at the end of the driveway and sit there in the dark, imagining what they must be doing behind those walls. I used to call on the phone at all hours of the day and night, just to hear the sound of his voice when he answered."

"Did you kill him?" he said softly.

She raised those elegant eyebrows. "Why, everybody knows that Kathryn killed him in a jealous rage because she found out he'd been whoring around on her. Michael had a lot of his daddy in him, Mr. DiSalvo. More than anybody knew, except maybe me, and his momma. Michael had his weaknesses, and one of them was beautiful women. I loved Michael anyway. Even after he betrayed me, even after he married that cold bitch, I still loved him. I would never have done anything to hurt him. But I wanted to hurt her. I wanted that power, that victory, over her. And I got it." Her smile was thin and cruel. "One Christmas Eve at the country club, when Kathryn was home sick with the flu, I gave her husband a very personal Christmas present in the gazebo on the back lawn. It was the high point of my life. You can't imagine how I felt, knowing I'd cuckolded that bitch."

Nick looked at her for a long time, at the elegant sweep of her jaw, the almond-shaped green eyes, the flawless skin. She had the body of a goddess and the soul of a reptile. "Bucky?" he said. "You got the cuffs?"

"Right here, Chief." Bucky held them up like it was show-and-tell day at school.

"Take her in," he said curtly, "and book her."

* * *

The FedEx envelope was waiting on his desk, sent overnight from the State Bureau of Records at Annapolis, Maryland. Timothy Ward Crumley's birth certificate. Nick picked up the package, looked it over, set it back down and brooded over a cup of coffee that was already going cold. He didn't like what he'd learned this morning. The soft, white, decaying underbelly of this town was beginning to be exposed, and he wondered what other surprises lay in store for him.

He set down the coffee and ripped open the envelope. Turned it upside down and shook it, and the photocopied birth certificate fluttered out onto the desk. He picked it up, wondering why he should feel trepidation at uncovering one more rock and finding a snake under it, coiled and ready to strike. He was a cop, for Christ's sake. It was his job to expose people's secrets when it became necessary. And during a homicide investigation, it became imperative.

So why did he feel like a damn Peeping Tom?

He cleared his throat, unfolded the sheet of paper, and began to skim it. Name: *Timothy Ward Crumley*. Date of Birth: *January 16, 1995*. Place of Birth: *Baltimore City Hospital, Baltimore, Maryland*. Mother: *Wanita Joy Crumley*. Father—

"Oh, shit," he said, and closed his eyes. "Oh, shit."

On top of everything else, this was just too much. Wanita could have lied. She was, after all, a whore and a junkie who'd lied under oath. Or had she? If what the birth certificate said was true, her sister's suspicions had been way off target. Whoever Wanita's sugar daddy was, he wasn't the father of her child.

He crumpled up the piece of paper and hurled it at the wall. "Damn it all to hell!" Furious, he got up and stalked over to it, picked it back up and smoothed it out, then read those damning words again, just to be sure he hadn't imagined them. Father:

Michael Jeffrey McAllister.

How the hell was he going to break the news to her that her husband really had been unfaithful to her, not just with one woman, but with at least two different women? He thought about how he'd felt when he'd learned that Lenore had cheated on him. It had been like taking a size thirteen combat boot hard in the gut. How the hell could he do that to her? How the hell could she get through something like that?

The same way she'd gotten through prison. By calling up that steely reserve she had in her spine and forging ahead, without looking to the right or the left. Kathryn Sipowicz McAllister was one tough lady. He wasn't sure he could have been as tough in her place. Her toughness had gotten her this far; it would get her a little farther. But he'd be damned if he was going to be the one to tell her.

The phone rang, and he picked it up absently. "DiSalvo," he said.

"I know," Kathryn began haltingly, "that you have every right to be furious with me. But you have to understand how long this has been eating up my insides. I can't let anything get in the way, Nick. Not until it's over."

He straightened slowly, let Timmy's birth certificate flutter to the desktop. "I'm not mad at you," he said. "Not any more."

"Don't lie to me, DiSalvo. I can hear it in your voice."

He cleared his throat. "No," he said. "Really. I'm just tired. Rough morning."

She hesitated, then said, "What about Georgia Pepperell?"

"We arrested her. I figure she'll make bail by noon at the latest, but it put a serious crimp in her plans for the morning. She had a very important tennis match scheduled with your former mother-in-law."

"What did she say?"

He picked up a pen and began to doodle. "She put up a tough front for a while, but then she crumbled like a cookie and admitted everything. You're not exactly on her top ten list."

"I just bet I'm not. She thought she had Michael all sewn up. It really threw her for a loop when he came home with me tagging along behind him."

He cleared his throat again. "Yeah," he said, "she, ah—she told us that."

"Nick? Are you sure you're okay? You sound funny."

"I'm fine." He doodled a three-dimensional picture of a box. In each of the four corners, he wrote a name: *Ruby, Kevin, Michael, Wanita.* What was the common denominator that brought them together? Where was the intersecting line where their lives collided?

"You sound so distant," Kathryn said.

"What? Oh, sorry. I'm just thinking. Trying to puzzle it all out. It's driving me crazy. I have this feeling that I'm missing something. Something so simple that I'm not seeing it, even though it's staring me in the face."

"We'll find it. We have to."

"We're getting close. The back of my neck is itching like crazy. Listen, Kat? I'm sorry for coming down on you like that last night. I had no right."

She paused. "I'd like to think," she said, "that you had every right."

His heart began to thud in a rapid, irregular motion. "What are you saying?"

"I'm saying that when this is over, when we've put it all to rest, we're going to talk about us, Nick. There's a lot that needs to be said."

"I would like to see you tonight," he said. "I would like to spend an evening with you, a nice, normal evening, one that doesn't end with a visitation from the entire Elba police force. Do you think we could accomplish that?"

"I don't know, DiSalvo. We could try."

"Janine's going to Sylvie's tonight to spend the evening trading Leonardo DiCaprio pictures. Why don't you come over to my place? I'll throw a steak on the barbecue, we'll put on some music. I have some great jazz CD's. Do you like jazz?"

"I love jazz."

"Great. We'll put on some jazz, and then we'll turn out the lights and sit on the couch and make out like a couple of teenagers."

"You do know how to tempt a woman, DiSalvo. What time should I be there?"

"Seven-ish okay?"

"Seven-ish is fine. I'll see you then."

He hung up the phone, feeling good for the first time since he'd left Georgia Pepperell's house. He picked up Timmy Crumley's birth certificate and looked at it again. And then he crumpled it up and tossed it in the trash.

The less she knew about Michael McAllister's sordid past, the better.

* * *

She and Elvis went running, along her favorite route, around Lake Alberta and up the County Road, circling back along Myrtle Street to home. Elvis was the ideal running companion. He always stayed at her heel, and he kept his mouth shut. It was a perfect combination. When they got back home, she collapsed on the couch, and he lay his head in her lap and worshipped her with those big, yellow eyes. "What a good doggie you are," she said, rubbing at his ears and his chin. She bent down and he raised his broad snout and lapped her ear, a kiss that was amazingly dainty for so large a dog. "I love you, too, sweetie," she said, and then wondered what kind of twisted priorities allowed her to admit tender feelings for a dog but not for Nick DiSalvo.

"It's complicated," she argued aloud. Christ, she barely knew the man. Had known him for all of two weeks, two weeks that they'd spent alternately sparring with and lusting after each other. It was too soon for tender sentiments. Not to mention that after last night's little exchange between Nick and his daughter, she suspected he was still harboring feelings towards his ex-wife.

"Christ," she said, "what a mess."

Elvis tilted his head and looked at her. "You're lucky," she told him. "For you, love is simple. Be grateful you're not human."

He smiled at her, tongue lolling halfway to the floor. "Get out of here," she said, shoving at his massive chest. "You're drooling all over me."

The phone rang, and she hurried to answer it, grateful for the distraction. She didn't want to examine too closely her feelings for Nick. Not yet. "Hello?" she said.

"Stop asking nosy questions, or you're going to wind up dead."

The voice was low-pitched, muffled, deliberately disguised. She couldn't even tell if it was a man or a woman. Her fingers tightened on the telephone receiver. And then fury bubbled up through her. "Go to hell!" she said, and slammed down the phone.

She was still trembling five minutes later when Elvis let out a short, sharp bark, and somebody knocked on her door. She went to answer it, Elvis by her side. "Who is it?" she said.

"Francis Willoughby."

It took her a moment to recall the name, and then she released Elvis's collar and opened the door. A stubby, balding man stood on her porch, ball cap in hand. "Mr. Willoughby," she said, surprised. "What can I do for you?"

"Nothing, ma'am. I mean, I need to do something for you." He reached into his breast pocket and pulled out a slip of paper. "This here's for you," he said. "I never shoulda kept the money. It was yours. Yours and Mr. McAllister's."

She stared in amazement at the check he held out, made out to her in the amount of two hundred and fifty dollars. "I always figured I'd pay it back some day," he said, "and now's my chance."

"You don't have to do this," she said.

"Well, yes, ma'am, I do. Will you please accept it?"

She softened. "Of course I will. Come in." And she opened the screen door for him. "Can I get you a glass of lemonade?"

With his sleeve, he discreetly wiped a bead of sweat from his face. "I sure would appreciate that, Miz. McAllister."

She hung the check on the refrigerator with a magnet, and got out the lemonade pitcher. "Nice little house," he said from the living room. "Squarely built."

"Yes," she said. "I'm renting it from a friend."

"Not like that Chandler place," he said. "Never saw any place such a mess. Crooked floors, sagging ceilings, bulges in the walls. Doorways all off kilter. If it'd been built plumb in the first place, it wouldn't have settled that way."

She returned to the living room and handed him the lemonade. "Thank you, ma'am," he said, and downed half of it in one long swallow.

"So the Chandler place wasn't exactly a contractor's dream?"

"Hell—I mean heck—no. And that kitchen was straight out of the nineteenth century. Mr. McAllister was insistent that everything be new and modern for you. Said he didn't want to see you working so hard. And that crooked little wall between the kitchen and the dining room just had to go. It wasn't a bearing wall, so it really wasn't necessary, and all it did was block the light from the dining room windows. Somebody'd replastered it a few years back, and they didn't have a clue what they was doing. It was an eyesore, all lumps and bumps and bulges. So we was gonna take it down when we gutted the kitchen. It woulda opened that space up right nice."

He finished the lemonade, thanked her again, and went on his way. After he was gone, she sat back down on the couch, wondering why she was so unsettled by his visit. There was something, something right at the edge of her mind, the tip of her tongue, something that just wouldn't break through from the subconscious to the conscious. Frustrated, she tried to call Nick back, but Rowena said he was out. So she shoved it aside, concentrated instead on the threatening phone call she'd received. *Stop asking nosy questions, or you're going to wind up dead.* It was the same thing Wanita had told her, only Wanita was the one who'd turned up dead.

She was getting closer to Michael's killer. The phone call was proof. She was on the right track and closing in, and the killer was getting nervous. As well he should be, because Kathryn McAllister was going to nail his hide to the wall.

She was in the shower, washing off her morning run and thinking of something else altogether when it broke through, so simple she couldn't believe she'd overlooked it, couldn't believe Nick hadn't thought of it yet. If it hadn't been for Francis Willoughby's visit, it might never have occurred to her.

The house. There was something in the house.

* * *

She found Michael's spare house key right where she expected it to be, scotch-taped to the inside of a turquoise folder labeled *mortgage*. As long as Kevin and Neely hadn't changed the locks, what she was about to do couldn't technically be called breaking and entering, since she had a key. She hoped that the worst they could get her for was tresspassing. She dressed in black jeans and a black tee shirt, pocketed the key, shut Elvis in the kitchen, and went outside to her car.

When she turned the key, the engine made a soft growling sound, then died. It figured. She'd spent sixty bucks this morning for a new tire, and now the damn thing wouldn't start. She popped the hood and looked under it. The battery terminals were old and corroded, and the battery itself looked like there was a good chance it had come over on the Mayflower. She glanced at her watch. It was already 6:45, and Nick was expecting her at seven. Disgusted, she slammed down the hood and headed off on foot.

It was nearly ten past seven when she reached his house. She went into the entry hall and knocked on the door of his apartment. When he didn't answer, she opened the door a crack. "Nick?" she said.

There was still no answer, but Pat Metheny was playing softly on the stereo, and she let herself in. She found him just beyond the French doors, on the backyard patio, standing over a sizzling steak. "You're late," he said.

She brushed the hair back from her face. "My battery's dead. I had to walk."

He glanced up, saw the expression on her face, the way she was dressed. "Why do I have the feeling," he said, "that this isn't going to be a nice, normal date after all?"

"It's the house, Nick."

He looked at her blankly. "What house?"

"There's something in the house. I don't know why I didn't think of it sooner. But Willoughby came by today and paid me back the money Michael gave him, and—"

"Whoa. Slow down. Willoughby who?"

"Francis Willoughby," she said impatiently. "The contractor. Michael hired him to remodel the kitchen a couple of weeks before he died. I think that's why he was killed. There's something in the house, and he was about to stumble across it. The killer couldn't let that happen, so he had to get rid of Michael."

He digested her words, and an odd gleam lit his eyes. "Ruby Jackson," he said.

She nodded, adrenaline racing through her veins. "Ruby's in the house somewhere, Nick." Now that she was so close, she could barely contain her excitement. "And I think I know where."

chapter sixteen

It was an overcast night, a mixed blessing, for the darkness gave them cover, but there was no moonlight to illuminate their way. They parked the Blazer out on the shore of Lake Alberta, in the turnout where she'd waited in vain for Wanita, and she led him in the back way. In the darkness, all she could see of Nick was his hands as his shadowy form preceded her through dense forest, shoving aside hardwood branches, tangling in kudzu vines, skirting stands of palmetto and squeezing past the massive trunks of loblolly pine. In her hand, she carried his high-powered flashlight. In his, he carried a crowbar.

They skirted the edge of the swamp that connected with one end of Lake Alberta. There were millions of live things out there in that murky water, creatures that came out at night to buzz and slither and croak. She'd even heard stories about alligators, although she wasn't sure she believed them. A bullfrog made his low, plucked-banjo sound nearby, and she gasped and stumbled, falling directly into Nick. He reached out a hand to catch her. "You all right?" he said.

"I'm sorry. He startled me."

"Are you sure this is the right way?"

"I'm sure. I lived in that house for four years. I know my way around."

He stood there for a moment, surveying the swamp, while her fingers clutched at the warm fabric of his shirt. "How frigging big is this damn swamp?" he said.

199

"I don't know. Huge. It goes on forever, all the way to the Old Raleigh Road."

"That must be two or three miles from here."

"Do you suppose we could move along?" she said. "This place is full of water moccasins."

"You've got me convinced. Hang onto my belt loop or something. I don't want to lose you in the dark."

The continued their slow progress, Nick leading, Kathryn navigating, until the denseness gave way to scrub brush and the occasional poplar. "This way," she said, and they broke free of the forest and found themselves at the edge of a grassy field that had once been lawn. "There," she said. "There it is."

The Chandler place sat in front of them, dark and ominous, windows boarded up, a single shutter dangling at an awkward angle. Nick looked to the left, then the right. In the distance, through the trees that bordered the property, there was a faint light. "What's that?" he said.

"That's Harriet Slocum's house. Don't worry, she's seventy-five years old and deaf as a post. She sits in front of the TV every night with the volume blasting so loud they can hear it downtown. The Concorde could take off over her head and she wouldn't know it."

They crossed the lawn together, climbed up the steps and stopped at the back door. "I want you to know," he said, "that I've been a cop for sixteen years. I've never done anything illegal in my life. Never even lifted a pack of cigarettes when I was a kid. But what we're about to do is illegal as hell."

"I know."

"I could lose my job over this."

"You don't have to do it, DiSalvo. If you want to walk away right now, I'll never hold it against you. I can do this by myself."

"There's nobody else in the world I'd do this for."

"I know."

He lowered his head and kissed her tenderly. Her arms went around him and she stretched up on her toes to reach him, hungry for his touch. He ended the kiss, and she fell against his chest, both of them breathing with difficulty.

"Nick?" she said into the darkness.

His fingers played in her hair. "What?" he said.

She ran a finger up the back of his neck and into his hair. Wet her lips. "Never mind," she said.

He patted her cheek, dropped a hard kiss on her chin and released her. "Key?" he said.

She fumbled in her pocket, handed it to him, rested her hand on his forearm and crossed the fingers of her other hand while he slipped the key into the lock. "Oh, baby," he said as it slid home, "the eagle has landed."

Her fingers tightened on his forearm as he eased the door open. It squeaked like a rusty coffin lid, and she caught her breath, afraid somebody would hear. "Careful," he whispered. "The threshold's warped. Don't trip over it."

"I won't."

Still holding onto him, she stepped over the warped threshold and into the house where her life had come to an abrupt end four years earlier. Perhaps it was fitting that this was where her life would begin again, on this night, with this man. "It's darker than the inside of a dog in here," he said. "Shut the door behind you so I can turn on the flashlight."

She eased the door shut, locking it for good measure, and they were in total darkness. Something scurried past her foot, and she gasped. Nick took the flashlight from her and clicked it on, and three huge cockroaches scurried away from the beam of light. "Jesus," he said.

The house had that musty odor that all abandoned houses have, a combination of dust and mold and mouse droppings. Beneath it, faint but still discernible, was the rusty tang of blood. Even if they'd had the carpets cleaned after the murder, she knew the smell would still be there. For a moment, she felt physically ill as it struck her again, the godawful ripe, sweet scent of Michael's blood as it pooled into the white shag carpet beneath his lifeless body. Bile rose in her throat and she retched, and Nick sat her down hard on the floor and shoved her head between her knees. "Kat?" he said.

Tears stung her eyelids as she struggled to bring her stomach under control. "I'm okay," she said, pushing him away. "I'm okay!"

"We shouldn't be here," he said. "This is too much for you. I should've just got a court order and come in here and got it over with. This skulking around in the dark is ridiculous."

"I'm all right now. The smell of blood hit me, and for a minute, I was right back there in that upstairs bedroom, with the rain falling on the roof and thunder rolling outside, and Michael dead on the floor."

"You okay now?"

"I'm okay."

He touched her cheek with gentle fingers. "You're one tough cookie."

She raised her head and looked up at him. "Damn right I am, DiSalvo!"

Still touching her cheek, he said gently, "Come on, McAllister, let's see if we can find Ruby."

He played the flashlight beam around the room, highlighted the ancient enamel appliances, the old-fashioned flowered wallpaper, the broken window over the sink. "Over here," she said, and led him to the wall that Willoughby had been talking about. It was only four feet long, and ran between the doorways that led to bathroom and dining room. It was thicker than most walls, and she suspected that at one time a chimney had run through it. On the other side, the dining room sat bleak and empty, and she wondered what had happened to the beautiful oak dining set she and Michael had bought.

"Here," he said. "Hold the flashlight."

She aimed it past his head, at the wall. It wasn't papered like the others. Instead, it had been painted a color that had probably once been white, but which was now a dingy gray. Nick brushed aside a spider and played his fingertips over the surface of the wall. "Rough," he said.

"That's what Willoughby said. That whoever plastered it didn't have a clue what they were doing. She slowly scanned the flashlight beam lower. "See how it bulges?"

"Doesn't necessarily mean anything. It's an old house. Everything's crooked."

"Don't shoot down my theory now, DiSalvo."

"I'm not shooting down anything." He lifted the crowbar and tapped gently. Held his ear up to the wall and tapped again, while she leaned forward, her chin almost digging into his shoulder in her eagerness.

"Do you hear anything?" she said.

"Shh." While he listened, he tapped again, lower. "Come here," he said.

They traded places and he showed her where to listen. "Okay," he said, "I'm going to tap in two different spots, and I want you to tell me what you hear."

She closed her eyes to concentrate, and he tapped the wall down low, about a foot above the baseboard. "Sounds hollow," she said.

"Now listen." He moved the crowbar up to her approximate shoulder height and tapped it. There was no echo. It sounded solid as an oak tree.

"Do you think something's in there?"

"Sure sounds it to me. Look, where I tapped up here—" He pointed with the crowbar. "—it's right in line with the hollow spot down here. If it was some kind of a joist, it would go all the way, floor to ceiling. But it doesn't. It stops right about—" He bent and tapped near her knees. "Here."

The full ramifications of what she'd suspected hadn't hit her until now. If it were indeed Ruby Jackson inside that hollow wall, there were ethical considerations that must be taken into account. Ruby had lived her life with joy, and dignity. But what kind of dignity would she maintain with strangers gaping at her fleshless skeleton?

Outside, on the street, a car slowed and turned into the driveway. Nick spun around, his eyes wild as they met hers. "Turn off the damn light!" he said.

She plunged them into instant darkness as a car door slammed outside. "Shit," he said, grabbing her arm. "Upstairs! Now!"

Flashlight in hand, she guided him through the darkness to the stairs, moving as silently as possible up the staircase she knew so well. "Hurry," he whispered as somebody slid a key into the kitchen door lock and turned the handle.

She all but dragged him through the nearest door. Her old bedroom. The bloodstained carpet muffled their footsteps. "There's a closet," she whispered, feeling for the door, her heart hammering as footsteps walked across the kitchen floor. Frantic, she felt the wall, and then she found the closet door. They dove inside and Nick yanked it shut behind them, catching it at the last minute before it could slam. "If you crawl," she said, "the storage space extends under the eaves."

"Go!" he said, and shoved her in ahead of him. On her hands

and knees, she scrabbled like a crab, until she hit solid wall and realized she'd come to the end.

"This is as far as it goes," she whispered.

"Set down the flashlight," he whispered. "Trade places."

In the cramped space, he squeezed past her and sat on the floor, his back against the wooden studding of the eave. Leaning forward because there was no head room, he pulled her up tight between his thighs. Hearts hammering in unison, they sat glued together, his arms around her from behind, his legs wrapped around hers, while beneath them the heavy footsteps moved slowly from room to room. In that small, enclosed space where there was no room to move an inch, it must have been well over a hundred degrees. Sweat dampened her forehead and fear quickened her breathing. Something with more than four legs ran down her arm. She gasped, opened her mouth to cry out, and he clapped his hand over her mouth. "Shh," he whispered into her ear, and rocked her back and forth. "Shh..."

Terror twisted her insides as those slow, deliberate footsteps climbed the stairs. They turned down the hall, and behind her, Nick let out a hard breath. The heat was nearly unbearable as her overtaxed lungs sucked in humid, searing air. They were both sodden with sweat, and she was starting to feel faint. The footsteps returned, came into the bedroom, and stopped. Nick's hand tightened on her mouth. The closet door opened, and they both stopped breathing. She could feel the erratic racing of Nick's heart as a flashlight beam, thin and weak, played around the corners of the closet, poked into the crawl space, missing them by inches. Her heart was thundering so loudly she was certain the intruder must be able to hear it.

Except that in this instance, they were the intruders.

The door shut, and still neither of them dared to breathe. Her lungs burned as though she'd inhaled chlorine, and then the footsteps went back out into the hall and down the stairs to the living room.

She let out a huge breath, gulped in another one while behind her Nick did the same. Kathryn uttered a tiny sob, and his hand again closed over her mouth. He tightened his arm around her, dropped a feather-light kiss on her temple. "We'll be okay," he whispered. "He's leaving now."

The kitchen door opened and shut, and moments later, they heard the car back out of the driveway and head down the street.

Nick removed his hand from her mouth. Limp and wet and ragged, she scooted across the floor on the seat of her jeans until she reached the opening that led back into the closet. She scrambled to her feet, then turned and held out a hand to help him up.

The crowbar still in his hand, he swept her into his arms and they stood together, limp and trembling violently, for a very long time. "Come on," he said finally, brushing a cobweb from her hair, "let's get the hell out of this creepy place."

* * *

"Who do you think it was?" she said as she sipped at the coffee he'd spiked with rum especially for the occasion. In his kitchen, their freshly laundered clothes tumbled in the clothes dryer. They'd both showered, and she was sitting on his couch, feet up on the coffee table, wearing the ugly striped bathrobe that Lenore had bought him years ago. It made him look like a troll, but on Kathryn, it looked sexy as hell.

In the rocking chair across from her, he sipped his coffee and considered her question. He'd been considering it since long before she asked it, since the moment that car had pulled into the driveway of the Chandler place. Nobody could possibly have known they were there. Even the eyes and ears of this town weren't that good. Which could mean only one thing. The killer knew damn well they were hot on his ass, and he was keeping close watch over his most closely guarded secret. "It was a man," he said.

"Heavy footsteps," she said. "It could have been a large woman."

"He was wearing men's shoes. I could tell by the sound."

"What do you think he would have done if he'd found us?"

He looked at her levelly over the rim of his cup. "You don't really want me to answer that question, do you?"

She set down her coffee and rubbed both hands over her face. "What happens next?"

"Next," he said, "we get a court order, and we go in and open up the wall."

"Without asking Neely and Kevin for their permission?"

He rested the coffee cup on his knee. "If we spook them, there's always the chance they'll run. I'd rather not take that chance."

"You think it was Kevin, then?"

"Whoever it was had a key to the place."

"True. But so did we."

"Mmn." He studied her in the ratty old robe that was five sizes too big. "Kat?" he said. "Come sit with me."

She hesitated for just a moment, and then she got up and crossed the room to him. He held out his arms, and she settled herself on his lap. He drew her head down to his shoulder and buried his face in her hair and began to rock the chair in a slow, easy rhythm.

He'd missed this in his marriage to Lenore, this simple pleasure derived wholly from being close to another human being he cared for. Lenore had preferred that he show his affection in more material ways. She'd been more concerned with making sure her hair and her nails looked just right, more concerned with ensuring that their Christmas display had at least as many colored lights as any on the block, than she had with taking any pleasure from just being with him.

But Kathryn understood the simple pleasures, understood the importance of something as elementary as touch, possibly because for four years she'd been deprived of it. "You smell like soap," he said.

"Mmn."

"You tired?"

"Mmn."

"Stay here tonight. Janine's staying over with Sylvie. Her new best friend. We can sleep in her bed. Which," he added, "come to think of it, was my bed until she showed up."

"I don't know," she said. "I'm not sure I feel right about it."

"What? I assure you that my intentions are thoroughly honorable. Even I'm not cheesy enough to make whoopie in my daughter's bed. I just want to sleep with you. That's all."

She touched his face with her fingertips, and he caught her hand in his and kissed it. "All right," she said. "I didn't really want to be alone tonight anyway."

He turned out all the lights and locked the doors, and they fell into bed, exhausted and drained. He drew her into his arms, his breath fluttering the hair that lay against her cheek. She snuggled closer against him, this human dynamo who had survived things that would destroy most women, and he closed his eyes and followed her into sleep.

It was the ringing that woke him. It tore him out of sleep, and he reached out blindly to shut off the alarm. But it wasn't that. It wasn't his pager, either. He finally came awake enough to realize it was the telephone, and he fumbled for the cordless, pushed buttons until he got the right one. "DiSalvo," he said, his voice still thick with sleep.

"Sorry to wake you, Chief," Teddy said. "But I thought you'd better hear this right away."

He came instantly awake. "What?" he said.

"The fire department just got a call from Minnie Rawlings. That house Kathryn McAllister's living in? It's on fire."

* * *

By the time they got there, the house was engulfed. A sheet of flame licked at the roof, and black smoke billowed out the shattered windows. He brought the Blazer to a screeching halt in Minnie's driveway, and he and Kathryn both went running, tripping over fire hoses and trying to stay out of the way of Elba's stalwart volunteer firemen. A powerful spray of water shot up into the air and fell on the roof, but it was clear to any observer that the house was going to be a total loss.

Kathryn paused on the lawn, her hand over her mouth in horror. Nick left her there, climbing over hoses until he found the fire chief. "What the hell happened?" he said.

Ashley Dillon gazed at him through red-rimmed, smoky eyes. "Some joker poured gasoline all around the place and then lit her up."

"Son of a bitch! Son of a fucking bitch!"

Kathryn came up behind him and grabbed his sleeve. "My dog," she said in an odd, high voice. "Christ, Nick, my dog was in there."

He put an arm around her. She was trembling like a willow in a high wind. "The dog?" he asked Dillon.

"I dunno. We were a little more concerned about whether she was in there. Car's in the yard, you know. Whoever set it must've thought she was inside."

It hit him between the eyes like a twenty-pound ball peen hammer. This wasn't just arson. It was three o'clock in the morning, and Kathryn's Toyota was sitting in the driveway. Whoever set this fire thought she was inside the house.

And he wanted to make damn sure that she came out in a body bag.

"My dog," she said again, faintly, and then she sat down hard on the wet grass and began to weep with a fury that, once unleashed, sent harsh sobs through her entire body. It was the first illogical woman-thing he'd ever seen her do, and Nick stared at her in disbelief. After all she'd been through, after everything they'd done to her, after they'd tried to fucking *kill* her, it was a goddamn dead dog she cried over. "I'll buy you another fucking dog!" he roared. "Don't you understand, it could have been you that got turned into a freaking Tater Tot!"

She raised her head, her wet eyes narrowed with fury. "I happened to *love* that goddamn dog, DiSalvo! Not that I'd expect you to understand!"

"Kat. Sweetheart." Ignoring the raised eyebrows and the knowing looks exchanged by the firefighters and the curious crowd of onlookers, he knelt beside her on the grass. "Whoever set this fire was trying to kill you. Jesus Christ, Kathryn, it could have been you in there. What if you'd gone home tonight?"

Up until now, he'd managed to maintain a certain distance from what was going on around him. As a police officer, it was his duty to maintain that distance. Until this moment, he'd been able to do it. But this fire had turned it personal. And if he ever got hold of the son of a bitch who did this, he'd rip off his balls and shove them down his throat.

"Miz McAllister?" Sonny Turcotte paused beside them, his face sooty and his hair standing up like rooster tails on top of his head. "You missing a dog? A big ugly one?"

They both looked up, and hope lit her face. "Yes," she said.

"He went out through a window, ma'am. Got himself cut up a bit in the process. I sent him over to Doc Winslow to get patched up, but he looked okay. I imagine you can swing by and pick him up in the morning."

She scrambled to her feet and threw her arms around the surprised firefighter. "You don't know how important that dog is to me."

Sonny patted her back awkwardly. "I understand, ma'am. I have a dog myself."

* * *

It was a somber group that gathered at the Chandler place the next afternoon. Kathryn, wearing the same jeans and tee shirt she'd worn the night before, now the only clothes she owned. Nick, wrinkled and unshaven, running on caffeine and two hours of sleep. Bucky, his uniform pressed and his customary exuberant expression tamed into one of appropriate solemnity. A nervous Francis Willoughby, pressed into service fifteen minutes earlier, when the court order finally came through. Dwayne Sampson, one of Willoughby's construction workers, who was there for the muscle and told Nick that it might be cool to see somebody who'd been dead that long.

And last but not least, the Reverend Aloysius Kingston, pastor of the church Ruby had attended as a girl. He was there at Kathryn's insistence, and Nick hadn't even bothered to try to argue with her. It was a battle he wouldn't have won.

The back door had been left open, and they'd brought several battery-powered spotlights and a variety of tools. They stood around in a hushed semi-circle, each of them looking at the wall and thinking private thoughts, and then Nick said, "Okay, boys, let's open her up."

Dwayne hefted the pickax over his muscled shoulder and swung it mightily. It made contact with a heavy thud, and plaster fell in a hail of powdery pieces to the floor. He raised it again, and again it hit the wall, making a huge indentation. "Stuff's tough," he said. "Just like cement. It don't want to come down."

"Give it another good one," Nick said. "Just try not to destroy what's behind it."

Kathryn moved to Nick's side, leaned against him, and he put an arm around her. Dwayne swung the hammer again. This time, it broke through. When he pulled it from the wall, they were all holding their breath and straining to see what was behind it.

It was the smell that hit her first, the smell of old decay, trapped inside the wall for nearly thirty years. She felt Nick's body stiffen, and she knew he'd smelled it before. Dwayne looked at them uncertainly, and Nick nodded. "Keep going," he said curtly.

The pickax swung again, and a huge chunk of plaster fell from the wall. Ruby had been wearing a red dress on the day she died. Fragments of it still clung to her slender frame. As Dwayne swung the ax again, Kathryn turned away from the sight and buried her face against Nick's shoulder. "I didn't want to be right," she said. "Oh, God, Nick, I didn't want to be right."

Nick patted her shoulder absently. Reverend Kingston said, "Gentlemen—and Miz McAllister—I think we should take a moment to pray for Ruby."

There was a moment of silence, and they all bowed their heads. "Lord," the Reverend said, "we're all here today, asking you to look kindly upon the soul of Ruby Jackson, who departed this world for a better one twenty-six years ago. We're praying also that those of us here today won't be judged harshly for disturbing her resting place. We thank you, Lord, for your wonderful mercy in allowing us to return Ruby, finally, to the folks who love her, the folks who for twenty-six years never let a day go by without hoping she'd come home to them. And last, Lord, we ask you to forgive the one who's responsible for her being here. We pray for his immortal soul. Amen."

There was a chorus of murmured amens, and as Dwayne raised the ax again, Nick drew Bucky aside. "Get the coroner over here," he said, "and an ambulance. Try to keep it quiet, I don't want it getting around just yet. Oh, and call Eloise Fitzgerald and tell her we're pretty sure we've found her sister. Ask about dental records."

"Yes, sir."

He patted Bucky on the shoulder. "Think you can handle things from here?"

"Yes, sir!"

"You're in charge. I have to go see a man about a horse."

Kathryn followed him out into sweet, fresh air. She filled her lungs with it, emptying them of the scent of decay. "I'm coming with you," she said.

When he turned around, he was wearing his cop face. "This is a police matter, Kat. I can't take you along."

"Damn you, DiSalvo! This was my deal from the beginning, and I'm not through until I get answers!"

He stopped and took her by the shoulders so hard his fingers bit into her tender flesh. "I have no idea," he said, "what's going to go down here tonight. I want you where I know you're safe. Last time somebody tried to kill you, they missed. Next time, we might not be so lucky."

"It's not fair," she said. "You know it's not fair."

"I'll let you know the minute I know anything. I promise. It's the best I can give you, Kathryn." He lowered his head and kissed her, but her lips remained stiff and unresponsive. "Don't be this way," he said.

She ran her fingers up the side of his neck, over his ear and into his hair. "You're the most infuriating man I've ever met."

He fumbled in his pocket and pulled out a set of car keys. "Here," he said, putting them in her hand and closing her fingers around them. "Take the Blazer. Go home and get Janine and get the hell out of Elba. Both of you. Drive to Fayetteville or Raleigh and take a motel room." He pulled out his wallet, gave her his ATM card and fifty dollars in cash. "The PIN number's 5163," he said. "That's my birthdate. There's about eight hundred in my account. You can use the card to pay for the room. Don't trust anybody. Don't tell anybody where you're going, and make sure nobody follows you. Call me tonight and tell me where you are."

She looked up into those melted-chocolate eyes. "I'm not one of your officers," she said, "that you can push around."

"Why the hell do I torture myself, keeping you around?"

"It must be my magnetic personality."

He fingered a strand of her hair. "Look, I know you wanted to be there. But this is getting nasty. I want you and Janine as far away from it as you can get. You remember what I said? All of it?"

"I remember."

"What's the PIN number?"

"May 1, 1963."

He cupped the back of her neck in his hand. "Be careful," he said. "I don't want to lose either one of you." He kissed her a final time, and then he released her and stalked off toward Bucky's police cruiser.

The Blazer was a man's vehicle, with a massive stick shift and a clutch that would have given a lumberjack pause. She adjusted the mirrors and left the police radio on, just in case something interesting should come across the wire. She drove at a sedate pace through downtown Elba, then cut off onto Myrtle Street and swung by the smoldering remains of her house. The Fire Marshal was parked out front, and several grim-faced men sifted through the ruins. Kathryn stopped for a moment to watch, sickened by the sight. She'd managed to get through to Raelynn this morning in Atlanta, and with typical good humor, her friend had told her not to worry, that the house was fully insured. "I'll be home tonight," she'd said. "I'm just glad that you and your ugly dog are both all right."

Minnie Rawlings, seeing her in the Blazer, scuttled across the street. "Ain't it something?" she said. "Why, that little house has been there since my momma was a girl. It's a pure shame. And how's your poor dog?"

"He's going to be fine," she said. "He had a couple of pretty deep cuts that Doc Winslow had to stitch up. Doc's keeping him in the kennel until I have a place to take him. Look, Minnie, I have to run. I'm in a bit of a hurry."

"Sure, honey. Now y'all take care of yourself, you hear?"

She drove to Nick's place and let herself into the apartment with his house key. "Janine?" she said.

Her greeting was met by silence. The apartment was empty. She went upstairs and knocked on Caroline's door. "Have you seen Janine?" she asked Nick's elegant landlady.

"Not since yesterday," Caroline said, "when my sister picked her up to spend the night with Sylvie. Want me to give Karen a call?"

"Would you?"

"Sure. Come on in."

She waited in the foyer while Caroline talked on the phone. "Nope," she said when she returned. "Janine's not there. Karen dropped her off here around three o'clock this afternoon. I wouldn't worry, she's probably just gone downtown. She's been pretty restless, all alone in that apartment every day while Nick's at work."

Kathryn went back downstairs and flicked on the television. At this time of day, the airwaves overflowed with talk shows that were little more than a hopped-up version of the sleazy confession magazines she and her girlfriends used to hide under their mattresses when they were teenagers. *I Slept With My Sister's Husband, and Now I'm Pregnant With His Baby.* Sensation and cheap sex. She wondered if Janine watched this garbage. Home alone all day, she probably did. What else was there for a thirteen-year-old girl to do in this place? And God only knew what kind of ideas that sort of sleaze put into the mind of an impressionable young girl. She would have to talk to Nick about it. The girl needed some kind of guidance, and she certainly wasn't getting it from either of her parents.

She turned off the television and began pacing the kitchen. It was getting later by the minute, and if she didn't follow his orders, Nick would probably tear her head off. He was a man accustomed to being obeyed. But she couldn't very well leave town without Janine. And the truth was that she didn't want to be in Fayetteville or Raleigh anyway. She wanted to be here, in Elba, right smack in the middle of this whole stinking mess. *Her* stinking mess.

She opened each of the kitchen cupboards in turn, hoping to find something to distract her. Everything in Nick's cupboards was either canned or instant. The man lived like a barbarian. He was badly in need of a woman to take care of him. It seemed that the only thing he knew how to cook was steak. She grimaced, imagining his arteries clogged with all that saturated fat. If somebody didn't take him in hand, he'd die of a heart attack before he was forty-five.

The telephone rang, and she automatically went to answer it. "DiSalvo residence," she said.

And the voice, that raspy, muffled voice, said, "I've got the girl."

* * *

The McAllisters were entertaining. There were four or five cars in the driveway besides Neely's Caddy and Kevin's Lincoln Town Car. From somewhere behind the house came the soft tinkle of laughter and the charred odor of barbecued beef. "Prepare yourself," he warned Linda Barden when Althea opened the door. "You're about to enter an alien universe."

The maid eyed them coolly from beneath raised eyebrows. "I don't believe I saw your names on tonight's guest list," she said.

"Good evening, Althea," he said jovially. "No, I imagine you didn't. I'd like to speak to Judge McAllister. And his lovely wife."

"They're busy," she said flatly.

"I can see that. And while I'm sure their social obligations are of the utmost importance, what I have to say to them can't wait. Now be a good girl and get them for me, before I have to arrest you for obstruction of justice."

She looked at him from beneath lowered lids. And sniffed. "Wait in the parlor," she said.

"Of course," he said. "Wouldn't want any of the guests to be offended by our uniforms."

The parlor furniture was upholstered in pastel shades of peach and green. "Poverty," Linda said, looking around the room, "is such a tragedy."

"Isn't it, though?"

It was a good ten minutes before he heard the rapid *click-click* of Neely's heels on the parquet floor of the hall, followed by Kevin's heavier, more leisurely footsteps. Were they the same footsteps he and Kathryn had listened to last night while they hovered in terror in that tiny crawl space beneath the eaves?

"Mr. DiSalvo," Neely said, her reptilian eyes cold with fury. "How dare you come to our home when we're entertaining guests and embarrass us this way? I demand that you come back at a more appropriate time, like any civilized person would do."

"Before we get started here," he said pleasantly, "you might want to shut the door. Lower the embarrassment factor a little."

Neely gazed at him without speaking, and then she walked across the floor and quietly shut the door. "All right," she said, and folded her arms across her bony chest. "State your business, Mr. DiSalvo, so that Kevin and I can get back to our guests."

Amiably, he said, "Actually, Mrs. McAllister, my business is kind of complex, you know? So I thought it would be easier if we dealt with this one issue at a time. Is that okay with you?"

"Make it quick!" she snapped.

"I couldn't have said it better myself. Issue number one is Wanita Crumley. A close personal friend of yours, Judge, according to my sources. Would you care to tell us about your relationship with her?"

Kevin McAllister's face paled, and his nostrils flared. "I didn't have a relationship with her," he said.

"That's not what I hear. I hear she had a rich gentleman friend who paid her bills and gave her spending money. Dewey kept asking her to marry him, but she kept turning him down because she didn't want to let go of her sugar daddy. Are you telling me that wasn't you?"

McAllister opened his mouth. Closed it. "It was me," he said. "But it's not like you think."

"Please, Kevin," Neely said. "I've known about your sexual escapades for more than thirty years. Now's hardly the time to start lying about them."

"I'm not lying," he said.

"Oh, for pity's sake," Neely said, "any idiot could see—"

"It was the boy," he said. "I gave her money because of the boy."

Neely's mouth clamped abruptly shut. "The boy?" she said.

"Timmy. Wanita's oldest boy. He was Michael's."

Neely turned the color of an old bedsheet. "Are you telling me that Michael fathered a child with that awful woman?"

"He's our grandchild, Neely. The only one we're ever going to have."

"The woman was a tramp. She probably lied. Michael wouldn't have—"

"Have you ever looked at the boy, Neely? Blond hair, blue eyes. Built just like Michael was at that age."

"Which brings us to issue number two," Nick said. "Michael. Your son."

They both looked at him. "I have this theory," he said. "It goes kinda like this. Wanita Crumley was killed because she knew who killed Michael. The killer couldn't risk being exposed, so he had to do away with her. Ditto for Michael. Except that he was killed because he was about to stumble across something huge, something that would have put a certain somebody behind bars for a very long time."

"I don't understand," Kevin said.

"Bear with me. It'll all make sense in a minute. Issue number three: Ruby Jackson."

Neely gasped, and Kevin's forehead wrinkled in puzzlement. "Ah," Nick said, "I see you remember her. But I imagine you don't know that a couple of hours ago, we pulled Ruby's body out of the kitchen wall of the Chandler place. Now, we all know the rather seamy history of that particular address. Home to the Businessmen's Benevolent Association, an organization of which you were a charter member, Judge. Considering that you and your wife currently own the property, not to mention that according to Ruby's older sister, at the time she disappeared, Ruby was carrying your child—well, I have to say, sir, this doesn't look very good for you."

Kevin went white as a corpse. Neely clutched at her husband's arm in a protective gesture. "That is the most preposterous accusation I've ever heard!" Her voice trembled as her composure began to unravel, one elegant thread at a time. "You're actually suggestin' that my husband murdered that girl? And placed her inside a wall?"

Nick shook his head in sympathetic disbelief. "I know," he said. "Shocking, isn't it? By the way, Judge, feel free to jump in at any time if something should occur to you."

"I didn't kill her," McAllister said quietly.

"So I guess you folks can see the pattern emerging here. Our good friend Judge McAllister, at that time only a lowly barrister, finds out that his young black mistress is in a family way. Since he already has one family, this could prove to be quite a nuisance. But Ruby's insistent. Marry her, or she'll go public. Of course, this would ruin this up-and-coming young man's future as a judge. So he does the only thing he can think of. He knocks her off, and he hides her body inside a wall, where nobody will ever find it and nobody will ever be the wiser. Time goes on, his career flourishes, and everybody forgets Ruby Jackson. Twenty-two years go by, and then, by chance, he hears that his son Michael, who now owns the house in question, is planning to renovate the kitchen as an anniversary gift for his wife, Kathryn. Part of that plan is to tear down the wall where Ruby's body is hidden.

"If the truth came out, it would ruin his life, his career, his reputation. All those years he worked so hard would be for nothing. He can't let that happen. This man who's sent so many people to prison can't go there himself. So he kills his son and frames his daughter-in-law. She gets to take a twenty-five-year vacation, courtesy of the state, instead of him.

"Everything is working out just fine, until Kathryn unexpectedly gets her conviction overturned and comes back to Elba, armed for bear. Things start to deteriorate rapidly, and then Wanita, with whom our boy Kevin has become friendly enough to let a few things slip, decides it's time to 'fess up. But we can't let that happen, can we, folks? So Wanita, like Michael and Ruby before her, gets to take the long sleep. Is everybody following me? Do I need to back up a bit?"

"Kevin did not kill our son," Neely said, her voice quivering. "I can't believe you could think such a terrible thing."

"Judge? Am I anywhere in the ball park?"

"I've done some things in my life," McAllister said through gritted teeth, "of which I am not exactly proud. But I have never killed anybody, Mr. DiSalvo."

"You know, Judge, I really wish I could believe you. You seem like an all right guy. A little twisted sexually, maybe, but hey—that's your business. Different strokes for different folks, right? But at the moment, you're my number-one suspect. You know as well as I do how the system works. You had motive, and you had access to each of the victims. Now all I need is a signed confession. I'm sure you know that the court will look more leniently on you if you admit your guilt."

"I want my lawyer," McAllister said. "This is preposterous."

"Of course," Nick said. "We'll give him a call, soon as we get downtown. Linda? Did you bring the cuffs?"

"Right here, Chief."

"Excellent. Now just hold out your wrists, Judge, this won't hurt a bit. You have the right to remain silent. You have the right to an attorney. If you can't afford an attorney—oh, hell, we might as well not bother with that one, eh, Judge? Let's see, where was I? Anything you say can and will be held against you in—"

"Stop it!" Neely shouted.

He paused dramatically, turned slowly to look at her. "Why, Mrs. McAllister. Is there something you'd like to say?"

Her face was ashen, her body trembling violently. Her eyes began to fill with tears. "Kevin didn't kill Ruby Jackson," she said. "I did."

Kevin McAllister took a step forward. "Neely?" he said.

Nick removed the cuffs from the Judge's wrists. "Ma'am?" he said gently. "Would you like to tell us about it?"

Neely began to weep huge, silent tears. Nick nodded to Linda, and she helped the woman into a chair. "She came to me," Neely said, "and told me the whole story. About the Benevolent Association, and what was going on there. How they took advantage

of young colored girls and used them for their own personal whores.
She was pregnant, said it was Kevin's child. She told me that if he
didn't divorce me and marry her, she was going to the *Gazette* with
the story. I didn't know what to do. If it came out, my life would be
over. It would all be ruined. Kevin's career, his reputation.
Everything. Why, neither of us would have ever again been able to
hold up our heads anywhere in the state of North Carolina." Her eyes
begged Nick to understand the terrible position she'd been placed in.
"So I did the only thing I could do. I strangled her with a silk scarf
that Kevin had given me for my birthday. And then I hid her body
inside that wall. I thought it was fitting, since that's where Kevin's
indiscretions with her had taken place." She looked at her husband
through narrowed eyes. "And then," she said, "I called every one of
the wives and told them what was going on in that place. What their
men were doing there, night after night, while we were sitting home,
playing canasta. And that was the end of the Businessmen's
Benevolent Association."

McAllister was looking at his wife as though he'd never seen
her before. "Michael?" he said hoarsely. "Tell me you didn't kill our
son."

"Of course I didn't kill Michael! He was my child!" She looked
at Nick beseechingly. "My baby," she said. "My only baby. I could
never have any more children after he was born, you see. I had
difficulties with the birth, and they had to remove my womb. I nearly
died. So Michael was special to me, my precious only child. I would
never have done anything to hurt him. I've always believed it was
Kathryn who killed him. But you're saying the murders are related. I
don't understand. I don't understand at all."

Nick rubbed his cheek with the palm of his hand. "Who
knew?" he said. "Who else knew, besides you? You must have had
help, Neely. You're a little tiny thing. You couldn't have plastered
Ruby into that wall by yourself. There had to be somebody else.
Somebody who helped you. Somebody who has a key to the house."

She looked at him in disbelief. "But he wouldn't have—" She
paused, her mind obviously working, trying to fit the pieces together.
Her eyes slowly widened in comprehension. "Oh, blessed Jesus," she
whispered.

"Who, Neely? Who helped you?"

"Shep," she said, covering her eyes with her hands. "Shep

Henley."

chapter seventeen

Kathryn's tongue had turned to sawdust. She moved it around inside her mouth, licked at her lips with it. "What girl?" she said.

"You know what girl," the voice said. "I tried to warn you. I tried to get you to leave it alone. But you wouldn't listen. Now you gotta pay."

Her heart thudding like a sledgehammer, she said, "If you harm a hair on that girl's head, I'll kill you."

He chuckled, soft and low, as though she'd said something clever. "That would be hard, now, wouldn't it, since I'm the one holding all the cards?"

"What do you want?"

"I'll make a trade. The girl for you. You come to me, I let her go."

"How do I know you're telling the truth?"

"You don't. But you can't take the chance, can you?"

Fury swelled inside her, rising up to sit side-by-side with the fear. "Where are you?"

"I timed it, Miz McAllister. Nine minutes. That's how long you have to get here before I kill the girl. If you stop anywhere along the way, if you take the time to call Lover Boy, I'll slit her throat and leave her there for you and DiSalvo to find. It'll be just like Michael all over again, won't it?"

Her stomach turned over. She tried to stifle the sob that rose in her throat, but she wasn't quite successful. "Stop it," she said firmly. "Stop it right now."

"I really hated having to kill him," the voice continued. "But that was before I found out how good it felt to see the look in his eyes when he knew he was dying."

The rage burst, red-hot, inside her. "Put Janine on the phone," she demanded.

"One thing I can say for you, girl. You got a lot of moxie. You still haven't figured out that you ain't the one calling the shots, have you?"

"Who are you?"

"Sorry. You'll have to wait and see. You know the road to Lake Alberta?"

She forced herself to remain calm. If she lost it now, Nick would be pulling his daughter's body from a ditch somewhere. She tried not to think about that possibility. "Yes," she said. "If I remember correctly, it's where you tried to kill me the first time."

He chuckled again. "Good girl," he said. "Now, a half-mile past the lake, there's a dirt road on the left. Just a couple of tire tracks with grass down the middle. Turn in, drive exactly three-tenths of a mile, and stop. And don't bother to try calling anybody on the radio. I got a police radio, and if I hear anything I shouldn't, I kill her. Understood?"

Her heartbeat was steady and rapid. "Yes," she said.

"You got nine minutes. Starting now."

The connection was broken. Kathryn stared for a moment at the phone, then dropped it on the floor. Nick's keys were on the kitchen table. She grabbed them up and flew out of the apartment and down the stairs. The Blazer's door squawked open, and she slammed it shut behind her. Her hands were trembling so hard she fumbled with the keys, finally fit the right one into the ignition. The Blazer started with a roar, and she crammed the stick shift into reverse and shot out of the driveway and into the street, directly in the path of an oncoming car. The car swerved and the driver laid on the horn.

Ignoring him, she shifted into first gear and shot down Oak Street. She took the corner on two wheels and raced toward downtown. The main street was clogged with traffic in Elba's version of a rush hour. She swerved out around a blue minivan and screamed past Carlyle's Barber Shop. On the sidewalk, the old men gaped. A young man attempting to cross the street leaped back out of her way as she pressed the accelerator to the floor and shot straight through the red light.

By some miracle of fate, nobody was coming the other way. She took Cypress Avenue, where the speed limit was a sedate twenty-five, at fifty miles per hour. You never could find a cop when you needed one. Not when they were all tied up somewhere else. At the outskirts of town, she reached the fifty-mile-per-hour speed limit sign, and punched it up to seventy.

She almost missed her turnoff. Kathryn hit the brakes hard, and the Blazer fishtailed. She brought it around, tires screaming, and skidded onto the gravel-topped Swanville Road. Her left front tire hit the soft shoulder and it sucked her in, bringing her to a stop so abrupt that she slammed into the steering column and her head snapped back. For a moment, she saw stars. She shook her head to clear it, and crammed the shifter into reverse. The tires spun. "Come on, you son of a bitch," she said. She shifted it back into first and eased the gas pedal, then reversed it again and punched it. The tires spun, then with a loud whine, they caught traction, and she bounced back up onto the road.

Dust billowed behind her in a thick cloud. She passed Lake Alberta, the lowering sun turning its sparkling water to a soft rose. Passed the turnout where she and Nick had parked the Blazer last night, a lifetime ago. Began watching the shoulder for the dirt road the caller had told her about.

The entrance was overhung with greenery, and she almost drove past it. She skidded to a stop and paused for a moment, not sure the Blazer could navigate terrain this rough. The road was cut through thick forest, and it didn't look passable. But she didn't have a choice. There was no time for debate. Kathryn took a deep breath and cut the steering wheel sharply to the left.

It was like being plunged into night, the foliage was so thick. She glanced at her odometer as she bumped and rattled along what was little more than a path through the woods. The road took a sharp turn to the left toward the lake, and she followed its path through deep grass. When she'd driven precisely three-tenths of a mile, she brought the vehicle to a halt and turned off the engine.

The silence was overwhelming. She sat there, acrid sweat pouring from every possible orifice, her breathing the only sound. The forest was a deep, dark green, shot through with random shafts of sunlight that filtered through leafy treetops. From out of the darkness, Shep Henley appeared in front of her, wearing a police uniform and carrying a hunting rifle. She sat silently, her chest rising and falling, as he approached her.

"Very good, Miz McAllister," he said. "Seven-and-a-half minutes. I'm impressed."

"You son of a bitch."

"You always were a feisty one. Fought like a wildcat that day we arrested you."

"Where is she? Where's Janine?"

Instead of answering, he glanced in the window, checked the back seat, walked around the vehicle and returned to the driver's side. When he opened the door, it squawked loudly. "Needs oil," he said. "Come on. Get out."

It was the dogs she heard first, yipping and whining as Henley's hard fist on the small of her back propelled her forward over uneven ground. Overhanging branches slapped at her face. Brambles caught at her bare arm, tore her skin, and a single drop of red blood beaded up and trickled slowly toward her elbow. "Why?" she said. "Why did you do it? You were a cop. You're supposed to be one of the good guys."

"Kevin," he said in a conversational tone, "was never good enough for Neely. Weak, that's what he is. Always has been. She thought his womanizing would stop after they got married, but it didn't. He wasn't even man enough to hide it from her. Left her home alone four or five nights a week while he was out sticking it to other women." His face hardened. "I begged her to leave him, but Neely's a proud woman. Said she'd made her bed, and she was gonna have to lie in it. I wanted to kill the son of a bitch."

The sound of the dogs grew louder. Kathryn stumbled over a tree root that was hidden in the underbrush. "Where's Janine?" she said.

"And then," Henley said, as though she hadn't spoken, "he got himself mixed up in that Benevolent Association. Nothing more than a damn brothel for spoiled rich boys. Then Neely found out the little tramp was pregnant, and she killed her. She was so scared when she come to me. She didn't know what to do. I couldn't let her go to jail. A woman like Neely—it would've killed her. So I did what I had to do."

"You put Ruby in the wall," she said dully.

"And nobody was ever the wiser until your damn husband decided to remodel the house. It was his own fault he died." Henley's voice rose, thinned, the voice of madness. "I had to keep Neely from going to jail. That was my job. That's why the good Lord put me here on this earth. To take care of her."

They broke through into a clearing and she saw the pickup truck. Four or five hunting dogs were caged in the back, and the dogs broke into loud yapping when they came into view. "Shut up!" Henley yelled.

The dogs fell silent, stood there wagging, watching. "Where's Janine?" she said.

He walked around to the cab of the truck and opened the door. Janine sat on the bench seat, her eyes terrified above the rag he'd used to gag her. Henley pulled a key from his pocket and used it to unlock the handcuffs that bound her to the steering column. He untied the gag, and she ran to Kathryn and flung her arms around her.

"Oh, baby," Kathryn said. "I'm sorry. I'm so sorry."

"It's not your fault. Daddy told me not to trust anybody. But he was wearing a uniform. He told me he worked for Daddy. I believed him."

"It's all right," Kathryn told her, glaring at Henley. "You didn't do anything wrong. And Mr. Henley's going to let you go now. Aren't you, Henley?"

Henley pulled a package of Camels from his pocket. Pulled out a lighter and lit one. He took a long drag, and let out the smoke. "I lied," he said.

She couldn't let him see her fear. She had to keep the upper hand. She had to set a good example for Janine. In a voice that was remarkably strong, she said, "What are you going to do with us?"

He leaned against the side of the pickup and took another drag on the cigarette. "Well," he said, scratching the tip of his nose on his sleeve, "in an hour or so, when it starts to get dark—" He paused, and then he broke into a grin. "We're gonna have us a hunt."

Her heart began to thud slowly, as though it already knew something she hadn't yet quite figured out. "A hunt?" she said.

"That's right, Miz McAllister. The dogs and me, we're the hunters. And you two ladies—well, you're the huntees."

* * *

The Elba police station hadn't seen this much action in its eighty-five-year history. The phone was ringing off the hook, Teddy fielding call after call from curious citizens who wanted to know what was all the commotion at the Chandler place. In the employee lounge that doubled as an interrogation room, Linda Barden was processing Neely McAllister, while the Judge spoke *sotto voce* to his lawyer on the pay phone just inside the front door. Bucky was at Nick's desk, feet planted firmly on the floor, his face somber as he talked on the phone. "That's right," he was saying. "Jackson. That's J-A-C-K-S-O-N. Ruby. Yes, I'll hold."

He looked up at Nick and rolled his eyes. "Damn woman at the dentist's office doesn't know her ass from her elbow."

"Bucky, Bucky, Bucky," Nick said. "What happened to that sweet young boy I took under my wing just a few short months ago?"

Bucky grinned. "You taught me how to be a real hardass. Sir." His attention swerved back to the telephone. "You got 'em? Excellent. You got somebody that can courier 'em over here to the police station? We're a little busy. My name? I already told you my name. It's Officer Stimpson. S-T-I-M-P—"

There was a quick rap on the door, and Teddy stuck his head in. "Earl just radioed in," he said. "Henley's not at his house. His wife says he took off with the dogs two, three hours ago. She hasn't seen him since. Says it's not unusual. He goes off hunting at all hours, sometimes doesn't come home until morning."

"Wonderful. Okay, let's put out an APB. This guy isn't a fool. If we're not careful, we'll lose him. And call his wife and find out who his hunting buddies are. And where he likes to hunt."

"Will do, Chief."

He poured himself a cup of coffee and went in to where Linda was sitting with Neely McAllister. All the starch had gone out of her, and tonight, even in the silk and pearls, Neely looked every day of her fifty-seven years. "I don't understand it," she was saying. "I thought he loved me. How could he have killed my boy?"

"Maybe," Nick said, "he thought it was the only way out. He knew if the truth came out, you'd go to prison. And he'd be going right along with you."

"Oh, but I could never do that. I'd never survive in a place like that. I—" Her words came to an abrupt halt and her eyes widened as the realization dawned on her that it was extremely likely she was headed to a place precisely like that. "Oh, my Lord," she said, and began to weep again. "How will I ever get through this?"

Nick headed for the door. "You could take a few lessons in courage from your daughter-in-law."

Teddy waved him over to the dispatch desk. "I don't know what this means, Chief, but Raelynn Wilbur just called. Said she was driving home from the airport when she met Kathryn headed out Cypress Avenue in your Blazer, going like a bat out of hell."

His stomach did a hard somersault. "Was my daughter with her?"

"Raelynn said as far as she could tell, Kathryn was alone. But she was going so fast, it was hard to say."

He was pondering the implications when Linda popped her head out the door of the interrogation room. "Chief? Can you come back in here for a minute? I have a question about these damn forms."

Paperwork. The bane of his existence. "Yeah," he said, "I'll be right in."

He refilled his coffee, his mind still on Kathryn. Judge McAllister hung up the phone, his face pale and frightened. "My attorney, Elliott Lancaster, is on his way over," he said. "You're not putting her in a cell, are you?"

He couldn't deal with this right now. "I'm sorry," he said, and left McAllister standing there, open-mouthed. Inside the interrogation room, Neely was still weeping softly, and Linda rolled her eyes and beckoned him in.

"These damn forms are new," she said. "and I've never filled one out. Will you look it over and make sure I haven't missed anything?"

Nick made a mental note to schedule a staff workshop on the topic of paperwork. He picked up the form and squinted at the tiny print, wondering if this meant his vision was about to go. Next thing he knew, he'd be wearing stocking garters and whistling Glenn Miller tunes through his dentures.

"Chief?"

He looked up blankly at Teddy, who was leaning in the doorway, his face ashen. "It's the phone, for you, sir. It's Henley."

He dropped the piece of paper and stalked across the lobby to the dispatch desk. Picked up Teddy's headset and put it on. "DiSalvo," he barked.

"Evening, DiSalvo."

Henley's voice was scratchy, fading in and out, and Nick realized he was on a cell phone. "Henley," he said. "We've been looking for you."

"I imagine Neely's been running her mouth. I tried to protect her, but there's nothing more I can do."

"We know all about Ruby," he said. "And all the rest of it. Turn yourself in, Henley. You know the score. If we have to come after you, it'll look a lot worse."

"Oh, you'll come after me, all right. I have something that belongs to you."

His heart slammed into his throat as Kathryn's voice said, "Nick? Christ, Nick, I'm so sorry."

"Kat." He closed his eyes. "Ah, Jesus, Kat. What happened?"

"I'm sorry. I never meant to cause you trouble—"

She was cut off abruptly, and Henley was back on the line. In the background, the hunting dogs yapped and whined. "We're going hunting," Henley said. "Your lady friend, me, and the dogs. It gets dark real early out here in the swamp. And there's all kinds of wild critters out here. Bugs and snakes. Maybe even a gator or two. Not to mention the dogs. They got real sharp teeth, DiSalvo, and they been itching to track down a coon. Or something bigger."

"What do you want?" he said grimly.

"Well," Henley said, "I figger at this point, I got nothing to lose. But I'm a reasonable man, DiSalvo. So I'm gonna give you a chance to show me what kind of a lawman you are. You get to her first, you get to keep her. Fair's fair. But if I get to her first—" He paused, then chuckled. "—you get to watch me kill her. Oh, by the way, I almost forgot. There is one other thing."

His heart, already beating rapidly, went even faster. "What?" he said.

At the other end, the phone was fumbled. It buzzed and sputtered, and then his daughter's voice said, "Daddy?"

And his blood turned to ice water.

* * *

Dusk came early in the swamp, and all its sleeping creatures awoke. Kathryn swatted at a mosquito as she stumbled along the damp, spongy ground behind Janine, the nose of Henley's hunting rifle pressed against her spine. "Why don't you just kill us now?" she said. "It would be easier."

"Well," he said, "I suppose it would be easier. But it would take all the fun out of it, now, wouldn't it?"

Her wet sneakers squished with every step she took. Henley had changed into hip waders before he led them out into the swamp, but she and Janine were still wearing their Nikes. The dogs trotted along ahead of them, yanking at the leashes that Henley held with grim tautness, eager to get on with the night's excitement. Beside her, Janine trudged along, silent and stoic. She had more than a little of her father in her, Kathryn thought, and an inexplicable pride shot through her at the courage the girl displayed. "You okay, Janine?" she said.

"I'm okay," the girl said.

Henley paused to look at the sky. "Stop here," he said, reining in the dogs.

The swamp lay before them, miles of dark, murky wetlands, thick with cypress and crawling vines, dotted with mossy hummocks and clumps of cattail. "Take off your shoes," he said.

"That's right, Henley," she said. "Make it a fair fight."

"Shut up!" he said, and swung the barrel of the gun at her head. It connected with her temple with a sharp crack, and everything in her vision went red. She swayed on her feet, and Janine caught her.

"Stop that!" the girl shouted. "Leave her alone, you pig!"

"Take the damn shoes off!" he roared, "or you'll be the next one to get it!"

Janine kicked off her sneakers, helped Kathryn into a sitting position. "Kat?" she said as she rapidly untied the laces to Kathryn's sneakers. "Are you okay?"

After trying for a while, she located her tongue. Her vocal cords. "I'm okay," she said. "My head hurts a little, but I'm okay."

It was an understatement. Her head felt like a melon that had been slammed onto the sidewalk and burst into smithereens. But she couldn't let the girl see. Barefoot, sitting on her rump on cold, wet ground, she patted Janine's hand. "Thanks," she said.

Henley pulled a bottle from his pocket and handed it to her. "Rub it on," he said. "Both of you. Starting with the feet. I want it all over you."

She stared at the bottle without comprehending. "What is it?" she said.

And he gave her that smile she'd come to hate. "Coon scent," he said. "Dogs got to know what they're after."

She looked at him stupidly. "Fuck you," she said.

He grabbed a fistful of her hair and yanked so hard that tears filled her eyes. "Rub it on, bitch," he said, "or I kill the girl right here."

He released her, and with clumsy hands, she silently poured a puddle of the oily substance into her palm. "Here," she said as she passed the bottle to Janine. "Baste yourself up real nice."

They both rubbed it on their feet, their legs, their arms and necks. "Faces, too," he said, and silent, steaming, Kathryn complied. The dogs, who'd already caught the scent, were getting restless and excited, yelping and growling and straining frantically at the leashes. Without a word, she handed the bottle back to him. "That's more like it," he said. "I like my women obedient."

"You'll fry in hell, Henley. That's my only comfort."

He nudged her with the rifle barrel. "Get up," he said.

Janine held out a hand to her. When she stood, her head screamed, and the sky tilted above her. Her stomach lurched, and for a moment she thought she would vomit, but she regained her equilibrium and the nausea went away.

Darkness was descending rapidly now, and Henley clicked on the flashlight he carried. "Lover Boy's on his way," he said. "Care to wager on whether he gets to you before the dogs do?"

"We're not afraid," Janine said, looping an arm through Kathryn's. "My father's smarter than you. He'll come. Won't he, Kathryn?"

Kathryn turned her head in slow motion. Christ, she was proud of the kid. "That's right," she said. "And when he does, Henley, you're dead meat."

As the dogs yelped and strained, he spun around. "Shut up!" he yelled, and they paused mid-yelp, cowering as he swung the rifle through their midst. It hit one of them, and the injured dog let out a sharp yip before falling silent and staring at Henley through soft, accusing brown eyes.

"You're just a prince among men, aren't you?" Kathryn said. "Abusive to women, children, and dogs. An equal opportunity offender."

"Shut up," he said, "and listen good. I'm givin' you a ten-minute head start before I turn the dogs loose. Now, this is up to you, of course, but I'd advise you to move fast. Them dogs can cover a lot of ground in damn little time. And they been trained to tear a coon to shreds when they get hold of it."

"You thought of everything, didn't you?" she said. "Covered all your bases."

"You sure do have a mouth on you, Miz McAllister. I kinda hate to have to kill you. I've enjoyed this little sparring match. Almost as much as I'm gonna enjoy the hunt. But duty's duty, and if the dogs don't kill y'all, I'll have to finish off what's left. While DiSalvo watches, of course." He turned off the flashlight, plunging them into darkness. "And then," he said, "I'm gonna kill him, too."

"You bastard."

"You got ten minutes, ladies. If I was you, I'd leave now."

* * *

"Chief?" Teddy said. "You okay? Chief?"

"The son of a bitch has my daughter," he said. "The goddamn son of a bitch has Kathryn and my daughter!"

Teddy's eyebrows nearly disappeared into his hairline. "Holy shit."

Nick ripped off the headset and threw it at Teddy. "Call Doc Winslow, tell him I'm coming by to pick up the dog. Get Earl on the radio and tell him to meet us out at the turnoff by Lake Alberta."

"Yes, sir.” Teddy spun around in his chair and put on his headset.

He strode toward his office door. *"Bucky!"* he bellowed as he shoved it open so hard it crashed up against the wall.

Bucky was still sitting there, still on the phone, still looking beleaguered. He looked up, saw the expression on Nick's face. "I'll call you back," he said into the phone, and hung it up.

"Hunting rifles," Nick said curtly. "Do you have hunting rifles?"

"I've got two at home, Chief. Loaded and ready to go."

"Give me your car keys, officer. We're going after those rifles."

Bucky dug out his keys. "Yes, sir," he said, flipping them across the desk. Nick caught them in mid-air. "May I ask—"

"He's got Kathryn," Nick said grimly, already heading for the door, "and Janine. Out in the swamp. He has the dogs with him. He's going to hunt them down and kill them."

"Holy mother o' God. Has Shep finally lost his mind?"

"I'd say he lost it a long time ago. *Linda!*" he yelled as he strode across the lobby.

"Yeah, Chief?" She popped her head out of the interrogation room.

"You're in charge until we get back. Try to keep the roof on the place."

"Yes, sir!"

The cruiser's powerful engine purred like the monster machine it was. He pulled out at full torque with lights on and siren screaming. "Listen, Chief," Bucky said, "I've been hunting that swamp since I was a boy. I know damn near every inch of it. And I know where Henley's favorite hunting spot is. I've been there with him. I've hunted with the son of a bitch."

"Good," he said. "You'll have to navigate. How big is the swamp?"

"About three miles long. Three-quarters of a mile wide. Shep usually goes in off the Swanville Road, half a mile or so past the turnoff."

He took the corner onto South Hickory with his tires squealing, and came to a screeching halt outside Doc Winslow's veterinary clinic. A lamp was burning in the window, and the old gentleman was waiting for him with Elvis, who was perched on a green Naughahyde settee. The dog had a large bandage on his right shoulder, evidence of the stitches he'd needed after he went through the window.

"Come on, boy," Nick said, and the dog hopped off the settee and ran to greet him. "Thanks, Doc," he said, rubbing the dog behind the ears. "I'll settle the bill later."

When he opened the back door of the cruiser, Elvis jumped in.

"That sure is one big dog," Bucky observed.

"That's a trained police dog," Nick said, "and I just deputized him. Which way to your house?"

"Turn at the end of the block, go down two streets, and hang a right. Third house on the left."

The thirty seconds Bucky was inside the house seemed more like thirty years to Nick. Bucky emerged with the hunting rifles wrapped in a blanket. He loaded them into the trunk and hopped back in the car, and Nick tapped the siren switch and floored the accelerator. "What are we likely to run into out there?" he said.

"Besides snakes? There's all kinds of small mammals. Otters, beaver, that kind of thing. But they're not dangerous. Lots of pesky insects. I've heard tell of a gator being found out there once, but that was twenty years ago, and nobody's seen one since. There's all kinds of waterfowl, and of course, bats—"

"Of course," he said.

"—but mostly it's the snakes. Cottonmouths and copperheads. Big and mean."

He slowed for the Swanville Road, fishtailed a little in the gravel, but the year-old Crown Victoria cornered like a race car. Siren still blasting, he shot down the gravel road doing ninety. He slowed near the turnoff, where Earl sat waiting in his patrol car, and pulled up to Earl's open window. "I don't understand," Earl said. "I worked with Shep for twenty years. He always ran things his way, but I never thought he'd do anything like this."

"He's gone off the deep end," Nick said. "Listen, Bucky thinks he knows where Henley would've taken them. You in shape to go with us? It's rough terrain."

"I can try. Damn lumbago's been bad."

"Maybe it would be better," Bucky said, "if Earl drove around to the other side. If they get across, they'll probably be coming out on Old Raleigh Road."

Nick considered it for half a second before he made his decision. "You head over there," he told Earl. "Cover that area. We'll go in from this side."

"You got it, Chief." Earl fired up the cruiser and sped off down the road.

"It's about a half-mile," Bucky said. "The car'll never make it in, Chief. We'll prob'ly have to go in on foot. There! Right up ahead, where that opening is."

Nick parked the cruiser on the shoulder, put on his four-ways, and they got out, Elvis bounding around their feet. They took the rifles from the trunk and pocketed the spare ammo. As he slammed the trunk lid, Nick said quietly, "I don't know how this will turn out. I just want you to know, officer, that it's been a pleasure and an honor working with you."

Solemnly, Bucky said, "Likewise, sir."

"And my name," he said, "is Nick."

"Yes, sir. I mean, Nick."

He clapped Bucky on the shoulder. "Come on," he said grimly. "Let's go do what the town hired us to do."

The going was rough, hindered by overhanging branches and kudzu vines. An owl hooted as they passed, an eerie sound in the night. They followed the fresh tire tracks, took a sharp left turn, and there, in the beam of their flashlights, sat the abandoned Blazer. His heart stuttered and he let out a breath as Bucky shone his light in each of the windows. "It's empty," Bucky said, and he was able to breathe again. "But she left her sweatshirt," Bucky added. "It's on the seat."

"Let me have it. I want Elvis to smell it."

He let the dog take his time smelling the shirt. "It's Kathryn's," he said. "We have to find Kathryn."

Elvis looked at him with those mournful eyes. "Do you think he understands?" Bucky said.

"Damned if I know."

He tied the shirtsleeves around the dog's neck, and together they followed the beam of Bucky's flashlight. "How the hell could anybody drive through here?" Nick said.

"That truck of Shep's," Bucky said, "it'll go anywheres."

They broke through the heavy undergrowth and there, in a clearing, sat Shep Henley's pickup truck. The dog cages in the back were open and empty, a grim reminder of why they were here.

"Remember," Bucky warned him, "you gotta watch for the snakes. They're deadly. Sometimes they hide in the trees. You gotta watch every minute."

"I'm watching," he said. "Believe me, I'm watching."

And then they heard it, a sudden frenzied burst, coming from somewhere in the darkness ahead of them. Elvis pricked up his ears and whined, and Nick rested a hand on his head. He exchanged a look with Bucky, and grimly, they surged forward, listening to that wild, inhuman keening.

The baying of the dogs. Shep Henley had let his hounds loose.

chapter eighteen

"Go!" she told Janine, shoving her from behind. "Through the water. It's harder for them to track us that way."

Around them, a million live creatures sang and twittered in a nocturnal chorus that would have been beautiful under different circumstances. But barefoot, in the dark, with Shep Henley's flashlight still shining behind them, it was eerie. With each footstep she took, her bare toes sank into the slimy bottom. Something brushed past her submerged leg, and a shudder ran through her body. Ahead of her, Janine was panting, splashing through the water with a deliberately elongated stride as they tried desperately to put ground behind them in the ten minutes that were all that stood between them and death.

Vines tangled in her face, her hair. She tore them away, stubbed her toe on a submerged root and cussed violently. Her head was still pounding, her balance still off-kilter. She had one hell of an egg on her head where Henley had hit her with the rifle, and her hair was encrusted with dried blood.

They found semi-solid ground again, climbed up onto a mossy hummock. "Run!" she told Janine, and gave her a hard shove. The girl stumbled, caught herself, and together they ran through brambles and tangled vines, over sticks and stones and giant cypress roots, and she tried not to think about the pain, tried to distance herself from the feet that were bruised and cut and throbbing in agony with each step she took. "We can do this," she gasped. "We can do this!"

"I have to stop," Janine said. "Just for a minute."

"We can't, baby. We don't have enough time. It's already been eight or nine minutes. We have to keep moving!"

"Where's Daddy? I thought he'd come. Why isn't he coming?"

She caught Janine by the chin. "Your father is coming after us!" she snapped. "He would never leave us out here to die! You're the most important thing in his life!"

"It's you that he loves," Janine said. "Not me."

Furious, she said, "You listen to me, young lady, and you listen good. You come first with him. Before his job, before me, before everything. And he'll come to get you. Or he'll die trying."

Janine began to cry softly. "I'm scared," she said.

"So am I. But we don't have time to be scared. Come on, sweetheart, let's go."

Janine took her hand, and they began moving forward again, shoving aside moss-draped branches. Without warning, the land mass came to an end. Kathryn lost her footing on the muddy verge and plunged headlong into the water.

It was dark and cold and rancid, and she retched, sucking water into her mouth, her lungs. Somewhere above her, Janine was shouting her name. She scrambled for a hold on the mucky bottom, but everything was in motion, the underwater plants slimy with algae, and she knew she was going to die.

And then a hand on the back of her shirt lifted her up and out of the water. Dizzy, she fell back against a cypress stump, gagging and retching, her head bursting with each spasmodic motion. "Kathryn!" Janine said. "Kat! Are you okay?"

She spat into the dark, murky water. Her head felt as though she'd been kicked hard by a mule. She tried to regain her balance, but the world was tilting at a crazy angle. "Kat?" Janine said. "We have to hurry!"

She leaned her head back, gasped air, her chest heaving with exertion. Nearby, something plopped into the water and began moving toward them. *"Come on!"* Janine roared. *"You can't quit on me now!"*

And the words got through to her. Somehow, they got through to her. She squeezed Janine's hand and nodded her head. And then she heard the siren. Distant at first, it drew nearer, louder. "Daddy," Janine said. "It's Daddy."

Her heart began to hammer so hard she thought it would burst from her chest. "Yes," she said. "It is."

She prayed he wasn't walking into a trap, and she tried not to think about him, a city boy lost in the bowels of the swamp. She couldn't think about him. She had to take care of Janine. If she let anything happen to Janine, it would kill him, as surely as if he'd taken a bullet from Shep Henley's rifle.

The siren stopped. "Come on," she told Janine. "Let's go."

And then she heard the dogs. Like banshees, they yelped and howled, snarling and baying in excitement as they followed the scent of coon. Hand in hand, she and Janine ran, splashing through the water, tripping and stumbling, catching each other, shoving aside vines and hanging moss. Something flew past them, darting and diving, and she knew it was a bat. "Move!" she said. "Faster!"

In the darkness, Janine scrambled up onto another mossy hummock. Kathryn followed her, the dogs yipping and snarling in the distance, and then Janine stopped so abruptly that Kathryn slammed into her. "Kat," she whispered. "Oh, Kat."

The cottonmouth was coiled a foot from Janine's ankle, a faint shape in the darkness, its head drawn back in fighting position. Kathryn slung an arm around the terrified girl's waist, and then the snake struck. Janine screamed as its fangs sank into her ankle once, then a second time. Engulfed in rage, Kathryn shoved the girl aside so hard she went tumbling. Picking up a huge stick, she slammed it as hard as she could against the snake. The animal hissed and tried to strike, but she'd stunned it, and it fell short of its target. Head spinning, she swung the stick with another huge thwack. The snake began to twitch and jerk. Kathryn slammed it a final time, and its death throes gradually halted.

Dizzy, with the sound of the dogs in her ears, she crawled on her hands and knees until she found Janine. "Christ," she said. "Oh, Christ, baby, I'm so sorry."

"It hurts," the girl said. "It hurts bad."

"I know, baby. We have to get you out of here. Can you walk?"

"I think so."

"Come on." She hoisted Janine's arm over her shoulder and pulled her to her feet. The girl was weak, trembling violently. They took a couple of steps and faltered. "I can't do it," Janine said. "I think I'm going to throw up."

"You're going to be fine!" Kathryn snapped. "Hang onto my

neck."

Janine clung to her, the only solid thing left in the young girl's world. With a strength she'd forgotten she possessed, she hoisted the girl up into her arms.

And with grim determination, she continued walking.

* * *

The swamp was murky and black around him. He'd long since ruined his shoes, and his arms were exhausted from holding the hunting rifle out of the water. "Henley!" he shouted. "Show your damn ugly face. Come out and be a man!"

His voice echoed around him, amid the buzzing and the chirping and the slithering. In the distance, the dogs were still baying. He and Bucky carefully picked their way through the water as Elvis sloshed ahead of them, pausing every so often to sniff as they passed something solid. "How far are we from the other side?" he asked Bucky.

"Hard to say. But from the sound of the dogs, I'd say Kathryn's gone in deep. Unless she's circling around. That'd be the smart thing to do."

He cupped a hand to his mouth. "Kathryn!" he shouted.

Around him, the swamp was alive with sound, but there was no answer except for the echo of his own voice. He slogged through the water, grabbed hold of a slimy cypress knee and hauled himself up onto spongy ground. Elvis was already there, shaking water from his fur. "Turn off the light," Bucky said sharply.

The darkness was eerie, the twinkling stars above their heads providing minimal light. In the distance, he saw the wispy glow of a flashlight. "Henley," he said.

"Henley," Bucky agreed.

With renewed vigor, they continued, lights off this time as they sloshed through water up to their waists, slapping at insects, jumping each time a frog plopped into the water behind them. He'd thought he was in good shape, but he felt twenty years past his age, huffing like an old man. If it was this difficult for him, how must it be for Henley? The man was in his sixties. He couldn't keep this up forever.

Ahead of them, the light bobbed and then stopped. "He's

resting," Bucky whispered. "Can't take the pace."

They continued their silent progress. The light ahead of them didn't move. "Take the dog," Nick said, "and circle around. I'll keep going this way."

Like a wraith, Bucky disappeared into the night, and he was alone. He moved silently toward the lantern in the darkness, through the water and up onto dry land. Creeping on his knees, he approached the light. Thirty more feet. Twenty. Ten.

The light sat in a clearing, by itself, beam pointed upward into the treetops. Disgusted, Nick stood up and raised his face to the sky. "Come on out, Henley!" he shouted. "Or are you afraid of me?"

Fifty feet away, Shep Henley came walking out of the shadows, his rifle cocked and pointed directly at Nick's heart. "So," he said, "you made it. Not bad for a city boy."

He didn't dare look for Bucky. He kept his face carefully noncommittal. "That's right, Henley. You invited me to your little tea party, and here I am."

"Well, then, maybe we should be having us some tea."

"Let them go, Henley."

"It's too late for that," Henley said. "Any minute now, the dogs'll catch up to 'em. And when they do, they'll rip them girls to shreds. There won't be enough left for you to tell which pieces belonged to which one. Damn shame. They were both real pretty."

He forced himself to remain calm. He was a police officer. He'd been trained to stay calm. It wasn't supposed to matter that one of the intended victims was his lover, the other his daughter. "I know why you killed Michael McAllister," he said casually. "It was because of Ruby. But why'd you kill Wanita?"

"She turned on me," Henley said. "The mother of my own kid. I didn't have a choice. I had to kill her."

"Wait a minute. Back up. What do you mean, the mother of your own kid? Which one?"

"Timmy," Henley said. "He's my boy."

"But I thought Timmy was Michael's. The birth certificate said—"

"That was my idea," Henley said. "Just in case anybody started sniffing around later on, doubting the story she told the court. The whole thing was my idea. She went along with it because I'd helped her out when she was in trouble."

"You mean, she never had an affair with McAllister?"

"She didn't even know McAllister. They didn't exactly run in the same crowds. You know," he said, "Wanita was a right pretty little thing, back before she put on all that weight. A man gets to be my age, his wife loses interest in that kind of thing. So he gets it wherever he can."

"And you got it from your wife's niece."

"Everything was working fine, until the little bitch decided to squeeze me. Told me if I didn't pay up, she'd tell your girlfriend who really killed her husband."

"So you killed her."

"Damn right, I did. Rid the town of one more piece of vermin."

"Just like you tried to do with Kathryn," he said, "the night you burned down her house."

"Hell, boy, I shoulda figured she was off shacked up somewhere with you, the way the two of you been carrying on, right in front of the whole town. Thought I could take advantage of you sleeping in her bed. Use it to scare her off. The little message I painted on your truck. And the brick through the window. I thought that was a real nice touch. But she's tough, your little girlfriend. She don't scare easy."

"Neither do I," he said. "I'm going after 'em, Henley. I'm walking out of here, and I'm finding Kathryn and Janine. And if your dogs have touched a single hair on their heads, I'll come back and cut off your balls and stuff 'em down your throat."

"I was gonna wait," Henley said with great good nature. "Make you watch me kill the women first, before I killed you. But you're getting to be too much trouble, DiSalvo. I guess I'm gonna have to get rid of you first."

Nick stood his ground. "Go ahead, you son of a bitch. Try me."

"Good-bye, DiSalvo. Have a nice time in hell."

And Henley squeezed the trigger.

* * *

The dogs were almost upon her when she heard the shots, three of them, one right after the other. "Nick," she whispered. "Oh, Jesus, Nick."

Janine raised her head. "Daddy?" she said groggily.

"He's coming, baby. Hold on a little longer."

The girl was feverish, close to delirious, and the dogs were closing in. She'd been carrying Janine for what seemed like years. Her knees buckled, and she nearly fell. Raising her head, she scanned the treetops. If she could just get off the ground, out of reach of the dogs, they might still have a chance.

"Janine," she said.

"Mmn."

"Janine!" She slapped the girl's face, hard, and Janine's head rolled.

"Stop," the girl said.

"You have to help me. Do you understand? If you don't help me, we'll both die."

Janine opened her eyes, and Kathryn saw in them the same stoic determination that was in her father. "Okay," the girl whispered.

Kathryn had never experienced mother love, but in that instant, she knew what it was. "We have to climb this tree," she said. "We're going to do it together. I'll help you."

Janine nodded, and she put the girl down on wobbly legs. "You first, chickie," she said. "Grab this branch."

Janine's grasp was weak. She tugged, and her fingers slipped. The dogs were getting closer. "Come on, Janine," she said, frantic. "You can do this."

"I can't. I'm too weak."

"You will do this! Do you hear me? I will not allow your father to find you in little pieces! Do you understand me, Janine DiSalvo?"

The girl opened her eyes. They were glassy, feverish. And angry. She grabbed the branch, and Kathryn guided her up into the tree. "Higher!" she ordered. She caught the branch and swung herself up, pushing Janine higher, and then the dogs burst through the trees and threw themselves at the trunk in a wild frenzy, leaping and snapping, inches away from her feet.

She hovered there with Nick's daughter cradled in her arms, trying not to cry, trying not to wonder whether he was dead or alive. Beneath her, the dogs barked and howled, and then she heard a huge splash, and at the water's edge, like a savior come to her rescue, stood a wet and glistening Elvis. He shook the water from his coat and, fangs bared, dove into the fray. He singled out the lead dog, snapping and biting at his heels. While the others continued to bay, the two dogs rolled like a dervish, biting and growling and snapping at each other.

And then she saw the lights through the trees. Twin flashlight beams, scanning, seeking. She held Janine tighter, her heart thudding in her chest. If it was Henley, she wouldn't give in. She wouldn't break. She would fight him to the death to save Nick's daughter.

And then she heard it, faint but distinct, the sweetest sound she'd ever heard. Nick's voice. "Kathryn?" he shouted. "Where are you?"

She let out a sob, wet her lips, and took a deep breath. Putting all her strength into her voice, she shouted, "Nick!"

Beneath her, the dogs continued to fight. "Kathryn?" he shouted again, closer this time.

"Over here! Hurry!"

Nick splashed through the water toward her, with Bucky Stimpson directly behind him. Bucky raised his rifle and fired once into the air, and the dogs separated, scattering in five different directions. "Kathryn," Nick said. "Oh, Christ, Kat, I thought you were both dead."

"We have to get her to a hospital," she said. "Snakebite. It's already been a couple of hours. We don't have much time."

"Oh, Jesus. Hand her down. Help me, Bucky."

In her arms, the young girl groaned. "Janine?" she said. "Wake up, honey. Daddy's here."

Weakly, Janine said, "I told you he'd come."

She delivered Nick's daughter into his arms, and then she slid down out of the tree. Bucky caught her before she could fall. "Where's Henley?" she said.

"He's dead," Nick said curtly.

She closed her eyes to ward off a wave of dizziness. "You killed him?" she said.

"I did, ma'am," Bucky said respectfully. "I didn't have a choice. He was about to shoot my boss."

"And it's a damn good thing for me that you're a crack shot," Nick said. "That bullet missed me by half an inch. Where the hell are we?"

Bucky looked around. "We're about a hundred yards from Old

Raleigh Road," he said. "Come on, let's go. Earl should be waiting there."

She could no longer feel her legs. Numbly, like a wooden soldier, she followed Nick's long-legged stride. They emerged from the swamp like creatures from some B movie, Nick cradling his limp daughter in his arms, Bucky supporting Kathryn, Elvis tagging alongside, those big yellow eyes fraught with concern.

In the distance, headlights came around a curve. The car moved down the road toward them, and Nick stepped out into the road and stood there, holding his daughter. The headlights outlined his shuddering form. The car slowed, and its dark shape turned into a police cruiser. "Thank God," Kathryn said softly.

Nick swung open the passenger door. "I'll radio for somebody to pick you up," he told Earl curtly. "I'm taking your car." He turned to Kathryn. "Get in," he said. "Can you hold her on your lap?"

She nodded slowly, the movement making her dizzy. When she sat down, Nick finally got a good look at her. "Holy mother of Moses," he said. "What happened to you?"

"Never mind. I'll tell you later."

She cradled the limp girl in her arms, and Nick slammed the door shut. "I'll call you," he told Bucky as he raced around the front of the car and climbed into the driver's seat. He hit the siren and the lights, and punched down hard on the accelerator. "Fayetteville," he said. "We'll go to Fayetteville. It's the nearest hospital."

The drive took them a half-hour, doing ninety over back roads. In her arms, Janine moved restlessly, every so often moaning softly. Kathryn brushed the damp hair back from the girl's forehead. "Her fever's going up," she said. "We have to hurry, Nick."

He glanced once at his daughter, then at the speedometer, and stepped it up to ninety-five. They hit the Fayetteville city limits doing a hundred and ten. She'd never in her life been in a vehicle moving at that speed. Yet she was as calm as if they'd been sipping lemonade at a church picnic. Nick was driving, and she had complete faith in him. He would take care of them. He wouldn't let anything happen to them.

"I was so furious," she told him, "when that snake bit her. I just saw red. It's amazing what you can do when you're angry."

He slowed to seventy as he neared the hospital. "What did you do?" he said.

"I picked up a big stick," she said, "and I beat the son of a bitch to death."

At the hospital, he brought the car to a shuddering halt. Opened his door and came around to hers. "You okay?" he said, prodding at her temple with gentle fingers.

"I'm okay. Get her inside, DiSalvo. Don't worry about me."

"Get that head looked at," he ordered. He took Janine from her arms, gave Kathryn a last look, and stalked through the emergency entrance. She climbed out of the car and followed at a slower pace. The world was tilting, darkening, and when she walked up to the nurse's desk, the attendant stared at her.

"Good evening," she said. "My name is Kathryn McAllister."

And she passed out cold on the floor.

chapter nineteen

When she came to, she was in a hospital bed, and sunlight streamed through the window. Her headache had died down to a dull roar, and somebody had stripped off her ruined clothes and bathed her. Her arms were peppered with infected insect bites that itched like a son of a bitch. While she lay there studying them in puzzlement, a white-frocked young doctor came in. "Well," he said jovially, "it's about time you decided to rejoin us. How are you feeling?"

"I'm starving," she said. "How long have I been here?"

He checked the bump on her head, looked into her eyes, prodded at the glands beneath her jaw. "Two days," he said.

"Two days?"

"That was quite a bump on the head. Nasty concussion." He held up two fingers in front of her face. "How many?" he said.

"Who do you think you are, Shecky Greene?"

"Ah, yes, I was warned about your infamous mouth. How many fingers, Kathryn?"

"Two. Where's Janine?"

"Janine who?"

"Janine DiSalvo. We came in here together. Where the hell is she?"

"Oh," he said. "The girl."

"Well?"

"She's in ICU," he said, "but—"

"Oh, Christ." She sat up and the room tilted. "Holy shit," she said.

He caught her before she could fall ass over teakettle out of the bed and onto the floor. "It's going to take a few days," he warned.

"I have to go check on Janine."

"You're not up to walking yet."

"In a pig's eye," she said, and proved it by sliding off the edge of the bed and standing on her feet. "Now," she said, "unless you plan on everybody in the hospital getting a good close-up look at my backside, you'd best find me a robe."

He found her a robe, and she shuffled off barefoot down the hall to the nurse's station. There was a pretty young Asian nurse sitting at the desk, writing something on a chart. She looked up and her eyes widened. "Yes?" she said.

"How do I get to the ICU?"

"Why do you ask?" the nurse said cautiously.

"I have a friend in there. Listen, you can tell me, or I can ask somebody else. It's up to you."

They eyed each other while the nurse debated. "Down the hall," she finally said, pointing her pen. "Take the elevator to the third floor. Hang a right out of the elevator, take your first left, and you can't miss it."

She ignored the people in the elevator who stared at her bare feet and her funky mode of dress. When the doors opened on the third floor, she squeezed through people. "Excuse me," she said, elbowing her way through. "Excuse me."

The ICU nurse looked up at her through square granny style glasses. "Yes?" she said. "May I help you?"

"I'm looking for Janine DiSalvo. The young girl who was brought in here a couple of nights ago with snakebite."

The nurse looked her up and down, and pursed her lips. "Are you a relative?" she said.

"I'm a friend of the family."

"I'm sorry," the nurse said, and returned her eyes to her paperwork. "Nobody's allowed in except immediate family."

Kathryn leaned over her desk, and the nurse looked back up, startled. "Look," she said, "we came into this hospital together, and you will damn well tell me her what her condition is, or I'll be speaking with your supervisor. And if that doesn't do the trick, I'll work my way right on up the line until I get what I want."

Seconds ticked by while they faced off. "She's in critical condition," the nurse said. "For a while there, it was touch and go. But today, she's showing signs of improvement. Her folks have been with her night and day. Her poor momma was a wreck when she got here."

It hadn't occurred to her until this moment that Nick's ex-wife would be here. But of course she would. Under the circumstances, any mother would have flown immediately to her daughter's side. "Can I look in?" Kathryn said. "Just take a peek through the glass?"

The nurse pointed to the door. "One peek," she said sternly, "and then back to your room."

Kathryn moved toward the window, propelled by equal parts concern for Janine and curiosity about Lenore. She peered through the window. Janine lay pale and silent in the bed, tubes protruding from every possible orifice. Near the window, standing in a pool of sunlight, Nick was talking with a lovely dark-haired woman. Janine had inherited her mother's facial features, her bone structure. Nick's ex-wife was pretty enough to be a model. She had been crying, and Nick wiped a tear from her face. He closed his eyes, and they embraced with a ferocity that was both poignant and heartbreaking.

Kathryn looked again at the girl in the bed, then at the parents who so obviously loved her. And each other, if their behavior was any indicator. She squared her shoulders. This was, after all, the way it should be. Nick and Lenore had created this perfect child together, and at this critical moment in her life, she needed both her parents, together, as a family. As one who had grown up without the full complement of parents, Kathryn knew how important it was to a teenage girl to have all the right people in all the right places. It was the natural order of things, and nobody, least of all Kathryn McAllister, had the right to interfere with that.

Besides, it wasn't as though she and Nick had made any kind of commitment. He'd never even told her he loved her. And she'd been too hell-bent on finding Michael's killer to see beyond the end of her own nose. It wasn't his fault if she'd discouraged him from thinking about a future that included her. It wasn't his fault if she'd been fool enough to fall in love with a man who probably considered their relationship to be nothing more significant than a few nights of great sex.

The fault was all hers.

So she would do the gracious thing and walk away. Even if it ripped the heart out of her chest.

Kathryn turned away from the window. The nurse was watching her oddly. "Shall I leave a message?" the woman said.

"No," she said. "No message."

She went back to her room and called Raelynn. "I need something to wear," she said. "Can I impose on you one more time?"

"Sugar, I have already been shopping. I would have loaned you something of mine, but, well—we aren't exactly of a size, if you get my drift."

She hung up the phone and walked to the nurse's station and badgered the young Asian nurse until the poor woman finally gave in and called the doctor to come in and sign her release papers.

Raelynn picked her up at eleven o'clock, and loaned her the Mustang. "One scratch," her friend said, "and I'll have you back in Carolina Women's."

"Idle threats," she said, then drove away and left Raelynn standing on the sidewalk in a powder-blue suit, grinning and shaking her head.

Her afternoon was fruitful. She sold the Toyota to Dwight Harvey's boy for a hundred dollars, then swung by Gabe Holden's office to discuss Michael's life insurance policy. "Shep Henley admitted to me and to two police officers that he killed Michael," she said. "That should be proof enough for even your tight-assed insurance adjuster that I'm entitled to collect on his life insurance."

Gabe wiggled and squirmed and wiped his beet-red brow with a snowy white handkerchief, but finally agreed that since her conviction had been overturned and the real killer located, she was, indeed, entitled to Michael's insurance. "You have to realize," he said, "that these things take time, Miz McAllister. You'll have to give me a few days to process the claim. Explain things to the comp'ny."

"Fine," she said. "I'll be back on Monday afternoon to pick up the check."

She left him sputtering as she drove back to Raelynn's place and sat down with the Boston *Globe* that she'd picked up in Fayetteville this morning. She spent an hour perusing the want ads, circling anything that looked promising. And then she started making phone calls.

A half-hour later, she had three job interviews scheduled for the end of next week, and flight reservations for Tuesday morning. Elvis probably wouldn't appreciate flying in the cargo hold, but there was no way she was leaving him behind, even if it meant she had to drive him to Boston.

Her Aunt Elena cried when she heard Kathryn's voice on the phone. "Oh, baby," she said through tears, "I've prayed for this moment."

"So have I, Auntie. Listen, will you open up the house for me? Get it aired out?"

It would seem so strange without him there, the man who'd tried so hard to give her a normal childhood after the death of her mother. But it was all she had left of him, the small wooden frame house in Somerville where she'd grown up. And her memories of living there were good. Pop might be gone, but he would live on in her memories. And maybe, some day, in her children. It was a fitting legacy for the man with the twinkling blue eyes, that she should come back to live in the house that Frank Sipowicz had worked so hard to turn into a home.

Raelynn was shocked to hear she was leaving. "But, sugar," she said, clearly bewildered, "I thought you and that spectacular Chief DiSalvo were an item. What happened?"

"His wife is what happened. He's still in love with her."

"Ex-wife," Raelynn said, and raised a brow. "And you're not even going to fight for him?"

"I've been fighting for four years," she said. "I don't want to fight any more. I don't have to fight any more. I'm going home, and Elvis and I are going to live like normal people. Do you have any idea how long it's been since I lived like normal people?"

Raelynn eyed the dog with distaste. "I hate to break it to you, sugar, but Elvis isn't people."

Kathryn fed him half a doughnut. He caught it in mid-air, and swallowed it whole. "He is to me," she said.

"Personally," Raelynn said, "I think that bump on your head must have been bigger than they thought. You leave DiSalvo behind, and take that damn ugly dog with you. There's something wrong with this picture."

"Thank you for the unsolicited advice. Now you can butt out."

Monday afternoon, she picked up the insurance check, and

strode directly across the street to the First National Bank of Elba to deposit it. "Good afternoon," she said, stepping up to the teller's window. "I'd like to open an account. Here's my first deposit."

The teller looked at the check, and her mouth fell open. When she recovered, she quickly pulled out the necessary paperwork, and Kathryn left the bank twenty minutes later with two thousand dollars in cash and the other $148,000 in savings.

There was one last thing she had to do. She drove to Mount Hope Cemetery, to the McAllister plot, to say good-bye to Michael. His parents had buried him in a style befitting a McAllister, beneath a polished marble monument that rose to the sky in an elegant sweep that would have pleased the architect in him. Etched into the stone were the words *Beloved Son.*

"Well," she told him, "it's over. I promised you I'd find justice, and I kept my promise. I hope you're at peace. Now we can both go on with a clear conscience and the knowledge that we did the best we could."

She'd loved him so much that the absence of that love surprised her. The Kathryn who'd been so in love with Michael McAllister had been a girl. This Kathryn was a woman, seasoned and hardened and ripened into something that didn't even vaguely resemble Kathryn the girl. "I'm sorry," she said, "about the way it turned out. But maybe it wouldn't have lasted anyway." Certainly not here in Elba, where their every move had been scrutinized and turned into gossip and public information. She wasn't sorry to be leaving.

Behind her, footsteps crunched in the gravel. She swung around and looked steadily at the man who stood at the foot of Michael's grave. "Hello, Judge," she said.

"Kathryn," he said. "I heard you were leaving town."

"Word does travel fast around here, doesn't it?"

A faint breeze blew a lock of his blond hair into his face. "It seems," he said, "that Neely and I owe you an apology."

"It's a little late for that, Kevin. About four years too late."

"You have to understand, Kathryn, he was our son. We loved him."

"And my husband. I loved him, too."

"Where are you going to?"

"Home," she said. "Boston. Where I belong."

"And I imagine," he said, "that you won't be coming back."

"Michael told me once," she said, "that there were two kinds of people in this town. Those who run things the way they've been run since the beginning of time, and those who let themselves be run. We were different, he said. Mavericks. We wouldn't let that happen to us. Well, he was right. He escaped from this town the only way he could. Now, it's my turn to escape. And you're right. I won't be back."

He held out his hand. "Good luck, Kathryn. I hope you find your peace."

She looked at the outstretched hand for a long time. "I've already found it," she said. "Good-bye, Kevin."

And she turned and walked away.

* * *

Raleigh-Durham International Airport was busy on a Tuesday morning, mobbed with business travelers, denizens of the academic and research worlds, and the occasional tourist, all of them rushing to get to their destinations. "Sugar," Raelynn said, "I am gonna miss you so much."

Kathryn returned her hug. "I'm going to miss you, too. How will I ever thank you for everything you've done for me?"

"I did my job," Raelynn said. "And after that, I helped out a friend. That's all."

"I even got your mother's house burned down."

Raelynn leaned close. "You want to know a secret?" she said. "I always hated that house. I bought it for Momma, because she liked it. Why do you think I wasn't living in it?"

"I think you're a bullshit artist of the highest caliber. But I love you for it."

"I do, however, have one particularly fine bone to pick with you. I can't believe you really thought I could have had anything to do with that awful snake business."

"I was running on fear," she said. "I didn't know who I could trust. Nothing was what it seemed."

"Yes, well, I suppose I'll have to forgive you. Maybe you can make it up to me somehow. Say, a couple of weeks in Boston during skiing season?"

"They're yours. My house has plenty of room. And Elvis will

be thrilled to see your smiling face."

"That is the ugliest dog I ever saw," Raelynn said.

"Beauty is as beauty does."

Raelynn looked past her shoulder, and suddenly her face lit up like Times Square at New Year's. "Hallelujah, Jesus," she said under her breath. Her smile broadened, and charm oozed out of every pore like rich, thick molasses. "As I live and breathe," she said, "if it isn't our own Chief DiSalvo. My word, Nicholas, you are a sight for sore eyes!"

Kathryn spun around, her breath trapped in her throat. He was dressed in jeans and a cotton plaid shirt, and had a black Nike duffel bag slung over one shoulder. "Morning, ladies," he said. "And it's private citizen DiSalvo. I resigned from my job yesterday afternoon."

"What?" Kathryn said.

While her heart hammered double-time, those soft, dark eyes met hers and stayed there. "I gave Bucky a glowing recommendation as my replacement," he said. "Told the city council they didn't realize what a gem they had right there under their collective noses."

Raelynn beamed. "And where are you flying off to on this fine morning?" she said.

"Boston," he said, his eyes never leaving Kathryn's. "I've always had a hankering to see Boston."

"Why, isn't that just the most amazing coincidence? Our little Kat here is flying to Boston, too." Raelynn looked from one to the other. "Well," she said briskly, "I can see that my presence here is no longer needed. Or even acknowledged. And on that auspicious note, I shall take my leave. Y'all can thank me later."

And they were alone. Softly, Kathryn said, "How's Janine?"

"She's fine. Gave us one hell of a scare, though. She's flying home tomorrow with her mother." His voice softened. "I came to see you in the hospital," he said. "Three or four times. But you were out cold, every damn time. You scared the hell out of me with that concussion. I thought I was about to lose both of you. And then, the minute you woke up, you left. You didn't even say good-bye."

"I thought—you and Lenore—"

"That was over with a long time ago," he said. "I was married to her for fifteen years, Kat. She's the mother of my child. There'll always be feelings there. But I'm not in love with her any more. I haven't wanted anybody but you since the day you walked through the door of my office, wearing that flowered skirt and those sexy shoes."

"Both of which," she said wryly, "went up in flames."

"So did I, the minute you walked through the door."

She wet her lips, tried to think of something to say, but all the blood had left her brain. "We've only known each other for three weeks."

"A lot can happen in three weeks." He set down his duffel bag. "I have an appointment first thing tomorrow morning with a Captain O'Sullivan of the Boston PD. He says he's willing to take a chance on an old war-horse. I was hoping maybe you would, too."

She went weak and fluid inside. She wondered if, when they were ninety, he'd still have the ability to do that to her. "Are you sure, DiSalvo?"

"You know what I want, McAllister? I want to take you ice skating, when it's so damn cold outside that your teeth ache. I want to build a snowman in our front yard, and eat real Chinese food again. I want to walk the city streets and complain about rush hour traffic and fight for a seat on the subway. Most of all, I want to come home after a long day at work and find you there, waiting to rub my aching feet and fight with me over the remote."

"Sounds incredibly romantic," she said.

"There's just one other thing I want," he said. "Do you suppose we could honeymoon some place where there aren't any telephones? Just once, I'd like to sleep beside you all night without getting dragged away to attend a murder. If it's not too much to ask?"

She looked into those chocolate eyes. Nick DiSalvo was warm and sexy and smart. Not to mention stubborn, hot-tempered, and overprotective. And he was all hers, every spectacular inch of him.

Over their heads, the loudspeaker crackled to life. *"Flight 1202 to Pittsburgh and Boston is now boarding at gate nine. Y'all have a nice flight."*

She held out an arm, looped it through his. "Come on, DiSalvo," she said. "Let's go home."

THE END

Author Bio

Laurie Breton started making up stories in her head when she was a small child. At the age of eight, she picked up a pen and began writing them down. Although she now uses a computer to write, she is still addicted to a new pen and a fresh sheet of lined paper. At some point during her angsty teenage years, her incoherent scribblings morphed into love stories, and that is what she has been writing, in one form or another, ever since.

When not writing, she can usually be found driving the back roads of Maine, looking for inspiration. Or perhaps standing on a beach at dawn, shooting a sunrise with her Canon camera. If all else fails, a day trip to Boston, where her heart resides, will usually get the juices flowing.

The mother of two grown children, Breton has two beautiful grandkids and two precious grand-dogs. She and her husband live in a small Maine town with a lovebird who refuses to stop laying eggs and two Chihuahua-mix dogs named River and Bella who pretty much run the household.

Made in the USA
Monee, IL
20 March 2024

55116183R00152